A Knife in the Back:
Seven Tales of Murder and Madness, and Raleigh's Prep, a Novel

Third Edition

James Noll

*To Meredith,
Thanks for the read!
James Noll*

This is a work of fiction. Names, characters, places, and incidents either are products of the author's imagination or are used fictitiously. Any resemblance to actual events, locales, or persons, living or dead, is entirely coincidental.

To my wife, Angie, who has supported me in all of my creative endeavors. And to my daughters, Haley, Taylor, and Elena, who inspire me everyday with their wit, humor, and intelligence. Ya'll rock.

James Noll

CONTENTS

BETA

Here in the mountains it starts to snow in early November, so by the time we found one of the local farmers dead in a frozen bank, we all thought it was wolves. Wolves. In January the idea is not as comical as you think. Wolves howl around our village all winter, and during the long brutal seasons, when we are covered for months at a time in a thick carpet of white, they steal across our fences, feed on our livestock. Our village is not completely isolated. A lake lay only a twenty-minute walk away, we are a few hours ride from the river, and with it the city of P—. In the summer the hills in the river valley are covered with roses, vegetables, fruit, glowing gold and maroon, blue, green, and red, like a painter dropped thick globs of paint all over the hillside. We have our goats and cheeses and our wool from our sheep. They come highly prized in the valley and lowlands, and the river affords us trade as deep as Mnichov.

Bednan the Cooper said wolves had killed three of his chickens the week before, and that one of the shepherds told him some of his sheep had disappeared, too.

"He found them halfway to the river, near the old cemetery. Not eaten, but cut. They bled to death. A waste of good wool and chops." He spat on the ground.

"Why didn't you tell us?" someone asked.

"Why should I? It was just a wolf. My son Han and I went out into the woods and hunted it down. We're not sure if we got the right one, but we killed a wolf."

Some of the older men standing around the dead man scolded Bednan for not staking the head on a stick as a warning to the other wolves, but Bednan waved his hand at them and turned away muttering.

All evidence pointed to wolves. It is a fact. I am an old man now, and my joints may creak and my eyes may water, but back then I was just a boy, yes, and my mind was sharp and my eyes were keen. I remember the poor farmer, his throat torn out, his stomach a rose in full bloom. His face was more horrific, frozen in wide-eyed surprise, mouth half open. A rivulet of blood painted a crooked line from one corner across his cheek. His arms and legs stuck out of the snow bank, and it looked like he was trying to leap out at us, fingers rigid with rigor and cold.

You get the idea. An altogether horrible death. To die like that no one

9

deserves. The curious thing was the lack of blood—like the sheep, the lack of blood. Only with the sheep they'd fallen down, or maybe were just attacked and then left, or maybe they died and bled out before the carrion fowl got to them. With the farmer we expected the snow to be saturated black with it, but this was simply not the case. There were some orange stains around him, some red and maroon splatters, but not near as much as should be.

"It's been a long winter," the konstabl said.

We all looked to him for an explanation. The konstabl, a fat man with a few wisps of hair stretched over his bald pate and, like the rest of the men, a thick, full beard, pouted his lips and looked around at all of us like we were stupid.

"They're hungry."

The next day was cold and crisp and clear. The konstabl gathered some local men, shop owners, Fleischaka the butcher, Bednan, and a few shepherds, and led them higher up into the mountains to kill the pack that killed the farmer. Bilko the priest blessed their weapons himself, the muskets and swords, the pitchforks and axes, all with rusted red metal or wood-wormed, handles smooth and worn from decades of use. He pitched holy water in the winter air and it stung their cheeks.

I wanted to go, of course, but my mother forbade it, and my father (who probably would have let me) ordered me to help him in the shop. He was a cobbler, and the long, cold winter created an unusual demand for mending boots and shoes. His little shop stank, and the open hearth and ever burning fire made it worse. Even now as I tell you this I remember the smell: hot feet and mildew, burning hair where the sparks shot out and singed the wool-covered boots, and beneath that, mud and dirt, always the mud and the dirt. I moped around the shop like a scorned puppy. My long face, stooped shoulders and deafening silence must have been unbearable because by ten o'clock my father sent me out to retrieve some nails from the kovar's son, and leather from the kozeluh. He did this because he knew I'd have to go by the Inn, which was where all of the news gathered before disseminating into the village. There I could pass the time and wait for reports from the hunting party. What he didn't know was the way also brought me past the butcher's, and the butcher's daughter, Beta.

Beta was older than me by five years, and at nineteen she possessed a beauty unrivaled in all the surrounding villages. Her skin was milky white, and she had long, blond hair that fell down to the middle of her back, even when she wore a thick parka and woolen hat. Her mouth was wide and lips full, and they were soft pink, and her eyes so blue that they glowed in the night.

Beta.

Her name dripped off my tongue like honey. Tasted like sweet red wine. Every man was in love with Beta, even the married ones (especially the married ones) but the problem was that she knew it. When she walked through the village she held her nose so high as if to keep it above the stench of we lowly rabble, and she spoke very little to anyone, or sometimes not at all. She was also very dedicated to God, and spent a large part of her day at the church with Bilko the priest.

The butcher was very proud of Beta, and he bragged about her beauty to everyone. His wife had died giving birth to her, so we all gave him leeway with this. There were some who ascribed unnatural things to the pair, but they were shouted down. The idea was unthinkable, and besides, she spent all her free time with the priest.

I often strolled by the butcher's whenever I could, just to catch a glimpse of her, hoping she might look at me or even say hello. On that day, slogging through the ankle deep snow and churning mud that comprised our lanes, the sun bright and blazing but the air cold and sharp, I went by to see if that would be the day Beta acknowledged my existence. It was cold enough to keep everyone in their homes and away from the shops, barring a few of the women hurrying on one or another errand, or the odd shop-owner shoveling snow off his stoop. As I approached the butcher's from behind, I heard voices from the slaughter yard, where Fleischaka rendered his animals, capturing their blood and inedible organs in a huge stone tub, which he emptied into a fire pit and burned. He kept a barrel there, too, double fortified, in which he sometimes cured the meat. It was huge, and on occasion when he cleaned it, it held hundreds of liters of water. The stench coming from the yard was at all times unspeakable. The voice I heard was high and keening, a whine as if from a child. It stopped me dead cold.

"I know I know I know." It gasped and sobbed. "Don't make me do it again. Don't make me do it."

Could that have been Beta? Were the sick rumors of the old lechers at the Inn true? What had her father done? I'd kill him! But then I remembered that he was out with the hunting party. No. As I listened I knew that it was not her voice. Beta afraid of wolves, afraid of her father who doted on her, was laughable.

The voice I heard belonged to the priest, Bilko.

Then another voice spoke up, nothing more than a low murmur. I couldn't discern anything it said, but I understood the tone, at once calming and threatening, and over that came Bilko's whining voice, pleading "No! Of course I do! I'll do anything. Anything at all!"

More murmuring, and then I heard a whisper of water, as if someone were stroking his hand on the surface of a pool. I had to know who he was talking to, who had made him so upset. How could it be Beta? Her father, though he loved her so, would thrash her if he found her alone with a man in the back yard. Fleischaka had built a tall, handmade fence. I always thought it was out of deference to the rest of the village, so that we wouldn't have to see the repulsive course of his work, but his designs were not out of respect but practicality. He built the fence to keep as many animals as he could from raiding his fire pit and slaughter tub and befouling his workspace. As I said, the fence was sturdy and tall, but Fleischaka was a butcher for a reason, and some of the slats were misaligned. I found a crack and pressed my eye up to it to look inside.

There it went wide. My knees went weak. I pushed myself away, and some snow shifted off the top and plopped on the ground.

"Ssst!" I heard Beta hiss, but I was already running away.

All of the sudden I never wanted to see her face anymore. I ran as fast as I could away from the slaughter yard and the image that burned my eyes. I didn't care if she heard me; at least she didn't know who I was.

The konstabl and his hunting party returned at dusk carrying the carcasses of three full-grown wolves. Fleischaka gutted and cut the meat in his slaughter yard and we held a feast around a bonfire in the middle of the village. The heads were cut off and staked on pikes at three points around the village. Beta sat close to the fire, her cold smile appraising every face of the attendees, meeting their gazes and holding them until they could no longer bear to look, then moving on to her next mark. I did my best to avoid her completely, but at one point she caught me across the fire. My face flushed and I jerked it away. Then, aware of my obvious guilt, I glanced up again.

She was still staring at me, her smile like icicles. It broadened and broadened until I could see her teeth.

The priest did not attend the feast. Beta went home soon after.

The next murder occurred a week later.

We had gotten arrogant and careless. The new snow piled another three inches into the lanes, blanketing (at least for a little while) the black mud in pure, clean white. The men resumed ice fishing at night, and tromped to and from the Inn. Mothers let their children out to chore before the sun came up. The innkeeper stayed open at all hours, working himself around the clock to make up for the custom he lost during the panic after the first murder. He gave me a job, calling me his "Assistant," and while the pay was good, being an "Assistant" innkeeper consisted mainly of clearing the tables of empty mugs and half eaten food, and mopping up the contents of the drunks' stomachs if they couldn't make it outside into the snow. Still, father allowed it as it brought in a few extra korunas and gave him an excuse to start training my younger brother as a cobbler.

They found Bednan the Cooper east of the village, staked through the heart with one of the pikes we used to mount the wolf heads. His throat was torn out just like the farmer's. His stomach was another rose in bloom. And there was again very little blood in the snow.

This time with no wolves upon which to blame the murder, the villagers' eyes turned on each other. I was at the Inn one night after they found his body, working what looked to be my last shift, judging by the sudden drop off of customers. The men whispered and grumbled, casting gossip as carelessly as a cat toying with a bird.

".. . naturally it's the butcher. Only he can wield a knife so expertly."

"Why not the chirug, the surgeon?"

"Did you see the wounds? No respectable surgeon would be caught making such ragged filth. A common beggar could have butchered . . ."

"Ah ha! See a butcher!"

"No, no butcher. No surgeon."

"Why then, do you mean to say it could have been any one of us?"

"Of course. Where were you yesterday morning?"

"Me!"

"I know what it is," growled a voice from the corner.

The men at the bar continued to argue and shout.

"I said I know what it is!"

The men stopped and turned their heads toward the corner.

It was Martinek, the old blacksmith. His shoulders were wide and round, his chest broad, his hands thick and scarred. He broke his arm at the elbow the year before, and it healed strange. His son had since taken over the iron and anvil, leaving the old man to recover and dissipate at the Inn.

"Do I have to spell it out?"

"We can't read your mind, Martinek," said one of the others.

Martinek muttered under his breath and took a swig of beer. Finally he said, "In my village when I was a boy we had several such murders. We, too, thought it was wolves; we, too, hunted a few and pegged their heads on sticks. But the deaths continued. Our konstabl questioned everyone. Jailed a few drunks and travelers. Still the murders continued. Every time the same. Throats torn out. Intestines yanked like yarn.

"A godless old crone, she never went to church, she said it was a monster, an Upir, pah!" He spit on the ground. "We all laughed at her. The konstabl would have jailed everyone in the village but it wouldn't have done a thing. We would have all died in our cells. A girl was found dead on the church stoop, only twenty years old, just married. Finally we started to think about what the old crone said. Some wanted to kill her but she couldn't be found, so we searched the graveyards, the mausoleum beneath the church, the ruins out in the woods. We found it in a tomb in an old, desiccated cemetery hidden behind the church by an old copse, sleeping in an iron casket in the middle of the day.

"It had two inch fangs like a snake in front of its mouth, and long, brown, curled fingernails with blood and dirt crusted under them. Its hair barely covered its withered scalp, it was long and greasy and ran down its back. We pulled it out of its tomb and drove a stake through its heart, cut off its head, and set the body out in the sun.

"Upir, pah!

"It burned to dust in seconds."

There was a shocked pause during which I heard the Innkeeper, his eyes searching the room for signs of trouble, rub a glass squeaking clean. The fire popped and crackled. Then the group at the bar burst out laughing, clapping each other on the back. They ordered another round and gave one to Martinek for the story. He took it begrudgingly and cursed their disrespect as he drank, and when they were done the Innkeeper threw them out because one of them broke a chair.

That night a storm dropped half a foot of snow on the village.

In the light of the next morning, as the winter sun burst through the snow heavy clouds, the miller's daughter, only nineteen years old, was found gutted by the creek. The miller swore she'd been in bed the night before, before he went out to the Inn, insisted over the howls of his wife and sons that she'd been safe and sound. No he couldn't remember when he'd gotten home. Nobody recalled seeing him at the Inn. They buried her immediately and cleared the murder site then set a bonfire there to cleanse it of evil.

The konstabl took the miller to jail but had to let him go the next morning when they found another man, a traveler nobody knew, lying dead on the ashes of the bonfire.

The hunt for the vampire started the next morning.

It was led by the men who'd laughed at Martinek the blacksmith at the Inn. They stayed up all night, first at the Inn drinking beer after beer, then after they were thrown out, at the ringleader's house in the village. They asked for Martinek to come with them, but he refused.

This time the priest didn't bless the weapons. Nobody saw them off, bid them farewell. They merely stole out of the village in the near dark, five drunken men slipping and cussing in the churned-up mud snow, axes resting on their shoulders. We stayed in all day long. Mother wouldn't let us out, not even father to go to the shop. By dusk he'd had enough, and he ordered me to the Inn for news of the hunt. I slipped out before mother could object and slogged my way through the lanes, trying to avoid the icy puddles that formed as the sun set.

It was dark by the time the Inn came into view, only five minutes since I'd left home. The village was deserted; no lights warmed the windows, only smoke from chimneys trailed in the air. The wind howled down the lane as I trudged forward, and then I heard other footsteps behind me. I stopped and turned but could see nothing in the darkness.

"Who is it?" That was a mistake. Now they knew I didn't know. "I have a knife!" I didn't have a knife.

A whisper of sound came from behind me, and as I turned again something hard and flat struck me hard in the face. My vision went black and I was on the ground. Snow and ice shot down my jacket. I heard commotion all around me, footsteps and cursing. A hood was shoved down over my head, and rough hands gripped me by the armpits and feet and then we were moving.

I cried "Help!" but my voice was muffled by the hood, and no one answered.

We jogged forward three more feet and I struggled, went stiff, kicked out and lashed around like a fish in a net. My kidnappers cursed and hissed but neither spoke. Finally I freed my right foot, pulled back, and launched a hefty kick out into the air, hoping it would connect. I hit something solid, my kidnapper grunted, and my other foot was free.

"You oaf!"

My other captor's voice was high and thick and gruff and I couldn't make out who it was.

Then I heard other voices, manly voices, boisterous and loud. They were singing victoriously. The hunting party. I reached out to grab my other captor and felt my fingers grip onto an arm. He grunted in disgust and pulled away, but I didn't let go, even as I was dropped to the icy lane. I held on as he yanked and yanked. His shirt ripped and I fell free. Footsteps chunked in the snow, then another blow struck my face. I fell unconscious to the sounds of the shouts of the hunting party as they ran to my aid.

I woke on the floor of the Inn. My head was bandaged, and someone had placed hunks of snow in an old rag and rested it against my temple. My mouth was sore where I'd been kicked, my lips swollen. One eye wouldn't open.

The hunting party sat at a table, hunched over plates of food. Their eyes were red from hangover and effort, and their faces long and pale. A sack hung from the ringleader's belt. It was brown and oily, and something round hung low in the bottom. A dark, black stain infused the burlap. I watched as some kind of thick liquid gathered to a head and dripped to the floor.

"Well?" Martinek growled from somewhere. "Did you find it?"

The men in the hunting party dropped their eyes to their cups and planted them at the bottom. Only the ringleader stared straight ahead, sipping froth off the top of his drink. Finally he said, "Yes, we found it."

The others' eyes shook up at him in doubt, then a few over at me. I quickly closed my one good eye. *Catch what?* I thought. *A vampire? There was no vampire. The murderers are among us!*

The ringleader read their unease and put his mug down on the wooden table with a clunk. He stared around at his friends in disbelief. Most kept their eyes glued to the table, though one or two glanced nervously up at him like guilty dogs.

"I said we found it," the ringleader said. "We found the vampire."

"Did you burn the body?"

The ringleader glanced at him and returned to his beer, but not before letting his eyes fall on me.

"Yes."

"Did you cut off its head?"

A pause.

"Yes."

Martinek eyed the innkeeper who shook his head. He nodded at me.

"Then let's see it."

The ringleader set his mug down again and sighed. Then he stood abruptly up and disengaged from the table. The men there continued to eat in silence, didn't move, fixed their eyes even more permanently to their food. He strode over to Martinek, sitting at his place by the fire, the sack swinging at his side. It bumped his leg as he moved, dripped down his trousers. There were red tracks in his wake. He pulled the rope that cinched the sack shut off his belt and, gripping it by the top, set it on old man's table with a thud.

"Here," he said, turning his back. "You look."

Martinek eyed the sack and the stain and puffed on his pipe. The smoke drifted out of his mouth, past his dry, cracked lips and over to the fireplace, where the night's heat glowed orange and red. It turned over and over, gray as stone, and mingled with the wood smoke and was sucked up into the chimney and up and out into the night.

The konstabl would not commit to the theory that my attackers were the murderers.

"Probably just common robbers. It's no secret that we're under siege here. They're just trying to take advantage of our terror."

He took the patch of clothing I'd torn off one of them but I could tell he'd do nothing with it. It was just a swatch of cloth to him. Oh he hauled several men in for questioning, but they were soon released. The vampire hunters left the village after on a legitimate hunting party, looking for meat to last the rest of the month, and into their vampire hunt the konstabl probed no further.

Still, no one relaxed, and for good reason, too. In the darkening final days of winter there were three more murders. The first happened two weeks after my attack. A woman was found hanging from a tree near the church. She died of strangulation, that much was clear, but her blood had been drained, too. All that remained were the splatters blossoming in the snow under her brown, swinging boots, and leading away into the woods like fairy footprints. No one knew her, where she came from, and no inquiries were made about her in the days that followed. We left the body hanging from the tree. It disappeared the next day. The second murder was only assumed. A farmer disappeared during the night, his body, too, never recovered. And finally, finally, old Fleischaka the butcher. His was the worst.

They found his head staked on one of the wolf pikes, his body burned in the snow beneath, charred and black, as if mocking the hunters who'd left the village. They hadn't returned either, by the way, and their wives and families frantically petitioned the konstabl to put together an armed search party. It was assumed their bodies would show up in the woods after the thaw.

And that was it.

The thaw came early in March. By April the lanes of our little village were black again with mud. The hunters were never found.

I tried to avoid the butcher's as much as possible since the day I heard the priest crying and the low murmuring voice alternately calming and provoking him. In fact, I didn't want to see Beta at all anymore, which was easy as she, like the rest of us, stayed in-doors for the rest of the winter.

But one night my father killed a deer nibbling on mother's vegetable patch, and he sent me to the butcher's to get some tools so he could process it.

"No." I said it before I knew it was coming out of my mouth.

He smacked me across the face so hard that it echoed in the spring night.

"Go," he ordered, and that was that.

I approached the house from the front this time. All of the windows were dark. The sun had just set, and the cool spring mountain air raised the goose bumps on my arms. In the winter the wind whooshed down the middle of the village, bringing with it snow dust and dead leaves; in the spring it is flower petals and fresh pine. Noise from the Inn up the way wafted down toward me: men shouting, a fiddle high and merry, the clink of mugs. I thought about returning home without the tools, telling father that nobody was home, but father would have seen through the lie, and the beating I would receive would leave more than just the red welt of his handprint on my cheek.

I took a deep breath and cast a glance at the Inn. Maybe Martinek was there? A raucous shout answered my thought, followed by breaking bottles. No. If he was there he'd be drunk by now. A useless old man.

I heard the unmistakable sound of water as I crept around the side of the house. My spirits sank. I'd hoped the house would be abandoned, and perhaps I could have stolen the tools father needed. But no, there it was again, like someone was taking a bath. The butcher had set stones in the mud as a path around his house and I used them, thankful that my feet wouldn't make the sucking sound in the mud and give me away. The moon was high and bursting, illuminating the night in its eerie, pale light.

There were no voices this time, not at first. I found the slat in the fence I'd peered through months ago when I saw them the first time. I'd had my doubts, but after she looked at me during the wolf feast, and after my attack, I was sure it was them.

They were there again.

Beta lay in the large tub her father used to render the animals, to catch the blood. The moon painted the water dark and opaque and cast shadows all around the slaughter yard. Bilko the priest stood at the head, looking down at her. As I watched he produced a ladle from his sleeve, a silver ladle with strange markings on it. He whispered something as if praying, then dipped it into the water, swirling it around as Beta waited patiently, her face serene, a cold smile played across those pale, pink lips. Her hair was wet and dark and spilled out over the back of the tub. Bilko withdrew the ladle and poured its contents over her face, and she let it wash over her. Even in the moonlight I could see.

The liquid left dark red trails across her pale skin.

THE UNHOLY TRIUMVIRATE

Just . . . just get your leg up there and . . . whoa, whoa! Got a kicker here! Maybe you should just calm down and listen to the story, huh? Okay? Hold on, hold on. I gotta feed the kitties.

Okay I'm back. Let's start from the start, huh?

See, Frankie was this guy, he was like . . . he was this tough guy in the neighborhood. Lived around the corner with his Pop what ran the newsstand, you know, where you can buy gum and smokes and, uh, newspapers, right? That kinda stuff. His pop's name was Giuseppe. Real old school old like. Real old country. Come over here in what? '96, '97? Been here forever. When the Hindenburg went down? And when they lost that Lindbergh baby? Tragic, tragic. And this Frankie was a big guy, you know, no slouch. Told everyone he got them bulging biceps hauling around all them crates of merchandise and stacks of papers for his old man, who was a boozer by the way, and he'd racked up some pretty big debts playing the ponies, playing the boxers, playing the pretty much anything what could be played. And the guys he owed? Bad news.

And Frankie? He loved his pop and all, but he didn't know what to do about it. Probably because he had his own problems to worry, especially them rumors. What kinda rumors? I dunno. I mean, you know, it was just . . . kinda personal rumors about the guy and, well. . . some people thought he was a . . . that he preferred . . . .

Well . . . I'll tell you later.

So look, the day he disappeared, it was like what, three, four in the afternoon? And little Ronnie Resnick was messing around in the street, chucking a baseball at the steps of that old abandoned townhouse, and . . . What? No, it wasn't little Ronnie what disappeared. Frankie did. Pay attention.

Little Ronnie came up to Frankie at Frankie's pop's newsstand with tears just streaming down his face, a freakin' busted fire hydrant this kid. Frankie looked around to see if his Pop was anywhere in sight, and he wasn't, so he said, "Hey kid. Whatsamatta?" And the kid, Ronnie, he just kept on crying and crying, I mean who would have thought such a scrawny little kid had so much water in him? Don't they fast for Hanukkah or something? Anyway, Frankie said, "Hey, you want some candy?" I mean, really, but the kid fell for it, and Frankie snuck a Hershey from the stand and handed it over to little Ronnie, who was sitting on The Widow Mrs. Feldman's front stoop now.

So Frankie sat down next to him and kinda looked around real quick. One of them cats that was always around in the neighborhood came sauntering over and rubbed up against his leg, and Frankie just pet it a little. And then he licked his lips and he put his arm around the kid. Ronnie didn't even notice. He just chomped away on his Hershey's, chocolate smeared all over his mouth like a, like a, like a kid . . . eating a big chocolate bar. You know, getting it all over his face. Then The Widow Mrs. Feldman opened up her window and stuck her head out and Frankie's arm whipped off the kid's shoulder like a snake bit him.

"What'dja do, Frankie?" The Widow Mrs. Feldman asked, kinda shocked. "What'dja do?"

"Nothin', I-I didn't do nothin'. He just come here like this."

"What, with his face all swole up and cryin'? You beat that kid up? He steal somethin' from you?"

"Nah, nah, he didn't . . . hey, Ronnie. Why you crying like this?"

So the kid told him. He was over there throwing the ball against the stoop when some big goombahs came riding through and took the ball and when he put up a stink they threw the thing through the window of the old abandoned house.

Oh, look! It's widdle schnookums. See this little kitty? Started hanging round lately. Can't blame him. Got about ten out there. They like to prowl around the back yard.

So at this point in the narrative it becomes necessary to describe our old abandoned townhouse. It looked like any other townhouse on the block except for the fact that it was "empty". And that emptiness weighed on it like, uh, like eating too much hamburger lasagna on a hot summer day.

No. That's an awful comparison.

How about, "it weighed on the house like a wet, wool straightjacket?"

Eh, not perfect, but better.

It was just, I dunno, it was just the fact that the windows was all the time dark, you know? And not just your 'the lights is out and it's midnight on Halloween' dark, but black. Pure black. Opaque. Is that the right word? Just nod if it's—oh, that's right you can't. Just blink your eyes twice if it's—yeah, I thought I'd heard that word before. Opaque. The windows was opaque. Blacker'n asphalt, deader'n lead.

During the day they seemed to stare at you, them windows. And the door was all stripped and gray, and there was moss and vines all creeping all over the stoop like friggin' snakes. It was like the house'd been transported all the way from a swamp or something. Real ju-ju Louisiana stuff, you know? And all kinds of rumors spun around about the place, too. Blood oozing out the walls, knives slicing through the air. Friggin' nightmare.

Well, back to Frankie. He was sitting there with that poor kid just bawling and bawling about the ball. Said his dad gave it to him, and the old bastard kicked the bucket in the war. And Frankie was sitting there, and all the old pluggers on the block what hung around his Pop's newsstand all day started to show up, shuffling around with their canes and such, and they was looking at him all funny, and so finally he said, "Alright, alright I'll go an get it."

Thing was, it was getting dark all the sudden. The setting sun cast shadows of the houses on the street, and the old townhouse was all covered in them. And there Frankie stood at the stoop, lookin' up at the windows, and them window's was just staring right back at him. He folded his arms across his chest, not 'cause he was trying to look tough, though looking tough was exactly how he was trying to look, but more cause he was cold, standing there in his white tee shirt with the sleeves rolled up, and his brown trousers and his newsboy's hat. And them windows was just daring him to come in. "Yeah, that's right," they whispered. "Put your foot on my stoop. Lay your hand on my door. Come on in, Frankie. Come on in."

What? What happened to him? Whaddaya think happened to him? He never come back out, that's what. They never found his body. Never found his clothes. Not a peep. Nothing. His pop raised a ruckus with the peelers, but this place was well-known to anyone with half a brain, and most of the coppers grew up around here, so there was no way any of them was gonna set foot in it.

Hold on a minute. Gotta get this thing rolling here. It's pretty heavy, you know, and if I don't keep the stainless steel bleached and shining it craps out on me. Believe you me, it's no picnic.

Anyway, about a month later there was these guys, right? Couple of thugs in real nice suits. Herringbone. Italian leather shoes.

"Hey," the tall one said. Gray, wool long coat. "Look who it is. Giuseppe Malone!" He kinda held out his arms, palms up, expecting a hug or something.

The other one was as short and squat as the first one was tall. Wore a wool long coat, too, but it was black. His fedora was black, too, just like the other one was gray. Couple of fancy dressers, them two. The fat one didn't say nothing, just grabbed a Hershey's off the stand, unwrapped it, and chucked the trash on the street.

"What's this?" The Widow Mrs. Feldman said, leaning out her window. "Ain't you got enough sense to find a trash can?"

The tall one eyeballed her out of the corner of his eye, kinda like this. He didn't say nothing for a second, and the fat one just looked at him like a dog waiting for directions. Finally the tall one hissed something in Italian at his partner, and the little one said, "What? What'd I do?"

"Just pick up the wrapper, huh?"

Frankie's pop just stood there, and he looked a billion years old since

Frankie's went missing. Sure he was bald before, but now his skin was all . . . chalky? Is that the right word? Jus blink if . . . yeah, chalky. And his wrinkles'd grown wrinkles, and he had a hitch in his step where there wasn't one before, and he was all the time sighing and breathing heavy for no reason at all. A real Job.

The tall thug tried again.

"Giuseppe! Haven't heard from you in a long time, huh?"

Giuseppe gave him this withering glare, you know, like he didn't really care. Then he leaned on the stacks of newspapers on his counter and said, *"Che cifai qui, Basilio? Te l'ho detto prima, non ho nulla per te."*

The smile on Basilio's face fell just a little, but his hands stayed up.

"Nothing?" He made this grand display, like he's—oh don't mind this, it's a little cold—like he was just seeing the newsstand for the first time. He peered at the rows a Hershey's, ogled the newspapers all bundled up in brown paper, squinted at the boxes a smokes. "Nothing? What's all this, then? Peanuts?"

Meanwhile the short little guy came back from the trashcan clapping his hands like he just built the pyramids or something, and Basilio said, "Arko, you hear that?"

"Hear what?"

"Giuseppe. He says he ain't got nothing for us today."

Suddenly Arko was all concerned. His eyebrows bounced up, and his mouth dropped open a little. "Vincent's gonna be pissed."

Then Giuseppe did something really stupid. He waved his hands at them like they was one of them urchin's come begging for candy.

And then he turned his back.

Basilio's bemused smile quickly dropped into a snarl, and with a grunt and a growl he lunged over the counter, and he grabbed the old man by the collar, pulled him back over, threw him on the street and . . . well, you get the picture.

When they was done, Basilio, and he was breathing all heavy, and his coat was all ruffled and his hat lay in the gutter, Basilio screamed, "That's right! You got nothing! And you better have all that nothing by the end a the week or you'll have even more nothing than you already ain't got!"

Arko leveled a kick right at the old man's ribs, just to rub it in, like a rim shot at the follies, right, 'cept there wasn't no minstrels, there wasn't no go-go girls shaking their cans, and there wasn't nobody laughing.

And then they just left him there, newspapers soaking up the rain in the gutter, his teeth all bashed in and bloody, jagged gashes crisscrossing his face from where Basilio's rings cut him, and now in addition to not having his son Frankie no more, he lost the sight in his left eye, not that he'd notice on account of his eye was swole up to the size of a grapefruit: big, black, purple, and yellow.

Monday came and went, and Giuseppe didn't do nothing. He set up his stand, he sold his newspapers, he made jokes with The Widow Mrs. Feldman, but he didn't do nothing else. If he got a gun he wasn't showing it around. If he planned on skipping town, nobody seen no suitcases. Other'n that pumpkin for an eye, you wouldn't have known anything happened.

'Cept this.

Every night he just stood there on the sidewalk outside the old abandoned town house, looking up at it. It was creepy, just him an the house, staring at each other. Some people thought they seen his lips moving, like he was talking to it or something, hands hanging by his sides, the full moon hanging in the sky like a fat spider sack, casting his black shadow on the street.

Then it was Wednesday, then it was Thursday, and Friday morning rolled around cold and clear. You could see your breath fogging the air. Dew froze on windows in leopard spots, and the puddles of muck was skimmed over with a stained glass layer of ice. Fall in the big city. Basilio and Arko showed up right after sunrise, and Giuseppe was the only one out on the street. The Widow Mrs. Feldman's curtains twitched, and little Ronnie Resnick's ma paced by her window. Even the peelers, strolling by at the top of the street, hands clasped behind their backs, disappeared as soon as them two goombahs showed up.

Giuseppe didn't say a word, just stood there when they walked up. Basilio said, "You got your nothing for us today, Giuseppe? Or we gonna have to wipe the gutter with your face again?"

"My son, Frankie."

Giuseppe's good eye wandered over to the townhouse.

Basilio and Arko exchanged a look.

"Your son Frankie what?" Arko spat. "That fruitcake?" He slapped the back of his gloved hand on Basilio's chest. "I hear he hangs out down the docks during fleet week."

Giuseppe's face went dark, and a sneer swiped across it.

"He won't let you do somethin' like this. He won't let this happen *maggio le vostre anima per sempre camminano la terra nel dolore.*"

Them two guys just burst out into laughter. And not just a few giggles neither, but full-on belly laughs. Basilio hit Arko in the shoulder with his gloves again. Giuseppe remained stone-faced and cold. Then without warning, Basilio slapped him across the face three times real quick, like a machine gun that one, and grabbed him by the back a the neck and slammed his face into the stack of newspapers on the counter. Poor old Giuseppe cried out something horrible, but there wasn't much he could do except flail his arms. Arko pressed his thumb into the old man's grapefruit eye.

"Frankie ain't here no more, is he? That friggin' homo's burning in hell now. It's you you should be worried about. Now you gonna give us your nothing or what?"

"Yes, yes," Giuseppe whispered. He's got their money. And so they let him go and said, "Where?" and he said, "Follow me."

And where did he lead them? You guessed it. Right over to the old abandoned townhouse. He slogged up the stairs to the door, but Basilio and Arko didn't go no farther than the sidewalk, staring at the place like the whole thing was a joke.

"You gotta be kidding me," Basilio said. "You think this is funny? Come here. I'm gonna close your other eye."

Giuseppe put his hand on the door.

"You want your money, you come in here."

The other two didn't say nothing. Basilio nodded, grimacing. Arko frowned, confused. "All right, old man," Basilio finally said. "But if there's anything—"

Giuseppe didn't let him finish. He opened the door, went inside, and gently shut it behind him.

You never seen two old garlic cloves move so friggin' fast! They charged up them steps and burst into the house like a herd of elephants. You could see them standing there, looking around for the old man, then a shadow passed by the door and slammed it close.

For minute there was nothing. Then the heaters started firing like lightning through the windows. It went on and on, then the door flew open and fat little Arko fell out. Didn't run, didn't walk, but fell out, flat on his face. He was covered in blood, and his hat was gone, and you couldn't tell if the blood was his or not. He just lay there for a second, and then he started to crawl forward, pulling himself along with his pudgy fingers, inch by inch, trying to make it to the steps.

What's he gonna do once he gets there nobody knows. Blood dripped off his face, and his greasy hair fell in his eyes. He opened his mouth to cry for help, but he was only able to gurgle a little. Then something pulled him back a foot, almost all the way into the house. Arko dug his nails into the concrete, leaving red marks and skin. He stopped long enough to let out a broken sob, and then whatever was on the other side of that door pulled him all the way back in and slammed it shut.

A few minutes later the peelers strolled by and waited for a while next to Giuseppe's newsstand. Then The Widow Mrs. Feldman came out of her house, picked up some of the papers that'd blown into the gutter. When one of the cops puts a nickel down on the stack, she handed him one.

Here. Raise your head. There you go. Just a sip, okay? Don't want to choke it all back up.

So that's the way it stood for a while. The house was like the, uh . . . the whatchamacallit? The monkey in the oven. You know, everyone went about their business, going to school, going to work, and everybody knew it was there but nobody wanted to admit it. Politicians lied and paid the rich; businessmen lied and paid the lobbyists, lobbyists lied and paid the politicians. Nothing ever changes, and nothing ever will. Only thing different on the street was who was screwing who. And there sat the old abandoned house in the middle of it all, black eyed and dirty and covered in moss, daring anybody to come near.

What? What's that? Yeah! The elephant in the room. That's what I meant.

Huh. "Monkey in the oven."

Anyway, then the kids started disappearing and everything went to hell.

Someone set fire to the place, but the flames didn't do nothing more than blacken the foundation, burn away some of the moss and clear the weeds. The funniest thing was when the guy who did it was standing there, watching it burn, and wouldn't you know it? A window fell out of the top floor and impaled the jerk right through the head, like a spear, killed him dead on the spot.

And after that they called you.

You.

A priest.

They sent a priest.

In here.

With me.

It'd be funny if it wasn't so stupid.

'Cause, I mean, take it from my perspective. There you was in your vestal robes and your funny hat and your holy water and your silly little book. And you're chanting and reading in the living room, sprinkling water all over the brown stains on the carpet, your feet crunching on all the dirt and stuff, and you're trying to ignore that stench floating up from down here in the basement. I could see it in your face, you was thinking, "What does that smell like?"

That's when I sent widdle schnookims here at you, and while you was distracted by the sight of this perfect little kitty cat in all this filth, you didn't even hear the whisper of my footsteps coming up behind, did you? Didn't know there was anybody there till the cloth was over your mouth and nose, huh?

What's that, pop? Wha . . . hold on a minute. I'll be done down here soon.

That's my pop, he don't hear so good since them goons did a number on his ears. Looks like he won't have to worry about them no more, huh? And pretty soon I won't have to worry about you. Nobody'll ever have to worry about you again, huh father? You remember me yet? Huh? Yeah, I bet you don't. But I remember you. And here we are. I wish I had someone like me around when I was a kid.

The three biggest scourges of the Earth is violence, vice, and veneration. All three of them in some way responsible for all the wrongs done to all the people in all the world. Think of all the brutality done to poor children by the people who should have been taking care of them, and the stupid church that said it was okay.

Well, look up there on the wall. See that? Good old Arko. Well. Just his head. He was the first one so it was a little rough going on the skull there. Had to do some patching up in those bare spots. Next to him you got your standard goon, Basilio. His face got a little . . . how to say this . . . exploded? Don't blame the artist.

And in about a minute or two you're gonna join them there, father. The unholy triumvirate. A masterpiece, complete at last.

Whaddaya think? Oh that's right. You should be losing feeling in most of your face right about now.

Anyway, this won't hurt a bit. Just a little pinch in the arm and . . . no, no, don't worry about those.

I sharpened them up nice just this morning.

SALVATION

We was all setting out on the porch, it being evening and after dinner and all, and everybody was sipping tea and telling stories. There was me, of course, my sister Bonnie and her husband Cherish, and Daddy and Mama, and his daddy and Mama, my Grandaddy and Mamaw. Then there was my best friend since we was little, Miranda, and her husband, Joe. Sun was red behind the trees, and in the distance I could hear old John Walters, Mr. Kennedy's black lab, barking to raise the roof.

Mama said, "Why don't you tell about that time you found that ol' bum out by the fence?"

I flapped the fan Daddy made me right up to my face.

"Naw, Mama. I don't wanna tell it again. Everybody already heard it before."

Miranda said, "Nonsense girl! You know we all love that story! You go ahead now and tell it."

Well, rest of them people all started raising their voices and hollering for me to tell it, so I don't see how I couldn't have said 'yes'. And right then was the first time it hit me: I was going to have to tell this story till I was old and gray, setting in a rocker like Mamaw does all day, telling the story telling the story. I took a deep breath and let out a weary sigh.

"All right. I'll do it. Ya'll go ahead and stop me anytime, though. Must have heard this about a thousand times."

Everybody just sort of mumbled along in agreement, staring at their shoes like they did every time, so I went ahead and started telling it.

Y'see, *I* saw that ol' Raggity Man first, not Jimmy Walts like he'll tell you even today if ya'll ask. I saw that old Raggity Man lying right there in a heap of shredded up Federal soldier clothes. He was curled up on the dead brown grass around the electric fence at the edge of the compound. It was summer of '56? '57? I can't remember if I was ten or eleven. Don't matter.

Anyway, Mama was always telling me to look out for strangers when we was playing out Fence Line way, especially around that time. We had news of all them refugees coming from the north. Federal soldiers. And by God Himself there was one right there breathing right beneath my nose, not fifteen feet from where me and Jimmy and all them other kids was playing ghost in the graveyard! He was laid up against the fence so his clothes pushed through the holes. That meant that the electricity wasn't working,

27

and somebody had to go and tell somebody about it, and that somebody had to be me.

I stole a look over my shoulder at them other kids.

Fat Maynard was running away from Jimmy, and Jimmy, who was bigger than Maynard, caught him up in about two steps and pushed ol' Maynard right down on his face in the dirt.

Keeping my eyes on Jimmy, I reared back and kicked that Raggity Man real hard through the fence, hurling my leg into it like I was kicking Jimmy himself. Fence shook and made a jingly noise, but ol' Raggity? He ain't move or make a sound or do nothing. Dumb Jimmy was chasing the little kids round with a stick held over his head, and them kids was screaming like he'd bash them straight to hell! Miranda glanced over at me, frowning, so I turned around real quick and glared at the Raggity Man again. I thought he might have been dead, so I kicked him harder. Pretended his rear was dumb ol' Jimmy's face. Raggity Man moaned and stirred.

Then Jimmy called out, "What you doing, girl?"

Oh Lord.

If you couldn't tell already, I hated Jimmy Walts. He beat me up twice when I was little, and he did it just because he could. But he sure was dumb. I mean real dumb. One time, me and Miranda, we saw him tie his shoelaces together and fall down twice before he realized it.

Jimmy and Maynard came on over to where I was standing, and I swear they all let up a gasp like they'd seen Jesus strolling out Savior Bay, a grimace on his face, wrestling a shark.

"What is it?" Jimmy asked.

Fat little Maynard said, "What you think it is, Jimmy? A cat?"

Jimmy shot him a look like he was gonna beat him up, but Maynard wasn't afraid of Jimmy neither.

"Shut up, Maynard."

"Let's see. It don't look like no cat—"

"I said, shut up!"

I giggled.

"And it ain't look like no Hoop Snake."

Jimmy just shot me a look, but he didn't say nothing. I'd like to say that he was afraid of me because I'd hit him, or because I'd kicked him, or beat him up once, but that wouldn't be the truth. Truth was it was around that time that I'd cured Missus— of the blisters, and people had already started talking about me. Jimmy wasn't scared of me. He was scared of The Witch.

I bent over and picked up a stick and poked the Raggity Man through the fence.

"What you doing?"

Maynard said, "She going to wake that fool up, fool."

Then he picked up a rock and threw it at the fence. Jimmy started kicking the bum, and between the three of us we all finally got the Raggity

Man to hollering and crying.

"Leave me be, leave me be!"

We all backed away, and Raggity Man rolled over. His eyes was red and shot through with pain, his face was all scrunched up, and the way he grit his teeth reminded me a dog caught in a trap. I had to force myself not to run while he took us in.

Maynard stepped up to the fence.

"Who you? What you want here?"

Raggity Man's left leg was all twisted up under him, broke right in two, so he propped himself up on his elbow best he could. Then he pulled that broke leg up from under him an set it out in front, screaming as he done it. He was weeping by the end.

"If I was you, I'd be gone," said Jimmy. And he was serious. More serious than I ever seen him. It was almost like he was afraid for the man.

"Leg's broke," Raggity Man groaned. "I ain't going nowhere but here. I'm gonna die here lest you youngins go an get me some help."

I said, "Ain't nobody going to help you here."

Raggity Man fixed me a look, and he said, very patient, like I was deaf or stupid, "Girl, I broke my leg. I'm in a horrible pain. Now one ya'll go an get your mammy before I climb that fence and give you a whopping."

Jimmy's back was already ramrod straight, but now he puffed out his chest, and his eyes set hard. Me and Miranda shared a glance, but Maynard, he seemed to relax a little. His eyes softened.

"You ain't know where you at, do you?"

Raggity Man didn't said nothing after that, just sat there, thinking. After a while he lay back down in the leaves.

"What we gonna do?" Jimmy hissed at me.

"I know what I'm going to do. I'm going to run on back an get Mama, and we going to get some people out here."

"Now you're talking, little girl," Raggity Man called out, still on his back. "You go on and get your mama. Get me some people out here."

"You ain't telling yo mama," Jimmy said. "Get all the credit. You ain't going to watch. Nuh-uh, I'm going to tell my mama. *I'm* going to get all the credit."

And then he was off, and that's when the race started.

Out Fence Line way it was all winding dirt roads and pine trees. Us kids'd cut paths through the woods at certain spots for short cuts, and me and Jimmy knew them pretty good. But we ain't never *run* through them before, and now we knew why. Branches whipped our faces and hands with every step, and Jimmy and me was grunting, crying out every time a branch switched across our cheeks. Two times Jimmy just ducked out the way of a low, thick one, and two times I got hit in the eye with pine needles.

When we finally bust out onto Ring Road, we was so bloody and covered in bruises you would of thought we'd been tangling with a pack of wild dogs. We was both tired out from the run, and we both bent over right then, chests heaving, agreeing to a unspoken truce so we could each catch our breath.

Jimmy said, "Which way you going?"

I stood up, my heart still beating hard, my lungs burning. I could see what he meant. To the right was Ring Road. It circled round The Ring about two miles, then brought you straight into town, right smack up to Main Gate. But that wasn't the only way, cause in front of us was The Ring itself.

Both of us knew all the old stories about The Ring. How they was hants in there, old dead zombies from the Battle of The Ring, how there was quicksand and bugs the size of a dog with stingers that'd lance you right through. None of us kids ever dared cut no paths through it cause of them old stories, even if we all knew it was the fastest way from the Fence Line into town. When Jimmy asked me which way I was going, he meant, 'Are you going through The Ring?' And it wasn't no polite question, neither. He meant it as a dare, as a challenge.

Well, I was young enough and stupid enough to be offended by it, and I was too proud to back down. So I drew myself up, took a deep breath and said, "You can take the long way 'round, you scrawny little redneck. I'm going through The Ring."

And I didn't even wait for his reply, I just bust on through the brush and straight in.

I was fine at first. Found one of them old paths, probably something the soldiers used in the battle, and even though it was weedy and grown over, it was there, so I ran down it. The air grew heavy and strong, and the trees blocked out the light of the sun. I knew it was the middle of the day, but it felt like the middle of the night.

I ran along pretty good, only a few scrapes and scratches here and there. The trees didn't grow close to the path, and they were too tall and mangled and gnarly anyways. Wasn't a sound neither but the thump thump thump of my feet hitting the ground, and I thought to myself, 'I'm gonna cream Jimmy by a half hour, at least!'

Of course, just when I was thinking that, my shin hit a log hidden in the brush, sending me straight out in the air for a hundred feet. Well, that's how it felt. I hit an open patch of path with a thud, right on my chest, knocking the breath straight out of me. I skidded for another foot, skidded on my face, skidded forever, the gravel and rocks and dirt ripping my lip open and blinding my eyes and I felt like it wouldn't never stop but then finally I did.

I waited for the pain to hit, and when it did it swelled up and over my face, pulsed in my chest and belly, and knotted up in my shin. I rolled over on my back, moaning, barely able to breathe. My ribs felt like someone had hit them with a sledge, and my lungs was paralyzed. I struggled for breath, eyes bugging out, until finally I was able to take a deep one. Ain't no feeling in the world like getting the wind knocked out of you.

And that's when I heard the growling.

I sat up straight right then, staring around the clearing with wide, white eyes.

The thing was behind me.

I slowly turned my head back around, my breath coming in quick bursts. The growls increased in volume, and I stared down at the leg that'd hit the log. A bruise the size of a horse swelled up on my shin, and I wondered if I'd be able to run. Where'd that ugly old monster come from in the first place? Then I remembered: the electricity in the fence was down, probably had been for a while. Nasty little devil probably dug underneath it and holed up in here, living off the birds and swamp frogs and lizards and such.

I rose up off the ground as carefully as I could, and as I did the growling got louder, gruffer, meaner. I leaned on my left leg and slowly turned around to face it. My leg was tender, and painful, but I could put my weight on it. If I wanted to live, I'd have to run. Even if I couldn't, I'd have to.

The thing was all nasty fur and boils and clotted blood and raw skin. Its mouth was sharp teeth and drool; in its black eyes I saw death. Then I heard its voice, clear as a bell in my mind.

"Don't try to run, little witch," it said. "You lame, and you small, and I'm the serpent, the adversary, the Liar."

My eyes skittered over the path around me, looking for a weapon. There in the brush on the right, a fat tree branch about as long as my arm. I squatted down and picked it up, sucking in my breath at the pain in my right shin. It wasn't a tree branch. It was part of an old post. Oak. Petrified. Probably left over from the war.

That's when the thing leapt at me, snapping its teeth. I stood, swung the post back, and knocked it across the snout with all of my strength! It yelped and crashed into the brush. Instead of running like I should have, I waded into the weeds to finish it off. It lay on its side, panting and whining. It's eye rolled as I approached, and it bared its teeth and growled deep in its chest. I'd bashed the side of its head in.

"Take that you stupid devil! I ain't no lame witch! I'm of Salvation. And you a dead demon."

I raised the post over my head to bash the rest of it in, and that's when I heard more growls.

I paused, and my eyes swiveled to the left and the right, that post still held over my head in my shaking arms. The devil's generals was all around me in the brush: one in front, two down the path.

I slowly stepped back onto the dirt, the post still raised. I'd regained my breath, but my leg was giving me more trouble than I thought. Every step was agony, and the center of the bruise pulsed every time my foot touched the ground. It was now or never.

I spun and sprinted away. Well, I tried to sprint. It looked more like I as lunging forward every other step. The beasts let up a yelp and gave chase. Blood pounded in my ears as I tore though The Ring. The post slowed me down, but if I ditched it I was dead for sure. One of them things nipped at my heel. "Hi!" I cried, swinging behind me. I felt it connect and heard the thing yelp and I ran faster.

Quick glance over my shoulder. Two left: one about two feet behind me, one farther back. The one closest to me nipped at my heel again.

I swung the post but it ducked. Then it opened its jaws and clamped down on my calf. I cried out and fell to my knees. Soon as I did, the creature let go and lunged for my throat. I shoved the post up and into its jaws, heard a sick crack. It yelped, but jaw was locked. It twisted its head back and forth and drooled and snarled, but I didn't let go. One more second and the other monster would be on me, and it would chomp on my face and eyes, and it would tear out my throat.

I gritted my teeth.

If them things was going to kill me, I'd take at least one of 'em with me.

Then I heard shouts and a thud. I shoved the post in deeper, and the thing whined and whipped its head back and forth one last time, but I still held on. Then something pierced its side with a thud, and it sagged over to the left. A spear had stuck clear through it, and wiggling there in the air. I didn't even have time to wonder what was going on when two more spears zipped in and spiked the monster to the ground. It's eyes glazed over, and then it stopped breathing.

I got to my feet, shaking. A familiar voice said, "Didn't your Mama tell you not to go through The Ring?"

I turned around and there stood Miranda, hands on her hips, head cocked, a crooked smile on her face. Next to her was little ol' Maynard, clapping the dust off his hands.

Well, the whole porch just blew up. Joe kissed Miranda on the cheek, and Daddy punched Joe in the arm, laughing.

"Don't you mess with that one!"

Mama said, "I always knew Miranda was the smart one of you two." And that brought more laughs.

"Man, I tell you," Miranda said. "We wasn't going to just let you face no devil by yourself."

"How'd you know she was in there?" Joe asked, like he always done.

Miranda shrugged. She smiled at me.

"Just figured. She wasn't going to let ol' Jimmy Walts beat her, and she was slower than him in a straight up race."

"Hey now!"

"It's true."

"Where'd you get them spears?"

"Ol' Maynard found 'em," Miranda said. "Just settin' on the road like they was waiting for us."

Paw Paw whistled long and low.

"Hand of the Lord, hand of the Lord."

"Well we too old to find out now," I said. "You going to let me finish the rest of my story?"

"Ain't nobody stopping you!"

When they got a look at me, Maynard whistled.

"You look like hell."

Miranda's jaw dropped at the curse. Maynard never really was one to mince words.

"What? You seen her, too."

I have to admit, ol' Devil worked me over pretty good. My smile was cracked lips and a wall of bloody teeth. Dress shredded in a dozen places, right leg all swole up and bleeding, left eye all swole up and bleeding, face lashed and welted, my whole body covered in dirt and mud, and little sticks sticking up out my kinky head.

"Well? We saved your butt. Don't stop now. Jimmy's probably about ten feet away from Main Gate."

That was enough for me. I turned tail and ran.

"Don't worry 'bout us!"

And I didn't, neither.

Ten minutes later I limped out onto Ring Road, about three hundred yards from Main Gate, which was to my left. Just when I did, I seen Jimmy turn round the corner about a quarter of a mile to my right.

And then I smiled, cause I won.

Dingalingaling! Ding Ding Ding! Mayor Bram rang the Noticing Bell until it bout cracked in half. People come out of their homes and from all over the place, crawled out the woods like ants, slunk down the street like spiders. Mama and me was standing on the platform facing everybody, and I was looking for Daddy, but he was fishing in the cove so I knew it'd be a while. Meanwhile, Mayor Bram was talking before everybody was even there, and he was loud, too. More he talked, though, quieter everyone got, until it was still as the bay at dawn.

He told everybody that there was Others on the edge of the fence. Everyone's eyes flicked over me and I could feel the hate rolling off them. I just wanted to crawl away into a hole and cover up forever.

Then he told about when The People moved here after the war broke out between the Federals and the New States' Confederacy. He told about The Battle of Ring Wall with his daddy and Grandaddy, and about the time they was up north and seen them people suffering from the blisters. And he told about our rules, and about what happened last time refugees tried to get in.

"But we have prevailed! We have survived against all odds. Preserved our lives and the lives of our children and our religion for almost a century of strife. All around us they fight *their* wars, they exert *their* power. But not over us."

He paused, looked out over the crowd, and his voice became hushed, almost pleading.

"Now, our families, our children, our homes and our peace have been threatened once again." He pointed out a man in a red flannel standing in the crowd, and the man blushed and shuffled nailed his eyes right on his feet. "You, John Gray. You lived in Helena not sixty years ago. What did you see?"

John Gray didn't look up when he spoke, but his voice was clear and strong.

"I seen me some death and poverty. I seen despair and lies."

"That's right. That's right! And you, Christine Thompson. Your parents was from Old Capital. What was it like there?"

"It was like the end of the world, Mayor. So my daddy used to tell me. Folks dying off like flies. No food, no meds, nothing at all. Anybody had anything, it was for the soldiers."

Bram strode up and down the platform, finger pointing at Christine Thompson like he'd pin her to her spot. "For the soldiers!" He jabbed that finger at the sky. "For the soldiers!"

Whole town was looking up at the Mayor, eyes wide open, not blinking. They followed him while he paced back and forth, back and forth.

"You know what needs to be done. It is our way."

He stopped and dropped his chin to his chest, crossed his hands solemnly in front of him. I heard the wind rushing through the trees, the gulls squawking down by the water. Finally, the mayor raised his head and fixed the crowd with his steely eyes. "As you all know the harvest is going to be a small one this year."

Nods and murmurs from the crowd.

"The bay is not producing enough edible fish."

More nods and acknowledgment. Some angry cries.

He stuck out his neck, bent over at the waist.

"Now why is that, I wonder? Why is that?"

Everybody's eyes were cast down, staring at their shoes, pawing the dirt. Breeze picked up, mussing the mayor's hair. He didn't fix it. Mama gripped my shoulders, and I could hear her whispering a prayer.

He stood up, scowling at everybody.

"I'll tell you why. Because it's been two years! Two years!"

A soft shudder ran through the crowd, a murmur and gasp, and Mayor Bram held up two fingers.

"Two!"

Then he cast his cold eyes over the crowd, and he said in a low, dark rumble, "Well, I'm here to tell you today that we're going to end that bad habit."

About a half an hour later, the men Mayor Bram sent out after ol' Raggity came jogging back into town, holding him over their heads like he was some kind of trophy. He was screaming because of his leg, but that didn't slow them down at all. They ran right up to the Sunday school house behind the church.

Mayor Bram whispered in Mama's ear, and Mama took me back there to the side door. She opened it up and brought me into the stairwell, then dragged me down into the basement and into the classroom. Raggity Man was tied down tight to one of them long desks we used for painting and crafts. I could see the pink stain from a jar of paint Molly Lavalle spilled there Sunday before. Mama turned me around and held my face in her hands.

"You be good, girl. And don't be scared. This here for the good of all of us. Fear of this is foolishness."

I nodded, and Mama spun on her heel and left me in the room. The door shut behind her with a click, and I heard her footsteps echo up the stairs, and then the door to the outside squeaked open and slammed shut, and then it was just me and that Raggity Man. I peered at him real close. He was sweating, his face was bright red, his teeth was clamped down on his bottom lip. He didn't make no sound, just lay there, breathing through his nose. I could hear the swoosh of the wind, and every now and then he shifted on the table.

Finally he looked over at me, and with a face pinched tight in pain, he spoke.

"Little girl. Cut me loose."

I didn't say nothing. Just stared at him.

"Little girl, look." His voice was rocks in a barrel. "Cut me loose. I won't come back. I swear I won't. I know who you are now. I won't come back and I won't tell nobody. Just cut me loose."

I shook my head real slow, and the Raggity Man stared at me. He stared so long that I couldn't take it no more, so I just looked at the floor. I heard the swoosh of the wind outside. There was a pair of shears on Teacher's desk. I strolled over and was just about to reach out for them when somebody rapped on the window above.

I jumped about ten feet.

The windows were thin little rectangles set up near the ceiling. They let in just enough light to see by. I looked up, and there was dumb ol' Jimmy Walts, bent over and pushing his nose against the glass! I waved at him and smiled real big to make him jealous, and he made a face and all the sudden he was jerked away. I seen two pairs of legs, Jimmy's and his Daddy's, stalking away from the Sunday School House.

I padded around the desk and up to the window, pulled out Teacher's chair and stood on it, then stood up on my tip toes to see what was going on outside. I seen the people around the bell and Father Harris reading from the book, his voice getting louder over the groans and cries of his flock. Some was already starting to shake.

There was a clunk behind me, and some shuffling, and some low voices. I turned around and it was five men, one of them was Andy Rawlins. I knew him because I he was always gruff and mean and I was afraid of him. They each held a wood bowl in one hand and a copy of the book in the other.

"Get down, girl," Andy Rawlins said, and I did. I straightened my dress.

Rest of them men gathered around ol' Raggity, each coming to a halt at five points: one at each arm, one at each foot, and mean ol' Andy Rawlins at his head.

Four of them started reading a passage from the book I ain't never heard before. Then Andy Rawlins pulled out a big, flat, worn leather pouch he'd stuffed down his belt in the back. He set it on Teacher's desk and opened it up. I saw all kinds of shiny knives flashing inside. He took one out that was as big as my arm and ran his finger along the blade. I'd seen daddy's hunting knives before. They were pretty big, but not nearly as big as this one. This one looked like as sword. Like it could take a man's head off in one swipe. The other men put down their books and grabbed the Raggity Man's arms and feet.

"Hey!" Raggity Man yelled.

He started kicking with his good leg, and shouting, and he kicked one of the men clean off him. Kept on struggling till Andy Rawlins come up an grabbed him by his broke leg and shook it round a bit. Raggity howled something fierce and all the blood drained from his face. Then he started to weep, and he stared right at me, tears cutting pink patches through the dirt on his skin.

"Little girl."

Outside I heard the Noticing Bell rattle softly over the thick moans of the people. I turned to look out the window again. I wanted to be out there, out there with Miranda and Mama and Maynard and even dumb ol' Jimmy, but I wasn't. I was in here.

"Little girl. Please."

Andy Rawlins put the knife against his neck and drew it across. Blood fanned out and flooded down like a river.

He and the other men took up the bowls to catch what spilled over the edge. Ol' Raggity gagged and gurgled, moaned and gasped, and the blood splashed into the bowls, and he started shaking and twitching. Got so bad they had to hold him down by lying cross his chest. After a while he stopped, and Andy Rawlins got up and reached for the worn leather pouch. He turned and fixed me with a stare to freeze mercury, and thrust out a skinning knife. Held it by the blade so its fancy, polished ivory handle shivered in the air. He shook it at me like an order. I heard it loud and clear.

There was a lot more cutting to do.

James Noll

CITY OF SALT

I'm on the floor of someplace I've never seen, looking at a boot worn by a man I don't know. The carpet is plush and full, decorated with blue and yellow in swirling patterns. Head aches. Blood in my mouth from when the boot on the man I don't know kicked me, or where I fell. I don't know. I can't remember. I lose time.

Try not to let the blood drip on the carpet. It's a nice carpet, and I don't want to ruin it, but the blood drips onto it anyway.

Last thing I remember is the house on the edge of town. Looted. Porch stooped and leaned like a dirty old man. Black windows like black widows. Spider web in the corner of the porch blew in the breeze and I remember think "This is good." I stared at the web for a while. It was caught in the full cracked moon, and then I felt it creep across my brain, an electric spider web spreading out like a wash of prickers, and then I wake up and I'm on the floor, looking at the boot and bleeding carpet. I try to speak, but my voice is little more than a croak.

"Salvation?"

Laughter from the room. More than just the boot-wearing man. All around me.

This isn't Salvation.

"Water."

More men laughing. Gravelly and bitter. One snorts.

My hands are tied behind my back to a chair. Feet to feet, leg to leg, so we're like one crooked thing spilled out on the floor.

"Set him up, please" someone says. Male, high-pitched, smooth.

The chair swings up and I get dizzy, skyrockets in my head in the back, right where it meets my neck. Spider web lightenings across my eyes, but none in my brain. I lose no time. And then I'm up, head pounding whump whump whump with my heart. Fat man on the other side of a fat desk in front of me smoking a fat cigar. The smoke burns my eyes and throat and I cough. You can smell smoke in somebody's hair from fifteen feet away. Fifty if the wind's right.

"Give him some water, Chuck," the fat man says. He doesn't drop his letters, doesn't say "'im," asks politely. He's educated; he's in charge. Then he coughs, harsh and hoarse, like an old man on that dirty old porch.

Something wet pours over my head. Water. Chuck giggles. I can't see him but I know he's looking over his shoulder at his friends. The fat man leans forward and clasps his pork roll fingers in front of him on the table. He chews on the cigar in the left corner of his mouth, lips shine with spittle.

"Now to drink." He raises his eyebrows. "Please."

Laughter stops. Bottle to my lips. Water cools my mouth, my throat, my belly. No sediment. Clean. Bottled. I gulp so hard that it spills down my chin and neck. I gasp when Chuck takes it away.

"Fugee," he snarls, and smacks the back of my head so hard that my hair falls in my face.

My hair is long, and it's wet with the water he poured all over it, and when I whip it back the water flies off and spatters all over him.

"Goddammit!"

Fat man motions him away with one impatient and thick hand. Cigar smoke trails above his head in waves.

The cigar smoke masks the other scents. Good scents. I let my nostrils flare.

Chuck smells like manure.

Manure means animals.

Animals mean food.

The fat man smells like alcohol and soap.

Soap means showers.

Showers mean hygiene.

This is a good place. I won't be allowed to stay.

Fat man is speaking:

". . . going to help us get it." Leans back in his chair. It creaks. His belly sticks out like a watermelon in a sheet, his white pants pulled up almost to his chest.

"Get what?"

Skyrockets in my brain. Pain in my temple. It takes a while to fight off the spider web, and I lose a little time. When I come back the room is empty but for the fat man and me and Chuck. Something running out of my nose, over my lips.

I run a dry tongue over them. Cracked. Blood.

"You back with us?" Fat man.

I nod. Keep my head down, hair in my face. People don't like the looks I make when I'm angry. It scares them. So I hide it.

"Get what?" I ask.

The fat man puffs on his cigar.

"Salt." A carpet of smoke erupts from his lips.

"Salt."

I think until I feel the spider webs creep up my spine, and then I stop. No salt on the way into town. I remember I smelled the river, dank and earthy. I smelled the smoke from the fires carried down by the wind; the ash burned my eyes, my nose, my throat. I heard the crickets and the frogs by the river. I saw the houses, most of them burned down to the ground or only standing halfway.

"For the meat?"

Fat man smiles.

"You're not as dumb as you look."

"Where?"

Fat man stubs out the cigar on an ashtray with the words Visit Niagara! written in thick balloon letters. Rolls the edges. It glows for a minute in the center until he plunges it down.

"The city."

The city. Fire flies streak the air. Screams. Blood running down my leg. Flash of rotten teeth, pale arms. A meat cleaver.

"No."

Fat man nods and leans back in his chair. His pig eyes fall on Chuck over my shoulder. Nods once. Curt.

Do it.

Flash of skyrockets in my head.

Spider web over my brain.

I lose time.

My hands are still tied behind my back. I'm in a car, moving fast.

I must have mumbled something because a voice to my right says, "Hey, Pete. He's up."

Chuck.

"Untie me."

Pete's driving. He says, "What's he sayin'?"

Smoke. Sweat. Manure. Alcohol. I can smell them all from fifty yards away.

"He wants me to untie him."

Pete laughs.

"Not yet."

Look out the window. Let my hands feel along the waistband of my pants. My knife, a little shank of metal, is still there. My head cracks against the window. Stars in my eyes. Chuck hit me.

"Water?" he barks.

I blink the stars away. Nod.

He holds a bottle to my lips and I gulp, gladly, once, then spit a mouthful out all over the seat in front of me. Piss.

Chuck, laughing, coarse, Pete cusses in front of me. I wait until Chuck closes his eyes for just one second.

Throw myself at him, aim my forehead for the soft of his eye. Stars for a bit, then I am on top of him. My mouth finds his ear.

Chuck yells, "Get him off me!"

Screams to squeals. Blood on my tongue, something hard lands on the back of my skull. Stars explode again, but I don't let go. A thud. More stars. I lose time.

On the edge of the city. Smell the ash. Burnt metal. Rot in the distance. Fires deep inside, I can see their glow, the heart of the animal. *Their* fires.

Chuck presses the barrel of a shotgun against my temple, the left side of his face is awash in blood.

Spider web around the base of my skull. I lose time and then I'm up and Chuck is under me, his arm at an angle. My knife is buried past the hilt in his skinny, red farmer's neck. Pete has the shotgun now, trained on me, but not against me, and his eyes are wide and his mouth is shut. The other man's mouth is shut, too. My mouth. Was wide. Open.

The other man says, "What should we do?"

Pete swallows.

"Fat man wants his salt." He nods at me. "Wants him to get it."

"Look what he done to Chuck."

Pete lowers the barrel a little. His eye skitters over Chuck. He says, "Maybe Chuck shouldn't have did that." He says, "Maybe Chuck deserved what he give him."

Lowers the barrel all the way.

"You wanna get it by yourself?"

The other man stares at Pete. Takes a step back. Pete smiles. His teeth are straight and white. Raises the barrel at me.

"He seems to know what he's doing."

"Yeah," the other agrees, fast, voice shaking.

Upwind as we pick over the barricade. Fires somewhere burning. Smell smoke and flesh burning. The asphalt is a river bed in drought. Half buildings, skeleton arms poking up into the sky. Jagged windows like broken teeth.

Pete says, "Where to?"

I don't speak.

Pete says, "Where to?" again, harder.

I don't speak.

"He ain't talking," says the other one.

I stop and turn around, hold up my wrists still bound.

They stare at me. A long time.

"What do you think, Pete?"

Pete pulls the keys off his belt. Throws them to me, jingling in the air. Can hear that a hundred yards away. Scrape on the broken concrete. Wind shifts when I kneel to pick them up.

We walk for a mile or so, me between the other two. Pete points at a tall, old apartment building.

"What about that one? Bound to be salt up in there."

I shake my head.

"Well why the hell not?"

"Palies."

"Pale what?"

"Palies."

"What the—"

Scrape of feet on the asphalt behind me.

"Whatcha doin'?"

Pete. He's next to me now. We're a triangle.

The other one says, "I ain't going a step more tilll he tells us what we're doin'."

Pete ducks his head. Eyes me.

"Don't seem like much of a talker."

"Shouldn't talk too much here," I whisper.

He eyes me. Says to the other one, "Fat man wants his salt."

"And he'll get it! But not till I know what's what!"

Pete eyes me. He says, "Well?"

Spider web on my brain. Knock it down. Not now.

Wave my hand at the burned-out holes of the building the other one wants to go into.

"Nothing there," I say.

Wave my hand at the street in front of us.

"Nothing there," I say.

The other one points up at the building again, leans forward, eyebrows up, head first, like a rooster. "How the hell do you know there's nothing in that building?"

I shrug.

"Been in there before."

He laughs, short and harsh, but he stops when he sees I'm serious.

"When?"

I shrug again.

"Been in."

"When?"

Blade teeth. Bloody black smile. Flash of pale arms.

Look away up the street. Look back. Spit.

"Week ago."

"Bullshit!" He points again. "What's in there?"

I look up and behind me. The top is bone fingers stretching for the sky.

"Nothing."

He makes a hissing sound.

Pete eyes me again. He says, "What about up over there?"

Points the barrel across the street.

Don't even look.

I say, "Nothing in there but rats and dry rot."

I say, "What you want's farther in."

Pete points the barrel at me.

"I didn't ask you that. Where'd you go in there?"

Return his stare second for second, wait until he steadies the barrel, leans it in at my chest.

"Number three one three. Corpse in a chair by the window."

Pete lowers the barrel, still looking at me.

"I didn't do it."

Pete says, "Go on up there and see."

I don't move.

"You heard him," the other one growls at me. "Go on up there and—"

Pete puts a hand on his shoulder, shakes his head.

"Not him."

Sit on a crack till the other one comes back. He's a little pale. Wipes his arm across his mouth. One arm behind his back.

Pete says, "What's tha—"

His friend shoves a corpse arm up in his face.

"A gooligooligoo!"

Pete smacks the arm away with the barrel. Shatters to dust. The other one left with a forearm splintered like a knife.

"Cut the crap!" Knocks the rest of the arm out of his hand and into dust.

"Aw c'mon, Pete. Least we know he's telling the truth."

"Well, I'm glad you're finally convinced, princess. Your curiosity satisfied? You ready to move on? Or do we have to climb another fence for you?"

Wind changes direction every minute. I can smell their sweat, the animals they raise. And so can *they*. I palm a handful of ash from the gutter, rub it under my arms, scrub my face and arms. The other one giggles at the sight of the corpse's shattered arm. It echoes in the empty street.

If I can hear him. The wind shifts.

I button my lip tighter.

Princess opens his arms, hands splayed.

"Ready when he is."

Later.

The sky turns from death gray to widow black. Search the skyline, what's left of the buildings, the broken bone fingers, the empty eyes, and listen, listen, always listen, and smell the air. The fires will grow bright soon. Then the drums. Then—

"Why ain't we going into any of these places?"

Princess. Whining again. He smells the strongest of the two. He'll be first.

I don't answer.

"Hey!"

Pete says, "Leave him be."

Princess stops walking. A pile of ash and dirt behind a husk of a car. I take a handful, rub it on my legs, rub it on my face. Wind shifts.

"How the hell do we know where he's taking us? How the hell we know there's any salt at all?" He raises his gun at me. "I mean, Jesus. Look at him."

We make it to the intersection. Green canopy on the corner, ripped, pools of ash weighing it down, nosing forward over the sidewalk like a stumbling drunk. Just like I left it. Strings of yellow traffic lights and wires and poles all in a tangled web in the middle of the street. The buildings surrounding us are hollow shells of broken metal and glass. Mountain of black rubble to the right. Burned out brick, half-jagged black windows to the left.

Pete says, "He's managed on his own so far."

I point at the torn green canopy.

Princess and Pete's heads swivel on pistons.

Princess says, "What? There?"

Flash of black teeth.

I nod.

"Salt," I say.

The canopy frame is metal. Solid. Salvageable. I pull on a leg. Ash sifts underneath, a snake under a pillow. Princess stands in the gutter at the end. He stares doubtfully up at the sign overhead. Pete puts the barrel of his gun on my forearm and I look at him. Don't let go, just look.

"Let go," he says.

I pull the leg hard, yank the leg out, break the leg, and the canopy let's loose a high pitched squeal and comes crashing the rest of the way down to the sidewalk. Piles of ash slough slowly off and all over Princess.

"Hell!" he sputters. Can't see him through the ashes, but when it clears he's a puppy in a fireplace. Shakes his hair, ash in all directions.

Pete is laughing.

"Dammit!" Princess snaps. His white eyes glow in the dark. They'll see that.

Pete says, "Well, he got the door clear," and points at the entrance to the restaurant.

Keep my eyes on the skeleton fingers behind. Keep my ears pricked. The wind shifts and I smell the air. Just a hint, just a hint, but I can smell them.

Princess kicks a leg of the canopy away along with small pebbles. A few bounce high in the corner of my eye, and I watch them until they disappear in the twilight. Up there. On the building across the street. A round head pops over the top of the finger. Princess reads the letters on the sign again.

"What's that say?"

Pete tries to read it, spelling out the words.

"M E X." He stops and shakes his head. "Who cares? It's a food place. Hot damn!"

"What's M E X?"

"Never mi—"

"Mexican," I say.

They both look at me.

"It was a Mexican restaurant."

The wind shifts. "What's Mexican?"

Princess.

I don't say anything.

Pete stares at me for a second, then says, "Who cares? It ain't been looted. Canopy must have blocked it. Let's go in."

Tables inside still whole, still clean. Chairs pushed under. Long counter on the left. Steel door behind. Smell of dust and fire and smoke. Under that, rats. On each table a full cellar of salt. Just like before. All the blood, the blood from before, is gone. But the floor is still sticky.

"Hot damn!" Princess yells. Pulls a plastic bag from inside his shirt. Throws the cellars in one at a time. They clack and click.

"Careful, you idiot," Pete says. He gently places his cellars into his own bag. "They're glass."

"Have you ever seen so much?" Princess asks, his eyes wide enough to drool.

I inch toward the metal door in the back. If I can get it locked from the inside . . .

"Hey!"

Pete.

I turn.

He has a pillowcase. Balls it up and throws it at me. I catch it on my chest.

"Fill it up."

Slink slowly to the nearest table. Drop a cellar in the case.

Keep my eye on the window.

Two more round heads on the skeleton finger across the street, perched on the tip like insects. Pale and glowing white in the darkness.

"Damn!" Princess calls out from the kitchen. He pushes through the saloon doors, a large cardboard box cradled in his arms. "Hit the jackpot back here!"

I shuffle to the window, the case dangling from my right hand. Peek out of the corner of my eye. Stop dead.

There. And there. And there.

Quickly shove more cellars in my case.

Pete snaps: "Hey! Careful with those!"

Drums roll in the distance.

Princess stops, goes pale.

"What was that?"

A firefly shoots off the finger across the street, two more behind it. They arch high and loop down at the window. An explosion of white and red fire washes against the glass. I jump behind the bar. The window cracks. Then the other two hit and glass explodes. The spider web swarms up the back of my brain, and this time I don't fight it.

I lose time.

Standing in a black hollow of rubble across the street and a block away from the MEX. Breath comes in heaves. Arms and legs and back ache. Covered in blood. Soaks my clothes, hair. Gash on my right leg. White meat. I have Pete's shotgun and both of their bags of salt. My pillow case is empty, covered in blood. Ragged red hole in the bottom.

I can smell them.

Hundreds of them.

Poke at the meat around the wound in my leg. I'll need to clean that, sew it up. Step out of the hollow and suck in a hiss.

MEX swarms with palies. Cover the place like a pile of ants, front, top, sides. Naked blue-white skin glows in the night.

Something pops out of the mass, arches high toward me. I lose it against the sky, then it bounces with a thick thud in the middle of the tangle of lights and wires.

A handful of palies disengage from the swarm, pounce on it. See what it is before they get to it. Pete. Mouth open, lips ripped off, teeth punched in, blond hair matted red.

Wind changes directions. The whole swarm raises their blind eyes to it, their slit snouts flaring, snuffling sickly. A hundred white eyes turn as one in my direction.

I raise the shotgun and back away.

The spider web flows over my brain.

Turn to run.

The fat man will get his salt.

THE NEIGHBORHOOD IS REALLY GOING TO THE DEAD

Grossman's house was a blight upon the neighborhood. The windows were all boarded up, the top of the chimney collapsed and overgrown with weeds, and cars littered the front and back lawns in a parody of a castle wall. It was impossible to navigate the front yard without getting snared in the makeshift wire fence he'd strung like a labyrinth across the grass, or stepping on the leftover rusty nails and screws, or getting tangled up in the hoses, or falling into the pits he'd dug for one abandoned project after another. Compared to the pristine gardens, the manicured Bermuda grass, the sealed driveways of the other houses on Swan Tail Lane, Grossman's property was an embarrassment. An ear torn off a starlet; a gash on a baby.

It was Halloween, and the porches and mailboxes were decorated with paper skeletons or fanged pumpkins. A few of the yards even had blow up goblins or ghosts, now deflated in the early morning sun. At night, bushes flickered with cheery orange and green lights, set on timers to turn on as soon as it got dark. All Grossman had by way of decoration was a crimson smear of a handprint splattered on his mailbox and door. It looked more like some kind of twisted religious symbol than it did a decoration, but then again, nobody ever recalled seeing him at church.

Robert had only been in the neighborhood for a few days, but to him it was now home. He and Berenice had traveled hundreds of miles to get there, drawn to it by the quality of the people who lived there. And the amount. How could he forget the amount? There were so many, so many, and it first overwhelmed him to have to deal with them all. They were so healthy and strong and virile that it took him and Berenice (and Jimmy and Betty and some others) a long time to get the job done. Those first couple of days were heaven, a feast of introductions, at least until they came across Grossman's house.

Robert and Berenice stood at the mailbox across the street, glaring at the hideous sight opposite them. Berenice's mouth hung agape.

I can't believe he thinks it's okay to live that way, she muttered.

I know, Robert sighed. *I mean, who leaves all that stuff on their lawn? Makes it so difficult to get to him.*

We're lucky we didn't go to his house first.

Robert nodded. Their first few days were so easy. All they had to do was walk right up and introduce themselves. Nobody had pits in their lawns or shot at them. It was so easy that they'd become used to it, and after a while they didn't even pause as they made their rounds.

His best friend, Jimmy, straggled up next to them. His overalls were savaged, and his long beard swung over his pendulous belly. Robert tried not to look at him. Jimmy and Betty had had a run in with Grossman a few hours before, and the former had clearly come out the worse for wear.

That damn Grossman's pissed me off for the last time, Jimmy groaned.

Robert didn't want to look at him.

Is it really that bad?

Jimmy let his head loll and stared madly at Grossman's house. His tongue popped out in concentration.

Never mind that. He cast a furtive glance them. Both were still staring at Grossman's house, trying not to look at him. *But Betty ain't gonna be walkin' no more.*

Robert finally let himself look at his friend, and his mouth dropped. Jimmy's face was peppered with black marks, shotgun pellets from look of it. Then out of the corner of his eye, something in Grossman's house caught his attention, some kind of movement, but it was gone before he could bring his head back around, and all that remained was a twitching curtain in an upstairs window.

Durnit all, Jimmy muttered. *They's in there, mockin' us.* He turned to Robert and Berenice. *I've had it. C'mon. Let's get him.*

Robert tried to reach out to stop him, but Jimmy had already lurched out into the street and stumbled over to Grossman's lawn. *Wait!* was all he could get out.

He wanted to remind Jimmy of the pits and the traps, the wire and the screws, but Jimmy was new, fresh, and much too fast. He was already in the yard by the time Robert stepped off the curb. He managed to side step the first tangle of hoses, and even avoided two of the pits. Robert thought he might actually have a chance. Jimmy groaned, *Comin' to get you!* but in doing so, he didn't watch where he was going. His right foot slipped into one of the smaller holes, and his ankle twisted. Robert heard it snap, and then Jimmy pin-wheeled into the razor wire, his feet suddenly caught in a nest of hose.

Aargh! My feet is all tangled up!

Robert started for him. *Don't move. You'll only make it worse.*

He didn't want to rush out into the open. A few days before, Grossman had appeared on his roof for the first time in a while. Mrs. Gouger, seeing her opportunity to confront him personally, started up the street. Grossman watched her calmly pick her way through the cars parked pell-mell in his driveway, then, right when she reached the last one (opening her mouth to hiss and curse at him), he pulled a shotgun out from behind his back and—well, there were still parts of her scattered on the lawn, hanging from the tree limbs.

So Robert pulled himself up behind one of the vehicles at the end of the driveway, then slowly, as slow as he could manage, he wheeled around the edge.

The sight he beheld made his stomach drop.

Jimmy's legs were entirely wrapped up in the green garden hose. He spun slowly on his good leg, groaning in frustration. Something flashed in the morning sun, and Robert saw the nails and screws protruding from his friend's feet. One of Jimmy's arms was caught in the coiled wire, and it cut into his flesh. His eyes rolled in his head.

Then Grossman appeared on his roof.

He was dressed as much as Robert expected. A wife beater, stained light brown with sweat and armpit, hung from his skinny little shoulders. Crusty old blue corduroys slumped on his narrow hips. His feet were shod in clunky, black boots. His hair was lank and greasy, and it drooped in his eyes. He smiled a brown smile at them, and pulled his rifle from behind his back.

Jimmy, Robert moaned.

Grossman put the rifle up to his shoulder, closed one eye, took aim.

Robert pulled behind to the safety of the car just as the first shot rang out. He heard another, and another, too many to count, followed by the sick splat of Jimmy's body parts as they rained all over the lawn. There was a pause, and Robert thought it was over, but then the firing resumed and he realized Grossman was just reloading his weapon.

"That'll teach you, you freaks!" Grossman screamed. "Stay the hell off my property!"

Berenice growled in response, a combination of pain, horror, and mourning. Grossman glared at her, re-shouldered his rifle, aimed, and squeezed the trigger. Robert clenched his eyes shut. The first bullet pinged off a mailbox, but the second hit her directly in the forehead. She stood still, her eyes wide, before finally falling backwards onto the pavement.

When Robert finally opened his eyes, more new neighbors from the surrounding properties had appeared on their lawns, all of them facing Grossman's house. Many wore dazed, puzzled expressions on their faces. Some glared. More poured in from the feeder streets, attracted by the noise. He recognized a few from his trip to his new home, others were just arrived, and some appeared to have lived there for quite some time. The sheer number of witnesses seemed to frighten Grossman. He shot a panicked look around him, uttered a foul word, and disappeared down behind his house again.

Robert waited until he was sure the murderer wouldn't come back before turning around the car. The rest of the neighbors shuffled at the edge of the property, unsure of what to do next. Something had to be done, that was clear, but they were too afraid to begin. A few of them stared, lips twisted, eyes goggled. They were looking at Jimmy's remains, or

Berenice's brains. Robert knew some of them were thinking of Betty, sitting on the lawn of her new home, waiting for Jimmy. And he knew some of them were thinking of Mrs. Gouger. But all of them, all of them, were thinking the same thing: *What if I'm next?*

Some kind of tacit agreement shuddered through the crowd, and they started forward, seventy five strong, and started for the monster, started for Grossman's front door. Nobody cared if he showed up on his roof. Nobody cared about the traps and the hoses. Nobody cared about the wire and the nails. He couldn't catch them all. He couldn't shoot them all. Robert tried to lead them, wanted to be the first in the hoses, the first to take the nails and the screws, the first to be cut by the wire. But the others were new like Jimmy had been, and they lurched onto the lawn in front of him.

Grossman! they wailed. *Grossman!*

The curtains on the upstairs windows twitched. Three neighbors went down in the hoses. The rest trampled over them, Robert included, unable to stop the wave of flesh.

Grossman!

Lights behind the boarded up downstairs windows flashed. Another line of them was cut down by the wires. A handful disappeared into a pit, their surprised moans cut off by an ugly thud as they landed on the spikes below. They were down to nearly one third their original number, all in an instant. Still, they crested and poured into the garden.

Grossman! Grossman!

Robert couldn't believe it. They were almost to the door! Over thirty of them, spread out in a line on the lawn. He reached out for the house, they all did, moaning his name in unison, moaning the name of the evil thing that waited just on the other side of the door, waited for them to tear him apart.

Grossman! Grossssman! Gross—

Suddenly, Robert's ears felt like they'd been plugged with cotton. A fantastic roar swallowed the air all around him, the ground disappeared beneath his feet, and he felt himself falling, falling into dirt and darkness.

Grossman's house was dim and dank inside. The boarded up windows disallowed much light from entering, and he rarely allowed them to turn on the oil lamps for fear of attracting any attention. Even so, it was clear the house had been in foul condition for some time. Ashtrays overflowed with cigarette butts, plates of stale food sat on every available surface, and the mantle to the fireplace was lined with whiskey bottles, beer bottles, vodka bottles. Even worse was the carpet, which was tacky and stained with gruesome brown and red splotches, acned where cigarettes had been hastily ground out.

Grossman himself paced back and forth in front of the door, weaving between the unopened boxes of computer gear, a new electric guitar on a stand, and three large screen televisions. An array of weapons—shot guns, 30 06's, boxes of ammunition, chainsaws and gas cans—lined the walls. He let the toggle for the C4 he'd buried under the garden dangle from his hand.

"Yes! Yes!" he cried, punching the air. "Got the bastards! I got them gotdamn sons-a-bitches!"

The three women on the sagging couch flinched with each punch. They were dirty and sallow, each dressed in the flimsy clothes they'd worn during their flight from whatever respective horror they'd managed to escape. One was dressed only in a nightgown, another in jeans and a tee shirt but no shoes, and the third in a brown leather bomber's jacket and panties and flip flops. They sat with their feet curled up beneath them, cowering against each other for comfort.

Grossman swiped a half-empty bottle of Jameson's from the coffee table, up-turned it and swallowed greedily, wiping his lips with the back of his hand when he was done. They'd seen it a million times. He set the bottle down with a clunk, and swayed, woozy, staring at them. Then he flung a finger at the woman on the right hand side of the couch.

"You," he snarled. "Your turn."

PREY

The old man barely looked Dan in the eye when he opened the door.

"You're here," he said, then turned around and shuffled away toward the kitchen.

Dan didn't follow. The day was as wonderful a day as he could remember, and it was made even more wonderful by the fact that, thanks to a very rainy early spring, the grass was green, the cherry blossoms were blooming in full force, and tulips, yellow, satin, and red, sprang up in freshly mulched beds. Birds sang. A soft breeze ruffled his hair. Watching a shower of yellow pollen blow across the street, Dan was grateful not to suffer allergies.

If the outdoors were an Audubon painting, the old man's house was Bosch. The shades were drawn, the furniture saggy and defeated, the air stale and cold, like a crypt. An old plant sat dying and brown on the mantle of the fireplace, which was neglected and black, a burned-out cave carved out of the wall. Dust motes flickered in the air, and the old man clearly smoked, as the stench of tobacco nearly choked the young reporter. Not an easy feat, as he was himself a heavy smoker.

Dan took a deep breath and put his sunglasses on top of his head where it held up his hair, still wet from a last minute shower. He'd stayed out late with his friend Wes, drinking dollar drafts at the local college bar, taking shots with some soon-to-be graduating coeds from UMW, and smoking way too much. His head pounded. His chest felt like it was stuffed with ash.

The old man banged around in the kitchen.

"You wanna do the interview, or what?"

The kitchen was not in any better condition. The appliances, a bisque refrigerator that chugged along on a dying compressor, and a tan gas stove with rusted grates, looked to be about sixty years old. He didn't see a microwave or a coffee machine. The single window was littered with dead cacti in miniature red clay pots. Spider webs hung between what needles hadn't fallen off yet. The surface of the table was decorated with yellow-orange daisies, as were the old, plastic-covered chairs. The old man tended to some water boiling on the stove, his back to the young reporter. Dan took a crumpled pack of Camels from his breast pocket and shook up a cigarette.

"Don't smoke in here," the old man said. When he spoke he glanced, just barely, over his shoulder.

Dan let the cigarette dangle from his lower lip.

"I'm sorry. It just smells like—"

"My wife." The old man turned from the stove. In each hand he held a mug of steaming liquid. "My late wife. She smoked a pack a day."

Dan nodded and put the cigarette back in the pack.

"Sorry."

The old man placed the mug before him and he eyed it. The liquid was brown, with an oily sheen on the top.

"She died last month," the old man explained.

"Oh."

Dan didn't want to talk about the old man's wife. Dan really didn't want to be there at all, but his jackass editor Bill Sweeny made him take on all of the human-interest stories for the Weekender section. This meant covering the latest community garden fundraiser, or talking to the new butcher who just set up shop on William Street, or interviewing old widowers who liked to garden. Still, he'd done his research. Before he went out drinking, that is.

It was close and dusty in the kitchen, and it made Dan's head throb even more. Other dead plants sat in pots atop the fridge. They were labeled "Mix 1," "Mix 4," and "Mix 7." Dan rubbed his eyes and placed his mini-recorder on the table between him and the old man and pressed record. Probably only take twenty minutes, then it was back to the apartment for a smoke and a nap.

"So how long have you been interested in horticulture?"

The old man took a sip from his mug.

"Not until recently. In October."

"While your wife was sick."

"Yes."

The man took another sip, warmed his hands on the mug.

"It was a long illness. She suffered greatly. It required my utmost attention. Toward the end I started to get depressed. Her doctor suggested that I take up a hobby."

Dan shifted in his chair. It made a funny sound. A crack in the upholstery pinched the skin on his thigh.

"It must have been nice to actually see something grow."

"Yes."

"But why such an exotic flower? Why something like . . ." he opened a little notebook in which he had written down the name of the flower, and pronounced the name slowly. "*He-li-co-di-ceros mu-sci-vorus?*"

The old man brightened a little.

"It's beautiful."

"Yeah, but didn't it require more care than you were able to give? Considering your wife's condition."

The corners of the old man's mouth tugged upwards in what Dan realized was his version of a smile.

"Not really."

"That's funny. From what I read, the Helio-whatever actually does require a lot of care for a flower. It's also expensive to import. I mean, what did you do for a living? To be able to afford this?"

"I was an accountant."

"Wow."

Dan waited for the old man to expound, but no further explanation was necessary. It made sense. A man who did not talk much at all, didn't seem to notice or even care about his surroundings or other people. An accountant. Probably squirreled away every last penny he ever made, which was probably what happened, judging by the ancient appliances. He stared around the kitchen in the uncomfortable silence that followed. The counter was decorated in the same ugly pattern of bright yellow-orange flowers. At least a dozen pill bottles littered the surface. The tile was scuffed. A fly buzzed.

"So you split the time between here and the hospital?"

"Ellen didn't want to die in the hospital. She wanted to be buried in our back yard. I honored that wish."

Dan nodded. According to his research, the *Helicodiceros muscivorus* needed to be watched very carefully, it's climate adjusted so that it never fell below a certain temperature. The old man must have built an expensive greenhouse, and he would have had to check on the thing every two or three hours. The image of the old man tending his flower while his wife expelled her last breath made him slightly nauseas.

The old man smirked, as if he read Dan's thoughts.

"Have you ever cared for the dying, boy?"

"Never cared for one, no."

"It's not the most pleasant experience, let me assure you."

"I didn't mean to imply—"

"Nobody does, nobody does. Nobody truly understands until it happens to them."

But I'd never neglect my dying wife for a flower, Dan thought.

"My wife was ill for nearly three years," the old man continued. "When she took to her bed I did everything. All of the cooking, all of the cleaning. Diabetes took her legs in December. I fed her. I emptied her bag. She was helpless without me, like an infant. But worse. She just got sicker and *sicker*. Her doctor suggested gardening, not me. He thought that I might improve mentally if I were to take care of something that would actually thrive under my care."

Dan's hangover was truly kicking in now. Light sweat broke out on his forehead, and his stomach flipped. He was thirsty but didn't want to drink the oily liquid in the mug the old man gave him. He swallowed and his throat clicked. The old man said nothing. Just sat there, looking at him look at the mug.

Finally he picked it up. The tea was no longer warm, but he didn't care. He needed a drink. He closed his eyes and took a sip. It was strong, a little bitter, but the old man had added honey to sweeten it. Actually, it was quite tasty. He finished it with one gulp.

"Did it work?" he asked, placing the mug on the table.

The old man watched him for a moment. Then he shook his head.

"Not at first. I didn't have the proper soil, and it cost too much to have some imported. I found the solution around Christmas."

"Oh? What was it?"

"This and that. Something special. My own creation."

"And it worked?"

The old man smiled a crooked smile.

"Would you like to see for yourself?"

For a moment, based on that smile, Dan thought the old man meant his wife's corpse.

The grass in the back yard was green, the air scented with lilac. In the corner, a garden flourished beneath a blooming dogwood, the bed freshly covered with rich, black mulch. The greenhouse sat in the back, in the opposite corner. It looked like it was worth more than the old man's house, and it was better maintained, too.

A new vinyl fence had just been installed, tall and white and solid; only birds and squirrels would be able to get over. Dan followed the old man as he tottered across the lawn to the greenhouse door, opened it, and let him in. The smell hit him full in the face, an overpowering wall of rot. He dry heaved. All of the research had told him that the flower let off a scent like rotten meat, but none of what he had read prepared him for the reality of it. A stench like that was primal, deep and full, seeming to revel in its rancidness. He swooned.

The old man said "Here," and thrust something under his nose.

A tangy, minty scent cleared his head.

"Ben Gay." He swiped his upper lip with a dollop of the greasy ointment. "Tried Vicks but it didn't work."

Dan took the tube and wiped more under his nose. It cut the rotten meat smell nearly in half, but not all the way. At least he wasn't as dizzy anymore.

"She's down there, around the corner," the old man said, and gestured for Dan to move.

They walked down a short path lined with dozens of hothouse plants, flora and fauna the names of which Dan didn't know. Everything was radiant and healthy, bountiful. The bushes looked twice the size of what Dan thought they should be, and the flowers glowed with color. He walked with his hand covering his mouth and nose, as if the rotten meat scent might lodge there and resurface later.

When Dan spoke, his voice was muffled.

"How long did it take for you to get the fertilizer right?"

"What?"

"You said it took a while before you got it right. How long did it take?"

"Oh, only a few weeks. It was touch and go there then. She was hovering on the edge of death, you know. The first blend perked her up initially, but it didn't last long. I had to find other sources."

Dan felt queasy. The old man talked more about the stupid plant than he did his own wife. They reached the end of the aisle. A few gardening tools, a rake, a pickaxe, a shovel, leaned in the corner. Dan saw some sneakers tossed carelessly next to a door in the back. Must have belonged to the old man's wife. The door was open just a crack.

"What's back there?"

The old man gave the door a cursory glance.

"Mulching room." He nodded at the flowers and fauna, his handiwork. "I had a breakthrough toward the end. Found a special mixture that worked magic. She perked up immediately and bloomed."

"Where is it?"

"Turn around."

Dan turned and saw the flower, the *Helicodiceros muscivorus*. The old man had separated it from the other flowers: a queen on a pedestal. To Dan it was an oval shaped, purple lump, spotted white, looking like an alien vagina. He was simultaneously repulsed and intrigued. He leaned forward to get a better look despite the stench.

"She's a beauty," the old man said.

"Yeah," Dan mumbled. "Sure."

He looked at the soil for any evidence of the special blend the old man had gone on so much about, wondering the whole time why anybody in their right mind would raise such an awful flower.

"So what's your secret?"

"Secret?"

Dan thought he heard a note of doubt in the man's voice.

"Your secret. The blend you've been talking about. Oh—"

A wave of nausea overwhelmed him, his damn hangover kicking in right then, full force, with the heat and the smell. His stomach rose up and he gulped several times to hold it back.

"Mostly it has to do with age," the old man said from behind him. "The younger the source, the richer the blend. Works on pretty much all the flowers."

Dan leaned on the table upon which the *Helicodiceros muscivorus* sat. He'd been hung over before, many times, but it was never this bad. In fact, this didn't feel like a hangover at all. The dizziness peaked, his legs shook, his vision blurred and sharpened, blurred and sharpened. He thought of the oily surface of the old man's tea. He leaned over again, weak, his face inches away from the horrid flower, and something caught his attention, something pale sticking up out of the dirt. He bent forward to get a better look, then drew back sharply. It was a finger.

A human finger.

Dan started to say something when he heard the scrape of metal against the concrete floor of the greenhouse. He turned around to see the old man swinging the pickaxe directly at his head. He had just enough time to let out the beginning of a scream.

The old man grunted as he pulled the corpse to the room in the back of the greenhouse, kicking aside the footwear spilling out the door. A white, clawfoot tub sat in the middle, rust stained and spattered with dark blotches. He heaved the body up by the armpits and draped it over the edge with a grunt, making sure to bend at the knees so as not to throw out his back like he did the first time, the past winter. He removed the boy's sandals, those stupid roman-styled things all the kids wore these days, and tossed them into the pile by the door. Most were size ten or eleven, although a few were smaller, more petite.

He'd have to burn them soon.

Maybe in November, after the leaves fell.

UNDER THE ROCKS

Jason Riddle stood at the window a for very long time, staring out at the Rappahannock as it flowed in the night, timeless and heavy and dark. The window reflected the scene behind him perfectly: three men holding drinks, watching him, waiting for him to turn around. One, middle-aged, bald, a significant paunch pushing out over his belt, relaxed on an expensive couch, his arms spread out over the cushions. Another, middle-aged, too, but wiry and muscular, coiled in the doorway. The third, a young man with long hair and the beginning of a scruffy Van Dyke on his chin, crossed his legs on the love seat. Riddle fingered the lip of his cup. He cocked his head and held completely still for a moment. One of the men coughed politely and Riddle shushed him and leaned closer to the glass. After several minutes his shoulders relaxed. Finally, he turned around.

"Dan?" His voice had a nasal twang to it. Not quite as gruff as northern voices, but not the smooth purr of the Georgian gentleman, either. "It's close to nine, isn't it?"

The man in the doorway, the Dan in question, Dan Gallup that is, Fredericksburg native, contractor, hunter, former punk rocker, nodded and disappeared into the other room without a word. He was laconic by nature, prone to doing more than saying. His footsteps receded up a staircase, then thumped around overhead.

The man on the couch was Cole Porter, a Biology professor at UMW. His parents were, of course, fans of the late crooner, something he'd had to live with his entire life. He asked his colleagues to call him by his middle name, David, and they, of course, complied. For a while, when he'd first started teaching, one of his students would invariably discover his first name and some kind of juvenile wonderment would ensue, but as the years progressed and popular tastes skewed elsewhere, that sort of activity slowed and then ceased altogether. Every now and then a savvy student might express surprise upon discovering his name, but his classmates didn't understand the allusion or were too captivated by the all encompassing lure of their screens to care.

"So, what are you saying, Mr. Riddle?" Porter asked. "That somebody murdered these people?"

"Not somebody, but some*thing*."

Porter rolled his eyes.

"Now now, now now," Riddle said, patting the air with his hands. "Let me tell you a story, gentlemen. If by the end of the tale you're not convinced, you can leave. Minus my fee, course. Agreed?"

Porter paused and then shrugged.

"Why not. I'm here."

Riddle looked at the young man in the love seat.

"Dean?"

Dean Goodman was a hard news reporter for *The Free Lance Star* in the same way that Elton John was a linebacker for the Pittsburg Steelers. He was twenty-three, fresh out of college, and, like many young men, hungry to prove himself in his new career. Unfortunately, he graduated right in the middle of the Great Recession, which meant that despite his degree from Cornell, despite his glowing recommendations from his professors, despite his perfectly groomed writing samples, the best job he could land was as a cub reporter covering local events in Fredericksburg, Virginia. The job was not without some intrigue; Dean's predecessor was assumed to have been murdered the previous spring. Just disappeared one afternoon after an interview, his body never found.

He honestly had no idea what he was doing here, had merely responded to an invitation from Mr. Riddle out of curiosity. He supposed none of the "real" journalists at the paper would take the invite seriously, for why else would the kid (whose biggest scoops consisted of covering a concert by some interchangeable old guys playing grunge covers at one of the three dives around town, and august cultural events like the June craft fair in Market Square) be summoned?

"Sure. Go ahead."

"Very good."

Riddle sat down in one of the cushy chairs next to the fireplace and sighed. Took a sip of his drink. The ice clinked against the glass. "It started for me almost seventy years ago, in the summer of 1933."

I'm the youngest of three sons. My older brothers, Lee and Mitch are, bless em, dead. Died of natural causes, mind, not because of the river. As boys growing up, we knew the Rappahannock like we knew our own bedrooms. Every summer we spent lounging about on its banks, fishing and swimming, sometimes all day.

Summer of '33 was terrible hot and dry. We were in the middle of a long, disastrous drought, much like we are now. The river was at the lowest point I'd ever seen. There were sections up by Falmouth that'd run dry, exposing rocks that hadn't seen direct sunlight in over a century. Even so, there are others that will never run dry, and there are depths unknown to even the most experienced river rats.

Well, right around mid-summer the drownings started. First there was Lonnie Harris, a schoolmate of mine. Drowned in the middle of the day, surrounded by six other boys in my class. I wasn't one of em, but I would've been had my mother not decided to take me out to visit my grandparents in Culpepper. Then there was Michelle Phipps, an older girl, friend of my brother, Lee. Drowned on the Fourth of July. Back then the fireworks show was held over the river, not like it is now at that load of concrete and asphalt out there on Route 3. Families would picnic out on the banks all day long, watch the display at night. Michelle's mother said one second she was sunning on Diving Rock, next she was gone. Then there were two more, a Stafford man, a high school English teacher out with his daughters, drowned in late July, and my cousin Amanda in mid-August.

Now, my cousin Amanda was the sweetest thing in Fredericksburg. Even at ten years old I knew that. She was nineteen, beautiful, smart as a whip. She and my brother Lee had always been close, but as they got older her father, my Uncle Kenny, began to notice that they were a little too close. At the time I didn't understand what all the fuss was about, but early that summer there were some heated words between dad and Uncle Kenny, and then all of the sudden Amanda and her family didn't come around any more. Well, I guess Lee and Amanda found some way to meet up, usually at night, usually at the river. In fact, that's where they were the night Amanda went missing.

Of course nobody could prove what they were doing, or if Lee was even with her. In the summer Hurkamp Park was often filled late into the night by people trying to escape the heat. All anybody knew was that a few old timers hanging round the park said they'd seen Amanda heading that way around midnight, and the only evidence they had was a dress of hers slung up in some branches on the bank. Like the other victims that summer, nobody ever did find her body.

Uncle Kenny and my father repaired their relationship following Amanda's disappearance. I guess they figured one family tragedy was enough to bear. We all went to her funeral. Lee tried not to look distraught, but the pain on his face showed. He didn't cry until they started lowering her empty casket into the ground, and Uncle Kenny came over and put his arm around him.

It rained that evening, and we thought it would cool things off but it didn't. As soon as the storm passed, a thick front of heat and humidity settled over the city like a wet blanket. The rain did at least provide one benefit; I remember my parents talking about how the river had swelled up pretty high. Not up to flood levels, but high enough. Because of the heat, my parents and I slept in the living room, Lee and Mitch in the basement. The night of the funeral it got to be too hot for me even in the living room, so I went and made my bed on the screened-in front porch. Later on, I guess it had to be close to midnight, I was woken by the sound of angry words. When I sat up and looked out, I saw Lee and Mitch out front on the little walk under the screen.

" . . . don't care what you think, Mitch," Lee said, his voice raising from a whisper to nearly a shout. "I know what I saw and I'm going back there for it."

"Well, you're crazy if you think I ain't goin' with you."

I was foolish enough to stand up.

"Ain't going where?"

"Oh Lord, Jason!" Lee moaned. "What're you doing out here?"

"Too hot inside. Couldn't sleep. Where are you guys going? Why you got daddy's gun?"

Lee looked at the rifle in his hand like he hadn't realized it was there. He tried to hide it behind his back.

"I ain't got time to explain." He looked at Mitch. "I'm going."

And he stalked off across the lawn.

I'd been around long enough to know when Mitch and Lee were up to something interesting, and I wasn't about to let this one slip by, not with Lee toting daddy's rifle around and acting like he was crazy. I slipped on my old fishing shoes, which I always kept on the porch, opened the screen and hopped down to the lawn. I wasn't wearing anything else but my tightie-whities.

"Lee, wait! I'm coming, too!"

Lee stopped. "No you ain't." He walked up to me and knelt down to look me in the eye and put on that voice he used when momma put him in charge of me and Mitch. "Jason," he said. "You're staying right here till me and Mitch get back. It's for your own safety."

"Like hell I am. You step out this yard without me, I'll wake daddy up, and tell him you got his gun. I'll holler so the whole neighborhood'll hear. I'll start right now!"

I opened my mouth to scream and Lee clamped his hand over it. It was hot and sweaty.

"All right," he hissed. "Dammit. But you ain't going dressed like that. Go get some clothes on. Your fishing clothes. Hurry up. And don't wake up mom and dad."

I hurried upstairs to my room and got dressed. When I came back out I half expected Lee and Mitch to be gone, but there they were, waiting for me. Lee handed me the old machete daddy used to cut the kudzu in the back yard.

"Here, take this."

"What for?"

"Listen, if you're gonna ask too many questions don't bother coming along. I don't care if you do wake up the neighborhood."

With that, he turned and walked away, daddy's rifle slung over his shoulder.

"What about me?" Mitch called after him.

"You're a big boy, Mitch," Lee said over his shoulder. "Get your own weapon."

I waited for Mitch while he went and got an axe from the shed, and both of us took off after Lee. Mitch explained what was going on as we snuck across town.

"Lee was with Amanda the night she disappeared," he said.

"What you mean, they was together? Like they was—"

"Shut up, Jason. You don't know what you're talking about. Besides, she wasn't a blood cousin or nothin. Daddy and Uncle Kenny just fought in the war together."

This was news to me. I'd grown up believing Uncle Kenny was family.

"Anyway, Lee says Amanda wasn't drowned. Says something got her. Something pulled her down and took her away, and there wasn't anything he could do about it."

"What was it?"

"He don't know. But he said he's going to find it and kill it."

Fredericksburg was still and silent as we stole through her streets. We lived on Sunken Road back then. To get to the river we had to cut past the old Canal and head west up Princess Anne. Way off in the distance I heard the clock on the Presbyterian Church knell. It was quarter till one. Nobody was on Lee-Jackson, so we struck off north toward the river, then crossed Riverside and plunged down the hill and into the woods on the bank.

Lee stayed at least twenty yards in front of us the whole way, his gait sure and fast. Mitch had to call out for him to wait up more than once, and Lee'd stop for a few seconds, pawing at the ground with his shoes. When we got within ten feet he'd take off again. When we reached the woods we lost him almost immediately. The sound of the river drowned out everything but the sticks cracking under our feet and the crickets on the bank.

"Mitch, it's gotta be past one in the morning."

"So?"

"So were gonna get in trouble if we get found out."

"Jesus, Jason. We're already in trouble. You're the one made us take you."

"But mama wakes up earlier than the sun rises! She's gonna go looking for me, and if she don't see me—"

"Shhh!"

Mitch stopped abruptly and crouched down in the bush, his head cocked like he was listening for something. I crouched down next to him.

"What is it?" I asked. "You heard daddy? I knew it! I knew he was gonna find us."

"Shut up!"

"Both of you shut up," Lee spat.

He was crouched down about five feet in front of us, daddy's rifle in his left hand, spying at the river around a thick growth of bushes, past the hanging branches of a river tree. The water shone black and silver in the full moon, and though it was lower than I'd ever seen it, low enough to expose more than the top of Diving Rock, it was still strong and swift. All I heard was the rush of the current, and the occasional fish splashing in the distance.

"Stay down," Lee whispered.

"Why?"

"You hear that big splash a minute ago?"

"Yeah."

"That was it. The thing got Amanda. I seen it jumping off Diving Rock."

It was enough to make both me and Mitch mute with fear. Then suddenly that fear evaporated.

Two summers before, when I was eight, Lee and Mitch took me out to the movies. Daddy let Lee drive his car, and afterwards we stopped at Carl's and got some ice cream. Lee drove out to the docks and we ate our cones in the car, watching the river.

"I gotta piss," Mitch said, and got out to go shake it off in the bushes.

We sat and listened to the crickets and cicadas sing their night songs, and under that the calming sound of the river. Every now and then there was a mechanical whirr as a car drove across the bridge, or the echo of a dog barking in the distance.

"You ever hear of the Hook 'n Eye killer?" Lee asked after a while.

"No," I said, concentrating on my cone. I hated it when the ice cream dribbled down on my hand, so I was focused on licking the base clean.

"Never learned it in school?"

"No. Course not."

"Don't surprise me."

"Why?"

"Well, your teacher's a Yankee. She wouldn't know about it."

Lee was right. My third grade teacher, Mrs. Tucker, was from Chicago. She'd just moved down here with her husband, who was in the Marines. She was young and pretty, but she had the funniest accent I ever heard. She said the same thing about us.

"What's that got to do with it?"

"Never mind."

While Lee could be less than skilled when it came to reading and writing and school, he had a Harvard degree in child psychology.

"C'mon, Lee!" Suddenly the ice cream cone wasn't all that interesting anymore.

"Okay, okay." He finished his cone and chucked the paper napkin out the window. "See, when I was your age, all the third grade teachers had to tell this story. It was like a . . . a public service announcement. About twenty years ago, a couple of kids were murdered. Right around here, as a matter of fact. Right near the docks."

"Really?"

Lee glanced up in the mirror. He knew he had me.

"Heads tore clean off," he went on. "Hands, too. And their eyes was plucked out. Or so they thought. Nobody ever knew, cause there was just holes where the eyes should have been."

"Oh man."

"That's right. Anyway, nobody thought nothing much of it till about three weeks later when two more kids was found murdered, same thing again. Heads tore off. No eyes. The rumors started up from the first one, but this time everybody knew. It was the Hook 'n Eye killer."

Oh, he had me good.

"Who was it?" I asked. I bet my face'd turned completely white.

Lee stifled a smile, but I was too young to see it. I thought he was trying not to get too upset.

"Nobody really knew who it was, but a few years before the same thing happened. Some people thought he was an escaped mental patient from up north, some thought he was a hobo lived out in the woods. Didn't really matter, though. All that mattered was that he liked to kill kids, 'specially kids who hung out late at night in his neck of the woods."

I let my eyes wander out to the trees to our right. A little ice cream dribbled down my palm and I licked it, letting this new information set in.

"Why'd he take their heads off and poke out their eyes?"

Lee nodded.

"That's a good question, Jason. See, the Hook 'n Eye killer was blind. Lost both hands in the war. He knew he couldn't ever get his hands back, but for some reason he thought he could with his eyes. So he put hooks on his hands, sharpened them up real good, and went around looking for victims."

By this point I was wound up tighter than a cat's ass. You could have bounced a nickel off my head and I wouldn't have noticed. Lee swung his hand out the window, started tapping lightly on the roof.

"And the story goes that before he killed his victims, he'd drag his hook along something nearby, something loud, like the asphalt, or a light pole, or a car."

Just then something scraped along the side of daddy's car, right on my side.

I hit the deck, screaming. "Oh Jesus, Lee! Start the car! Start the car!"

The driver's side door opened.

"Oh God, Jason!" Lee screamed. "God help me!"

"Lee! Lee! Lee!"

Then suddenly I heard laughter.

Mitch's laughter. And Lee's.

I sat up, poked my head over the head rest.

There they were. Outside the car. Holding onto each other, belly-laughing.

My cone was mashed up on the floor; ice cream was smeared all over my face.

"You sonsabitches!" I cried. I didn't even know what it meant, I just heard daddy say it whenever he was mad.

I scrambled out of the car and leapt on Mitch, started hitting him in the face.

"That wasn't funny, you sonsabitches!"

Lee tried to pull me off, but only managed to topple us over, and we ended up in a big pile on the ground, and then we were all laughing.

And that's what they were doing right now. Playing a trick on me, just like they did before.

"Now I know both of you is full of it," I said. "There ain't no river monster. Just like there ain't no Hook 'n Eye killer. You're just trying to scare me, that's all, you sonsabitches!"

Lee leapt for me and clasped his hand over my mouth.

"Dammit, Jason, shut up! We ain't trying to do nothing but kill the thing that killed Amanda. I didn't want you here in the first place, so you can go on home if you won't take it seriously."

I bit his hand and he held it there until he couldn't take it anymore, then he pulled it away with a bitter curse.

"See. You're just keeping it up now,"

"Listen, you idiot. Really listen. You hear anything?"

I cocked my head and listened.

"No."

"That's cause all the crickets stopped chirping. You ever hear the crickets stop chirping down here?"

Lee was right. It was dead silent, nothing to be heard but the rush of the river. The crickets *never* stopped chirping by the river. All of the sudden I was very afraid.

"Same thing happened right before that thing got Amanda."

I looked at both of them, and my voice wavered when I spoke.

"Ya'll ain't messing with me?"

Lee shook his head.

"This ain't no Hook 'n Eye killer?"

I must have looked about as pale as a ghost, because Lee's attitude changed. He smiled.

"Listen. Ain't nothing gonna happen to you if you do what I say. I got daddy's rifle, you got a machete, an Mitch's got an axe. It's more than what it's got."

"What're you gonna do?"

"I'm gonna wade out to Diving Rock. That's where it likes to hunt.

Then I'm gonna kill it."

"I'm going with you," Mitch said.

"No. You stay here with Jason."

"You're gonna need another set of eyes. What if it comes at you from behind?"

Lee thought about it for a minute.

"Okay. But I'll go first. Jason, you sit tight here on the shore, make sure ain't nothing coming at us from anywhere else."

I started to protest but Lee cut me off.

"We can't see everything from out there. You got to be another set of eyes, too."

I couldn't argue because I knew he was right.

"Okay," I said.

Then Lee did something he rarely did. He hugged me.

"You're gonna be all right, okay? Anything comes after you, you just chop it up with the machete, got it?"

I nodded meekly. My eyes felt like they were like big, fat basketballs.

"All right, then. Mitch, wait until I'm about halfway out then come on in after me. Keep your eyes on the water around me."

He patted me on the shoulder, took off his shoes and shorts, and waded into the river. When it got too deep to walk, he put the rifle over his head in one hand and started to paddle with the other.

When Lee was halfway out, Mitch said, "All right, Jason." Then he waded into the river, too.

I crouched at the bank to watch. Lee reached the rock, threw the rifle on top and scrambled up after. Mitch was a strong swimmer, but the axe weighed him down. He struggled to keep a straight line in the current. Lee strained to see down into the water. All of the sudden he shouldered the rifle, aimed it toward Mitch, and fired. The report echoed up the river.

"Jesus, Lee!" I heard Mitch shout. "You almost shot me!"

"Mitch, drop the axe and hurry up." He aimed his rifle at the water near Mitch again. "Now!"

Mitch opened his mouth to speak and then he was gone. One second his head was there, bobbing above water, perfectly visible in the full moonlight, then he was gone.

"Mitch!" I cried, standing.

"Jason, get down!" Lee yelled.

"What about Mitch?" Tears streamed down my face.

"Get down!"

I obeyed immediately and crouched back down in the bushes, keeping my eyes where I could see the river. Lee fired into the water again. A second later something popped up against Diving Rock, gasping for air. It was Mitch, extending his hand.

"Get me out!"

Lee put the rifle in his left hand and grabbed Mitch's forearm with his right. As he pulled, I saw a huge black form shoot out of the water. It was aiming right for Lee. Lee fell back, still holding onto Mitch, and shot from the hip. The form squealed and spun in midair, knocking the rifle out of Lee's hand. Then it crashed back down into the swift moving current. Lee pulled Mitch up onto the rock then dove back into the river. He resurfaced and yelled, "Jason don't move!"

Mitch dove in after Lee and began to swim toward the bank with strong, determined strokes. He overtook Lee and made it to where he could stand. I stood up out of the bushes.

"Get down!"

But it was too late.

The huge thing burst out of the water almost as soon as I stood up, roaring and snarling as it shot straight for me. Then all of the sudden I was on my back. Didn't even remember getting there. Both of my arms were out on either side, and I discovered with some amazement that I had managed to hold onto the machete. It struck my chest, claws ripped into my shoulder and neck, and an unearthly roar rumbled out of the monster's deep lungs.

The beast reared up to deliver what I was sure would be my deathblow; its arms, chest, and head were etched inky black against the white moon. I drew up all my strength and blindly swung the machete out in front of me. The monster's weight shifted. Its arms were falling, falling swiftly for me, for my head, and that was it, I was dead, my head'd be cut off only not by the Hook 'n Eye killer but by some ugly, disgusting Thing, some horrible beast from my worst, most terrible nightmare.

Then I felt the blade connect with something hard.

Wetness splattered my face, my torso.

A horrible squeal filled the air.

Then the weight was off my body and I heard a huge splash. I opened my eyes. Mitch was standing over me.

"Jason! Oh my God."

I tried to sit up but the pain in my neck was too much. The corners of my eyes went black.

"He's bleeding all over the place," Mitch said. "We've got to get him home, Lee."

I saw spots in the corners of my eyes.

"Did I get it?"

Lee came quietly up behind us and squatted down next to me. He had something in his hand.

"You got him, Jason. You got him all right."

He handed me something wet and muscular, covered with scales. I held it up in the moon light. It was the monsters arm, severed clean through the bone at the elbow.

"Sonsabitches," I groaned, and everything went black.

Riddle was finished. He stood up and walked over to the window, his hands held behind his back. They no longer shook. Dean leaned forward and placed his empty Coke can on the coffee table, and Gallup came over and placed an Igloo cooler next to it. He glanced at Porter.

"Is that the reason you brought us here?" Dean asked. "Has it come back?"

Riddle stirred as if from deep thought.

"June 26th, 28th, and 30th. July 3rd, 4th, and 7th. August 9th. August 11th."

Porter said, "Okay. So?"

"Nine people, Cole. Nine people this summer so far. Three teenagers, a six year old, and five adults. All gone. All dead. All killed by that thing."

"Couldn't they have just drowned? I mean, I know a lot of people have gone missing out here this summer, but that doesn't necessarily mean anything."

"You're right. Maybe they did drown. Maybe that thing got them. But —" His intensity softened, and he took a step closer to the professor. "Think of it, Cole. Find of the century."

"It's a little far fetched," Porter said.

Riddle nodded and turned around.

"Yes it is. And if it hadn't happened to me I'd agree. I'm a businessman. The only boogie-men I know are lawyers and bankers. But it did happen to me, and I'm telling you that the monster is real. Very real."

He crossed the floor and opened the cooler on the coffee table. Cold fog permeated the air, as if whatever was inside had been in frozen for quite some time. "Maybe this'll prove it." Porter leaned forward, then Dean. "Go ahead. Take a look. It's no longer any danger to anyone now."

The fog cleared, then Porter gasped. Dean exclaimed something short and vulgar. Riddle laughed out loud.

"You boys remind me of the look on Dan's face when he first saw it," he said, nodding at the handyman.

Porter reached for it.

"May I?"

"By all means."

Porter dipped his hands in and withdrew a portion of an arm, a very muscular arm. It was gray and withered with age, and scales ran its length, from where it had been sliced off in the middle of the forearm to the top of the wrist. Two black digits grew out of the hand, connected by a thick, rubbery membrane. Out of these sprouted black talons, curved, sharp, and brutal.

"It seems real," Dean said. He poked at the old flesh with his forefinger. "Ice cold." He grimaced and winced, but could not take his eyes off it.

Porter turned the limb over and over in his hands. He inspected the end that had been severed, marveled at the jagged cut bone. "Have you kept it frozen all these years?"

"Not me," Riddle said. "First Lee kept it. When he died five years ago, Mitch took it. Then last year Mitch passed and it was my turn. We never showed it to anybody else. Until now. And now, as I'm the last living brother, it's my duty to kill the beast once and for all."

Porter paused. He and Dean looked up at Riddle

"You mean you didn't before?"

Riddle shrugged.

"We thought we might have. Lee shot it and I cut off its arm. But we never saw the body. None of us ever said we'd kill it if it ever came back, but the responsibility was ours, hanging over us. Now Lee and Mitch are dead, and it's come back, and I'm going to kill it."

"And you want me to document it."

"Yes, Dean."

"But I write for the Weekender section. I write about bluegrass music and Eagle Scouts. I'm sure you could have gotten somebody better."

Riddle waved the question aside.

"You're young, talented, hungry for success. More importantly, you live nearby, and you were available. What more could I possibly ask?"

"I can guess why you want me along," Porter said.

Riddle smiled.

"Once we kill it, I mean to show the world. A lot of money to made. Affirmation from a well-regarded marine biologist will not hurt my case."

Gallup reentered the room. He had a rifle slung over each shoulder, and a long black duffle bag in one hand. He set the bag on the ground, unzipped it, and pulled out two .44s.

"Take these," he said, handing one to Porter and one to Dean. Porter handled his weapon like a diseased organ. "And these." He handed each man a key. "It opens the doors to the pump house. If we become separated or, worse, if I . . . you can take refuge here as long as it's necessary."

Gallup brushed off the suggestion.

"I don't think that'll be a problem. Them there is forty fours, Jason. You and me are armed to the teeth. Between the four of us, we'll blow a hole through just about anything." He looked at Porter and Dean. "You boys ever shot a gun before?"

"No."

"Uh-uh."

Gallup nodded.

"Well, I guess you're gonna learn real quick."

He gathered up the bag and started for the stairs.

"Ready boys?" Riddle asked.

Dean and Porter exchanged a look.

"What makes you so sure we'll go?" Porter asked.

Riddle arched his eyebrows at them, then gave them an equally arch-smile.

"Come on now. Who could say no to this?"

The clanging of the steel barred doors sounded like a death sentence to Dean. He took a deep breath and listened for the sounds of the night. Crickets, mainly, but every now and then a revving engine echoed in the air, or an owl hooted. They crossed through the narrow path of thorn bushes to the trail that ran along the river, walking in single file: Gallup first, lugging the bag full of weapons, then Riddle, still spry even for his age, followed by Porter, his .44 dangling carelessly from his right hand. Dean took up the rear. He'd shoved his gun into his belt. The river was flat and black, and it didn't seem to be at all low. He could make out the line of the far bank, Stafford side. The black trees towered overhead; the thick brush ran right up to the water. The crickets were raucous this close to the water.

He tripped over a root and cussed. A few hundred yards later he stepped into a puddle and made a loud splash. Gallup stopped at least three times, head cocked, listening intently. They finally stopped on a little beach rounded out of the bank. The outline of a huge rock sat in the middle of the river, about twenty-five yards out.

"The Diving Rock?" Dean asked.

"The one and only," Riddle replied.

Gallup set the bag down and dug around inside.

He pulled something long out of the bag and handed it to the old man. "Here."

"What's this?"

"Little something."

He turned and clapped Porter on the back, and they waded quietly out into the river, both holding their weapons over their heads.

Riddle gazed at the instrument with wonder. It was a machete, his father's machete, the same one he'd used to cut the arm off the river monster six decades before. Its blade flecked with rust, but it was still sharp, still whole.

"My God. Where'd he get this?"

He and Dean watched the other two swim slowly out to the rock, gently correcting their courses when the current pulled them too far down river. Porter made it first, and scrambled up the side to stand dripping wet on top. Gallup was less of a swimmer than the professor, and was still about ten yards away. They could see his head bobbing in the current.

"No monsters out here!" Porter called.

Dean had to admit that this was one of the strangest assignments he'd ever been on. That wasn't saying much. He was only in his twenties. He was an entertainment reporter in a small town in Virginia. Still. Five years before, if someone had asked him what he'd be doing with his life after graduation, he would not have answered, "hunting river monsters on the Rappahannock."

It was a beautiful summer night. The moon was full and bright, so bright that he could actually make out some of the details on Porter's face and clothes. The insects chirped and swelled, chirped and swelled.

And then they stopped.

"My God," Riddle said. "Cole!"

Porter turned around on the rock. He stood there for a moment, a black figure silhouetted against the sky. Then something exploded out of the water and he was gone. A muffled shot and flash lit up the current.

Riddle threw the machete into the sand at his feet and cocked his rifle.

"Get ready, Dean."

"For what?"

"For anything."

Gallup gained the rock. He turned and squatted, his body tense and alert. Suddenly he stood up, shouldered his rifle, and fired into the water.

"I—" he said, turning to the shore. Then he froze. "Run!"

"What?"

"In the woods! All around! Run!"

Dean squatted down and listened. The woods around him seemed alive all of the sudden, full of cracking branches and feed thudding in the brush. He backed away downriver, his gun held out in front of him in a hand that did not feel like his own. His eyes were wide, his ears open, but all he could see was Riddle standing on the bank, peering into the darkness. Riddle picked the machete up and tossed it toward Dean, who slowly knelt down and picked it up.

"No," Riddle muttered, suddenly panicked. "It must've . . . how could it —" His eyes were wide and jittery as he surveyed the bush. Then, just as sudden, the panic was wiped away and replaced by a cool calm. The old man nodded. "Okay. Get back to the pump house, Dean. We'll meet you there."

Gallup fired a few shots into the bushes upstream. Each one was met with squeals of pain and angry, inhuman roars.

". . . fire into the bush!"

The water exploded behind him, and a dark form swept him off the rock. They tumbled in the air, spinning, spinning, and hit the water with a smack. A spray of droplets twinkled in the light. Gallup resurfaced once, wrestling with something large and slick and muscular. His hunting knife flashed in the moonlight as he brought it down again and again, then he rolled back into the water.

Two black forms shot out of the brush, aiming for Riddle, who fired, twisted, fired, and the things squealed and collapsed on either side of him, black blood spilling onto the sand.

"Run, Dean!"

Dean spun on his heel and sprinted away. Branches whipped his face, his arms. He parted tangles of spider web, tripped over roots. More shots rang out behind him, and he heard the old man cry out. Then silence. No crashing, no cracking, no insects. Just the inexorable rush of the river and his footsteps. He stopped. The blood rushed in his ears. He raised the .44 in his shaky fist, turning back the way he'd come.

Suddenly, just as suddenly as they stopped, the insects swelled again. Dean never thought he'd be so relieved to hear their music. He relaxed a little, let his arm drop to his sides.

"Riddle? Gallup?"

The insects stopped again, and a huge, dark form burst out of the water to his right, and Dean's senses were overwhelmed with the stench of rotting fish. The figure leaned back and loosed a horrid, bubbly roar. It lashed out and knocked the gun from his hand. He turned to flee, but the beast squatted down and launched itself at him. It struck his back, and then he was airborne. He landed his face, sand and rocks grinding into his skin, cutting his lips, and tumbled into the brush, ending the fall on his back, his left arm held up in front of his face. A searing pain ripped across his chest and belly. Wetness splattered across his torso.

The creature's talons struck his left arm.

It snapped.

The boy screamed in agony.

He sucked in a deep breath wondering if this was it, if this was the way he was going to die, slashed to pieces on the banks of some foreign, southern river, dragged into the bland churl of the Rappahannock and stuffed under a rock to rot. Then he realized that he still had the machete in his right hand. Time seemed to slow down. His left arm was a searing brand of pain. His chest was on fire. The beast reared up, straddling his body, its claws flailing madly in the midnight blue sky, its face turned toward the full moon, loosing another roar. Its claws started to descend, aiming straight for his head, and Dean saw the air part as they did so, saw the water wick off the monster's rubber skin, saw the leaves of the brush shake with the force.

He closed his eyes.

With all of his remaining strength, he swept the machete off the ground, aiming for the monster above him, hoping to cut it somewhere, anywhere, before those razor sharp talons severed his head from his body, ripped his throat from his neck. The young reporter did not have a violent bone in him. The last time he'd been in a fight was elementary school. The last time he'd thrown a punch was in a free aikido class six years before. But he wasn't a coward. He wasn't weak, and he would not go out like this; he would at least try to fight back.

The blade connected, he felt the shock run up his arm. More pain, this time not from a cut but from his muscles. They screamed in agony as he followed through his swing. The monster's roar, so thick and full and horrible milliseconds before, suddenly cut off. Something thumped in the sand next to Dean's head. More wetness splattered in his face. His arm completed its arc, and the machete thunked into the sand at his side. He waited, waited for the end. Would he feel anything? Would it toy with him? Would it eat him alive? What was it waiting for!

After a few seconds he realized that he was still alive. Nothing tore into his flesh. His head was still attached to his body, his throat still in his neck.

He opened his eyes.

The torso of the beast still straddled him, arms hanging limply by its sides. The head was gone. He moaned and shoved the body off. It collapsed into the brush. Standing was shaky. He'd lost blood. His left arm and chest were slashed to ribbons, and his right shoulder dislocated.

"Riddle!" he cried, not caring anymore. "Gallup!"

Nobody answered. No more shots rang out. The insects continued their mute vigil. Then he heard something crash in the bushes behind him and he ran again.

How long did it take to make it back to the pump house? Twenty minutes? An hour? Dean couldn't be sure. All he knew was that he was exhausted, and every step was agony, made him dizzier and weaker and sicker. He had to stop twice, had fallen to his knees, breathing in ragged strips, and twice he thought he heard something crash in the brush behind him. He'd turned and thrashed the machete wildly, desperately, but nothing was there.

He collapsed against the door when he reached it, sank to the concrete stoop, suppressing a shudder. It was a long time before he was able to breathe without thinking he'd vomit. Then finally his lungs relaxed. Oxygen flowed easily, and though it hurt his ribs to expand, he took long, deep breaths, two, three times, until his vision cleared and his body settled.

He fit the key in the lock and turned it, pausing for a moment for some reason. It was amazing how everything and nothing had changed. There were monsters in the world, horrible things with talons and sharp teeth, and they were out to get him, yet moon was still full, still showered the woods with its cold glow. The air, thick with August humidity, cocooned him in heat. The crickets chirped and sang, the peepers in the brush by the river sent up their musical call. Dean marveled again at their melody.

And then they stopped.

Raleigh's Prep,

Book the First

of the

Topher Trilogy

CONTENTS

"There is no terror in the bang, only the anticipation of it."
—Alfred Hitchcock

"I don't believe in using too much graphic violence, although I've done it. It's better to be suggestive and to allow the viewer to fill in the blanks."
—Tobe Hooper

"There is a thin line that separates laughter and pain, comedy and tragedy, humor and hurt."
—Erma Bombeck

"Tragedy plus time equals comedy."
—Steve Allen

POUNDS OF FLESH

The dead body sat in the middle of the playing field, looking like a pile of rags melting into the ground. Zorn saw it and stopped jogging, thinking it might be a drunk student passed out after a night's partying. Why hadn't his friends dragged him back to campus?

"Topher, look," he said.

Topher stopped a few feet away, jogging in place.

"Quit making excuses and run, you slug. You'll never survive this place in your condition."

"No, really."

Topher rolled his eyes and looked, squinting against sun rising over the campus.

"I'll be damned."

The smell hit them at the thirty-yard line. It reminded Zorn of the time the meat freezer in his parents' basement died. He and Topher pulled their shirts up over their noses and came to a stop on either side of the pile. There were scraps of clothes and shards of bone and red stuff all mixed together like a salad, and it was big and wet and sticky looking. Flies had begun to gather.

"Phew," Zorn said. "I am ripe."

"Not as ripe as that."

Gertrude (whose real name was Kenneth) finally caught up to them, winded and confused.

"What are you doing?" Then, seeing the bloody mound, "what's that?"

Topher crossed his arms. "Well," he said, squatting down to get a better view. "That's a finger."

"Where?"

"Right there, next to the spleen."

Gertrude put his hands on his knees.

"How do you know that's a spleen?"

"It's either a spleen or a bladder."

A buzzard swooped down and landed on the mound, which shifted. Something plopped on the grass. Gertrude turned green. The stench, the offal, the machine-like buzzing of the flies, it was all too much. The bird plucked something out of the mess, something long and stringy, and he trotted off to the edge of the track and threw up. At the same time, a pickup truck, primer gray with calico patches of rust, came bounding over the maintenance road, engine revving.

"Oh no," Zorn whispered. "Mr. Floyd."

Mr. Floyd was the grounds keeper. Though the boys had only been at Raleigh's for a few weeks, they'd heard rumors about his meanness, and his drunkenness, and his mean drunkenness, and now they were about to experience all of it first hand, beginning with being bounced along in the payload of his truck, plastic zip ties binding their hands. Gertrude looked miserably out at the passing fields. He had been hit hardest by the whole ordeal: the accident, the fire, the trial and incarceration. His family was tightly knit and, unlike his friends', still alive. He had promised his mother there would be no more of the shenanigans that landed him there in the first place, and now he was already tangled up in the death of another student. There were no second chances at Raleigh's Prep: any student caught breaking any rule was subject to the sternest possible punishment. In some very few cases that meant some kind of beating or flogging in the courtyard, but for most it meant one thing and one thing only. Expulsion. And expulsion meant prison.

Real prison.

With prison cells and prison food and prison rape.

Not that there weren't rapists at Raleigh's, but at least they were wealthy rapists.

Topher watched him for a while, looking for signs of weakness or instability. Would he cry? Was he angry? The latter was more his worry than the former. Gertrude was easily a foot taller and fifty pounds heavier, even without the furs and beard. He'd once seen him lift an entire keg over his head in a drunken rage and throw it through a sliding glass door.

"Are you all right, Gertrude?" he cried over the wind. Gertrude continued to stare at the passing fields. "Gertrude! Are you all right?"

Gertrude said nothing. Topher kicked him. Gertrude still didn't respond. Zorn put a hand on Topher's foot.

"Leave him alone. I'll talk to him later."

The payload hit a bump, sending them all a few inches into the air with startled cries. Zorn ended up on the truck bed.

Topher beat on the window with his fists.

"Damn your hide, Mr. Floyd!"

Mr. Floyd shot them a glance, then whipped the window back.

"You mind yourself there, boy. You three in a heap of trouble already."

Then he slammed it back and locked it into place.

"The man is a moron," Topher cried to the wind.

Gertrude nudged him with his foot.

"Here comes the campus."

Topher craned his neck to see how fast they would get there. Who would be awake in the courtyard at this hour to witness their arrest? What a wonderful rumor that would create. Whispers in The Grotto: The new kids were caught eating a dead student! His standing with the older boys would skyrocket. Especially if they were all flogged or beaten.

"Do you think that ass, Brimstone, will be awake at this hour?"

Zorn stretched his legs, resting his feet on the tailgate.

"Why do you ask?"

"He wants somebody to see us," Gertrude said. "He wants to be associated with the murder."

Topher was offended.

"I do not want just anybody to see us. I want that ass Brimstone to see us. How do you know it was a murder?"

Gertrude shot him an incredulous look.

"You saw the body. How could that not be a murder?"

"Perhaps he had a virus. Maybe he died of natural causes, and then was eaten by wild dogs. Did I not tell you of the bloodcurdling howl I heard this morning?"

The pickup emerged from the path and stopped parallel to the forest.

"It doesn't matter," Gertrude said. "We'll be expelled before breakfast."

"Oh don't be such a baby."

Mr. Floyd cut the engine, which knocked and pinged before finally coming to rest. The door opened with a crack and a whine and he jolted out, his boots crunching on the gravel as he stalked around to the tailgate. He surveyed the grounds, but other than a few voices floating out of the dorm windows, the coast was clear. Satisfied, he turned on them and snarled, "Get out! Get!"

Topher stared back like a dumb beast. Gertrude merely glanced at him. When it was clear they weren't going to move, Mr. Floyd leaned in, yanked Zorn out by his wrists, then Topher, then Gertrude.

"Line up against the truck."

They did as they were told, shooting each other wary glances.

"Aren't you going to bring us to the headmaster?" Topher squeaked.

"Shut up," Mr. Floyd growled. "Now listen. I'm gonna ignore the fact that you boys was out of your rooms before morning roll. I'm gonna ignore the fact that you been sass talking me all morning. Now one of ya'll tell me what you seen out there on the field."

"A bloody cor—" Zorn began, but Mr. Floyd backhanded him across the face before he could finish. The crack echoed in the morning. Crows in the nearby trees cawed in complaint and flapped away into the distance. A red welt swelled on Zorn's cheek.

"Now listen to me very closely," Mr. Floyd repeated, breathing hard. His breath smelled sharp, like rotten apples. "Tell me. What you boys seen. Out there. On the field."

"Well," Topher said. "I believe Zorn was trying to tell you that we saw a dead body befo—"

Mr. Floyd backhanded him, too. He fixed his eyes upon Gertrude, who shrank back a little

"You. Tell me what you seen out there on the field."

"Certainly not a dead body."

Gertrude shut his eyes tight, waiting for the blow. The birds in the trees awoke and sang, and a strong breeze whooshed through the leaves. He opened one eye. Mr. Floyd was smiling at him, which was a terrible thing. He raised his chin at Gertrude.

"This one here's the smartest one of all ya'll. Now listen, I'm gonna tell you boys what you seen out there." He pulled a hunting knife out of a sheath on his belt and waggled it menacingly. "You ain't seen nothing, got it?" Gertrude nodded furiously. "Now, if you go around spreading any rumors—" He shoved the knife between the boy's wrists and began to saw back and forth.

"No!" Gertrude cried, but then the zip ties were cut and he was free. Zorn was next, then Topher, and then all three were standing there, free, frowning in their confusion.

"Get outta here," Mr. Floyd spat.

They didn't move.

"I said GET!"

They took a few cautious steps away from the truck, waiting for some kind of trick. Mr. Floyd twirled the knife in his hand, then Zorn reached over and grabbed Topher by the sleeve and pulled him away, and all three sprinted off.

The grounds keeper watched them cut across the grass and head up the brick path that led to the courtyard. When he was sure that they weren't coming back, he limped to the driver's side door and eased himself inside. The pickup started with a throaty roar. He put it in gear and spun the wheel around, heading back the way he had just come, back to the field.

When he was sure they were out of earshot, Topher said, "A near miss. We'll have to be more careful."

Zorn patted his belly.

"I'm hungry."

"Today's sausage day at The Grotto. I love sausage day."

The thought of sausage links reminded Gertrude of the corpse on the field, particularly its—

"Perhaps I'll just have a fruit cup."

Topher fell silent, which unsettled his roommates. When Topher fell silent it meant one of three things:

1. that he was plotting to vomit.
2. that he was plotting some kind of tomfoolery.
3. that he was plotting to vomit as a measure of tomfoolery.

It was just such the combination that landed them in Raleigh's in the first place, only in that case it wasn't "vomit" and "tomfoolery," but "arson" and "premeditated murder".

Fortunately, all he did was remain silent and continue to walk, and Gertrude, feeling better now that they hadn't gotten in to trouble, began to think about his family.

"I wonder if my parents have built the new house yet."

"Hardly," Zorn replied. "They'll have to wait for the check from the insurance company."

"At least that'll allow father's wounds to heal. How long does it take skin to grow back?"

"It would make an excellent research project. I once burned my calf on the tailpipe of a moped. My doctor prescribed this greasy salve. I was supposed to rub it on the burn for two weeks, and so I did, but all it did was make the skin melt. I got a violent infection, and my leg nearly fell off. It took a full two months to recover."

"Father's in an oxygen tent. He's fed intravenously."

Brown shirted boys burst out of dormitory's side doors, screaming like drill sergeants. Assistants. The worst of the worst, chosen specifically for their lack of empathy and daddy issues, sycophantic psychopaths assigned by administration to boss the other boys around, bully them, snoop through their belongings, and report any and all non-conformists, weirdos, oddballs, introverts, rebels, radicals, mopers, and ononists to Headmaster Stoneman .

"Get to breakfast!" they cried.

Topher despised them. He despised their short clipped hair and their crisp, button-up shirts. He despised their shiny black shoes, their pressed and pleated khakis. But most of all he despised their whistles, which they blew incessantly, red faced and angry, directly into the face of any peon who dared not immediately react to an order. Fortunately, they were unarmed. Stoneman was severe, but he wasn't an idiot. Still, he ignored the little homemade blackjacks some of them carried, unless they were crazy enough to use them in the open, or if one were used in the commission of the death of another student, in which case his preferred method of punishment was more biblical than progressive.

"Beat the cur with his own tail and it will never disobey again," he often said.

The door to Burleigh's flew open, and Topher saw the Assistants that were assigned to their floor, Brimstone and Burr, stomp out onto the cobblestones, carrying on in their usual fashion, screaming at everybody to exit the dorm immediately, maggots, and get to chow.

"Just fall in with the crowd," Topher muttered, and they did exactly that, wending their way into the mass of adolescents nearly trampling each other to get to breakfast and away from the brown shirted menace.

When he was sure they'd escaped detection, Topher said, "I think he knows who we are."

"Gertrude's father?" Zorn said. "He knows *exactly* who we are. He's the reason we were sent to this place. Weren't you at the trial? It was quite dramatic."

"I'm aware of Mr. Hughes's roll in our internment. I was referring to Mr. Floyd."

"But we've only been here less than a month," Gertrude said.

"Yes, but Mr. Floyd is everywhere. He could probably tell us the time and date of your last bowel movement."

"What?"

"Didn't I tell you he approached me the third day after our arrival? 'Six thirty in the evening,' he growled. 'Tuesday.' It took a while before I understood exactly what he was talking about, but when I did I shuddered for nearly an hour straight."

"Then he knows exactly who we are. Among other things."

Topher waved the comment aside. "The question I propose is this: Why did he let us go?"

"Maybe he didn't see the corpse?"

"How could he *not* see it?" Zorn said. "It was right there in front of him, despite Topher's, er, best efforts to draw away his attention."

"I don't know what happened. My buttocks usually have a mesmerizing effect upon people, particularly adults."

"Perhaps, then, he didn't understand that the corpse was a corpse?" Gertrude offered. "I mean, I know it was obvious to us, but he didn't really get a good look at it like we did."

"Don't be an idiot, Gertrude. What else could he think it was?"

"From that distance? Maybe a pile of rotted squirrels? Odious little vermin, them. I was once attacked by squirrels when I was three years-old. Nearly bit off my thumb. See the scar?"

He presented his thumb to them for inspection.

Zorn peered at the tiny white line just below the nail.

"I thought that was a badger?"

"I was also attacked by a badger, but not until I was six. An altogether different story. It was mostly to blame."

"You told me you swatted it with a walking stick."

"I did, and when it leapt at me I compared it to several unfavorable things. I believe the beauty of the metaphor was lost in the violence of the moment. I was forced to run for my life."

Topher began to get heated.

"The corpse was neither a pile of deceased squirrels, nor was it a pile of deceased badgers."

"Then there was the time that baboon bit me on the arm at the zoo," Gertrude continued. "It would seem as though I'm not held in high regard by mammals at all."

"Shut up! What we found was obviously the body of a dead student. Correct me if I'm wrong, but isn't there something about not murdering one's classmates in the Student Code of Conduct?"

"If there isn't, there should be," Zorn said.

The gold dome of The Grotto loomed ahead atop a short incline, growing larger and more mythical as they approached. Pillars framed the wide wooden doors, and marble benches were bolted into the concrete next to them. Zorn's belly growled at the thought of the impending feast.

"Wait, are rodents mammals?" Gertrude finally asked.

If the exterior of The Grotto was a romantic approximation of a gothic cathedral, the interior resembled more of a late nineteenth century booby hatch. Beige tiles covered the floor, and the walls (also beige) weren't made out of brick, or wood beams, or anything else stylish, but sheetrock. Even the lime-streaked windows were square. Rusty iron bars were bolted into the frames, and the glass panes were warped and bubbled.

"Look," Zorn said as they joined the queue. "It's I, Dennis. Hello, I, Dennis!"

He waved at a tall, skinny boy in the middle of the line. He was wearing black celluloid pants that crinkled when he walked, a matching black shirt, and a black plastic helmet, all of which shined dully in the buzzing overhead lights. His nose was angular and prominent, his cheeks sallow and sunken, and his Adam's apple protruded like a painful tumor. Topher had never been very impressed by the helmet, though everyone else seemed to think it was magnificent. That knot in his throat, however, was unnerving, bobbing like it did whenever he spoke, or breathed, or did nothing. It was like it had a mind of its own.

He didn't say anything, but he did let them cut in line behind him.

Gertrude eyed the camera mounted onto the back of the helmet.

"So, are you still, er, still modifying your body?"

The camera jerked in symmetrical polygons, making little mechanical sounds as it scanned Gertrude's every movement. I, Dennis turned around, blessing them with his white, scar-puckered countenance.

"Hello, Zorn. Hello, Kenneth." He nodded at Topher and his Adam's apple bobbed and Topher jerked his eyes toward the ceiling.

Gertrude beamed. It was rare that anyone referred to him by his given name. Zorn pointed at some wires sticking out his neck.

"What are those for?"

"Performance enhancers. The kids at my old school used to tease me. They don't anymore."

"The wires stopped them?"

"No, I did."

He let that hover in the air.

"I did these before I came here. The kids at my old school liked to throw soggy bread rolls at me. If someone here throws a soggy bread roll at me, my camera will identify it as a hostile object and send electrical impulses to my various muscles. Then I'd burn it to bits with my eyeball lasers."

A soggy bread roll sailed through the air and hit him right in the back of the head. It splattered, thick and wet, the sodden dough squirting into the helmet, which sparked and fizzled.

"Duck, Jean-Claude!" someone yelled.

"Why do they call me that?"

He took the helmet off with a twist and a click, revealing his puckered skull. Irregular strands of greasy gray hair sprouted like witch-weed, and where there wasn't hair the skin was corpse white, and where the skin wasn't corpse white it was scarred and bruised, and where it wasn't scarred and bruised it was wrinkled like the neck of a bulldog. Topher found another spot on the ceiling to stare at.

"It's an allusion, I think," Gertrude said.

"An allusion?" I, Dennis scraped bread off the components and out of the cracks in the plastic. "To what?"

"A movie. A late-eighties, science fiction flick called *Cyborg*, to be specific. It starred Jean-Claude Van Damme. He's a Belgian karate expert."

I, Dennis flicked the last few specks bread from his helmet and twisted it back on his head. It clicked and whirred, buzzed and droned, and dinged three times.

"I don't watch Japanese films."

"How did you get your hands on all of this?" Zorn asked. "Isn't that considered contraband?"

"I told you. Most of my upgrades were completed before I was sent here. I'd have Internet service if we weren't so far out of range."

Topher continued to stare at the ceiling.

"You're lying. Who's your contact? Can you get me some candy bars and a revolver?"

Someone grabbed him by the shoulder and spun him around and he came face to face with a muscular Assistant. Phyro Brimstone, his nemesis. He was a little taller than Topher, and he kept his head shaved. The shiny slug of a scar crossed his left cheek. His partner, Burr, stood behind him like a dog, his hands clasped behind his back, fawning and obsequious and ridiculously intense.

"Did I just hear you threaten to shoot somebody?" Brimstone asked.

"My goodness, Phyro," Topher said. "Your uniform is spotless. Did your boyfriend wash it for you?"

Brimstone sneered.

"Didn't see you in the hallway this morning, Bill."

"Oh?"

"You weren't sneaking out, were you?"

"Of course not. That would be against school rules."

Brimstone took a step closer so that his nose almost grazed Topher's.

"If I find out you've been sneaking out before wake-up call, you know what that means, right?"

"That I've been banging your mother without you?"

The satisfied smile on Brimstone's face turned into a snarl. He clenched his fists. Topher bounced on his toes, trying to seem taller. Then a voice, cool and collected, said, "Is there a problem, boys?"

Brimstone whipped around, ready to pummel whoever said it, but then panic swept over his face.

There, standing in the entry, was the new Headmaster, Mr. Stoneman. He was very thin, with sunken, snakelike eyes, and a sharp nose and sharp cheeks that emphasized his full lips. His skin was smooth and ruddy, offset by jet-black hair streaked with gray. He wore it long and swept back off his forehead. His suit was also black and expensive, and his shoes were polished within an inch of exploding into flames.

Brimstone's fists unclenched and he stood at attention. Burr followed suit, the bloodlust in his eyes replaced by terror.

"Mr. Stoneman," Brimstone said. "How nice to see you, sir."

"Spare me, Brimstone. I asked you a question."

"A question, sir?"

"Don't be an ass, boy. What's going on here?"

"Nothing. Nothing at all, sir."

Burr nodded furiously. Stoneman smirked. He hung his head a bit and let the smirk turn into a creepy half-smile.

"Aren't you going to introduce me to your friends?"

Brimstone blinked and swallowed.

"Yes, sir. This is Topher Bill. Behind him is his roommate, Michael Zorn. And this is Ger . . . Kenneth Hughes."

"Zorn? That's an odd name."

"Yes, sir," Zorn said. "It's a family name. My mother's mother's maiden name, sir."

"I see."

He took them all in, a little half-smile on his face.

"Topher Bill, Michael Zorn, and Kenneth Hughes. I remember you now. I just read your files the other day. Positively murderous." Gertrude shuddered. "I trust you boys will stay out of trouble while you're in my care? No more 'accidental' fires?" The boys nodded in unison. He held their attention for one last uncomfortable beat. "Very good. Brimstone?"

Brimstone stood even straighter, and Burr tried to mimic him.

"I need you and your little friend to come with me, please."

Marvin Grimm was almost six foot six and weighed over two hundred pounds. His hunch was legendary. Usually it was all anybody could see as he waded through the sea of chairs, bobbing on his back like a gull on the waves. His head was huge, too; a stylist's nightmare, a haberdasher's wet dream. He scanned the cafeteria for an empty table where he could spread his full bulk, an empty table, preferably, far away from the others, but there wasn't one. Then he saw his roommate, I, Dennis, and the other new kids whose names he didn't know yet. They were sitting in the middle of the cafeteria, surrounded by a forest of chair legs and backpacks, but he decided to risk it. He was big and strong, and that'd saved him before, but he'd never been sent away to a place like Raleigh's where his size and strength didn't seem to matter. There were kids in there that had done unspeakable things and had no problem telling him about it.

Those unfortunate enough to be in his way were knocked aside or shoved into the tables. When he was forced to stop at some impasse, his hunch was assaulted by a variety of fruit, mostly apples, which ricocheted off like a marble on a trampoline. One shot straight up into the air and hit the ceiling. He grunted a greeting when he reached the table, prompting one of the bearded newcomers below cry out "Marvin Grimm! Nice to see you. Please, have a seat."

Marvin gently placed his heaping lunch tray on the table and allowed his backpack to slip off his non-hunched shoulder. He placed it carefully on the floor, pulled out a chair, and engulfed it with his buttocks. The chair protested with a creak.

"I forgot your name."

"I'm Michael. But you can just call me Zorn."

"Okay. Hi, Zorn."

Topher, a wicked gleam in his eye, said, "What's in your backpack, Marvin?"

The table hushed. The contents of Marvin Grimm's backpack were the subject of wild, and often ludicrous, speculation. Marvin shrugged and shoved a small stack of pancakes into his face. Topher pressed on.

"I like to imagine it is your storage container for hacked up limbs, all wrapped in cheesecloth."

Marvin shoveled a mound of beans into his face.

"How would you like to find out?"

"Yes, Topher," Zorn said. "How would you like to find out?"

An apple struck Marvin directly in the forehead and he didn't bat an eyelash. It fell into his lap, defeated and embarrassed. When he was done with the pancakes, he started in on entire second breakfast that he'd hidden underneath: bacon, eggs, steak. He devoured this in much the same manner he had the pancakes. Another apple sailed by and he swatted it. It exploded.

Zorn caught another apple as it zipped past and took a bite.

"Who's throwing all of this fruit?"

I, Dennis adjusted his eye plate, studying the images.

"Two boys next to the window in the back."

"Oh?"

Zorn stood up, the apple in his paw, and scanned the cafeteria for the offenders. He spotted them, two older boys in the corner, ducking and giggling. He threw the apple as hard as he could, hitting one of them in the back of the head and sending him face first into his bowl of oatmeal. There was a brief break in the cafeteria din, and then the room burst into applause and laughter from all directions. The boy stood up, angry and ready to fight, but when he saw who threw it he paused. The boys around him booed and called him names, and he glanced at them, sheepish, before he sat down and wiped the oatmeal off his face with a napkin.

Zorn sat down.

"It seems Mr. Stoneman isn't the only one who knows about our past."

"We need to get down to serious business," Topher said.

Gertrude swallowed.

"Oh, yes. I've been meaning to ask you about those weird slapping noises you make in the bathroom."

"No, not that! We must discuss the heer-haw that we found in the wee-oow."

"The what?"

"You know." Topher jerked his head in the direction of the athletic fields. "The thing."

"I'm not following you."

"The windows?" Zorn ventured.

"The body! On the field!"

Gertrude's eyes nearly popped out of his head.

"Topher, don't be an idiot. Mr. Floyd told us not to mention that to anyone."

"Yes, yes. But I interpreted that as more of a dare than an order, and the Bill family has never backed down from a dare."

"Which is more important," Zorn said, rolling his eyes.

Gertrude worried his fingers, doe eyed.

"Topher, please."

"What? Did you really think I would let something as colossal as a dead body go uninvestigated?"

Gertrude hunched over the table.

"You yourself said it was dangerous." He put on his best conspiratorial whisper. "Mr. Floyd is omniscient. He knows when I've pooped!"

"I know. But what can he do, after all. Turn us in for pooping?"

Zorn tried reason.

"Topher, it does seem risky. And considering that just by being here we are in enough trouble as it is."

"Dead body?" Grimm grumbled.

"Sssssst!" Gertrude said, his face sinking to the table, his eyes gone wild.

"Gertrude, shut up," Topher said. "And get up. You draw more attention to yourself like that than were you sitting there naked with a flaming torch sticking out of your ass. And yes, Marvin. A dead body. On the athletic fields. This morning."

Gertrude jabbed his finger at Zorn.

"He found it."

"I did not!" Zorn jabbed back. "He . . . he!"

"Me!"

"It doesn't matter who found it!" Topher said. "What matters is that we saw it. It exists. And now we must discover the murderer."

"Why?" Gertrude said. "Why can't we just let it alone?"

"Because, that boy wasn't just killed. He was mauled. Turned into organ meat salad. Any one of us could be next." Gertrude wanted to respond but couldn't. Topher was right. "If we want to be prepared, we need to know what did this to him."

"What exactly did it look like?" I, Dennis asked. "The body?"

"Ah, I, Dennis," Topher said. "Now you're thinking like a sleuth. The condition of the body is directly related to the method of murder. A gunshot wound to the head yields a hunt for the specific gun that fired it. Same for a knife wound or a bludgeoned skull. Alas, our task is much more difficult."

"Why's that?"

"Because," someone else said. A boy sitting right behind Topher. "Like you said, the body you found was all mangled up."

Topher turned around. He was nice enough looking, with a mop of curly black hair that fell into his eyes. But nobody was entirely innocent, especially someone who ended up at Raleigh's Prep.

"Were you eavesdropping?"

"It's not really eavesdropping if I can hear you without trying. I wouldn't be talking about this to anybody if I were you."

Gertrude nodded eagerly. He liked this person.

Topher was not as impressed.

"Oh really? And you're an expert on organ meat salad?"

The boy smiled.

"Over the summer they found a body out there, too."

"Organ meat salad?"

"Organ meat salad."

He had their full attention now. Even Marvin Grimm stopped feeding, leaning as far forward as his knees would allow. The boy offered his hand to Topher, saying, "My name is Crews."

Topher ignored it.

"*Who* found a body?"

"Some new kid." Crews put his hand in his lap. "And my roommate and me."

"Did the administration do anything to you?"

"The administration? You mean Stoneman?" He shook his head ruefully. "No. Nobody did anything. Not at first."

"And Mr. Floyd didn't catch you?"

"Nobody caught us. It was dark out, and . . . and we ran." Crews paused, seeming to gather his nerve. "Me and Banks, we told the new kid not tell anybody, but he couldn't resist. Next thing I know, he up and disappeared."

"Maybe his sentence was over?"

Crews shook his head.

"Nobody's sentence is ever over here."

"Ours will be," Gertrude said. "Five years. Three with good behavior."

"And Gertrude's parents are rich," Topher added. "So it might be even shorter."

Crews opened his mouth to speak, but right when he did, somebody popped a paper bag. All five boys jumped. The cafeteria erupted in a chorus of 'Oohs! and Ahhs!' Crews joined in, crying, "Bravo!" Then to Topher he said, "Everybody here has rich parents, and nobody ever leaves."

Topher pondered this, swirled his juice around in the cup. When the noise died down, Crews continued.

"The day after we found the body, Stoneman called an assembly. Told us that 'Wesley Watts was out early in the morning helping Mr. Floyd cut down a tree in the woods that had been damaged in a storm.' He told us Wesley fell and broke his neck, ruled it an accident, but I knew he was lying. I saw the body. That kid didn't fall. It looked like he'd been eaten."

"Are you saying there are wolves in the woods?"

The boy leaned forward again. "Not just any kind of wolves. Werewolves."

All of them stared at him, transfixed. Then Topher laughed aloud.

"Balderdash!" he declared.

"Poppycock!" Zorn added.

"Sssssst!" Gertrude hissed.

Topher wiped a tear from his eye.

"Oh dear. You really had us going."

The boy stared back, clenching his jaw.

"I'm serious."

"Fine. There are fairy tale monsters in the woods."

"Is your roommate around?" Gertrude asked. "We could ask him what he thinks."

The boy opened his mouth to say something, then he shook his head.

"Banks has a big mouth. I'm surprised he was able to keep it to himself this long. He got up early, I think. We were supposed to meet up for breakfast, but—"

There was a commotion at the front of the cafeteria. They all turned and saw Mr. Floyd wheeling in a lectern with a microphone on it. Stoneman followed close behind. Everyone fell into a tense silence as Mr. Floyd plugged a mic cable into the wall. Stoneman took the lectern and spoke, his voice coming out of the speakers bolted into the walls all around the cafeteria.

"Your attention, please. We regret to announce that at six o'clock this morning, the body of John Banks was discovered floating in Lake Perish." He voice did not quaver. "It appears to be a suicide, though the investigation is ongoing."

93

He allowed for the whispers to diminish before speaking again.

"Grief counselors will be available at Merton Hall for those of you who need someone to talk to. There will be an extra room search scheduled at a time of our choosing. Classes will still continue as usual. Please do not try to visit the athletic fields or the lake today, as they are closed for the investigation."

The lunch bell rang, signaling the ten-minute transition to post-meal room inspection. Chairs scraped against the tile, utensils clattered, and chatter dinned the air. Topher got ready to leave. The boy didn't move. He sat where he was, processing what he just heard.

"What did you say your roommate's name was?" Topher asked him.

Crews didn't answer. He stood up and picked up his tray, keeping his back to them, wiped his face on his sleeve.

"Wait," Topher said.

Crews walked away from the table, then paused, seeming to think. He turned abruptly and came back, his eyes red and brimming. "John's the third one to die this year. You don't have to believe me about the wolves. Full moon tonight. Go out into the woods and see for yourself." Then he left, saying over his shoulder, "I bet you won't."

Topher was incensed by the challenge. All evening long he struggled with the absurdity of what Crews told him and the desire to prove him wrong. Finally, when he could take it no longer, he stood up from behind his desk and said, "Dammit! I'll not be made a fool of. Grab your gear, boys. We're going werewolf hunting."

Zorn, who was reading *The Awakening* for English class, had not expected such an outburst. Nor did he expect the codpiece Topher threw at him. He welcomed the diversion, though. He thought Edna a weak, pathetic little woman, and the sooner he could get away from her, the better. Even if it took gallivanting around with a metal contraption clasped up his, to his . . . around his waist.

"Why a codpiece?"

Topher lowered his voice and growled, "Incubi."

Zorn stared at it.

"Should I wear it in front or in back?"

"What do you think?"

Topher tossed an iron collar at Gertrude, who was trying to complete his Historical Math Analysis homework for his Historical Math Analysis class. He had no idea how or why learning nautical navigation would benefit him in the future, as he thought sailors a rather surly and unapproachable lot, known more for their salty language, high seas sexual desperation, and questionable career choices than anything else, and the sooner he could get away from thoughts of buggery the better. Even if it took gallivanting around with a piece of iron clasped to his, around his . . . hopefully Topher intended to clasp it around his neck.

"Why an iron collar?"

"Vampires"

Gertrude put the collar down on his desk and decisively pushed it away.

"Look, Gertrude," Topher said. "We're not going werewolf hunting so much per se, in a manner of speaking, as such, in and of itself. If you know what I mean."

Gertrude shook his head.

"I don't."

"What I mean is, we're going to summon a liderc."

"What's a liderc?"

"A liderc is a Romanian werewolf hunter."

"Oh! So a knight?"

Topher bobbed his head from side to side.

"Not really. More like a witch."

"Mother made me promise not to get caught up in any of your schemes."

"What about if it's a witch that can only do our bidding?"

"A zombie witch," Zorn offered.

"Yes," Topher said. "And no. More like a golem zombie. Well no, that's redundant. Gertrude, are you in or not?"

Gertrude studied the metal collar. Then his eyes fell on his textbook, the laboriously titled *Bloated Flesh and Lost Compass: History's Greatest Maritime Nautical Disasters*. He wanted to say no. He wanted to pick up that silly book and study. He heard his mother's voice, admonishing him to stay out of trouble, to stay away from "that boy." But he couldn't. He just couldn't. What Topher was proposing was just too exciting. Topher's propositions were always much more exciting than anything Gertrude originally set out to do. Going to a movie? Let's blow up frogs in the creek instead. Reading your favorite book? Let's throw rocks at cars from an overpass. Practicing the oboe? Let's look at these magazines I found in the woods. Okay, okay, okay.

He worked up a slow boil. Topher was the most selfish, careless, irresponsible person he'd ever known, but being his friend, his second right-hand man (Zorn would always be first) was both dangerous and thrilling. While Gertrude preferred to plan things out, carefully consider his options, and move through his day, dutifully checking off his list of things to do, Topher barreled through time like a hyperactive pit bull, destroying everything in his wake, barking gleefully has he did so. Gertrude was the guy who stood in the corner at parties, watching, carrying on a conversation with a few good friends. Topher was the madman doing keg stands and setting the couch on fire, dragging the poor schmuck standing in the corner into the back room to snort white powder off a mirror.

And then it struck him. None of this was really Topher's fault. He could have said no to all of those things but he didn't. He wanted to do them. He wanted to blow up frogs and throw rocks at cars. He wanted to look at pornography and snort drugs. He just needed someone to push him into it. And this is how it works out. He ends up at Raleigh's Prep. It was the only logical result. Nobody put him here. He chose to be here. He belonged here. As soon he realized that, the pressure on his chest was gone. The icy ball in his stomach melted. He had always gone along with what Topher said and he always would. He knew his place in the world. He understood his fate, and it was freeing, this knowledge. And terrifying. He looked up.

There stood Topher, waiting for an answer. Zorn had already snapped the codpiece around his waist and turned it around to guard his backside. He was checking it out in the mirror.

"Well?" Topher asked.

Gertrude sighed and grabbed the iron collar.

"Okay. I'm in."

The path snaked through the woods, leading the boys deep into the heart of Chainwrought Forest. Topher had no idea where he was going. He chose it because it looked like it had been used before. The bare limbs of the trees enmeshed overhead, creating a thick, knotty web that creaked in the wind. Outside the forest, the moon shone bright and full; inside it barely penetrated the canopy. Topher pulled a broadsword out to clear away a tangle of creepers and thorns that seemed to purposefully block his way. He sliced through for a couple of feet, but they reformed behind him. He hacked at a knot the size of his head.

"Magical prickers! I'd move quick if I were you."

"Where'd you get that sword?" Gertrude asked.

"I found it in the basement."

"You found a sword in the basement?"

"Where do you think I got your collar?"

"Where in the basement?"

"I don't know. Someone just left them out, so I took them." He pulled up his shirt, revealing his own codpiece and a mace, which he'd tucked into his belt. "And these!"

"Did you find anything we could use?"

"No, of course not. Well, maybe. Okay, yes. But I'm not giving them to you."

"Why not me?"

"You? Please."

They followed him as close as they could, pinching the vines and thorns between their fingers, trying to move them aside, but they scratched and bit and tore their furs. Gertrude was actually glad for the collar, though it rubbed his skin raw. At least it protected his neck. No telling what kind of poison magical prickers contained. The vine, no doubt, carried some kind of toxic oil. They'd all be covered in calamine lotion before the week was out. If they survived this. He sneezed. His belly was in knots. He began to chant the refrain that defined his life with Topher: thiswasabadidea, thiswasabadidea. On top of everything else, the wood was stuffy and humid, and it smelled like a trunk filled with old raincoats and apple cores.

"Cat urine," Zorn announced.

Topher shot him a glance over his shoulder.

"What?"

"It smells like cat urine in here."

"Oh."

"Why did you look at me like that?"

Topher shrugged. "I thought you said something else."

Zorn pondered this a moment. He brushed away a spider's web.

"What else could I have said?"

"Never mind. Listen to me, you two. We have entered the belly of the beast, to use a cliché. *Acta non verba*, as they say. Be mindful of all noises and smells. Ahab himself could not be more vigilant."

"Are we in any particular immediate danger?" Gertrude asked.

"Are you kidding? When have I not put us in danger?"

"Good point."

"No need to freak out yet. I've never been here before."

"What?"

"No need to worry. Crews is a ninny. Have we seen anything weird yet? Tonight," he added, cutting Gertrude off. "The only thing that's attacked me at Raleigh's so far was a titmouse out on the Badugby fields. And that ass, Brimstone. And a few other boys on our first day. And Zorn, but that was purely sexual and he was sleepwalking."

"It was not sexual!"

"Please, Zorn. You grabbed my nethers."

"I have strange dreams."

"I was attacked by a squirrel just last week," Gertrude said. "They're the natural enemies of simians. Ever since that baboon bit me at the National Zoo, I've been targeted by a variety of rodents. Especially Family *Sciuridae*."

"Wait, did it bite you?" Topher asked.

"The squirrel? On the contrary. I smashed it in the face and sent it crashing into the bushes. The beast will think twice before it startles a Hughes again."

"A regular Francis Macomber," Zorn said.

"Who's he?"

"Never mind."

Topher snorted.

Gertrude worried his fingers.

"Tell me."

"He's a fictional character in a Hemingway short story," Zorn explained.

"Oh? Big game hunter?"

"Of a sort. He runs from a lion, then his wife blows his head off."

"It's a shame, Gertrude," Topher said before his friend could respond. "That you were not bitten by that squirrel. We could have used your rabies-infested blood to summon an even more frightful liderc. Or a succubus. Whatever we can manage."

The more they walked, the darker it grew. Gertrude started to wheeze. He withdrew his inhaler from his pocket and triggered a blast.

"The pollen count in here must be phenomenal," he said. "I can hardly breathe."

"It could be all of the fur," Topher said. "Werewolves are terribly negligent groomers."

He raised his fist and stopped in his tracks. Zorn ran into him, of course, and then Gertrude (who was looking up at the trees) ran into Zorn.

"Careful, you oafs," Topher said. He pointed at a wall of thorns about ten feet in front of them. Dim light flickered behind it, a pale, icy fire. Garbled voices and strangled grunts wafted through the air. "This looks like a hant haunt."

"A hant haunt?" Zorn asked.

"A hant haunt."

"What's a hant haunt?"

"A haunt for hants."

Zorn pondered this.

"You have experience with hant haunts?"

"This one reminds me of the hant haunt outside the old Bill family manse. Oh how I loved our bi-annual hant haunt hunts. William Bill the Trembler once suffered the molestation of fourteen succubi during one. It's how he earned his nickname."

Topher crept forward to the wall of thorns, Zorn and Gertrude right behind, and carefully drew aside a few branches.

"How about that," he whispered. "Crews was right."

"He was?"

"Yep. There are four werewolves in there and only three vampires. That I can see. It'll be a blood bath. Ready lads?"

"Are you serious?" Zorn asked.

"My asthma," Gertrude said.

With an earsplitting ululation, Topher crashed into the wall, rebounded once, then shoved his way through, cursing the whole time. "Avaunt ye knaves!" they heard him cry, followed by anguished yelps and guttural snarls.

Zorn and Gertrude paused, mouths slightly ajar.

"Er—" Zorn said.

"Zorn! Gertrude!" Topher cried. "Damn your hides!"

Gertrude stepped aside and gestured elaborately at the wall.

"After you," he said.

Zorn cursed under his breath, then picked his way through the wall, like a cat walking in molasses.

The first thing he saw when he reached the other side was an afghan rug with teeth flying in his direction. It hit him square in the chest, bounced off with a yelp, and landed at his feet, unconscious.

"Don't just stand there, Zorn! Fight!"

Zorn pointed at the rug on the ground.

"Shall I throw this?"

"Throw it! Stab it! Do something to it!"

Gertrude stepped daintily into the clearing.

"Hello," he sang.

Topher was surrounded by afghan rugs larger than the one that attacked Zorn. His broadsword lay out of reach, but he still had his mace, which he used to strike at them repeatedly, causing minimal damage. One lunged forward and clamped onto his codpiece.

"Ha ha!" he cried, and brained it.

"He seems to having a devil of a time," Gertrude observed. A bat fluttered into his face. "Oooh, a bat."

It bothered his eyes, dodging his frantic swats, before transforming into a vampire in a grand puff of smoke.

He cried, "A sucker!" and then it lunged for his neck. There was a clinking sound as fangs met the metal collar. Gertrude laughed. "Topher, it works!" he cried, and the two stumbled backwards into the shadows.

Zorn bent over the thing at his feet and stroked his chin. Was there a specific way one should pick up a werewolf? He didn't want to strain anything, and he didn't want to touch . . . anything. He knew that he should lift with his legs, not his back, but where would he put his hands? And what if he brushed up against, or rub, or handle in any way, the thing's thing?

"Zorn!" Topher yelled. He ducked. A wolf flew over his shoulder.

"All right, all right," Zorn said.

He scooped the beast up and held it over his head. It was much heavier than he anticipated, and he hadn't stretched properly. His arms shook and he took a deep, gulping breath, then launched it into the air, leaning in to the throw with all of his strength. It spun once and collided with a mass of its fellows, sending them flying into the thorn wall. One hit Topher, knocking him to the ground where his head struck a stump and knocked him unconscious.

Zorn put his hand to his mouth.

"Oops."

He turned his attention to Gertrude, whose attacker labored under the delusion that its fangs could puncture metal. Before he could offer his services, he was struck from behind by an unknown force and driven face first into the ground. There was a brief moment when all was still. Then his pants were shucked violently, and something assailed his reverse codpiece with extreme force, driving his pelvis into the earth. There was another pause, and then the strikes were renewed, each one with mounting intensity and greater frustration.

"Good Lord!" he wailed.

Topher moaned. He shook his head and opened his eyes. Something wet and pungent lay next to him. A wolf's snout! The rest of it lay out in a great mound of muscle and nappy fur. It opened its eyes. They were dark and yellow and run through with red veins. A deep growl rumbled from its chest. Its foul breath blew Topher's hair back from his forehead. He scrambled backwards, trying to ignore the pain in his skull, and was relieved to find that he had been able to hold on to his mace.

The beast gathered its legs beneath its body and launched itself with a growl. Topher shut his eyes and swung blindly before him, swung as hard as he could. He connected, heard the wolf yelp, and his shoulder popped, and pain flared through his arm. The beast flew past him and crashed into a tree, its head crushed. Topher fell to his knees, his shoulder hanging at an odd angle. He looked around the clearing, and his heart sank. Zorn was trapped beneath some invisible weight, his pelvis shoved repeatedly into the ground. Gertrude struggled with a vampire, its fangs still clinking against his neck collar. He swayed. He was hit from behind and sent sprawling to the ground. His shoulder popped back in and he cried out.

"Stay down!" somebody yelled. He tried to get up but a boot stomped on his back. "I said, stay down."

And then, for the second time that night, something struck his head and knocked him out.

"If he's dead, I get his mace."

"Shhh! His lids are fluttering."

Topher moaned, rocking his head back and forth.

"Perhaps he was bitten."

"What if he's been bitten by both vampire and werewolf?"

"Maybe he'll become a werepyre."

"Or a vampwere."

"Depending on which bit him first."

There was a short silence, during which the stroking of beards could be heard.

"At least his neck isn't broken."

"What about his spine? I should kick him in the head."

"Do you think that's entirely wise?"

"Right. I'll kick him in the back."

A blinding pain seared through Topher's lower lumbar, and his eyes flashed open. Above him hovered the faces of Gertrude and the Crews boy. Zorn's face appeared shortly thereafter, his cheeks red.

"I kicked him with the strength of ten bulls," he said. "Is he well?"

"You," Topher groaned. "Idiot."

"He's well," Gertrude replied.

They pulled him off the ground, his head pounding. Crews gave him a swig from his water bottle.

"What are you doing here?" Topher asked.

"He saved your life," Zorn said, beaming. "Leapt into the clearing alone and cleared all the ghouls and what have you. A real professional."

"Did he?"

"Killed the vampire," Gertrude said.

"And the incubus," Zorn added.

Crews stood a bit away, measuring the trio. Upset at his roommate's death, he hadn't truly seen them in the lunchroom. The two large boys in furs with the strange names seemed impressive enough, but the one in the linen suit (Topher, was it?) was lacking in a variety of ways.

"Didn't expect to see you out here."

Topher allowed Zorn to help him to his feet.

"You told me to find out for myself!"

"I tell that to a lot of people. You were the first to listen."

Topher felt a little small.

"Well you're certainly the hero, aren't you? Is this what you do in your spare time?"

Crews smirked.

"Not by choice. It's about survival." A howl rang out behind them. "Come on. We've got to be going."

"Didn't you kill them?"

"I killed enough to get you out of there." Another howl shot through the air, this one closer than the first. It was answered from somewhere in a different direction. "Are you okay to run?"

"Not necessarily."

"It'll be really necessary here in about two minutes." Crews started to jog away. "I don't need anybody holding me back."

Topher's vision swam in the darkness. He was lightheaded, and his mace, now holstered in his belt, dragged him down, but he was determined to hold his own. Zorn tried to help by holding his elbow, but he shrugged it off. Branches whipped against his face, bloodying his cheeks, so he put his head down and thrust his arm up to deflect them.

"These thorns are a menace," he declared. "They're *still* trying to stop us!"

"Come on!" Crews called. Topher could just make out his white shirt ahead of them. "They're coming!"

The edge of the wood lay before them, the fields beyond lit by the moon. The boys made for it as fast as they could. More howls dogged their heels. Topher chanced a look over his shoulder; a dozen pairs of red lamps bobbed and weaved behind him.

"This is ridiculous."

The forest's edge wavered before him. He saw Crews break through it, then Zorn, then Gertrude. He stumbled on, nearly hitting his head on a tree.

"Come on!" Crews yelled.

How does one indicate that he was trying as hard as he could without stating the obvious? Rather than waste any breath on explaining himself, Topher gasped, "Don't leave me," but doubted anybody heard him. He completely expected to not make it. Right before he reached the tree line, right before he burst out of the woods, something horrible would bite into his calf and take him down. His friends would stand there, waiting, wondering where he was, and maybe he'd let loose a feeble "garg" as whatever horrid monster dragged him backwards, his one good hand scrabbling for purchase, trying to delay the inevitable. But it didn't happen. He kept running, un-chomped. He was two feet away. One foot away. And then he was through, stumbling onto the gravel maintenance path.

Of course they would be dead, lying there, gutted. Of course there would be no salvation, no team of well-trained student monster assassins whose job it was to take care of such brazen attacks. Of course he would merely run from one slobbering pack of beasts right into another, these uglier and more deadly, and as soon as he realized it, one would launch itself at him, all greasy, tangled fur and drooling, sharp teeth, and of course the last thing he would think right before it decapitated him or severed him in two would be "of course." But that didn't happen. Instead all he saw there were his friends standing around Mr. Floyd's truck, and Mr. Floyd himself, staring at them in disbelief, about to dump a shovelful of gravel into a hole in the path.

Without a word, he threw his shovel into the payload, lumbered around to the cab, yanked open the door, and leapt inside. The truck chugged and chugged, straining to turn over, finally roaring to life just as Gertrude, Crews, and Zorn leapt into the back.

"Wait!" Topher cried.

He grabbed the tailgate with both hands and was yanked off the ground as the truck peeled away. Gravel shot out from beneath the tires, striking his face, chest, and legs. One hit his eye and he saw stars. Zorn grabbed his wrist, trying to pull him aboard. Crews grabbed the other. The truck bucked as Mr. Floyd changed gears, and the boys were sent forward, teetering for one dizzy second over the edge, then they righted, and the truck bucked and shifted again, and they flew back, pulling Topher with them, and he was about to sail over the tailgate when something clamped onto the heel of his boot and pulled him backwards. He grew taut, stretching like a rope being pulled between opposing forces of equal strength and determination.

Gertrude tried to anchor everybody by hugging Crews around the middle.

Topher turned his head to see what had him. It was squat and ugly and foul, and it whipped its head back and forth so hard that he thought his ankle would break. Behind them ran a full pack of creatures of all sizes, gaining even as the truck whined at the top edge of sixty miles an hour. Some were as big as the payload of Mr. Floyd's truck; a few were even larger. Those in front were the smallest and fastest, their red eyes narrowing in on Topher, drooling in anticipation. They were covered in tumors, their white flesh poking through filthy fur.

Zorn tightened his grip on his wrist.

"Shake your boot free!"

Topher kicked once, to no avail.

"Harder!"

Topher pulled his right leg forward with all of his strength.

The wolf at his heel planted its feet in the ground.

Dirt shot up around as it dragged along.

Then Topher thrust his leg back, and the boot flew off and the wolf went spinning off behind them, tumbling along the path like a bowling ball, sweeping five more out of the way. The truck shifted again, and the boys hauled back as one, pulling Topher over the tailgate and crashing in a heap against into the pile of gravel. As the truck sped away, the monsters behind them gave up. They pushed their warty snouts into the air, sending up a colossal howl to befoul the night.

Topher wiggled his toes just to make sure they were still there.

"Did it bite you?" Crews asked. He picked up Topher's foot before he could say anything and inspected his heel. It was bruised and dirty, but whole. No blood. No bite wounds. He let it drop.

Mr. Floyd whipped the cab's rear window back and cried, "Lose anyone?"

"Just Topher's boot," Gertrude reported.

This, for some reason, tickled the man. He laughed out loud, raspy and harsh, and slid the window shut. The boys didn't share his delight. They just lay there, panting, nauseated, and terrified.

THE SECRET ROOM

Topher was uncertain about a lot of things. Physics and chemistry, instructions on shampoo bottles. He was uncertain about politics and sex, about technology and fashion. He was uncertain about the future of the environment, about the legitimacy of reality programming, about calculus and James Joyce's place in the literary pantheon.

But there were many more things of which he was certain. (He was a teenager, after all.) The sky was blue, naked women were awesome, and pickles should never be fried. Video games rotted the brain, bacon flavored ice cream was the devil's work, and . . . naked women . . . . Initially he was certain Gertrude's parents had shown the three of them mercy by commuting their sentence to Raleigh's Prep. All of the delinquent children of the fabulously rich were sent there at one point or another: Chad Mitchell after he curb-stomped his maid's son; Mark Bauer after he drunkenly plowed into that family in the minivan. The Chad Mitchells and the Mark Bauers and, for that matter, the Tophers, the Zorns, and the Gertrudes of the world were the reason for the invention of the word "affluenza," and while many derided the idea, he thought it an apt diagnosis. How on earth could he be held accountable for any of his behavior when all his parents had ever done was thrown money at him and given him anything he wanted?

But Chad Mitchell, he'd gone to Raleigh's Prep and nobody ever saw him again. Everybody just assumed he served his time and moved on with his life. Mark Bauer, too. But that wasn't the case, was it? No. Not at all. Their parents had bought off the judge, promised that Raleigh's would straighten out their children, and sent them packing, but not with the intent of reforming them. No. Not at all. Chad and Mark never served their time, they never moved on with their lives. The reason nobody ever saw them again was because they really were never seen again. They were sent to Raleigh's to die. Topher knew it. Knew it for certain, just like now he knew that the mercy bestowed upon him by Gertrude's mother and father was no more than a trick, and that the punishment they would suffer was not five years of prep school but death. A horrible, sad, painful, and undignified death.

He was also certain that the human versions of the beasts that had chased them out of the woods were students at Raleigh's Prep, and that they would reveal themselves by bearing the wounds delivered them during what he now thought of as The Battle of Chainwrought Den.

"We'll simply find them out and make a list," Topher said. "Then we'll hunt them down one by one, and rid this school of its supernatural filth once and for all."

When they reached the playing fields, Mr. Floyd, in a rare show of benevolence, threw them out of his truck with a "Get!", and so they did. They ran back to their dorm room. Now Gertrude sat on his bed and worried his fingers. Crews lurked by their door. Zorn paced back and forth, wild eyed and fanatic.

"Yes, yes," he said. "Kill them! Kill them all!"

"That's the spirit!" Topher chortled. "Now, it's first necessary to figure out who struck whom and how. I, for instance, brained at least a dozen of the bastards with my noble mace."

He hefted it in his hands, stroked the stalk with his palm.

"Topher, please," Gertrude said. "We don't know whether or not any of those poor creatures are fatherless."

"I didn't mean to insult them. I just meant it in the sense that they are horrible and despicable." He leaned the mace against his desk.

"Either way. They're already horrid beasts. Why rub it in?"

"Fine. What should I call them? Adorable balls of fluff?"

"I wouldn't go that far. How about 'critters'?"

"Critters they most certainly are *not*," Zorn said. "That implies some sort of cuteness."

"Badgers are critters," Gertrude said. "And I've never met a cute badger."

"Squirrels are critters."

"Oh shut up!" Topher spat. "Squirrels are in no way similar to werewolves."

Zorn said, "I believe these are were*pyres*."

"I," growled Topher. "Brained at least a dozen of the beasts. So we should be on the lookout for lads with horrible head wounds."

"I definitely caused some damage to the incubus that attacked me, if that is possible," Zorn said. "Grabbed him by the William Johnson I did, and didn't let go until I'd squeezed it to pulp."

Gertrude wondered if they should be on the lookout for a boy with a mangled penis.

"How will we check?"

"The incubus isn't a shape shifter," Topher said. "Zorn only managed to disfigure a ghoul. Plus, didn't you say Crews already killed it?"

"I threw at least half a dozen werepyres into the surrounding thorns," Zorn said. "So be on the lookout for anybody bearing minor dermal abrasions."

The next morning the boys were up much earlier than usual. Even Zorn rolled out of bed at a decent hour. They gobbled a cold breakfast at The Grotto and set out to begin their search.

"There's a Badugby game this morning," Gertrude informed them. "Everybody'll be at the stadium. Are you a fan?"

"Of Badugby?" Topher replied. He shrugged. "It's an interesting concept. I think one has to be here a while, you know, sink down into the boredom and drudgery before he grows weary enough of life to watch live sports for entertainment."

Gertrude sniffed.

"Well I love it."

"Yes, and you also like listening to smooth jazz. Anyone with as much bad taste to purposefully listen to someone rocking the clarinet would certainly enjoy something as inane as Badugby."

Gertrude ignored him.

"I prefer Dilque's Demons," he said, turning to Zorn. "How about you, Zorn?"

"Oh, I'm a fan of Trinkle's Timberwolves. Their uni's are so natty. I'm a sucker for anything gray or green, or any combination of the two. It's why I love the sea."

"But you can't swim," Topher said.

"So? I can't enjoy its symbolism? It's notion of the ocean that strikes me as romantic, not the actual physical properties of the water." He took a deep breath, as if inhaling some far off ocean air. "Aaaahhhhh."

The stadium was full. Fall in the north was often chilly, particularly in the mountains. The arena itself seemed to attract the most biting of the arctic air, and its design made for a fairly effective wind tunnel. All of the students, therefore, wore thick coats, heavy knit caps and gloves, which made it difficult, if impossible, to discern one person from the next. For some reason, everybody decided to wear neon ski gear that day, and the colors—the greens, the reds, the yellows—were blinding.

"It's best that we split up," Topher said. "The better to investigate a voluminous amount of afflicted."

Gertrude agreed, but Zorn wasn't convinced.

"Doesn't that conflict with your Scooby Doo Axiom?"

"Yes, but one can't live his entire life based on a cartoon featuring a drug addled hippy." He skipped away before anyone could disagree. "Don't be afraid to remove items of clothing should it be necessary."

He decided to first sit amongst the boys in the stands to try and blend in. He found a clear spot in the middle of the middle section, swiped the seat free of dirt and grime, and sat primly down. The crowd immediately erupted, buffeting him with cheers and cries and thighs.

"Good Lord!" he yelled, swatting at the surrounding legs with his hat. A cannon exploded, signaling some sort of success on the field. He screamed and thrust his head between his knees. When it became clear that they were not under attack, when the students around him sat down and calmed themselves, he sat up and surveiled the stands. Hmm. Figuring out who was normal and who was a wounded wereperson would not be as easy as he thought. First, he had no formal training in the matter. Nobody did, as far as he knew. Perhaps this would be a new career opportunity? For when he escaped? Second, almost everybody at Raleigh's Prep played Badugby. It was a dangerous, violent game, and these were dangerous, violent boys, therefore the stands were populated with scores of young men who had been physically maimed to one degree or another. A few were missing parts of their earlobes, many had fresh scalp wounds, and nearly all of them sported scrapes, contusions, cuts. Add to that the presence of known bruisers and the emotionally disturbed, and Topher felt the mission impossible. Third, oh dear lord, there wasn't a third reason; this whole thing was ridiculous. He gave up around the middle of the first period and decided to watch what was going on on the field.

Badugby was a game that operated similarly to Australian football, only with less rules and significantly more violence. The addition of the Badminton rackets added to the latter, while the former allowed for maximum carnage, a premium among the rich and depraved. The team consisted of a stoolie, of course (who would stop the birdie from going inside the net?), two killers (defense), three assassins (midfield), and two slaughterers (offense). The goal was to move the birdie up the field without letting it touch the ground, then somehow get it into the net. Balancing it on your racket was legal, but so was hitting, punching, tackling, biting, maiming, mauling and anything else. To Topher it looked like a massive brawl, an excuse for the boys to massacre one another, which, of course, it was. Judging from the way the others discussed the game at length and in great detail, there was apparently some finesse and skill needed, though what it was escaped Topher entirely. Every now and then the stands erupted in a deafening cheer, or the cannon went off, or a fight broke out, though he was never sure why.

"Who's that boy who just clubbed the other boy over the head?"

Perhaps the most violent of the players would also be werethings?

The boy next to him said, "Dirk or Dudley?"

Topher startled a little. He hadn't expected someone to actually talk to him, especially someone who looked as odd as this one. The boy had striking blue eyes, and thin blond hair that stuck out like straw from beneath his red wool cap. His red down jacket was so puffy that Topher thought it might be stuffed with an entire lake full of ducks. His ghostly complexion made him look even colder in the crisp fall air, and his mittens were as ballooned as his jacket. Even worse, he twitched and tapped his foot as he sat, and when Topher spoke, he'd turned his head sharply in his direction as if he'd been waiting for days for someone to talk to him and had finally gotten the chance.

Wonderful, Topher thought. *The one person who'll talk to me, and he's mentally deranged.*

The boy repeated his question.

"Dirk or Dudley?" he asked.

"There are two?"

"Henderson's name is Dirk. Dudley is a Hor."

"If you say so."

Topher spotted Gertrude on the other side of the field, chatting merrily with Marvin Grimm and I, Dennis, and wished he were there.

The crowd erupted, and Topher, trying to be social, said, "Oh dear! The Hor boy laid a whopper of a hit upon that poor Timberwolf person."

The boy next to him sniffed around his collar.

"Who are you?"

"Who are you?"

The boy's nostrils flared, and he inhaled in three short bursts.

"You must live in Burleigh's," he said.

Topher gave the lad a double take, and his eyes turned to slits.

"You know this just from smelling me?"

"I've been here for a year. When you're here that long, you'll understand."

"Understand what?"

"Each dormitory has its own smell."

One of the Demons suddenly made a break for the goal. He sprinted across the field, balancing the birdie on his racket, dodging diving opponents, spinning, shucking, jiving. Two Timberwolves zeroed in on him. At the last moment he tossed the birdie to a teammate, bashed one with his racket and kneed the other in the groin. The crowd went nuts, and his teammate tossed the birdie back to him.

"That's Dirk Henderson," the boy next to Topher said.

Henderson was twenty yards from the Timberwolves' net. Fifteen. Ten. He was certain to score. He drew back his racket, prepared to shoot, and then the keeper charged forward and launched himself right at his head. They collided with an audible crack and collapsed on the turf, unconscious. Or dead. The stands erupted.

When the noise died down, Topher said, "Each dorm has its own smell? And you can tell the difference?"

"Yes. Ipswich smells like fish. Dilque smells like rotten fruit. Trinkle smells like moldy books."

"What does Burleigh's smell like?"

"Feet."

Topher's exclamation was lost in another roar. The blond boy stood up and raised his arms over his head, exposing the skin on his forearm to the cold. Topher's jaw fell open. There. Spreading down his arm. A rash of little welled up scratches, as if he'd been in a tangle with a patch of thorn bushes. Topher continued to stare after he sat down. The boy noticed and crossed his arms.

"That's a nice hat," Topher said. "Would you mind if I tried it on?"

The boy shifted his eyes at him, and Topher tried to reassure him with a smile, but managed only to look like he was passing a thistle. (It was a family trait). "My father was a connoisseur."

The boy stood up with a energy that he seemed to draw from the crowd. Topher saw that he was a little shaky all of the sudden, as if he had not received enough rest the night before. A sheath of papers fell from beneath his coat. The boy either ignored them or panicked; either way, he scooted out of their row, trampling the feet and knocking the knees of the other students. Right before he made to the steps he tripped and his hat flew off his head, and there, right there, Topher saw what he suspected: a shaven circle on the back of the skull, a raw, angry wound that had been carefully, and recently, stitched.

The boy knelt and retrieved his hat and shot Topher a glare, and Topher pretended to find something of interest on the field. A grand roar erupted, and students stood all about him, cheering. He stood, too, trying to see where the boy went, but he was lost in the crowd. He briefly caught a glimpse of red bobbing through the foot traffic near the field after the cheering mass sat, but then it disappeared. He picked up the papers, then made his way down the row, crying "Out of my way!"

His shoes reverberated on the metal risers as he ran down the stairs. At the bottom, he leaned over the final railing, straining to see where the boy had gone. No luck. He clomped down the last set and pushed his way through the throng, hugging the papers to his chest. The going was difficult, and he ran into several people, and then Zorn was standing in front of him.

"Topher!" Zorn cried, smiling. He held a very long hot dog in one hand, and an equally large soda in the other. "I have purchased a hot dog and fountain drink."

Topher tried to nose around him, but Zorn wouldn't allow it. Topher head butted his friend in the shoulder, to no effect.

"Out of my way! I'm in pursuit of a mean and hairy."

He faked left and ducked right, just managing to evade his friend.

"A what?"

"A mean and hairy!"

Zorn took a bite of his sausage. A Mean and Hairy? Was this some kind of new hot dog? If it was, it didn't sound too appetizing.

The courtyard was normally empty during the games (school rules dictated that if students were not at the stadium, they were to be in their rooms), but this was Raleigh's Prep after all, and any boy gracing its halls was most likely one who felt that rules were something that applied to other people. Therefore there were always, of course, a smattering of sluggards and slackers skulking in the courtyard's corners, as well as a hefty contingent of smokers huddling beneath a pretty little trellis arbor decorated with vines and carnations. Brimstone and Burr were among the latter, trying to appear as menacing and as surly as anybody standing under a flowery garden decoration could manage. They had adopted a certain muscular stoop that, contrary to their intentions, only made them appear as though they suffered some kind of spinal handicap.

Into this den bumbled Topher, his gaze fixed upon everything except his immediate direction. He thought he'd spied the boy from the game run this way, and his head swiveled as he looked for him. In his arms he still clutched the sheaf of papers the boy had dropped; hurricane winds could not have separated them from him. He would have hurried straight through had Brimstone not extended his foot. Topher, momentarily consternated by the smoke, mumbled something about protocol. Then he saw the foot in his path and leapt awkwardly to avoid it, his body jerking in the air like a cat dropped from a short height.

He cried out a customary "Good Lord!" before landing clumsily on the outside of his feet. He stumbled forward, arms still wrapped around the papers, and fell to his knees with a crack, finishing the fall by skidding forward at least a foot. It worked out better than Brimstone could have possibly imagined, and the sadness of the fact that this particular accomplishment was one of the few things in his life that he'd been able to successfully complete was lost upon him. A stunned silence fell over the smokers, and then Brimstone and Burr burst out into laughter, braying like donkeys. Topher was not amused.

"Quit your disharmonious barking!" he barked, still on his knees. "You sound like hyenas with the stomach flu."

Something hit his ear, and he tumbled to his side. A kick to his ribs sent him onto his back, but he still managed to hold onto the papers. Then Brimstone straddled him, crouched down, and put his knees on his chest. He took a heavy drag from his cigarette, held it, and blew the smoke into Topher's face. Topher coughed and sputtered.

"Look, Burr," Brimstone said, smiling with his teeth. "It's my dog."

Burr giggled, and Brimstone joined him.

"It's my dog. It's my bitch," he said.

"Curse you, Brimstone. You've ruined a perfectly good pair of pants. Do you know how much white linen costs?"

Brimstone put his hand to his ear.

"What's that? I think my bitch's trying to talk." Burr guffawed. Sneering, Brimstone took another drag off his cigarette and blew it into Topher's face. "Speak, bitch. Speak."

"Get off my chest."

Brimstone cocked his arm and slapped him across the face. It echoed in the courtyard. The other boys under the trellis grew even quieter. Something was about to happen.

"Bark," Brimstone said. "Bark, bitch."

Topher glared.

"No."

Brimstone hit him again, harder this time, rocking Topher's head to the side.

"Whatcha got there?" Brimstone asked, his eyes falling on the papers. "Gay porn?"

"Why is everything 'gay' to you?" Topher asked. "Either you're gay yourself and repressing it, or you're just plain gay. Either way, stop trying to force me into your lifestyle."

Brimstone shot a panicked look around.

"I'm not gay."

"Methinks the boy doth protest too much."

Brimstone grabbed at the papers but Topher clutched them tighter to his chest.

"Gimmie the papers!"

"No."

Brimstone took another drag on his cigarette. He couldn't just let the fag get away with it. He had to teach his bitch to behave. An idea struck him and he smiled. Pinching the cigarette between two fingers, he leaned forward and held the glowing end over Topher's face.

"Do it," he said.

Topher spat on the cigarette and it winked out.

"Ha!"

The boys surrounding them laughed hesitantly, thinking the tension gone, but Brimstone was not as amused. He flicked the wet butt aside and started hitting Topher again, this time with a closed fist, again, and again, over and over until Burr pulled him off, leaving Topher lying there on his back, eyes bruised, lips split. Brimstone struggled against Burr, who grunted "Teacher, dude, teacher" into his ear until he stopped.

He looked out at the courtyard. There, standing in the middle, was an old man. He was leaning on a cane and staring up at the alabaster face of the clock tower. The old man didn't seem to be paying attention to them, but Brimstone didn't want to risk it. He shrugged Burr off, straightened his brown shirt, and stomped away. Burr gave Topher a tentative kick, then squirreled off after his friend. The rest of the smokers dissipated, not wanting to get into trouble for being a part of the scrape. Fighting was technically against the rules, even if it was encouraged by the staff. Broken noses and black eyes were assiduously overlooked, but if any students was caught in the middle of one, or even watching one, they'd be publicly whipped.

Topher stayed where he was, moaning. He had to get up and follow the boy from the stadium, beaten and bruised or not. He put the papers on the ground to his right and struggled to his feet. His face was a mess, and his teeth felt loose in his head. How many more blows to the head could he withstand?

Just then, Zorn sprinted into the courtyard, a hulking mass of fur and beard, trying to catch up to Topher. He ran as fast as he could, which was not very fast at all. It looked like nobody had ever taught him that his limbs were all supposed to work in concordance. His arms seemed to work independently of each other and his legs, almost resembling, but not quite, a windmill engineered by English majors. He looked like he was suffering from the fits, or better yet, like he was performing in some kind of avant garde street show. Still, he managed to build up a full head of steam, completely oblivious to the teacher leaning on his cane in the middle of the courtyard.

"Dear Lord," Topher said. "Zorn! Watch out you idiot!"

This did not achieve the desired effect. Zorn, rather than cease his progress, merely looked at the trellis arbor, upgrading his equilibrium from "somewhat eccentric" to "certainly spastic." His arms flailed, his feet flapped out to either side, he spun round, and soon he was a rumbling avalanche of bone and muscle, and the old man the meager chateau at the bottom of the mountain. Zorn hit him at full speed, and they collapsed in a mound of furs and hair and old man and broken cane.

Topher hurried over, certain he'd crushed the poor old codger into dust.

"Zorn, you brute!"

Zorn got up off the ground, wincing. The old man was gone. A book was lying where he stood. He leaned over to pick it up.

"Is this him?"

It was the simplest of tomes, thick, with a cherry colored leather cover. It looked old but well cared-for. Strange runes had been burned into the leather. He ran his finger along them. An electric shock ran up his arm, and he snapped his hand away. Topher reached for it.

"Let's see it."

Zorn clutched it to his chest.

"It's mine!"

"What's gotten into you?"

"This is my book. It's always been my book. It's a magic book."

"You? Own a magic book? Please."

"Why not? You can't own everything that's interesting or fantastic." Zorn caressed the cover. "It must have been the cute little old man's. He used it to escape."

Topher rolled his eyes.

"Do you mean to tell me you think he's in your book?"

"Yes. Like I said, it's a magic book."

"Fine."

"Fine?"

"Yes, fine."

"You believe me?"

"What's not to believe in this place?"

Zorn shied away, nervous. Topher was never this nice. Or this earnest.

113

There was always some kind of ulterior motive. He calculated the various ways he might be forced to give up his book.

"You're not going take it from me?"

"Good Lord, no! Magic books are dangerous. I know about as much about that book as you do the intricacies of the vagina."

"Topher!"

"I'm serious, Zorn. I would no sooner receive into my care that book than I would eviscerate myself. The last time I played with one, I nearly took off a toe. It's why I quit reading magic books."

Zorn gazed upon it.

"But it's beautiful."

"See? It's already got a hold on your psyche. You must remind me to thank you. Had I retained that book I would have undoubtedly lost my soul, as you are evidently in the process of doing—Zorn!"

"I'm sorry, I can't hear you," Zorn said. "I'm staring at the book."

Topher kicked him.

"That's a vile, despicable, malevolent thing! Get rid of it. Get rid of it, I beg you."

"Oh yes," Zorn said, petting its face. "The book is wonderful."

Two weeks later, Topher was leaning over his bed in his underwear, inspecting his bellybutton for lint before showering, when Zorn and Gertrude entered the room holding a mannequin smeared with ketchup. He clutched his linen pants to his chest and ducked behind a chest of drawers.

"I'm naked!"

Gertrude tried to think of something that would distract him.

"Are those canary yellow briefs you're wearing? What happened to your general strike on all undergarments?"

Topher sighed and shrugged.

"Waylaid by necessity, I suppose. Whereas my ten-point Free Ball Plan definitely had its merits, I fear it was sabotaged by callow idealism, doomed to comprehensive failure. Plus, I began to experience drop-sack syndrome. So it's back to the drawing board. And the canary yellow briefs, I'm afraid."

"Drop-sack syndrome?"

"Fairly self-explanatory. Visualize."

Gertrude grimaced.

"We thought you'd run off," Zorn said. "Don't you normally train at this hour?"

Topher tried to peer through their legs at the thing they were hiding. "What devil's gotten into you two? What's that thing you're hiding?"

Zorn remained mute. Topher shot him a look, then advanced around the chest of drawers, affording his mammoth roommates a full shot of his bare legs, his briefs, his chest and arms, all bristling with pubescent growth.

Zorn and Gertrude dropped the mannequin and covered their eyes with their hands. The mannequin clonked to the floor with an unexpectedly hollow sound, sprawling at Topher's feet.

"Where did you get this thing?" he asked.

"Well," Gertrude said. "We were in the basement, looking for weapons like the ones you found, and I saw her in the corner."

"I see. And why did you rub her down with ketchup?"

"That was Zorn's idea. He wanted her to look like she was covered in blood."

"Where did you get the ketchup."

"There was a bottle lying right next to her."

Topher examined the mannequin's torso.

"I don't think she's a she," he said.

"Oh, she's a she all right. She's a she."

They let that hang there in the air between them.

Finally Gertrude said, "She'll make a good prank someday. You'll see."

"I'm sure I will."

"You don't care?"

"I've no interest in your morbid perversions. I'm going to shower. And then I'm going to get dressed. Could you finish up with—whatever you're going to do with that—before I'm done?"

Gertrude opened his wardrobe door and threw the mannequin inside. It struck the back and thumped to the ground. The hangers tined.

"I'm done now."

Topher grimaced.

"You're keeping it in your wardrobe?"

"Her name is Sally."

"You're keeping Sally in your wardrobe?"

"Of course. Where else are we going to put her?"

Marvin Grimm was already at lunch when they arrived. He waved them over them over, calling out "Did you hear?" repeatedly until they had all taken a seat.

"I have not," Topher replied. "Zorn? Pass the salt."

Zorn handed the cellar to his friend.

"What have you heard, Marvin?"

"They found another body. In the middle of the courtyard. This morning."

Gertrude nearly choked on his eggs.

"Another one?"

"It was partially eaten," Marvin said. "They had to use a . . . watchamacallit? Wood handle? Picks stuff up? A shovel."

Gertrude pushed his plate away.

"Did they say who it was yet?" Topher asked.

115

Marvin shrugged. He scooped a heap of grits into his mouth.

"They haven't announced it yet. But I know who it was."

"What? How?"

"I saw it."

"You witnessed the murder?"

"No. I told you. I saw them shovel his body into Mr. Floyd's truck. This morning. I woke up to get a drink of water, and when I passed by the window I saw the whole thing."

Crews suddenly appeared behind him, carrying a tray filled with steak and bacon.

"Dieting are we, Warren?" Topher asked.

"They found another body," Crews said.

"We know. Marvin Grimm saw it this morning."

Crews looked at him.

"What did you see?"

Marvin shrugged. He plugged a piece of bacon into his mouth.

"I saw them shovel a body into Mr. Floyd's truck."

Crews finally sat down, a smug smile on his face.

"Did you know that there was a note on the body?"

"A note?" Topher asked. "What did it say?"

Crews withdrew a folded piece of paper from his jacket. It was dappled with red flecks.

"Read it yourself."

"How did you get this?"

"Mr. Floyd gave it to me. Take it. He told me to tell you to read it."

Topher wrinkled his nose. He reached over the table, past the ever-greener Gertrude, and pinched it by the corner.

"Excuse me," Gertrude said, and dashed away, one hand over his mouth and one on his stomach.

Topher read the note.

"It says, 'No more attacks'."

"No more attacks?" Zorn said. "Wonderful! Then we don't need to go back to that horrible place. Can I give back my codpiece?"

Topher slid the note back over the table to Crews, who folded it and put it back in his pocket. "Not quite. If I'm right, this note is meant as a warning."

"A warning? To whom?"

"To us."

"To us! Why?"

"I suppose because we infiltrated their lair."

Zorn chewed thoughtfully on a piece of sausage and swallowed.

"Well," he said. "I don't think this is meant for me. All I did was throw one."

"You idiot. They don't care. They're trying to scare us. 'Don't attack or we'll do you the same,' right Warren?"

Crews, who had been slowly cutting his steak into pieces, nodded.

"That's about right. I got mine a few months back. Welcome to the club."

"Well it worked on me," Zorn said. "No more forays into the forest. Pass the pepper."

Topher, however, was incensed.

"This is terrorism, and terrorists are cowardly assholes. The day I bow to the demands of gutless pricks is the day I wear a reverse codpiece."

"I've worn a reverse codpiece. Worked out fairly well for me. In the end."

"Exactly!"

"Topher, does everything have to be a thing with you?"

"Yes. Now, does anybody know who died this time? What did he look like?"

Crews paused for a moment, seeming to think. He scratched his cheek with this fork.

"Not sure. Little blond kid. Nasty skull wound."

Topher blanched.

"Was he wearing a red jacket and a red hat?"

"How'd you know?"

"I sat next to him at the Badugby match. I got suspicious, and then he got suspicious, and then he ran. I tried to follow him, but he was too fast. Then Zorn killed an old man."

"I did not! He disappeared."

"Right. Into that 'magic book'."

"You'll speak nothing of my magic book!" Zorn jabbed his fork at Topher. "Brimstone kicked the shit out of you, though. Didn't he?"

"Both of you shut up," Crews said. "Topher, if they saw you chasing that dead kid, then that note is definitely meant for you. They probably thought he was a traitor."

"But I didn't even get to do anything. I was waylaid by idiots before I could catch him." He pointed at the fading, greenish bruise on his face. "Brimstone tried to put his cigarette out in my eye, but I spit it out."

"I really did find a magic book," Zorn said.

Crews sighed.

"The kid had to have done something. Did he tell you anything? Give you anything?"

Though he only had a few minutes before morning classes, Topher sprinted back to Burleigh's and up to his room. He wrenched open the bottom drawer of his desk and removed the papers the now dead blond boy had lost during the chase. He spread them out over the surface of his desk. The boy had been hiding them, and so they certainly must have been of some importance. At first he didn't understand what he was seeing. Drawings of buildings, architectural plans, maps of woods and hills, the creeks and . . .

"Oh my God," he whispered.

Zorn and Gertrude entered the room with a clatter.

"Topher," Zorn said. "Why'd you leave breakfast so fast?"

"Aren't you going to morning classes?" Gertrude asked. "I mean, you have go to morning classes. We're not allowed not to."

Topher waved their protests aside.

"In a moment. Come look at this."

Zorn and Gertrude came over to the desk, the latter casting worried glances over his shoulder.

"What is it?" Zorn asked.

"The reason that boy was killed. Look."

"Maps. Building plans. So what?"

Gertrude plunked a finger down on one of the maps.

"That's Lake Perish. And that's The Grotto."

Zorn suddenly saw it.

"You're right! So that must make this area the Athletic fields, but they're not marked. And this must be Chainwrought, though it's about ten times as big."

"These are the plans for the school," Topher added. "See? Here's Trinkle. Here's Merton, Croix. Here's Scathewort. And this," he pulled out the biggest sheet. "This is Burleigh's."

Gertrude pointed at the last piece of paper.

"What's that one?"

First bell sounded. The students would be heading for class.

"I don't know," Topher said. He cleared the other papers out of his way. "It looks like it's underground somewhere."

"But where?"

"*I don't know.* We'll have to read over the rest of the maps to figure it out. But look." He pulled the maps of the woods and surrounding land out of the pile and poured over them.

Gertrude worried his fingers. "We only have a few minutes, Topher," he said. "We'll be late, and we can't be—"

"I know! I know! Dammit!" Topher swept the maps and plans off his desk. "Damn this place! Damn you both for landing us here!"

"Us?" Zorn said, mystified and enraged. "Topher, it was your plan."

"And if you two dolts had carried it out correctly."

The warning bell sounded, putting an abrupt end to the argument. All three scattered about the room, picking up books and bags and other random articles.

"Meet back here after lunch!" Topher cried as they thundered out the door.

Three hours later, Zorn entered the room with Gertrude close behind. They were hiding something in their furs, cradling their arms beneath their bellies to keep it from falling out. They looked guilty or sick, like they'd killed a puppy or eaten too much at lunch. Topher, seated at his desk, barely looked up when they entered. He kept playing with the maps. First he placed them side by side, then he rearranged them, then he mixed them up and rearranged them again.

"You weren't at lunch," Zorn said. "We smuggled you some food."

Gertrude gently closed the door and they shuffled around to Zorn's desk to dump their load: sandwiches and muffins, apples and bananas, silverware, three bowls of potato salad covered with plastic wrap, nine cookies, and a piece of chocolate cake, also covered with plastic wrap.

Topher stared at the buffet, angry at first, but then softening.

"Look, I'm sorry. For snapping at you. Both of you." He looked each in the eye. "It's this place, these things, all of this." He made a broad gesture around him. "The truth is that I feel responsible for us being here. It was my idea, my plan. I didn't mean for it to go as far as it did."

He stopped. It was as close as he would ever get to an apology, and he knew it, and Zorn and Gertrude knew it. He couldn't apologize. There were no apologies for what they did. It just was. And it would hang between them for the rest of their lives. They only way to move past it was to forget it, but they could never forget it. So he said, "Would you like to see what I've done?"

"Yes," Zorn and Gertrude said simultaneously, relieved.

Zorn handed Topher a sandwich, and he unwrapped it and started to eat.

"How much time do we have before afternoon classes?"

Gertrude said, "A half an hour."

Topher swallowed and set the sandwich aside.

"I've been trying to organize them in some way that would make sense. These are the buildings."

He arranged them on his desk so that they were positioned in the same places as they were in real life, surrounding the courtyard. The Grotto and Scathewort were on the other side of the clock tower. In between and around them was empty space.

"What about the academic administrative buildings?" Gertrude asked.

"They're not here. Either that blond boy didn't have them, or they weren't included in the original plans."

Gertrude pointed at three pieces of old, brown paper.

"And those three are the maps of the property?"

"Yep."

Gertrude moved them around. They were brittle and flaky, and he had to maneuver them around on the desk carefully or risk tearing them.

119

"Chainwrought takes up nearly the entire property." He reached out and put his finger down in the middle, right where all three maps joined. "What's that?"

There was a strange symbol drawn on the map of the forest, a six-pointed star, the points being of varying length.

"I don't know," Topher said. "But they're all over the woods. Look. Here, here, here and here."

Zorn joined in.

"Here's one in Dilque. And Trinkle. And Merton. And Burleigh's."

They studied the maps silently, in awe.

"There are walls within the walls," Gertrude said.

"Huh?"

Gertrude pointed at the Burleigh's map.

"Here. It looks like they made secret passages."

Topher peered closer. "By God, you're right. It looks like—" He stared up at him, suddenly amazed. "Your wardrobe."

"My wardrobe?"

Topher stood, wrenching the chair back against the hardwood. He went over to Gertrude's wardrobe and yanked the door open.

"What are you doing?"

"We're going to get into the secret passage."

"We?"

"Well, you."

"What?" Gertrude said. "Why me?"

"It's your wardrobe."

Sally shifted across the back, causing the hangers to chime. Gertrude coughed and gave Topher an apologetic look.

"I'll just, uh, I'll just fix her up." He reached in and adjusted her limbs a little. "Are you sure you want to do this? I've heard things scrabbling behind the walls before. At night."

"Things? What kind of things?"

"Critters."

"Critters? What kind of critters?"

"I'm not sure. But I've heard pattering, perhaps a squeak or two."

"The rats in the walls!"

"Or squirrels."

"Squirrels prance and chitter," Topher said. "They don't patter and squeak."

"How do you know?"

"I am a keen observer of nature. Emerson has nothing on me."

"He was a transparent eyeball!"

"And I am a translucent one!"

"There's no difference."

"'Translucent' is the better word."

Gertrude rolled his eyes and turned his attention to the back of the wardrobe.

"So what do you think I should do?"

"Pound on the wall or something."

Gertrude pulled out an armful of clothing and handed it to Topher, who handed it to Zorn, who put it on the top bunk. Then he went back in and proceeded to pound on several random spots, all to no effect. He stood back rubbed his chin and pondered.

"Let me try," Topher said, pushing his way in. "How about like this." He pounded on a few spots.

Gertrude didn't like it.

"Put more flair in your Ulna. Or is it your Radius?"

Topher pounded again.

"Like this?"

"No! *Twist* your wrist, but let your pinkie out the side."

"Okay."

He pounded again.

"No, that's more of a turn. *Twist* it. Like a French playboy."

"What?"

"Now you're rotating it!"

"*This* is a twist! *This* is a rotation."

"Mmm. I'd say that last one was more of a twirl."

"How does one twirl his wrist?"

"Like that, apparently."

Topher tried knocking a little softer while attempting the flair of French aristocracy. It didn't work. He tapped softly, so softly. Nothing. Then he knocked! Loudly, very loudly! Nothing. He hit it once, twice, and soon was throwing his fists at the wall like a featherweight boxing a gorilla. When it was over, he was breathless and red in the face, but nothing about the back of the wardrobe had changed.

"I've completely forgotten what we're doing," he said. "I'm starving. Get out of my way."

He pushed Gertrude aside only to see Zorn standing next to his desk, eating his lunch. He held up a muffin.

"Muffin?"

"Hello," Gertrude said from inside the wardrobe. "What's this?"

A noise like gears dropping into place vibrated inside the room, followed by the tremendous sound of two walls grinding against one another. A cool blast of stale air blew out of the wardrobe, and Zorn dropped his food and Topher turned around and all three of them crowded inside. The back had rolled away to the right, revealing a dirt floor and an old, gray cinderblock wall and a passage shrouded in complete and utter darkness.

"Oh my God," Topher whispered.

Gertrude stepped back into the room, still staring into the secret passage. At the same time, Topher stepped into the passage itself. He reached extended his arms, measuring the width.

"This is easily eight feet wide," he said. "And the ceiling must be the floor of the floor above us."

The bell rang. Five minutes to get to class. Topher stepped back into the room.

"Close that," he told Gertrude. Gertrude did as he was told, and soon the fake wall rumbled back into place.

"What are we going to do?" Zorn asked.

"I don't know," Topher said. He gathered up his books and bag. "But right now we've got to get to class. We'll figure it out later."

"But there's a secret passage in our wall, and—"

Topher bustled out the door.

"Figure it out later! Tell nobody!"

Marvin and I, Dennis were waiting in the hall outside the room when Topher returned from afternoon classes.

"What do you want?"

I, Dennis's camera looked at Marvin Grimm.

"Er," Marvin said. "Gertrude told us about the secret passage and the maps."

Topher's face turned red.

"What secret passage?"

His key was on a chain around his neck, and he had to lean over to unlock his door, which he did, and then he threw it open and rushed into his room and tossed his bag and books on his bed and quickly tried to gather up the maps in his arms before the other two could see it. Marvin Grimm and I, Dennis loitered in the hallway for a moment, then quietly stuck their heads in.

"Do you mind if we come in?"

"Yes!" Topher yelled. He opened up his wardrobe and pitched all of the maps and plans inside, but they bounced off Gertrude's clothes and fell straight down, getting stuck in the jamb and blocking the latch so that when he tried to close the door all he could do was bonk it repeatedly. Marvin and I, Dennis watched with bland indifference.

"Excuse me," Gertrude said, coming up from behind.

Topher turned, hearing his voice, and the wardrobe door swung open and everything fell out.

"Did you tell these nincompoops about the maps and the plans and the secret passage?"

Gertrude paused, thinking.

"Yes?"

"Damn you, Gertrude! Didn't tell you not to tell anybody?"

"Yes, but—"

"'Yes, but' what?"

"But this is Marvin Grimm and I, Dennis," Gertrude explained.

"So?"

"So? I mean, look at them. Marvin's as big as a house and triply strong, and I, Dennis can shoot lasers out of his eyes."

"No, I can't," I, Dennis said.

Gertrude ignored him.

"If you're going to explore a secret passage in a place known for werepyres, don't you think you'd want them to come along?"

Topher thought about it for a moment.

"Fine. But if we find any treasure or gold, they don't get any part of the loot." Zorn entered the room. "Zorn! Help me with the maps."

"Who said anything about treasure?" Gertrude wondered, and motioned for Marvin and I, Dennis to enter. Marvin sat on Topher's single bed, which creaked and bowed. I, Dennis chose to stand completely still in the corner, expressionless, unblinking. Zorn and Topher threw the maps back onto his desk.

"I've decided that your services will be primarily security in nature," Topher told Marvin. "If we're attacked by a werepyre, or a vampire, or incubi or succubi, we'll expect you to throw yourself in front of us and die. That way we'll all be able to run to safety, unmolested."

Marvin cracked his knuckles.

"No problem," he said. "Should I bring the Mind Sword?"

"Certainly." Topher set about reorganizing the maps.

"So what's next?" Zorn asked.

"Well. We have maps to secret tunnels and subterranean lairs. Let's explore."

Zorn gulped.

"Now?"

"No. We have to show up for dinner roll-call. And then there's study group. So it'll have to be tonight."

"What do you have in mind?"

Topher pointed at the crooked, six-pointed star. "There's one of these under each dorm," he said. "And three out in the woods somewhere. I want to find out exactly where they are and what they lead to." He turned to Marvin and I, Dennis. "Meet us back here after midnight room-check. We're going in."

I, Dennis and Marvin Grimm arrived just after midnight, right as Gertrude attempted to show Zorn how to unlock the secret passage door.

After the third failed attempt, he said, "No, like a French playboy!"

"Well, evidently I don't know what a French playboy knocks like!"

Zorn burst out of the wardrobe in a huff. Topher sat on his desk, shaking his head.

"Told you," he said.

"Hello," Gertrude said from inside the wardrobe. "What's this?"

A thunk and whirring of gears. The low rumble of the false wall rolling aside. A cold wind flooded the room. Gertrude stuck his head back into the room.

"Ahoy ahoy."

They filed in one at a time. I, Dennis' helmet had a high-powered flood light on it "for camera lighting," so he walked behind Topher, who held the map. Then came Zorn and Gertrude, with Marvin locking down the rear. The passage followed the line of the dorm on a fairly noticeable decline, so that they descended as they rounded the building. Periodically a small circle of light shot into the air around their heads. At the fifth one, Gertrude put his eye up to it.

"It's Brimstone and Burr's room," he declared, then pulled away. "They're not in."

Zorn moved him aside and had a peek.

"They have a poster of a half-naked fireman on their wall."

From that point on, whenever they passed a circle of light Gertrude put his eye up to it. Sometimes the students were home, doing homework, cleaning their rooms, listening to music, but just as many times they weren't.

"Where could everyone be?" Topher said.

Three turns after ground level, they came to a part of the passage lit by three naked bulbs dangling from wires. The bulbs were dim, and one flickered off as they walked toward it. At the end stood a door. It was old and covered in cobwebs. A Judas hole had been cut into it, but when Topher pushed it aside, he couldn't see anything. He rattled the doorknob.

"Well?" Zorn asked.

"It's locked."

"Does the map say anything about a key, or a magic incantation or something?" Gertrude asked.

Topher snapped his fingers at I, Dennis.

"Shine the light on this." He shuffled and crinkled the maps. "There's a lot of indecipherable scribble."

"No key?"

"Of course not!"

"I think I got it," Marvin rumbled.

Gertrude had to sit down in order to let the larger boy pass, as did Zorn. Topher ducked under him, quickly followed by I, Dennis. Marvin gripped the handle firmly and applied pressure. The knob cracked, and he pulled harder. The door groaned and splintered, and then there was a huge explosion of wood shards and slivers and chips. When the dust cleared, Marvin stood in the empty doorway, a warm, orange light suffusing the air in the room beyond, silhouetting his massive frame. He jingled the ruins of the metal knob in his fingers, a little pile of rubble at his feet.

"Opened it."

The room was long and wide, with walnut floors and colonial molding. It was full of plush furniture: velvet love seats, leather reading chairs, and a long couch which faced an old brick fireplace that glowed with a cozy fire. Topher pushed past Marvin into the room. He ran his fingers along the antique tables, warmed his hands by the fire, gazed at the stonework on the hearth, turned the lamps on and off.

"There's another passage down here," he said, pointing at the archway that opened to the left of the fireplace.

Then he saw the tapestries. Five of them hanging on the long wall. Each one featured a knight in some kind of battle pose. The first one held an elegant bow in one hand, a crossbow in the other, and a quiver of arrows on his back. The second wielded a mace and stood next to a beautiful white steed. The third weighed a morning star, an eagle resting on his shoulder. The fourth brandished a curved scimitar, and sneered out at them. Behind each one lurked foul, misshapen, creatures, tumors bubbling on their skin, their eyes blood red. There were names stitched across the bottom of each one, and he read them aloud.

"Smythe, Dyxsonne, Vyncent, Fyssher."

Zorn ran his fingers over the brick hearth.

"Who are they?"

"I don't know, but they're dead."

"How do you know?"

Topher waved his hand at the tapestries.

"Little holes in their bodies. Each one. This one on the neck, that one in the chest, that one in the head."

He frowned with interest at the fifth tapestry, the most impressive one. This knight was tall, fully bedecked in gleaming silver armor. He, too, stood next to a wondrous horse, but one ten times more majestic than the others. Instead of a weapon, he tucked a single book under his arm. While the other four were healthily tanned, and muscular, this one was rail thin and pale and hollow-eyed. And while the others seemed to brim with vigor and vim, as if daring any onlooker to attack them, this knight appeared sad, withdrawn; a reluctant hero. Around him stood spindly, evil looking trees, with intertwined branches that formed knobby fingers seeming to reach for him. The moon shone overhead, illuminating the words LORD BURLEIGH stitched in silver thread. There were no holes in this one.

"I'm going to record this," I, Dennis said. He pushed a button on his helmet, then strolled slowly around the room, pausing at each item of interest.

Zorn pulled the book out of his pocket and caressed the cover.

"This is the perfect place to read my book." He opened it. "Ooh! It knows my name."

Topher threw himself down onto one of the couches, and a thin layer of dust shot into the air around him.

"Don't be an idiot, Zorn."

"No, really." He pointed at a passage on the first page. "Here, listen: 'Greetings, Zorn. No doubt you are wondering—"

Topher ignored him. He propped his feet up on the coffee table.

"I bet Brimstone and Burr don't have a place as nice as this."

Gertrude wandered over to the dark end of the room. A pair of wooden totems had been positioned along the wall, leaning against one of the columns. They were carved wolves, all flesh and fang and matted hair, and red, beaming eyes.

He turned to his friends.

"Hey, look at these!" Topher looked over at him. "Cool, huh?"

One of the totems behind him raised a clawed hand. Topher's eyes widened.

"Duck, Gertrude!"

Gertrude opened his mouth to ask why, but before he could, the claw struck, tearing through his furs. He cried out and fell on his face and then the wolf was upon him, snarling and drooling. Its claws ripped the flesh on his back, its teeth snapping at his neck. Marvin Grimm rushed the beast, twirling his backpack over his head like a ball and chain. Zorn threw a coffee table at it. I, Dennis pushed a button on his suit and his performance enhancers misfired, paralyzing him.

The table struck the beast in the head, knocking it off Gertrude, who lay face down and lifeless, his back a chaos of flesh, blood, and fur. The wolf rose shakily to all fours. It whipped its head back and forth, then its eyes cleared and it bared its fangs. Marvin put his head down and thundered toward it, bellowing. The beast crouched and launched itself at him, jaws wide. Marvin struck it with his backpack, smashing it into a grandfather clock sitting against the wall. The glass shattered, and the weights gonged against one another. The wolf yelped and stumbled awkwardly away, leaving the clock to totter and fall forward, quelling the weights with a muffled bong. Marvin swung the pack over his head, aiming for the beast's face, but it sprung away at the last second. It struck out at him with its claws, tearing a hole in his ballooning trench coat, then sprang away toward the archway and the passage next to the fire.

Topher snatched up a poker from the stand and dashed into the tunnel.

"C'mon!"

Marvin dashed after him, followed by Zorn. They'd only made it a few feet in when Topher tripped over something and was sent flying. He popped up, his hands scraped and bloody, and limped back, wielding the poker. Why were Marvin and Zorn just standing there, doing nothing?

"Kill it!"

"But—"

"Fine. I'll do it."

He raised the poker over his head, and Marvin slugged it out of his hand.

"What are you doing!" Topher yelled.

Zorn motioned at the form on the ground.

"It's not a monster, Topher. Look."

Topher shot him a baffled look, then squatted down. It *was* human, a boy, a crumpled up boy. A crumpled up unconscious boy with his limbs splayed out in uncomfortable directions. Topher brushed the boy's hair out of his eyes.

"It's Crews."

Heavy breathing. Light bobbing on the dirt floor. Shuffling, boxy footfalls. I, Dennis led the way, followed by Topher and Zorn who carried Gertrude between them. Marvin Grimm took up the rear again, hauling the still unconscious Crews over one shoulder.

The lever for the secret door was clearly visible on this side, an ornate iron pedal, painted white. Topher pushed into the lead and stepped on it, the door rumbled aside, and they ducked inside, one by one, past hanging pants and towels, tripping over shoes and hangers and Sally, all the way back through the wardrobe and into their room and directly into Brimstone and Burr and a small handful of other Assistants who were, to say the least, a bit startled upon seeing six full-grown boys suddenly burst out of a closet. Brimstone recovered first.

"Look, it's my bitch. It's my bitch and his faggot friends. Still in the closet, huh boys?" He nodded at Marvin and I, Dennis. "Of course you'd be hanging out with these losers."

Burr snickered.

Brimstone stepped around Marvin's back to get a better look at Crews, who was still draped over his shoulder.

"What's this?" He picked Crews' hair up to get a better look at his face. "You fairies been drinking? Ugh, Grimm. You stink. Haven't they taught you how to bathe yet?"

"Get out of here, Brimstone," Topher said. "You've no right to be in our room."

"I don't?"

He snaked between Zorn and Gertrude and grimaced at the sight of the latter's shredded back.

"Oh my," he said, smirking at Burr and the other Assistants. "You boys get a little rough with each other out in the woods?"

Burr laughed out loud.

Topher got in his face.

"I said get out!"

"You were off-campus after hours, bitch. Reading gay poetry, screwing around with each other. Whatever. You're fucked, fags."

He grabbed Topher by the shirt.

"Get off me!"

Marvin slowly lay Crews down on Topher's bed. He and Zorn exchanged a look. Brimstone pulled Topher closer.

"Not until you tell me where you've been." His sour breath soiled Topher's nose. "Bitch."

"Okay."

Brimstone smiled and relaxed. He let go of Topher's shirt and tried to smooth it. Topher let him. "What do you think, Burr," Brimstone said. "Should we—" and then Topher grabbed him by the back of the neck and slammed his head down onto his desk.

There was a moment's pause as Brimstone fell to the floor, dazed. His forehead started to bleed. Burr and the other Assistants hung there, unsure of what to do without their leader. Then Brimstone, holding his left eye, wailed, "Get them, you idiots!" and all hell broke loose.

Stoneman sat behind his desk, glaring. His hair was disheveled, and his thin, blue bathrobe hung off his boney frame. On the other side stood Topher and his crew, an assortment of split lips and black eyes. A line of bleary-eyed instructors separated them from Brimstone and the assistants, who were in no better condition.

"Topher Bill, Michael Zorn, and Kenneth Hughes," Stoneman said. "I thought we agreed that you would stay out of trouble?" His eyes wandered over Marvin and I, Dennis. "I see you've made some new friends."

Zorn frowned. Perhaps he should make introductions?

"Er. Mr. Stoneman, this is Marvin Grimm, and—"

"I know who they are!" Stoneman's eyes narrowed for a moment on Crews, uncertain, and then he growled, "Who started it?"

Topher and Brimstone started talking at once.

". . . just came into my room and . . ."

". . . was out of his room after midnight . . ."

". . . leapt on me for no reason at all . . ."

"Quiet!" The words died on the boys' lips. Stoneman stared at them, furious. He pointed at Brimstone. "You. Speak."

Brimstone gulped.

"Mr. Stoneman. Sir. We were given a tip that those three would be sneaking out of their room tonight after midnight room-check. So we went in there a little after one to check on them. Sir."

"Which three?"

Brimstone leaned forward and pointed at Topher and Zorn.

"Those two, sir." Then he pointed at Gertrude, who was looking more and more pale by the minute. "And Ger—their roommate."

"And who gave you this tip?" Brimstone gulped again. He looked unsure. "Well?"

"I don't know, sir."

"What do you mean you don't know? Surely somebody had to tell you this information."

"Yes, sir. I mean, no, sir."

"Which is it, boy?"

"Nobody told us, sir, so to speak. I mean, p-pardon the pun."

"Boy. If you don't answer my question immediately—"

"We were left a note, sir."

"A note?"

"Yes, sir. An anonymous note."

Stoneman nodded.

"I see," he said. "Do you have this note?"

Brimstone smiled triumphantly.

"Yes, sir. It's right here, sir." He jammed his hand into his pocket, and his face fell. He searched his other pocket.

Stoneman tapped his finger on his desk.

"Well?"

Brimstone patted his body, eyes searching, confused.

"Boy? Do you have the note or not?"

"No, sir."

"What's that?"

"I said, no, sir. It must have fallen out in the fight."

Stoneman glared at the boy for a moment before finally saying, "I see what's going on here."

"But, sir. They weren't in their room."

Stoneman raised his eyebrows.

"But they were there, correct? You did engage in a brawl with them, yes?"

"Y-yes, sir."

"So were they in their room or not?"

Brimstone didn't seem to know how to answer.

"Well?" Stoneman growled.

"Sir?"

"If they weren't in their room, where were they?"

"They were—"

"Did they just appear out of nowhere?"

"No, sir, they—"

"Did they sneak in through the window?"

"No, sir."

"Then where were they, Mr. Brimstone?"

"Drinking, sir," he bleated.

Stoneman's eyes widened in horror.

"Drinking?"

The full force of his anger fell upon Topher and his friends. Even Marvin Grimm appeared to shrink.

"Yes, sir," Brimstone said, suddenly relieved. "Drinking. That last one there had to be carried in by Grimm."

Stoneman continued to glare at Topher and company. Finally, he said, "In what place?"

Again, Brimstone looked uncertain. He shuffled his feet and looked to Burr for help, but Burr was no help and just stared back, confused.

"Boy!"

"Their wardrobe!"

Stoneman suddenly looked deflated.

"In their wardrobe? *In* their wardrobe?" He pointed at the five grown boys. "Them?"

"No, sir," Brimstone said. "They came out of their wardrobe."

Stoneman's wide eyes fell on Topher, and the briefest flicker of something, some kind of emotion, or recognition . . . something . . . passed over his face. Topher was unsure, but for a moment it seemed to him like the headmaster seemed to consider him as an equal. It passed, and the old man's features hardened, and it was clear that he was sizing them up. A short boy in a linen suit, two beards in furs, a mammoth with a hunch, and a freak wearing a plastic onesie.

"Sir? I'm not lying. The rest of us saw it, too. Burr, tell him."

"Phyro," Stoneman said. "I may be an old man, and I may be new to this institution, but contrary to what your puny little adolescent brain may think, I am not stupid."

Brimstone's jaw set.

"They came out of that wardrobe. I saw them."

Stoneman shook his head, rubbed his eyebrows. He started to mumble to himself. "Monsters coming out of the woods, boys playing in wardrobes."

"Sir?" Brimstone asked.

"Thank you Mr. Brimstone," Stoneman replied, cool and abrupt. "That will be all."

"Mr. Stoneman!"

"I said that will be all. You and your friends may return to your rooms."

"Aren't you going to do something?"

Stoneman stared at him, daring him to speak.

"Do not forget your place here, boy."

Brimstone dropped his eyes.

Stoneman nodded at two of the instructors.

"Mr. Lewis? Mr. Hodges? Will you escort these boys back to their dorm?"

One took Brimstone by the arm, and Brimstone jerked it loose.

"Get your hands off me!"

The instructor held out his arms.

"After you," he said.

Topher waited for them to leave, waited for his doom. Stoneman would castigate them, and then they'd be expelled, and then they'd be handed over to the harpies at the public justice system. He wondered if the rumors about state institutions were true: that they showered in groups, that they ate tater tots and industrial pasta and something called "chili mac"?

Stoneman stared at the wall, seeming to think. Then he noticed them and performed a comic double take.

"What are you waiting for?"

Topher's jaw nearly dropped.

"We can go, too, sir?"

"Boy, don't try my patience."

Topher glanced at his friends, sure this was a trick. Gertrude and Crews wavered.

"Er—" he began.

"Get out!"

They funneled through the door like water through a sieve, even Gertrude and Crews, though they had to be helped along by Marvin. Topher looked back just before the door closed. Stoneman was still sitting in the same spot, staring at his hands, muttering to himself. He ran his fingers through his hair and drew a ragged breath.

Crews regained his strength once he was back in Topher and Zorn and Gertrude's room. His head ached and he couldn't remember what happened to him, but he was nowhere near as bad as Gertrude, who went from able to walk, to barely able to walk, to unconscious and pale and sweating on Zorn's bed.

Zorn worried his beard.

"He stopped bleeding, right?"

Nobody answered him. Marvin leaned against the door, his arms crossed, and Topher paced, trying to think. I, Dennis had begged off on the way back to the dorm. "My cpu is running hot," he complained, adding, though more to himself, "Power down . . . memory loss . . . ."

Zorn said, "The only reason I ask is because I left my Delmont and Bunny poster on my bed, and it's a collector's item."

"Damn you, Zorn!" Topher said. "Gertrude's ill. He was attacked by one of those things. We need to think of something to do to help him. Stop thinking of yourself."

"You're right. We should clean the wounds." He looked at the bloody mess that was Gertrude's back. "You should clean the wounds."

"But then what? What if there are werepyre cooties gooped together with his blood? How do we get rid of them?"

Zorn thought for a moment. Who? Who could help them? Suddenly, he brightened.

"Mr. Floyd!"

Topher paused, a light of hope dawning in his face.

Crews said, "That old drunk?"

"He's rescued us before."

Crews rolled his eyes.

"He's a grounds keeper. He lives in the basement of the stackhouse."

"What other options do we have?" Topher asked. "He's been here a while. He seems to know something about the menace in the woods."

Crews stood up.

"Do what you want. I'm going to bed."

He started to leave.

"You don't want him to look at your head?" Zorn asked.

Crews snorted. "No." He opened the door and stepped out into the hallway. "Listen, guys. Thanks, you know. For tonight. And good luck with Gertrude."

"Wait," Topher said. Crews paused, his hand on the knob. "What were you doing down there? What is that place?"

Crews shook his head.

"I told you, I don't know. I was out in the woods and I fell into a hole. There was a tunnel and I followed it, and it led to that room, and then something hit me on the head."

"Do you know who it was?"

"All I know is that it was there when I showed up. You guys must have startled it before it could finish me off." A deep quiet settled over the room. "Well. So long."

Topher watched the door for a few minutes after he left.

The drunken singing echoed all the way down the corridor as the boys hauled Gertrude to Mr. Floyd's room.

To see my lovely by the sea, it slurred.

They aimed for it, shuffling past an open door that housed rattling physical equipment, boilers, water heaters, and HVAC parts. The corridor ended in bricks, and to the left there stood an old door, thick, iron, and battleship gray. The drunken voice came from behind it.

She means so much to me.

A bottle smashed inside.

Topher couldn't get past Marvin and Zorn to knock on the door, so he told Marvin to kick it. The boom echoed in the hall, the door rattled on its hinges, and the singing stopped abruptly. Total silence, and then glass tinkled on the other side.

"Who's there?" Mr. Floyd rasped.

"It's Topher Bill, sir," Topher called. "And Michael Zorn and Marvin

Grimm. We've brought our friend. He's hurt, sir. He needs help."

"Then take 'em to the 'firmry," came the reply. "Don't come down here botherin' me!"

"But—"

"Who told you where I lived?"

"Warren Crews, sir."

"Crews! That stupid little cuss!"

"Mr. Floyd! My friend was attacked by one of those things."

The sudden silence deafened their ears. Topher bore holes into the iron door. Finally, when he could take it no longer, he shouted, "Mr. Floyd!"

Locks clunked and rattled, one, two, three, four, and dead bolts were clicked aside, and a bar was removed, and other metallic noises happened, and finally the door swung wide open with a wrenching whine and there stood Mr. Floyd in a pair of white boxers and a white wife-beater.

He wasn't as old and flabby as Topher expected. His chest was broad and ropey, with a thatch of gray hair popping out of the top of his under shirt. His belly was hard and flat, like he'd swallowed a cinderblock, and he had baseballs in his biceps and legs like a soccer player. He was holding a bottle of clear liquid in his hand, and he swayed as he stood, as if some private wind were rocking his frame.

"Well why didn't you say so," he growled, then stood aside. "C'mon, c'mon."

Marvin and Zorn carried Gertrude inside. Mr. Floyd's "room" was little more than an L-shaped space that he'd carved out of a storage area. The long part of the L was furnished with a tool-strewn worktable. He'd bolted a pegboard to the wall behind it upon which he'd hung a collection of saws: rip saws, panel saws, hacksaws, sash saws, miter saws, carcass saws. He also owned a lot of handguns and armor, about thirty different types of knives, a couple of swords, and a pair of nun-chucks, all of which lay around the room. A single mattress on a spring-frame occupied the shorter part of the L, with a crisp, flat, green military blanket tucked into it and a flat pillow sitting on top. Mr. Floyd swept the workbench clear, sending screwdrivers and screws and a few chunky pieces of metal clanging to the concrete floor.

"Put 'em up here!" He set the bottle down on the table with a thunk. "Where's he hurt?"

"On his back," Topher said.

Marvin and Zorn hefted Gertrude onto table face down. He huffed and groaned and mumbled something that sounded like "Corn shuffle."

"Take his coat off."

Gertrude didn't move while they tugged his arms out of the sleeves, but when they pulled the coat off his back, his eyes flew open and he screamed.

"I'm sorry! I'm sorry!" Zorn cried.

He let it drop, and Mr. Floyd pushed him aside and tore it off, oblivious to the howls.

"You're useless." He glared at Gertrude, blubbering on the bench. "Shut him up."

"He's in pain," Zorn said. "You're not exactly Mother Teresa."

"Shut him up, or I will."

Zorn patted his friend on the head.

"Shhh. Mr. Floyd's going to beat you if you don't quiet down."

Gertrude's undershirt was ripped to shreds and bloody. The old man pulled a box cutter off his pegboard, sliced it right down the middle, and peeled it aside. Gertrude whimpered. He'd been slashed three times, one across his shoulders, one diagonal from his right armpit to his left oblique, and the worst one, right down the spine. They were deep wounds, ugly, ragged, and red.

Zorn took the book out of his pocket.

"Maybe my book can help."

Mr. Floyd locked onto it, and the intensity of his stare frightened Zorn. He took a step back.

"Where'd you get that, boy?"

"I found it."

"Bullshit. Give it to me."

"No."

Mr. Floyd took a step for him and Marvin cut him off, crossing his arms. As scary as the old man was, he only reached up to Marvin's chest.

"You know what I could do to you, boy?"

Marvin smiled.

"My step dad used to say the same thing," he said. "One day, he tried to show me."

The old man's lip twitched, and for the first time, Topher saw a chink in his armor. How much of this was an act? Was he really all that dangerous?

Mr. Floyd grunted. He turned back to the table.

"Did he get bit?"

"I couldn't really see," Topher said. "It tried, but I think Zorn got there before it got a chance."

Mr. Floyd grunted again. He shot a look at Zorn.

"You were closer. You saw it bite him, right?"

Zorn shook his head.

"No, no bite."

"'Course it did! You seen it. Bit him right there on his shoulder."

"No, I didn't. It was slashing at him with its claws, but it didn't bite him."

"Bullshit."

"I saw it happen, Mr. Floyd. He wasn't bitten."

The old man squinted at him, waiting for him to change his story, or modify it even in the slightest. When that didn't happen, he said, "Okay. So he's not one of mine." He nodded at Topher. "You. Hand me that bottle over there."

Topher looked around him. There were at least a dozen bottles sitting all over the place, some old and half-empty, some overturned under the bed, a few littering the bedside table. They were filled with amber stuff, or black stuff, or clear stuff, and none of them were labeled. Just bottles. He picked up one with caramel-colored liquid in it and handed it to Mr. Floyd, who promptly hurled it away. It struck the far wall and exploded.

"You wanna kill him? Get me a clear one."

Topher quickly retrieved one of the clear liquid bottles and handed it to him. Mr. Floyd pulled a leather strap from the pegboard and said, "Put it in his mouth. Make him bite down on it."

Topher did as he was told.

"You and you," Mr. Floyd said, pointing at Zorn and Marvin. "Hold him down."

Without waiting, he bit into the cork stopper, pulled it out with a ploonk, and poured the rest of the contents over the wound on Gertrude's back. Liquid splashed into the wounds, and Gertrude began to flop like a marlin in a net. Marvin and Zorn, who had paused at Mr. Floyd's order, clamped down on his ankles and wrists. Gertrude bucked so hard that even Marvin had a hard time holding on to him. His breath came in great whuff's and chuff's as he bit down on the strap, and his eyes were wide with terror and pain.

When he could take it no longer, he opened his mouth and screamed.

Mr. Floyd clamped his jaw back down on the leather.

"You wanna bite your tongue off, do that again." Tears leaked out of Gertrude's eyes. "Let it ride, boy, let it ride. Be fit in a bit."

Eventually he stopped his violent thrashing, falling into tears and moans.

"Is he okay?" Topher asked. "Did you clean out the wounds?"

Mr. Floyd shrugged and finished the last of the liquor.

"I dunno."

"You don't know? Then why did you do that to him?"

"You brought him to me, boy. I ain't no doctor. Maybe that'll take care of any infection for the time. He'll need to get that cleaned out better, and he'll need stitches. Take him to Doctor Bowls."

"Who's Doctor Bowls?"

"He's the doctor, you idiot." Topher continued to stare at him blankly. "Medicine?" Nothing. "Christ Jesus. Just take him to the infirmary. Tell Bowls your friend walked into a door. He'll know what it means."

He staggered over to his bed, suddenly tired, dipping to pick up another bottle from the floor. He took a deep swig and sat down on his mattress. His belly rose up and down as he caught his breath, and his white, hairy legs stuck out like logs.

"Wait," Topher said, walking tentatively to the back of the room. "Aren't you going to help us?"

Mr. Floyd withered him with a bitter eyebrow.

"Boy. What do you think I just did?"

"But what's going on here? How did that help? Why are there monsters in the woods?"

Mr. Floyd waved his bottle in the air as if conducting a choir.

"Here it goes again," he said. "'Our friend's hurt,' they whine. 'I'm scared,' they whine. 'Help us, help us'." He took a deep pull and fixed Topher with drunken eyes. "There ain't no help for them."

"What's that supposed to mean?"

"It means there ain't nothing to be done, that's what it means. It is what it is, *ce la vie*, such is life. You want my advice? Do your best in class, keep your head down and your nose clean and maybe you'll get out of here with your skin still attached. Don't go poking around in the woods, don't go poking around in the fields, don't go poking around down here, and stop bothering me when I'm trying to get drunk."

He took another pull, his throat working like a piston.

Topher looked back to his friends for support. Gertrude was asleep, peacefully, having found some relief following his brutal procedure. Marvin assumed his usual position, leaning up against the wall near the door with his arms crossed. Only Zorn looked on, listening eagerly. He took a hesitant step forward.

"We found a room in the walls."

"Oh, so you found that, eh?" Mr. Floyd saluted them with his bottle. "Congratulations. Took you long enough. Your predecessors, who were much smarter'n you, found it in half the time. I'd stay away from that place if I were you."

"That's where Gertrude was attacked," Topher said.

"Where? In the woods, right?"

"No, in the room."

The old man brought his hand up to scratch his head, and it was covered in blood.

"Mr. Floyd?"

"What?"

Topher motioned at his hand.

The old man looked at it like he'd never seen it before. Then he cursed and poured some of the contents of the bottle over fingers, and rubbed it off on his boxers.

"Your damn friend bled all over me." After a while he glanced down at his empty bottle, cursed again, and put it aside. He stood woozily up and began to pace to and fro, hands on his hips. "Said they'd steer clear."

"Who are you talking about?" Topher asked. "And who were our predecessors?"

Mr. Floyd eyeballed him.

"Never mind," he grumbled.

He started to turn, but Topher grabbed his elbow.

"Tell me." Mr. Floyd turned around, staring at Topher's hand. Topher let it drop. "Please."

"Your predecessors are the boys who was here the last time this happened."

"Were you the grounds keeper then, too?"

The old man suddenly grew angry again, and Topher thought he was going to hit him. Then he took a short breath, let it out, and let his head drop slightly.

"No. I was one of them."

Gertrude moaned and stirred.

"What's happening?"

"Don't get up," Topher said.

"No, get him up," Mr. Floyd ordered. "Get him up and get him out. It's late, and I need to get to sleep."

Marvin and Zorn helped Gertrude off the workbench, and Mr. Floyd ushered them to the door and out into the hall.

"Mr. Floyd?" Topher asked.

"What?"

"The boys? The one's who were here before?" Mr. Floyd grunted. "Were they your friends?"

"Yeah, they were my friends."

"Maybe they can help us? Where are they now?"

Mr. Floyd started to close the door, leaving it open just a crack, peeking out with one, brown eye.

"They're dead," he said, and slammed it shut.

Doctor Bowls was a short, fat, balding, paranoid little man. His coke bottle glasses gave him an expression of perpetual astonishment, which may have caused him some little dismay were it not for the fact that he actually *was* in a state of perpetual astonishment, or vigilance, or astonished vigilance, depending on the events of the day. Those eyes were the first Topher ever saw of him, staring out of a crack in the door to the infirmary.

"What do you want?" the doctor asked. His voice was high and clear, as if he'd never completed puberty.

"My friend needs help," Topher explained. He stepped aside to let him see Gertrude hanging between Marvin and Zorn.

"Is he throwing up? Does he have cancer?"

"Well, no."

"Then I don't have any more room."

"He walked into a door."

Bowls' impossibly wide eyes grew impossibly wider, and he shut the door.

Topher turned around and looked at his friends in dismay, then there was a sound of locks turning, and chains being taken off, and metal bars being removed, and another lock and chain, and one last lock, and then the door swung open to reveal a tiny, round man in a rumpled lab coat standing on a step stool.

"Bring him in." He stepped off the stool and set it aside. "Come on, come on. Before anybody sees you." Once the boys were inside, he stuck his head out to make sure there was nobody around, then slammed the door shut. The locks turned and more chains rattled, then all was quiet.

"How long ago?" he asked, carrying the stool to the supply cabinet. Seeing them about to place Gertrude in a chair with a back, he said, "No, not there. On the bed. Not that one, the one with the curtain." He climbed up and opened a drawer and withdrew a pair of sterile gloves. He pulled them on with a snap. "How long ago?"

"A few hours," Topher said. "A little after midnight."

The doctor nodded jumped off the stool, walking quickly to his patient.

"Where is he hurt?"

"On his back."

Bowls directed the boys to push Gertrude onto his stomach.

"Take off his coat."

Gertrude sucked in his breath but didn't cry out. Perhaps the alcohol had numbed him. The doctor leaned over his back, inspecting the wounds.

"Who cleaned his wounds?"

"Mr. Floyd."

"What did he clean it with?"

"Vodka, I think."

The doctor tsked.

"I told him just to send them up to me," he said. Then, to the boys, "You may go."

"Go?"

"There's nothing you need to worry about, and he's in no immediate danger. I'll treat him accordingly. He'll be here a few days to make sure the stitches remain in place and that the infection doesn't spread. You may go."

"But what if we don't want to leave?" Topher asked.

Bowls stopped working and fixed his magnified eyes upon him.

"You may not know this from just looking at me, but I don't like people," he said. Then he sighed. It was no ordinary sigh. It was a weary sigh, a belabored sigh. A sigh that explained to the boys that he was about to embark on a strain of logic he'd obviously delivered many times before. "I especially don't like people when they hover and ask irritating questions. When they hover and ask irritating questions, I spend more time feeling irritated than I do actually focusing on the task at hand, which usually entails saving someone's life. Thinking about not being able to save a patient irritates me even more, and when I'm that irritated, I make mistakes. When I make mistakes, people die." He turned his back on them. "Shut the door after you leave."

Another boy arrived later that morning, complaining of a sour stomach. Bowls answered the door with his usual defensive air, but quickly let the boy in.

"Stand there," he ordered, pointing at a corner next to the door.

Then he hurried over to Gertrude, saying, "Get up. You'll have to move to the other bed. This one's closer to the bathroom."

Gertrude lay in his new bed for a while, dozing. The other boy kept throwing up, and he was glad the doctor had pulled the curtain around him so he didn't have to see it. He drifted off, waking later to hear the boy snoring and whimpering, drifted off again. Later he woke to the sound of a spoon clinking in a bowl. He had the strange thought that it was his mother. She always gave him sherbet when he was sick. Orange sherbet was his favorite, but he didn't mind lime, either. The doctor was shuffling around somewhere in the clinic, whistling "Come on Eileen."

Later. Another knock at the door.

The doctor's heels clipped on the linoleum, and the locks thunked and the chains rattled and the door creaked open.

"Bowls."

Even in his pain-filled stupor, Gertrude recognized that voice. Stoneman.

"Oh. Hello, sir."

Gertrude craned his neck around, trying to see something, anything, but all he could make out were two forms standing in the hallway, one short and fat, one tall and imperious.

Stoneman said, "It's been brought to my attention that one of our wards has had an accident."

"Oh, no sir. No accidents in here. Two cases of norovirus, though."

"Mmhmm. I'm sure you wouldn't mind if I inspected the infirmary."

Gertrude heard him enter. He imagined his eyes scouring the room, penetrating the cabinets, scanning the sink, looking for signs, clues. But of what? Him? He heard him sniff the air, and he tried to lie as still as possible, breathe as shallow as he could, just in case the headmaster had super-hearing or could smell his breath.

"Who is this?" Stoneman asked. Gertrude could see him reach for the curtain.

"I wouldn't do that!" Doctor Bowls bustled around and stood between Stoneman and the bed.

"Excuse me?"

"I'm sorry, Mr. Stoneman, but you don't want to be exposed to this one."

"What is the boy's name? Where is his information?"

"I don't know that." Bowls sounded suddenly combative. "*Please*, Mr.

Stoneman. I've been up for twenty-four hours, tending him, and then getting sick myself. I'll take care of the paperwork tomorrow."

Stoneman pushed the little man aside and ripped open the curtain.

The sick boy lay on his back, a soiled bucket next to the bed on the floor. He blearily opened his bloodshot eyes.

"Oh," Stoneman said. "Excuse me, young man." He drew the curtains closed. "Norovirus, you say?"

"Violent case, I'm afraid."

"And in the other bed?"

A slight pause.

"Same thing, only worse. Possible staph infection."

"Disgusting, these boys."

The door opened, and Gertrude felt cool air flow into the room. Stoneman said, "Very well, then." His voice had regained some of its officiousness. "You will send me the information on the afflicted?"

"Yes, sir."

A moment passed before the door shut. Bowls turned all of the locks, latched all of the latches, and slowly lowered himself to the ground with a deep, stressful sigh. After a moment, Gertrude heard him gag. Seconds later he was scrambling for the bathroom.

One week later . . .

Zorn woke up early, blinked the sleep out of his eyes, and yawned. The room glowed with the rising sun, the lonely light shrouding Topher's corner of the room in eerie half-shadows. He frowned at the condition of their abode, the clutter and the dust and the general muck, illuminated by pale beams of unflattering starkness. Topher's papers towered precariously on every available surface, threatening at the slightest sneeze to topple over and fan out all over the dusty floor. Scraps of toilet paper trailed in and out of bathroom, bits of cardboard littered the corners, and half-crumpled balls of paper, upon which Topher jotted down his "ideas," punctuated the area around his desk like huge, half-melted hailstones. He'd promised to organize it three weeks before, but clearly it hadn't been done. He always promised to organize his side, or clean the bathroom, or do his laundry, and he always forgot.

And there he was now, sitting in his chair, already awake. Zorn would have liked to describe his roommate as sitting "at" his desk. Certainly the boy was perched in his chair, and certainly the chair was only partially encumbered by his coat and knapsack (both of which hung from the back), but the clutter was so thick that he was more or less just kind of in the area, muttering and clucking to himself as he attempted to extricate a single scrap of one of his "ideas" from a balled up wad of papers bound together with rubber bands.

Zorn sat up and stretched.

"What's that?"

Topher turned around, startled, pushing the ball aside.

"This?"

"Yeah."

"I found it when I was in the basement behind the water heater this morning. I think it's a note from a former student."

He extended an old, coffee-stained piece of paper in his fingertips. Zorn took it.

"It's a letter," he said. "Dear father. Please take me out of this godforsaken hell-hole. Save me from the murderous beasts of Chainwrought Forest. Also, please tell mother not to put nuts in my next care package. I'm sorry about the dog and brother Talbot." He handed it back to Topher. "Sounds familiar."

Zorn inspected the letter.

"Which part?"

Topher turned and separated a different piece of paper from the wad. Inspired and feeling frisky, Zorn leapt out of bed and snatched it out of his hands.

"Hornet shot? How to bypass the gook—shoot them whole?"

"It's a weapon," Topher explained. "Maybe it can help us fight the werepyres."

Gertrude yawned and rose up on his elbow. He was no longer able to sleep on his back for the stitches and the pain, but he always slept on his belly, so it didn't matter. His hair stood straight up in the air on the left side of his head. He wore an expression of dopey satisfaction. Sleep had never been so good.

"Good morning, Gertrude," Zorn said.

"Morning."

He stretched. Carefully. He wanted to avoid Doctor Bowls and the infirmary if he could help it. At least until the stitches came out.

"What are you doing?"

Zorn showed him the idea for the hornet gun.

"Topher's going to build it to help us blind the werepyres."

Gertrude handed it back.

"Are you game for some breakfast?"

Zorn patted his stomach. He hadn't realized how hungry he was.

"Sounds delightful." He turned to Topher, who was pouring over his work. "Would you like to join us, T?"

"Excuse me?"

"I asked if you would like to join us for breakfast."

"And then you called me a name," Topher said, pushing back from his desk. He struck a tower of papers, which tottered. First a single sheet slipped off, then another, then three or four, and then more and more and more until an avalanche of paper, white and massive, gushed off the stack, a sluice of information pouring into a puddle on the floor, and Topher— maintaining eye-contact the whole time—raised an eyebrow as if to say "what?" until the whole thing collapsed to the floor at his feet.

Zorn smiled condescendingly and said, "No, no. I was merely truncating your first name to a single letter: 'T'. All of the hippest lads in the nation have gone crazy for it. It, apparently, is off the heazy?"

He sought confirmation of his pronunciation of the word 'heazy' from Gertrude, but received only a baffled look in return.

"Zorn, have you turned into a complete and utter moron?" Topher asked. "There will be nothing 'heazy' in this room, nor will I allow myself to be called 'T.' I'm a young man, not a beverage."

"Well, would you like to join us anyway, squareness notwithstanding?"

"After you just insulted me? No thank you."

"Have it your way, pizzle."

"Damn your hide!"

Zorn turned patiently back to him again.

"No no no. It's a compliment. It means pimp."

"That's a compliment?"

"In certain circles."

"Where are you getting this information?"

"I, Dennis. He hacked into a wireless signal."

"All the way up here?"

Zorn shrugged.

"If it makes you feel any better, he can only get onto one website, and it only has old episodes of Yo! MTV raps."

"I think I understand," Topher said. "So, how does one get 'pimp' from 'pizzle?"

"One retains the first letter of a word and simply adds an 'izzle' to the end."

"That is, without a doubt, the stupidest thing I've ever heard. How would anybody understand anything at all?"

"If one were schizzled in the wizzle of sizzle, one would hizzle no pizzle."

"Get out of my room!" Topher cried. "Now!"

"Nizzle!" Zorn corrected, pointing.

Topher looked down at his chest. Were his nipples exposed?

Gertrude had gotten up in the middle of the night to pee and stumbled into the wardrobe by accident. In the subsequent confusion, he entered the secret passage, turned right instead of left, got extremely lost, and discovered a secret door to the courtyard, which he showed to Zorn on their way to breakfast.

"Here we are," he announced.

As far as Zorn could tell, they had reached a dead end. The bricks in front of them appeared to be particularly solid, reminding him of a Russian matron, or a Russian tank. Something Russian.

"Stand here," Gertrude said. Zorn did. "Kick that." He said. Zorn did. Before Zorn could blink, they were whipped around in a circle and deposited, breathless, on the opposite side of the wall in full view of the courtyard.

"Spectacular!" Zorn cried.

Gertrude beamed. "I knew you'd enjoy it," he said. "I wasn't as pleased at three in the morning. I peed on that bush."

He pointed to a brown, withered boxwood.

"I'm glad Topher isn't here," Zorn said. They both took a step away from the wall. "Now we can talk about our physics project without worrying about his crazy ideas."

The wall whipped around again, depositing Topher into the courtyard.

"What project?" he asked.

"Ahhhhh," Zorn said. "Shit!"

"I decided to join you anyway, insulting hip-hop slang notwithstanding." He looked around. "The Assistants aren't out yet?"

"The less run-ins we have with Brimstone, the better."

"Agreed."

The clock rang out just as they reached the main walk. They heard the doors slam open, and the shouts of the Assistants as they flushed the students out of the dorms. Topher took a deep breath of the crisp morning air.

"I'm afraid the hornet shot is a loss. So I'm in the perfect position to help out. Describe your physics assignment. I have several great ideas for explosive devices and other weapons that might come in handy."

Gertrude felt his stomach drop. His physics teacher, a bald man with chemical burns on one side of his face and a prosthetic ear, had charged them with the creation of a device that would fire a twenty pound projectile into the air with enough velocity to enable it to ascend to a height of no less than fifty meters and enough force for it to penetrate a three-foot stone wall. If Topher got involved, he'd turn it into some kind of flame-throwing robot, just so he could say he screwed up their grade by building a flame-throwing robot. There was no way he'd tell Topher what the assignment was.

Zorn, however, hadn't thought about that at all.

"We get to build a cannon."

"Really?"

"Zorn, no!" Gertrude said.

"Oh, right. We're not building a cannon."

Gertrude let out a deep breath.

"We're building a catapult. Or a massive crossbow. Whatever. Just so long as it can fire a twenty pound weight through a three foot wall."

Topher was amazed.

"And Stoneman approved this?"

"He has no choice. It's part of the curriculum. Of course, we must be monitored during the display."

"And you get to fire it?"

"Of course."

"I should have taken physics."

"But in order to pass we must be very, very exact," Gertrude said. "Prior to the demonstration we must determine the projectile's actual height and apex, measure the distance it should travel from firing point to landing point, and from that calculate, within a few figures, the speed and force with which it will travel. We must be perfect! There can be no mistakes. AND NO FLAME-THROWING ROBOTS!"

"I have an idea," Topher announced.

"NO FLAME-THROWING ROBOTS!"

"Why don't we take our breakfast to go and eat it in the special room we found?"

Gertrude felt his stomach drop again.

"Perhaps not. Didn't Mr. Floyd tell us to avoid that place? Besides, I'm a little uncomfortable returning to the scene of the attack."

"Oh please, Gertrude. Don't be such a pussy. Get back up on that bike and ride!" He slapped him on the shoulder.

"Ahhh!"

"Wrong one, faker."

The room was in much better condition than before. The furniture had been replaced, the blood on the floor mopped up. Even the fireplace was cleaned and cleared of the charred husks of log and ash. Gertrude hovered in the hallway, stealing peeks over Zorn's shoulder.

"Someone's been here since we last visited," Zorn observed.

Topher moved from lamp to lamp, turning each one on. Soon, light warmed the room "Me and Marvin. We fixed the door."

The door was far from fixed. It looked like a team of six year olds had been let loose with scraps of wood and glue and nails. It hung cockeyed in the frame and wouldn't close or lock.

"Good job," Zorn said.

Topher disappeared under the archway next to the fireplace.

"Is it clear in there?" Gertrude asked.

"I'm not sure, yet."

"Check corner where the wolf was."

"Okay."

"And down the passage."

"I'm getting there."

"And look up the fireplace."

"Don't you think that's—"

"And don't forget under the couch!"

Topher returned a few minutes later, a little out of breath.

"All clear. Now can you come inside? I'd like to eat."

The weather outside was chilly enough, but the room, a few levels under the basement, was frigid. Gertrude wasn't truly able to relax until the Zorn started the fire, then he gathered his courage and wandered around while it hissed and cracked, filling the room with warmth and good cheer. He even dimmed the lamps.

Zorn decided to beat the cushions with the fireplace poker, and soon the air was choked with dust, whiting his face, hair, beard, and furs. Topher hunched over his food.

"Knock it off. You're getting dust in my apple fritter."

He finished eating, threw his trash into the fire, and stood up to look at the tapestries again. He stopped under Burleigh, enchanted.

"Maybe they were the founders? Why did they put a secondary school in the middle of a forest infested with monsters?"

"Maybe they didn't know it was infested with monsters," Gertrude said. "How could anybody?"

"Maybe they did," Zorn countered. He gestured around him. "We are being punished, after all."

Topher continued to stroll along the wall, hands held behind his back. He paused every now and then and leaned in to peer at some detail or stand on his tiptoes. Gertrude pulled on the top drawer of one of the chests that lined the room; it opened with a crack and a squeal.

"Books." He pulled one out and wiped a thin layer of dust from the cover. "The Abridged Field Guide to Hunting." He gently placed it on the top of the chest and reached in and pulled out another. "Metallurgy for Beginning Blacksmiths."

Zorn kicked a chest near the totem of the wolf Gertrude refused to go near. Something clinked and clanked and shifted inside. He opened the chest.

"Weapons!"

He pulled out a long, dull-looking sword and held it up, staring with wonder at its length, amazed at its weight and sturdiness.

"What's it for?"

Someone standing in the door said, "Killing."

All three gasped and spun. Mr. Floyd stood there, leaning on the jamb.

He limped down the short three steps leading into the room and placed his hands on his hips, gazing about him. "Been a while. Not much different from when I was a boy." His eyes fell on the books Gertrude pulled out of the drawer. He went over and picked up the metallurgy book, grunted, and put it down.

"Good read."

Gertrude gave the book a skeptical look, and Mr. Floyd continued around to the middle of the room.

"If you look on the bottom drawer, you'll find our yearbook. Catch a glimpse of us when we was young and dumb, like you."

Gertrude bent immediately over and opened the bottom drawer.

"Are you talking about our 'predecessors'?" Topher asked.

Mr. Floyd seemed to regard him as if for the first time.

"You remind me a lot of Smith."

"Oh?"

"Yeah. Bull-headed, silly little git that he was," Mr. Floyd answered. "Weird, too, like you." He twirled his hand in the air. "Head full of ideas." He sighed. "It was his idea, all this. Nobody liked what was going on, but nobody knew what to do about it. Smith was the first one who said we should put a stop to it."

"Did it work?"

The old man paused, thinking. Then he said, "For a while. Now ask me if it was worth it."

"Was it worth it?"

"Nope."

He stared around at all three of them.

"And that's why I'm down here. I'm here to tell you, one last time, to tell all of you, to back off. Just. Back. Off."

"But those things want to kill us," Topher said.

"You seen what they did to your friend." He motioned toward Gertrude. "You're all lucky he wasn't bit. 'Cause if he was, I would have had to kill him, and nobody here wants that."

Gertrude said, "Least of all, me."

Mr. Floyd looked at each boy pointedly, lingering longest on Topher. Then he nodded, not quite satisfied, and limped toward the stairs leading to the door.

"What else can we do?" Topher asked. "You act like we're going to get out, but we're not. They're not going to let us out. We're supposed to die here. You know that. Stoneman knows it. And I'm not dying without a fight."

Mr. Floyd stopped, rested his hand on the pane.

"So that's the way it's going to be, then?"

"I don't understand. Don't you want to help us?"

Mr. Floyd spit.

"I been helping you. Been helping you since the first day I seen you. Problem is, you just don't listen."

The boys studied their shoes. It was true. He kept telling them to stop, he kept telling them to just put their heads down and do the best they could, but they ignored him. But wasn't this they best they could do?

"It's not like we're doing it on purpose," Topher said. "Not all of it. Things just keep happening, and we have to fight back."

"Then that's it. Not much else I can do for you boys."

He knocked on the pane, gave the room one last look.

"You're gonna need a lot more help than a few dusty old books and rusty old swords." He clopped out. "A lot more help."

The boys trudged back to their room, dejected and nervous. Gertrude carried a few of the old books he found with him, including the one on blacksmithing and a stack of old yearbooks, and Zorn smuggled a long, sharp sword from the chest. When Topher saw it he ran back to the secret room to get one for himself. Then they sat in their room silence, pondering Mr. Floyd's warning. Zorn thumbed his sword, Topher thumbed bits of paper at him, and Gertrude thumbed through the yearbooks.

"Is it true, what you said?" Gertrude asked, not looking up from his yearbook.

Topher thumbed a piece of paper into Zorn's beard.

"Are you talking to me or Zorn?"

"You. Or Zorn."

Topher and Zorn shared a look.

"I'll answer," Topher said. "What did I say?"

"You said we were going to die here."

Topher didn't answer for a long time. There were multiple ways to approach his answer. He could lie and make Gertrude feel better, he could fashion an answer that sounded reasonable but which really didn't mean anything, or he could be brutally honest. He settled on the latter.

"Of course we are. You know we are."

Gertrude supposed he did know it. It shouldn't have come as any surprise. What they did was horrible. He deserved to die. He thought of his mother on that last day, how she was crying. "Don't get into anymore trouble," she said.

He wiped her tears away.

"Don't be sad. It's only five years."

She'd choked up when he said that. At the time he thought it was because five years felt so long to both of them. Now he realized it was because she knew where he was going, what she'd sentenced him to.

And so he looked at the yearbook photos of the boys who had come before him. Dead boys, all of them. What did they do to end up here? Were they just like him and his friends? Did they commit Murder? Arson? Or did they do something worse? He couldn't imagine what was worse than what he'd done. Maybe that's why so many of the boys avoided them. He paged through the yearbook. None of the boys were smiling. The pictures looked like mug shots. And then he realized that they were mug shots.

Why did they put a yearbook together at all? It seemed sick, all things considered, but then again, what wasn't sick about that place? It made him even sicker when he thought of the future, of some boy just like him, sitting in this room, helpless, hopeless, looking at a photo of Kenneth "Gertrude" Hughes, wondering what he'd done to deserve such a horrible fate.

"A whole bunch of the faces have been scratched out," he said, and held a page up for Topher to see. "See?"

Topher leaned over his desk and took the yearbook in one hand. A sea of young faces glared back at him.

"Look. This boy's name's Carol. What an awful thing to name a child, don't you agree, Gertrude?"

Gertrude smiled a tight smile.

"Just look at the photos."

Topher did. Gertrude was right. On each page, at least a half dozen faces had been scribbled out, or blotted with dark, black ink, or scratched into oblivion. Some had been defaced with the foulest phrases. Next to each one someone had scrawled a black claw.

"Marked for death, I suppose." He turned to the F-section. "Here he is. Mr. Floyd." He placed his finger below the picture of a round-faced, bespectacled boy of about thirteen. He looked just as angry before; he even wore the same crew cut, though his hair was thick and dirty blond, not thin and graying.

"Ha! His first name is Otis." He handed it over back to Gertrude. "Speaking of books. Zorn? Have you made any progress with the old man's book?"

"It's not his book. It's my book."

"Okay, calm down. Nobody's going to take it from you."

"I will rip the throat out of anyone who tries! I will smash his face in! I'll break his neck! And yes, I've made progress."

"Really? How far have you read?"

"I haven't read anything. I gave it a name."

"You gave your book a name? Doesn't it already have one?"

"It has a title, but a book as special as this deserves a name."

Topher tried not to laugh. He tried to take it seriously. So through pursed lips, he said, "What did you name it?"

"Admiral Tucker."

"You named your book of spells after a naval officer?"

Zorn put his new sword down on his bed.

"Gives it a certain maritime antiquity, don't you think?"

"Have you learned any spells of use? Something that might help us?"

"What do you have in mind?"

"Well—and bear with me now—but how about a Homunculus?"

"A Homunc . . ." Zorn began, then his eyes narrowed. How did Topher know about the recipe for the Homunculus? Had he been stealing glances in his book? The thought of this made him bristle with anger. How dare he molest Admiral Tucker? Why was he calling it Admiral Tucker? He hadn't really named it Admiral Tucker. He just said that to irritate Topher, that dick. Maybe he should punch him in the face?

His anger was so sudden and encompassing that it was frightening. He tried to ignore it by hastily removing the book from his breast pocket and flipping through the pages. Engaging with the book calmed him, and after a few minutes of muttering about a 'lack of an index,' he found what he was looking for. He thought for a moment about not saying anything, but then thought that not saying anything would pique Topher's interest and increase the odds of his molesting Admir—the book.

"I found it," he said.

Topher was surprised.

"You did? I was just joking. There really is a spell for creating a homunculus?"

Zorn's anger dissipated. He couldn't tell if Topher was lying or not (and he was an excellent liar), but right then he seemed sincere. The book had remained pure. All was well.

"It's right here, almost at the end. *A Spell for the Conjuring of Homunculi, or a Single Homunculus. See also Golem or Brownie.*" He read on a bit. "Seems simple enough. Find some human hair and the bones of the animal we wish our Homunculus to use for its bones. Then we bury them in a little hole and cover it with elephant dung. Two weeks later, a being one sixth the size of the person whose hair was used to create it will arrive on the doorstep."

"Smelling of elephant dung, no doubt," Gertrude said.

"You say that as if it were a bad thing," Topher replied. "Have you ever been covered in elephant dung?"

"No."

"Well, there you are."

Gertrude closed the yearbook, irritated.

"How will a pungent midget help protect us from the monsters?"

"First of all, they prefer 'little person'. And secondly, it will be a Homunculus, not a midget. Homunculi possess magical powers. It's eternally in debt to its maker, for one, and it's enormously fastidious to boot. It will dash the heads of our assailants against the cobblestones of the courtyard, then scrub the blood spot clean and do our laundry."

"Really? Because I've been wearing the same pair of socks for a month."

"I left out the part about its eventually turning on its creator. But as long as it solves our immediate problem—"

"Agreed!" Zorn cried.

"Very well then! With what animal shall we mix our Homunculus?"

"I've always been partial to guinea pigs," Gertrude said.

Topher rolled his eyes.

"Wonderful. And when the beasts attack, our Homunculus will run them to death on an exercise wheel."

"How about a cheetah and a spider monkey?" Zorn suggested. "Or a spider and a cheetah monkey?"

"I like the sound of that."

"Or an angry black bear and an even angrier black bear?"

"Even better! If a little redundant."

"Okay," Gertrude said, getting into the spirit. "What about an angry, or angrier, black bear and a sonic death panther? In keeping with noir conceit."

Topher stood up and started pacing.

"Now it only remains to find the bones of two such beasts and we're on our way to paranormal protection. First, however, we must have two human hairs. Gertrude, present your noggin."

"Why me?"

"Well it won't be mine."

"Why not you? What if it hurts?"

"Don't be a pussy!"

"Again. Why not you?"

"Please. Must I state the obvious?"

"Indulge me."

Topher waved the question away.

"I'm clearly far too important. Now, your head!"

In the end, they were only able to find a dead chameleon, the tail feather of a titmouse, some hardened dung, and a smattering of thin, mysterious bones.

Topher sighed and ran his hand through his hair.

"As hunters, we are miserable losers."

Zorn finished digging their 'fairy hole' (as he referred to it), and dumped their bounty within.

"My grandfather was an assassin for the Hungarian navy," he said, wiping his hands on his pants. "He murdered ten men."

"Dear me. Call the National Guard."

Zorn kicked some dirt into the hole.

"That we know of. One of them was another Hungarian assassin. I believe that was an accident, or maybe it was professional jealousy. My uncle said that Grandfather's prowess is quite evident in me. Judging by my critter take today, I must say that I agree."

Gertrude nodded enthusiastically while Topher rolled his eyes.

"Yes. Handling those worms and termites was the bravest feat of the day. You could have contracted some kind of pathogen. A termite could have infested your skin with eggs."

"Exactly."

Topher kicked the dung into the hole.

"Maybe a deadly spider will crawl into our magical incubator and die. It would at least add a perception of menace to our wee servant."

Gertrude looked sickened at the thought.

"Maybe he'll sport fangs and weave for us fine silken clothes."

"Don't be an idiot."

Gertrude jabbed his thumb at Topher, and leaning toward Zorn, he said, "Here's one who obviously never enjoyed the pleasure of a clean pair of silk jammies."

"Spider's don't spin silk," Zorn said. "Silk worms spin silk."

"Oh."

A week passed, and another. Nothing happened. To take their minds off the spell, they worked on Zorn and Gertrude's physics project. It did not go well. One morning, three weeks after they buried the bones, Topher was stirred from sleep by a faint knock on their dorm room door. The boys, in anticipation of the arrival of their own magical slave, had let the room go even further to pot. Drifts of papers and half-eaten food piled up in the corners. Dust coated the any available surface that had not already been covered with clothes and books, and the windows were streaked with grime. He had to slog through a full inch of discarded socks and undergarments, hazarding whatever might lie beneath: tacks, pens, pins, jacks, knives, jack-knives. Even in his semi-conscious state, he felt intrepid.

"Mother," he mumbled, shuffling through the mess. "I left the potato socks on the heater."

He slapped at the handle three times before he was able to grip it with any success, then he pulled the door open and stood there, eyes nearly closed, suffering the glare of the cruel overhead lights. Had anybody passed they would have seen a statue made out of white linen pajamas, topped by a wild thicket of curly black hair from which protruded a set of wet, red lips.

At his feet (well out of his current range of vision) stood the Homunculus. It was an exact replica of Gertrude, only one-sixth his size, dressed in fur from a squirrel it killed and skinned with its own hands. The man-thing above him smelled funny. It nicked his ankle with its thumbnail and tasted the blood. This was not Master. Master was in there, in the place that smelled like sour things and feet. Master should not live in such a place! It needed to get to work right away. It zipped between his legs and plowed into the first wall of filth.

A minute later, Topher found himself staring dumbly at the wall across from his room. What was he doing? Sleepwalking again? When he was a child, he used to have night terrors. He didn't remember much, just a general feeling of panic and dread, and images of faces breathing out of the walls. Apparently he'd run around the house, screaming at the top of his lungs, flicking lights on and off. Had he done that again? It wouldn't surprise him in a place like Raleigh's. Hmm. Better to deal with it tomorrow.

He shuffled slowly around and closed the door behind him.

A path had already been cleared from the door to his bed. The sink, formerly ripe with fuzzy green raiment, now sparkled in every crevice, even beneath the fixtures. Cobwebs that hung so brazenly from the corners were wiped clean. Sally, whom Gertrude had hung in the corner using a complex pulley/trigger system, had been straightened, her hair dusted, her one cockeyed limb mended and set.

Topher noticed none of this. Especially Sally, whom he had not noticed for weeks, much to Gertrude's dismay. He marched through the room, stomping as if the floor were still clogged, and collapsed into the plush warmth of his comforter and mattress, one leg hanging askew over the lip. In a moment, a tiny figure zipped by and pushed it under the covers.

THE BATTLE IN THE COURTYARD

Adolescence, like tofu, was weird. For example: Zorn never thought his survival would depend on his ability to create a Homunculus. Still, even though he had no idea whether or not the spell would work, he was fairly sure he enjoyed the whole process, so much so that he wanted to do it again, maybe with a different one this time. To be honest, until they'd completed the first spell he'd been a little afraid of the book, despite his attachment, his obsession. He'd never had any real experience with magic outside of church, which told him it was evil, and his old school, where the weird girls walked around in black tutus and black lipstick and called themselves Wiccans. Then there was the time his mother hid his favorite blanky and told him a faerie stole it.

But now he was ready. He took the book out from beneath his mattress and sat down to read. Color returned to his cheeks; he stood more erect than he had in days. He said, "It is a question that haunts my very soul," read further, clapped it shut, stuffed it in his fur, and bustled out the door.

It was late in the evening when he burst back into the room, nearly sending Gertrude (who was standing on a chair, readjusting Sally) plummeting to his death, most certainly the victim of a broken neck. At least that was how Gertrude envisioned his obituary as it would be read by a weeping Topher the next morning.

"Kenneth Hughes," Topher would bawl. "Yesterday. The victim of poor timing and a blundering oaf for a roommate."

"Watch it you oaf!" Gertrude meant to cry. Instead he just sputtered "Good Lord!" and flung his arms around the mannequin's torso.

Zorn shot an irritated look over his shoulder and plunked a paper sack down on his spotless desk. He strode to the window and yanked the yellowing shades down. Two eye-shaped holes had been cut into them, as well as a nose shaped one. Three beams of light, two ovals and a circle, pierced the murky evening air. He pushed his face up to them and peered out upon the courtyard.

"Good, good," he muttered. Then he turned to his bunk and lovingly drew his favorite Delmont and Bunny poster, which he just had laminated after ten years of ownership, out of its protective sheath. The poster, now tattered and torn, was nonetheless relatively intact, and he could admire the bizarre images for as long as the laminate held. Delmont. Young, sweater-vested, pearly smiled. Bunny. An actor of indeterminate age and sex in a bunny suit. He was never able to tell if their embrace was platonic or non-consensual. Psychedelic patterns swirled in the background. Farm tools littered the foreground. A picture of Leonid Brezhnev in a sparkling, golden frame sat on an easel. After a few moments of fingering its edges, he put it away, went to his desk, removed the book from his pocket, and opened it to page one.

"Greetings, Zorn," it read. "No doubt you are wondering many things, not the least of which being, 'What is the average rainfall in Portland?'

"Never mind all that now. As you might have guessed, this book is a magical book, passed down from magician to magician. You should revel in your discovery, Zorn, for the book chooses only those who are truly worthy, gentle of heart and deed, honest and forthright, and sagacious. You must embody all of these traits, my friend, and this knowledge alone should raise your spirits! Before you continue it is necessary to collect the following items . . . ."

Zorn reached into the sack and removed a long, smooth stick that, in accordance to the book's instructions, he had shaved and painted with intricate images. He read a few pages, stick in hand, then looked around the room. Gertrude had disappeared. Most likely he was in the wardrobe again, or creeping around the secret passages. He took a deep breath, focused, raised the stick in one hand, cried out a few words of gobbledygook, and brought his hand down with a decisive stroke. There was a great explosion and a cloud of sinister smoke filled the room, blackening his face.

"Great Hephaestus!"

He ran to the window and pulled on the shades (which whipped up with a whirr and a clatter) then shoved the window open and leaned out, coughing. The sun, blood red and glowing, set over the tops Chainwrought's skeletal trees. Topher sat below in the battery-powered golf cart he nicked from the security shed. He raised a bullhorn to his lips, eyeing the plumes of evil smoke issuing from his window.

"Zorn! What on earth are you doing to our room?"

"Nothing." Zorn coughed, trying waved the smoke away. Tears streaked white canals across his cheeks.

"Why are you in blackface? Need I remind you of the impropriety of your 'Massa Collins' act?"

"Lookee heah. All is well."

A spark fell out of the end of his painted stick and arced out over the courtyard. At the apex of its turn, the spark turned into a rainbow colored mouse, which plummeted to the cobblestones and exploded with a sickening plop.

Topher goggled at the multicolored gook.

"My God!"

Zorn pulled the stick inside and hid it behind his back, where it continued to spark.

"Where did you get the golf cart?"

"Ah, this," Topher said, proudly running his hand over the steering wheel. "I filched it."

"What?"

"Don't look so surprised. I'm a notorious footpad."

Zorn wiped some black soot from his face.

"Why?"

"It's for a little project of mine."

"Project?"

Gertrude reentered the room just as two enormous sparks shot out of the stick. A lion roared, a goat baaed, and Gertrude screamed.

"What's that?" Topher asked. "Are you harboring critters again?"

"Pardon me?"

"That noise? What was it?"

"Oh. I thought you were asking me what I was asking yourself."

Topher frowned.

"I asked you nothing?"

"You did too! You asked me what your new project was."

"How would you know that?"

"Exactly!"

More explosions lit up the room behind Zorn. Gertrude's form, in silhouette, played out a montage of poses: Gertrude fending off a lion. Gertrude head-butting a goat. Gertrude strangling a snake. A group of boys staggered up to the cart, entirely winded, red faced, and stooping with exhaustion. Topher beamed at them.

"This is my project."

He pressed the bullhorn to his lips and directed it into the face of a tall, gangly, skinny boy with his hands on his knees.

"Quit your panting, you lazy blacklung! You've run less than a mile!"

"Topher?" Zorn called, ignoring Gertrude's cries for help. "Are those the lads from the vestibule? Prior to the Eer-aw with the Hrm-Hrm?"

"I suppose so."

Something bit Zorn's non-wanded hand, and he made a strangled noise that reminded Topher of a badger he once saw choking on some garbage. Zorn stroked his beard with the hand holding the painted stick, and the stick, presumably aroused, exploded again, sending a majestic winged creature into the air. Every boy in the courtyard stopped what he was doing. Even Topher, who was used to such craziness, let his mouth drop open and watched.

It was a huge, marvelous dragonfly, colored all of the hues of the spectrum. It spread its translucent wings, and the gelatinous film that coated its skin wicked off as it flew. The setting sun glinted off its diamond eyes. It flapped once, but the film weighed it down, and rather than soar into the sky, it nosed dived, first at an easy angle, but then steadily steeper and steeper, its speed increasing as it plummeted straight down, straight for the cobblestones, where it splattered with a thick, wet, plop. The boys let up a collective groan. Some scattered. A few retched. One passed out.

Zorn quickly hid the painted stick behind his back, where it misfired again.

"Your project?" he asked.

Topher tore his eyes away from the leviathan mound of leviathan guts, now a bubbling mass of luminescent gook the shade and consistency of steaming neon bubble gum. He gagged.

"Yes, I—I am training them. We need all the help we can . . . My GOD, Zorn!"

Zorn stared at his friend with obvious forced inquisitiveness. He was jostled from behind.

"Heh," he said, disappeared for a moment, then reappeared, sweating and out of breath. He held his hands just below the window, like he was trying to suppress something from rising. "Cheers."

"Cheers my arse."

Gertrude clawed himself up from beneath Zorn. His hair was mussed, his face red and swelling, and a nasty cut ran jagged across his forehead.

"Dear Lord," he panted, and was pulled down again.

Zorn started beating at something below the sill, just out of sight.

"Get off! Off!" He swatted it with the stick, which shot more sparks into the room. When that didn't work, and as Gertrude's shrieks became louder, he bent over and violently yanked on whatever it was that was attacking his friend, once, twice, finally wrenching it loose (evoking a yowl from Gertrude) and thrusting it out the window, where it dangled at arm's length.

It was a miniature lion, golden and yellow, with a fantastic mane. A grey and white goat's head pushed out of its back. Its tail was a vibrant green and yellow snake. The lion roared a cute little roar, the goat bleated and tried to butt his hand, and the snake thrashed and hissed, striking at Zorn's arm, forcing him to twist and turn it to avoid getting bit.

Topher gasped.

"Where did you get a chimera?"

Zorn began to respond, but was cut off by a great collective howl that rang up from Chainwrought, roaring as if from the mouths of hundreds of beasts. Everyone turned toward it, and Topher clapped his forehead with his palm.

"Good Lord, the meeting." He shot Zorn a stricken look. "We were supposed to meet Warren Crews and the others at the fields."

Another howl rang out, this one closer. The boys in the courtyard began to chatter nervously. A few cried out in terror. Panic spread and they scattered, knocked each other down and cussed each other, and a fight broke out in front of Merton as people jammed the entrance. More howls erupted from Chainwrought. The sun, already low over the tops of the trees, sank behind them, shrouding the courtyard in shadow. Topher aimed the bullhorn at Zorn.

"Stay there!"

A few moments later he burst into the dorm room, patting his pockets.

"What are you looking for?" Gertrude asked.

Topher yanked the bottom drawer out of his desk, emptying the contents on to the floor. Pens and pencils, paper clips, and some very exciting looking knives.

"I found these in one of the trunks in the secret room. Take your pick, lads."

"I thought you had a sword?" Gertrude pointed at Zorn, struggling with the chimaera. "Him, too."

Topher pulled a knife out of the pile and staked it into his desk.

"They're dull and useless. These are not."

Gertrude reached for the most offensive looking knife out of the bunch. The white handle and sheath had been hand carved and fashioned to look like a leering face. It was quite frightening. Gertrude hoped that its mere presence would scare the monsters before he had to actually do anything with it. Topher slapped it out of his hand.

"You can't have this one," he said, picking it up. "It's mine."

He cut the air with a few short strokes, pretended to stab something. Then he put it back in its sheath and stuck it in his belt. He bent over and picked up a different knife, a very attractive one with tassels and interesting gold inlay, holding it up for his roommates to admire. He tossed it at Gertrude. It struck him in the chest and clattered to the floor.

"Gertrude, you idiot!"

Gertrude picked it up and unsheathed the blade. It was thin but deadly sharp; when he ran his finger along the side it sliced right into the skin without his having to assert any pressure.

"It's a Knight's Templar," Topher said. "Treat it with respect and it will slash the throats of a thousand of your enemies."

Zorn didn't need a knife.

"I'm bringing my painted stick." He held up the chimera. "And my this."

Another howl thundered outside, rattling the panes. Zorn looked out the window.

"They're here."

Gertrude proposed using the secret passage.

"Though we can't use the usual shortcut. It'll land us right in the middle of the courtyard."

"What do you want to do, then?" Topher asked. "Walk out the front door?"

"There are other passages. I just don't know where they are or where they lead."

"The maps," Zorn said.

Topher hurried to his desk, withdrew them from a drawer, and spread them out all over the floor. Outside, the snarls and growls of the beasts grew louder. Somebody screamed, high pitched and shrill.

"Here," Gertrude said, pointing at the Burleigh's map. "Here's our room. Here's where we usually go. And right here is the other passage. According to this, it looks like there's another door that opens into the tunnel connecting Burleigh's to Merton."

Moments later, they stepped out of the secret door and into the tunnel. The evening grew darker. Vicious snarls filled the air. A huge shadow shot by the opening. The earth shook. Topher gripped his knife. Another snarl, another scream. Something whimpered at his feet, and when he looked, he saw Brimstone, Burr and several other boys crouched against the brick wall, shivering.

"Hello, Brimstone," he said. "Peeing yourself silly, eh? I always knew you had a vagina."

"What are you doing, you idiots," Brimstone hissed. "Get down and hide. You'll bring those things over here."

One of the boys sobbed, and Brimstone snarled for him to shut up. Zorn gulped and attempted to pet the chimera, but it latched onto his thumb and he swallowed a yelp. Gertrude unsheathed the Knight's Templar. Topher frowned, hatred filling his eyes. He skinned the Definite Knife.

"Stay here with the children, then. The big boys will take care of you."

"Confounded chimera," Zorn muttered, shaking the snake loose from his thumb. It landed on the cobblestones, then leapt back into the air. Zorn held out his thumb. It latched on. He winced.

"Ready lads?" Topher asked.

"What's the plan?" Zorn asked through clenched teeth.

Topher laughed.

"Plan?" he said, and charged forward, Definite Knife at the ready, leaping into the courtyard. Zorn stood there for a moment, shocked, and then hurried after, leaving Gertrude to fret the tassels on the Knight's Templar.

The cobblestones were awash in blood.

Boys dashed about, eyes wide, hopelessly trying to outrun that which could not be outrun. A few climbed up what they thought to be the safety of the lampposts but soon discovered that the beasts could run fast and leap high. Topher watched as one boy, one of his trainees, was torn from a light; one second he was there, clinging to the post, then a huge figure shot by and he was gone, leaving it to shiver in its wake. Foul beasts dined on the bodies of the slain, emptied them out, severed their heads.

"At least there are no incubi or succubi," Zorn noted. The chimera bit his arm. "Ouch!"

He shook his hand and it flew off, spinning through the air, the goat's head butting, the snake's tale waving, and just as it completed half a revolution, a werepyre appeared out of nowhere and the lion sunk its teeth into the monster's face. The snake struck its eyeballs with mesmerizing speed, leftright, leftright, and the goat's head couldn't do anything as it was on the lion's back.

Gertrude jogged up to the end of the tunnel and joined his friends. The chimera-stricken werepyre, maddened and blinded, rushed them. At the last second they all took one, crisp step back, and it bucked past, the chimera striking and butting and clawing and generally tearing it to shreds. When the monster opened its mouth to roar, it jumped in and clawed down its throat, ripping and tearing the whole time, then burst out of its stomach. The monster collapsed in a heap, shook violently a few times, then lay motionless. The chimera popped onto the thing's back, triumphant. The lion roared.

"Well how about that," Zorn said.

Topher clapped him on the back.

"Your chimera's a valuable weapon. Now call it back before it attacks me."

"Or me!" Gertrude added.

Zorn nodded and stepped forward. He held out his thumb, turned his head, and squeezed his eyes shut.

Inspired, Topher dashed into the middle of the courtyard, brandishing the Definite Knife. He leapt onto the back of a werepyre eating a young boy and plunged the knife into its skull. The beast let out a horrified howl, its muzzle dripping with blood. It jumped five feet forward and collapsed, sending Topher into the air. He landed clumsily on his knees and was just able to duck another beast that sailed over his head. He held the Definite Knife above him as it passed, ripping its intestines out in the process. It showered him with offal, then collapsed in a ball and rolled to a sickening stop.

"See lads!" he cried gleefully, covered in gore. "That's how it's done!"

Zorn nodded and ran full steam into the fray. A beast shot straight toward him, and he threw the chimera at it. It attached itself to the monster's face and gouged out its eyes. Still running, Zorn shouted nonsense and aimed the painted stick at a creature climbing the lamppost after a boy cowering at the top. A silver jet shot out of the end and struck the beast right in its middle, severing it in two. The monster tried to continue its ascent as its lower half fell away, and then it realized that it had been cleaved and dutifully fell to the cobblestones. Zorn ran past, his thumb extended like a hitchhiker, and the chimera leapt aboard.

"Ouch!" he cried.

Gertrude did his best to avoid any interaction with anything at all, be it braying boy or malign monster. He entirely meant to bring down his fair share of the things, and he would gather up his strength and courage and run full steam toward one with the intention of decapitating it, or eviscerating it, or whatever it was he needed to do to kill it and prove his worth, but then at the last moment he would duck, or juke, or swerve, and the beast would fly over his head, or trip itself up, or chomp on thin air, and then he'd spring away, his Knight's Templar extended limply behind him lest another monster picked up the chase.

Finally, one of the things zeroed in on him. Gertrude yelped and ran. He darted and cut around the courtyard like a squirrel on the interstate, but the monster displayed similar alacrity, and it quickly gained on him. Gertrude waved the knife at it like a flaccid penis. Before him he saw another monster heading directly for them, not three feet away. He faked left, then leapt right, and the two beasts collided, creating a comical bonk, then fell over, unconscious.

"Ha!"

A horrendous ululation sounded from above. Gertrude looked up, and there was Topher, clinging to a lamppost, his linen suit gleaming with blood. He fell upon the beasts and set to them with the Definite Knife.

"Well played, Gertrude," he said when he was done.

Gertrude could only see the whites of his eyes. The rest was covered in blood. He recoiled.

"Thank you?"

Zorn ran by and tossed the chimera at Gertrude, who ducked. It attached itself to the face of a monster that had sneaked up behind him. Zorn aimed his pointed stick at something and spouted more nonsense. Silver streaks shot from the end, turning one of the werepyres into a rainbow colored mouse, which the chimera promptly ate. Another silver streak turned into a huge, rainbow colored dragon, cut a werepyre in half, and exploded in a remarkable spectrum of neon greens, pinks and golds.

Suddenly, they were trapped. The beasts had organized: six blocked their escape to the Athletic Fields, and each tunnel was guarded by another. They started forward, closing the nose. The boys stood back to back, Topher with his knife before him, Zorn wielding his stick, the chimaera hanging from his thumb. Gertrude just stood there, shaking.

Ten feet away.

Zorn could smell their foul coats, beading with whatever abominable fluids they produced. He drew back his chimera-hand, ready to fling.

"Zorn," Topher said.

"Yes?"

"If we don't get through this, I just wanted to tell you something."

Zorn nodded. This was good. His friend wanted to give him a tearful farewell.

"Go ahead, Topher. You can say anything to me."

"Well." Topher took a deep breath and let it out, very rapidly. "Your feet have the foulest odor I have ever smelled. There, I said it!"

"Finally!" Gertrude added.

The lead werepyre leaped forward. Gertrude closed his eyes and extended the Knight's Templar. A high-pitched whine cut the growl off, and when he opened his eyes, the werepyre was lying on the ground to his left, decapitated.

Topher watched the head roll away.

"Did you see that?"

Zorn nodded slowly.

Gertrude looked all around him.

"See what?"

The werepyres stopped in their tracks, fangs bared. They seemed uneasy, refusing to move forward. A little brown blur shot toward the monster nearest them. It screeched, and then the blur disappeared, leaving a hole in its side. The beast staggered forward a few steps and fell over, dead.

Gertrude jumped up and down, pointing the knife at the dead monster.

"Now I saw it! Now I saw it!"

The werepyres started to back away, frightened, enraged. One gathered itself for a leap at the boys, but before it could the brown blur sped by again and then its head was gone. Silence enveloped the courtyard. A breaze blew. Blood dripped. The beasts looked around, waiting. Then the brown blur struck one last time, cutting the legs out from under a monster, and the monsters scattered, wild, chomping at each other, searching for an escape, but everywhere they turned, the brown blur was there, cutting them in half, decapitating them, eviscerating them, until there were no more left.

Topher, Zorn, and Gertrude stood there, mouths wide open. Even the chimera seemed amazed, hanging from Zorn's thumb. The brown blur continued to speed around the cobblestones, and everywhere it went, a werepyre carcass disappeared, a puddle of blood was siphoned away, or an unpleasant pile demolished. Soon all that was left was the bodies of the dead students.

And that's when a spotlight froze the trio in place.

"What on Earth is this?"

It was Stoneman. On his electric cart. Surrounded by a bevy of armed guards from the front gate. Stoneman pulled up to the boys, staring in horror at the half eaten bodies. All three of them held up their hands, knives, sticks, mythological beasts and all. Stoneman turned around to speak to someone else in his cart.

"Disarm them."

"But, sir, didn't you see?"

"Of *course* I saw, you idiot, now do as I say!"

"Yes, sir."

And Crews stepped out of the car.

Topher gaped.

"Crews! You traitor."

He approached, his face perfectly opaque. He was wearing an Assistant's uniform, newly laundered, freshly pressed.

"Where were you?" he whispered. Topher didn't reply. "Fine, hand over your knife."

When Topher didn't move, Crews pried the weapon out his hand. Gertrude gave his up willingly. Neither he nor Zorn knew what to do with the chimera. Every time he reached for it, the snake struck or the lion bit or the goat tried to head butt him, so finally he just said, "Keep it.'"

He leaned into Topher.

"You shouldn't have forgotten. Stoneman's actually—"

The headmaster came up behind him and coughed, and Crews' demeanor changed. He straightened his posture, fixed his eyes straight ahead.

"All accounted for, sir. Two knives, a stick, and that."

He pointed at the chimera.

Stoneman gazed around the courtyard at the horror of blood and bodies and body parts flung about the stones, his eyes finally resting on Topher.

"Are you responsible for this?"

"What? No! We were defending them!"

"You call this a defense?" He pulled the Definite Knife out of Crews' jeans, grimacing at its gruesome appearance. "Disgusting." Something distracted him, and he looked over toward the tunnel where Brimstone and the other boys were hiding. "Sneaking off, are we, Phyro?"

Brimstone, who had been slinking toward Burleigh's front door, stopped in his tracks.

"No, sir."

"Cowering in the corner while others did your job for you?"

Brimstone's face reddened. He shot an evil glance at Topher.

"Why didn't you meet us at the appointed time?" Stoneman continued. "Did you forget? Or were you too busy trembling with the young boys?"

Brimstone found it difficult to control himself.

"I didn't forget. But those things got here before I could go."

"Likely excuse."

"That's not fair."

"Fair? Look around you, boy. Does any of this seem fair to you?"

"But Topher and his friends. They have weapons."

"At least they did something." He turned his attention back to the trio. "However unwanted." He weighted the Definite Knife in his hand, handed it back to Crews. Something in one of the dorm windows caught his eye, faces behind shades, watching.

"We'll continue this elsewhere," he said. "You men, clean up the bodies. Crews, bring them to my office. I'll be up shortly."

Gertrude peered out Stoneman's office window. Instructors and guards and other personnel stacked the corpses in the golf carts like cords of wood, used hoses and buckets to wash the blood off the stones. He grimaced and closed the shades.

"What do you think he'll do to us? He thinks we killed all those boys."

"No, he doesn't," Topher told him. "He was with Crews. Obviously he knows about the attacks."

"I don't think so," Gertrude said. "We'll be expelled."

He collapsed into one of the three plush chairs on the other side of Stoneman's desk. Topher was already in the middle chair, and Zorn sat next to him, trying to calm the chimera on his lap. This was his second time in Stoneman's office. The headmaster let them go the first time; maybe he'd do it again. Topher, however, entertained no illusions. He smelled treachery, and he said it aloud.

"You smell what?" Zorn asked, worrying about his feet.

"Perfidy and sedition."

"Are those even words?"

"Of course they are. Prepare to be blamed."

The door opened before Zorn could reply, and in strode Stoneman followed by Warren Crews and Mr. Floyd. The headmaster threw three folders on his desk, took off his jacket and hung it up on the coat tree. Then he sat down, clearing his throat, and placed a pair of bifocals on his face. They quickly dropped to the end of his nose as he opened the first folder. Topher suppressed the urge to push them back up. Crews stood next to Mr. Floyd, who was standing next to Stoneman's desk. A clock ticked.

Without looking up, Stoneman said, "Do you three know what I'm reading?"

Gertrude shook his head. Topher and Zorn exchanged a wary glance. The headmaster finally looked at them, his eyebrows raised, affording them an expression that was at once condescending, incredulous, and authoritative. Gertrude continued to shake his head, albeit with more vigor now that the headmaster was staring at him that way. Stoneman smiled, but it did little to calm him down. He looked like he was about to eat them.

"This is a description of the acts that brought you to Raleigh's in the first place. Care for me to read it aloud?"

Topher's smug expression fell. He sat forward a little in his seat.

"No."

Stoneman turned his eyes upon him.

"Such a naughty boy, aren't you Christopher?"

"I prefer Topher."

"I know."

His steely gaze fell upon Zorn, who wilted.

"And you go by Zorn." He chuckled. "I still think it's such an odd name. Why don't you use Michael?"

Zorn sat up, affronted.

"Zorn is a family name," he said. "It means 'maelstrom' in Turkish."

"I see. What's that in your lap? Is that a poppet?"

Zorn shifted uneasily. The chimera was asleep, but the snake refused to let go of his thumb. Was this a test?

"I never kept no poppets, not since I was a boy."

Stoneman sat back and looked at Mr. Floyd as if that were the most outlandish thing he'd ever heard.

"That's not a poppet, boy?"

Topher kicked Zorn in the ankle.

"Oh!" Zorn said. "Why, this is Gertrude's, er, Kenneth's."

Stoneman leaned forward.

"Would you please give it to me?"

"Why? Is there a rule about poppets now?"

The headmaster smiled, but there was no joy in it. He returned his attention to Topher.

"Mr. Bill. Topher. Crews informs me that the weapons you boys were using in the courtyard are yours. Is that correct?" Topher glared at Crews, who stared pointedly at a spot on the carpet. "No doubt you are aware of the punishment for possession of a weapon? Particularly weapons as deadly as these."

He revealed the Definite Knife. It had been cleaned. Not a drop of blood stained it. He let it clatter to his desk. Then he removed the painted stick and twirled it in the air. Zorn winced and shied away every time it pointed at him, but Mr. Floyd's eyes settled on it and widened just a little.

"I know that there probably is a punishment," Topher said. "But you know why we were using them."

Stoneman nodded slowly. He sighed and leaned back in his chair, tossing the painted stick on his desk. It rolled up against the Definite Knife. Mr. Floyd watched it, a cat tracing an insect.

"Indeed. This is such an interesting place. I've seen things here that boggle the mind. Boys, you've put me in a very difficult position. This is your second visit to my office. You're already in enough trouble as it is being at Raleigh's in the first place." He leaned forward suddenly and picked up a worn copy of the Raleigh's Code of Conduct, expertly opening it to page two. He pointed to a passage in the middle. "According to our covenants, 'No student shall be allowed to possess any contraband, contraband being defined as weapons of any kind, tobacco products, posters, books not on the approved list, and unsanctioned electronics. The punishment for which—"

"Is expulsion, we know," Topher said.

Stoneman paused.

"No. Nobody is expelled from Raleigh's. Surely you know this."

Zorn could no longer contain himself.

"This is a great miscarriage of justice! We were in the middle of a baOUCH!"

Stoneman was not accustomed to being yelled at by a ward, let alone in such a strange manner. His eyes widened. "Are you all right, boy?"

Zorn held his lips tightly to suppress the pain.

"Fine," he said through gritted teeth. "I only meant to explain what really wasOUCH!"

Stoneman pinched the bridge of his nose.

"Boys, I truly do not have time for this nonsense."

"But, sir, there were mOUCH! Stop pinching me, Topher!"

Stoneman leaned back in his chair, which creaked. He rocked a little, making a pyramid with his fingertips.

"All of you, please listen. Kenneth's parents paid a lot of money to send you here, and here is where you will stay. Do you understand? This is my job. To keep you here. Yet you broke not just a minor rule, but one of the most important rules we have."

Gertrude felt all of his energy leave his body. Topher merely frowned. Stoneman wasn't lowering the hammer yet on purpose. He liked to watch them squirm. He wanted them to suffer.

"I understand that there is a rather unfortunate situation here at Raleigh's Prep, but there are proper ways of handling it, proper avenues and steps that we can take to eradicate the problem. Avenues and steps that I am currently exploring. But you must know that I cannot have vigilantes running loose in this school, *particularly* this school, and I cannot have you wielding weapons and destroying property no matter what the reason." He stared at them. "Do you understand what I am telling you?"

They nodded, stunned.

Stoneman was satisfied. "Good. Unfortunately, you still need to be punished. Mr. Floyd?" The grounds keeper limped forward and waited for his orders. "You know what to do."

Mr. Floyd nodded curtly. He clasped a hand on Zorn and Gertrude's shoulders, his eyes still fixed on the stick, and then Crews sprang to life.

"Please, sir, let me," he nearly shouted.

Mr. Floyd's eyes narrowed.

"Warren Crews," he grumbled.

Crews shot him a panicked look, then forced his eyes back to Mr. Stoneman.

"Please, sir. I'll do it. Let me."

Stoneman seemed to think for a minute before answering.

"No. Since Brimstone is unable to do anything I ask him to do, I need you here. We have some more work to finish."

"Please, sir. It won't take very long. I'll just—"

"You heard the man, boy," Mr. Floyd growled.

"Yes, Warren," Stoneman said. "You're needed here. It's what you wanted, remember?"

Crews' body slumped. He nodded glumly and retreated to his spot against the wall.

Stoneman motioned to Mr. Floyd with his hand, dismissing him.

"Please, Otis."

The first thing Zorn heard as he came around was the sound of wind rushing through the trees, the creak of branches as they rubbed together. His back, buttocks, and legs were freezing, and his head was pounding. He'd been blindfolded, his arms and legs bound. He shifted on the ground where he lay.

"Topher? Gertrude? Hello?"

Someone groaned to the right.

"Topher? Gertrude?"

"My head," a voice said.

"Topher?"

"What?"

"Thank God. We're in the woods. Somebody tied us up and left us out here."

"Who?"

Zorn struggled to think for a moment.

"I don't know. What's the last thing you remember?"

Silence.

"I remember leaving Mr. Stoneman's office. Then I woke up here."

"Me, too."

"Hello?" Gertrude called. "Anyone?"

"Gertrude! You're awake!"

"What's happened?"

"I think this is our punishment."

The boys were quiet, letting the reality settle in.

"This is all Warren Crews' fault," Zorn said. "If I ever get my hands around his neck, I'll squeeze until my palms meet."

"Several offensive tortures for him have popped into my mind as well," Topher replied. "One of which requires a blow torch and a pair of needle nose pliers." He sniffed the air. "Boys, I must apologize. I fear it was my bravado that landed us here."

"At least you're honest," Zorn said, grimacing. The chimera was still attached to his thumb, asleep. "I still have the chimera."

Topher struggled to his feet.

"Perhaps you can get it to—"

"Shh!"

"What?"

"I heard a twig crack."

"From where?"

"Over there."

Topher hopped five feet to the right.

"Over here?"

"I don't know where you are. The noise came from behind me."

"Where are you?"

"Over here."

"Where?"

"Here!"

"Something just brushed my face!"

"Shut up and listen!"

The trio paused for what seemed like ages. And then, right behind them, came the clear crack of a branch being snapped in two, most likely by the crusty claw of some enormous nightmare. Gertrude uttered a strangled cry and hopped directly into Topher and their heads knocked and their teeth rattled.

"Damn you, Zorn!"

"It's Gertrude."

"Damn you, too!"

"Topher?" another voice called. "Zorn? Gertrude?"

"Who is that?"

Crashing sounds through the brush, combined with cries of "Over here!" Topher stumbled around, nose in the air, seeking the source of the noises.

"Found them!"

His blindfold was ripped off, and standing before him was the comfortably mammoth figure of Marvin Grimm. Behind him stood I, Dennis, hands on his hips, helmet clapped on his head, eyepiece firmly in place.

"Targets acquired," he said.

He went around to each of them, using a knife that seemed to emerge from the cuff of his plastic outer shell to cut the bindings on their hands and feet.

"How did you know we were here?" Zorn asked.

Marvin Grimm pulled a note out of his pocket. It was crumbled up and greasy, covered with smears and salad dressing. He handed it to Topher, shrugging apologetically.

"I had a buffalo chicken wrap for lunch."

Topher unfolded the note and read.

"Topher, Zorn, and Gertrude are in the forest. Save them, or they die."

I, Dennis cut the plastic zip ties around Gertrude's feet.

"It was shoved under our door." He stood up and the blade slipped back into his shell. "When I went out to see who'd done it, the hall was empty."

"Who could have known about this?" Zorn wondered aloud.

"Mr. Floyd, obviously," Topher replied. He balled up the note and put it in his pocket. "He knew Stoneman meant to have us killed, but couldn't do anything about it himself."

"Why not? He never had any problem before."

"Maybe Stoneman was watching him."

"I still don't think . . . shh!"

They all fell completely silent, adopting a semi-crouch, ready for anything, but all they could hear was sound of the wind in the trees. The saplings were thick, and Topher couldn't tell the difference between ten feet and twenty feet in front of him. His eyes focused and unfocused, giving him a headache, so he stared at the ground to regain his bearings.

Gertrude grew increasingly nervous and agitated. Finally he cried out, "Who's there? Who is it?"

"Gertrude!" Zorn hissed, but it was too late.

In the distance they heard the unmistakable sound of feet pushing through the leaves, heading directly for them. Shadows and dark figures shot through the brush with red, menacing eyes, floating as if bodiless. The chimera woke and wiggled anxiously on Zorn's thumb, and he put it up on his shoulder. The lion bristled and growled.

"What do we do?"

Topher stared around him.

"Which way did you two come?"

Marvin pointed toward the crashing forms in the woods.

The eyes loped toward them. One stopped, raised its snout to the sky, and sent out a gargling howl. A grey, lumpy form flew into the ring, aiming for Gertrude. He ducked, and the chimera leapt at the beast, attaching itself to its scraggly tail.

"This way!" Topher cried. He crashed into the brush, running blindly. The others followed: Marvin Grimm, I, Dennis, Gertrude, and Zorn. Zorn held out his thumb as he left and whistled for the chimera, which bounded off the fallen werepyre and onto his extended digit.

"Ouch!" he cried.

Branches whipped their faces and hands. Blood from a welt just above Topher's eyebrow stung his eye. Behind them they heard the crashing of the monsters. A tall hill loomed ahead, and they hit it at full speed, scrambling up, using their hands when the hill got too steep. Topher reached the top first and turned, breathing heavily. Marvin climbed just below him, followed Gertrude, who'd passed I, Dennis. Zorn took up the rear, having just reached the bottom. He made it to the midway point, several beasts pounding behind. One nipped at his heel, tripping him up. He cried out, and the thing leapt into the air, claws protracted, jaws wide and drooling, descending, descending, aiming for his back, to kill, to sink fang into meat and bone, to slash and rend and rip and tear and shred, when suddenly the brown blur streaked by, cutting it in half. It fell on either side of Zorn, wearing an expression that lay somewhere between, "I'm going to squeeze your heart into pulp!" and "What the hell was that?"

Topher's mouth dropped open.

"What was that?" Marvin Grimm asked.

The blur cut three more creatures in half as they watched.

"Help!" Zorn cried, snapping his friend's attention away from the blur.

Another werepyre had clamped onto his boot, and snarling and huffing, steadily pulled him backwards. He kicked at it, fingers desperately clawing the earth. Topher looked around his feet for something to throw. Nothing but dead leaves, a few thick branches, some rocks, and a rotting, but still solid, sizable portion of a fallen tree trunk. He dug around and found a fist sized rock, which he hurled at the thing. It struck the beast dead between the eyes, but the monster held on.

"Find more rocks!" he yelled.

They threw whatever they could find, rocks, sticks, branches. The beast weathered the attack with occasional growls but didn't let go. Marvin picked up a fallen tree trunk and staggered forward, holding it over his head.

"Move," he grunted.

His arms shook, and his face was red. He took a deep breath.

Topher cried, "Duck, Zorn!"

Zorn saw the trunk and pushed his face into the dirt. The chimera roared and tried to leap at the werepyre, but Zorn caught it and dragged it to him. The werepyre, sensing victory, let go of his boot. It growled, pushed its face over Zorn's head, teeth bared, drool hanging from its jowls. Marvin Grimm heaved, the log flew, the monster struck forward, and the tree trunk smashed into it, sending it cart wheeling to the bottom of the hill. It lay there, dead or unconscious, and the boys let up a cheer. Then another beast snarled past its fallen brother, bounding up the hill.

Zorn shot a glance over his shoulder, saw the new creature, and threw himself off the ground just ahead of it. He reached the top, the monster a dozen feet behind. Marvin Grimm grabbed his outstretched hand, and the werepyre hurtled itself at them, and the three were sent tumbling down the other side, Marvin, then Zorn, then the beast, end over end over end, tumbling in a mass of teeth and fur and limbs, and Zorn's head hit a rock and the monster squealed and Marvin's fist smashed into something soft and they slammed into ground and rolled into a pile of wet leaves and the n the ground opened up and swallowed them whole.

Zorn never did like it when people smacked when they ate. His father did it all the time, and it drove him crazy. It was even worse when smacking sounds were made by a chimaera feasting on the face of misshapen monster. He tried to shush it but was afraid the lion might roar or the goat baa.

They had fallen into a tunnel. It was about five and a half feet tall, maybe six feet wide. But it most certainly was a tunnel. The beast had broken its neck in the fall, but he and Marvin were okay. Once they saw what happened, they called to their friends. Now Marvin and Topher were holding sections of cracked and molding plywood over their heads, covering the hole; Marvin a solid statue, Topher red-faced and shaking. More beasts shuffled above, growling and snorting and snuffling, searching for their prey.

A solitary howl rang out, followed by the sound of paws tramping away in the leaves. Topher and Marvin held the plywood up for another few minutes before Topher finally gasped and dropped his end, dumping leaves and dirt all over him. He lay there, not caring, rubbing his shoulders.

A light glowed farther down the tunnel.

"Hey, fellows," I, Dennis said. "This way."

They hunched forward in the semi-dark. The tunnel was cold and dank. The dirt shifted, sending clumps into their hair, and roots scraped their skulls, and rocks tripped them up. After what seemed like twenty minutes of this, right when Zorn's legs were screaming with the effort of squat-walking, I, Dennis said, "Gosh!"

He backed to the side, keeping the light in front of him so they could see. There, at the end of the tunnel, was a door. He tried the handle.

"It's locked."

Marvin Grimm pushed past.

"Let me try."

He grabbed the knob and twisted. Metal cracked, the lock gave, and the door jerked in and they all pressed forward. They ran down a short passage and into an open space.

Chairs, couches, a fireplace.

Gertrude gasped.

"We're in the secret room."

They spread out on the couches while Zorn started the fire. His magic book fell out of his inside pocket once, nearly landing in the flames, so he placed it on the coffee table for safety. Gertrude returned from their room with the maps, which he spread out over the book.

"Here," he said, pointing at one of the six pointed stars in the forest. "This is where the tunnel lets out. This is where we were."

Topher agreed with a grunt.

"That must mean the other tunnels are attached to the other dorms," he said.

Zorn poked at the logs and blew on the flames.

"Maybe. Or maybe they were attached to this tunnel, and now they're collapsed."

"Or we just didn't see it. It was rather dark in there." Topher sighed and leaned back, exhausted. "It's all possible, I suppose."

The fire roared to life, casting a warm, orange-yellow glow over the room. It popped and hissed. He held up his hands to it, enjoying the heat.

"If Crews wanted us dead, why do it that way? Sitting us out there to wait for those things to come and eat us. It's like a bad James Bond movie.

Why not just shoot us, or stab us, or poison us?"

Gertrude shuddered.

"Who's James Bond?" I, Dennis asked.

Topher stared at the tapestries. He wanted to get up and inspect them again, but he didn't know what he was looking for.

"Mr. Floyd said he and his friends fought the beasts."

"What happened to them?" Zorn asked.

Topher glanced at him, then fixed his eyes on his hands. He mumbled something.

"What was that?"

"He said they're all dead."

The room grew very still.

Gertrude clapped his hands together.

"Well then it's settled."

"What's settled?"

"What we're going to do." He stared around at all of them as if the answer were obvious. "We run. We escape." Topher shook his head, Zorn hung his, and Marvin and I, Dennis continued to stare at the fire. "You really just want to stay here?"

"Nobody wants to stay here, Gertrude," Topher said.

"We can't fight forever. They'll get us. One by one. It'll be terrible." He folded his hands in his lap. "I know that we're supposed to die here. I know that, but I don't accept it. I can't. I want to live."

"It's not that we don't agree with you, Gertrude. But just how do you propose to do it?"

Gertrude paused. He knew he had to escape, but how to do it hadn't really occurred to him yet.

Topher said, "The gates are staffed twenty four hours a day."

"I know."

"And the only other way out is through the woods."

"I know."

He sat down, defeated and afraid, rested his elbows on his knees and clasped his hands.

"Occam's razor," I, Dennis said.

Topher made a face.

"What?"

"Occam's razor. The best solution is usually the simplest."

"Oh, shut up, Dennis. Hickam's dictum."

"Mr. Floyd told us to just put our heads down, go to class, and not get involved," Zorn said. "Maybe that's exactly what we should do."

Topher threw up his hands.

"Sure. Just push your nose in the air the next time the bloodthirsty death hounds attack. Whistle your favorite tune, that'll keep them from tearing out your throat." His sarcasm collapsed. "What else is there to do, then? If we can't escape, we fight."

"But Gertrude's right. We'll die."

"We're going to die anyway. I'd rather die fighting!"

Zorn rolled his eyes.

"Here we go again."

"What? You'll die lying down on the ground, like a coward?"

Zorn jabbed his finger at his friend.

"Don't you go lecturing me on cowardliness. It was your cowardly plan that landed us in here in the first place."

"How dare you!"

"If you had only the courage to stand up to your father—"

"I can't believe what I'm hearing. If only *I* had the courage? As I recall, Zorn, you didn't necessarily protest. I didn't drag you along behind me. You were the one who volunteered to buy the gas, and the matches, and the rags."

"How was I supposed to know you'd take it that far! I thought we'd just do his car. You were the one who firebombed th—"

Gertrude leaped to his feet.

"Shut up!"

Topher and Zorn stared at him, eyes wide, fingers still pointed at one another.

"Both of you! Shut up! We agreed about this already. We did it. All of us. That's why we're here."

Zorn, still angry, clamped his jaw shut and leaned back into the couch cushions, folding his arms and doing anything possible not to look at Topher, who pretty much did the same.

Gertrude yawned, deep and long.

"We have school in the morning, and I'm tired, and I'm going to bed."

Topher stared at him incredulously as he headed for the exit.

"How can you possibly think about sleep right now?"

Gertrude paused by the door, thinking. They all looked at him, waiting for some kind of answer, some kind of wisdom. Finally he turned and said, "What else can we do?"

BETRAYAL

Brimstone stormed out of his room, leaving Burr alone to cry at his desk. He stomped outside, through the courtyard, and threw himself down on the bench outside The Grotto. When he was little, before his father left, before his mother's boyfriend moved in, before all of the trouble that landed him here, he'd learned that the key to mastering his anger was in exercise. He ran, he lifted weights, he played sports. And if he wasn't able to do any of those things, if he were in a place where none of them were an immediate option, he could tense his muscles and release, tense his muscles and release.

So that's what he did.

He sat on the bench and flexed his fists and rocked a little, back and forth, back and forth. Next his biceps, his quadriceps, his pectorals. It worked just as it always had. Slowly his anger disappeared. He took a deep breath, able to think clearly again. Forget Burr. Forget what just happened. Unimportant now. Unimportant. What he really wanted to focus on what he'd come to think of as The Topher Situation.

His dog, his bitch, had gotten out of control. He needed to be punished. The fight in their room was bad enough, and he did not relish being made to look the fool in front of Stoneman. Now the bitch's friend, that greasy little shit, had taken his place as Stoneman's favorite. He'd loved being the favorite, loved the attention, the approval. It had never happened before, not at school, not at home. All he ever was, all he'd ever been, was The Loser. Someone made a bomb threat? Blame The Loser. Someone started a fight? Blame The Loser. Who left the gate open? The Loser. Who clogged the toilet? The Loser. Well, The Loser showed them, didn't he? He showed them all. Mother's boyfriend in his bed while he slept. His principal and math teacher and all those other bastards in the commons.

He didn't want to come here. He wanted to die. But they got to him before he could do it himself, sitting in the dugout on the baseball field, and again in his cell after they booked him. But then when he got here, he found a place, and the headmaster liked him, needed him. He felt something he'd never felt before, like he belonged. Being the favorite made him feel more in control, more in control than ever in his life. He had access to Stoneman's office, to secrets, to other avenues of power, and that was all gone now and he couldn't, no, he wouldn't allow that to be just taken away from him. Not by anybody, and definitely not by some fancy dressing faggot and his gay ass, fur-wearing butt-buddies. And embarrassing him in the tunnel? Having the nerve to insult him?

He flexed and rocked, flexed and rocked, shaking his head every now and then. The calm gradually returned, slowed his pulse, spread up from his spine and enveloped his brain like a warm blanket, quelling the dark thoughts, ensconcing him, zeroing his focus, leveling his energy, and he was finally able to think of what to do next and who to do it to and how to do it to them and how to make it hurt. Things he was good at, was always good at, something nobody UNDERSTOOD and so he had to show them . . .

Flex.

Focus.

Flex.

Focus.

Okay.

Who did he have to worry about? Marvin and I, Dennis he discounted immediately. Insignificant toads. The Gertrude fairy was easy enough to deal with. Fag jumped at the sight of squirrels. Zorn was a little more difficult, but he was stupid (they all were stupid), and maybe he could use Burr to distract him. It wasn't like they all traveled around together constantly.

He'd like to tear the little bitch a new hole, but that'd leave marks on his fists, and the little bitch might fight back. Any kind of sign that he'd been in a physical alteration and he'd be kicked out of the Assistants for good. Stoneman definitely wouldn't look the other way, considering that there was a new—

"Worried about something?"

Brimstone looked up and saw Mr. Floyd, the gay grounds keeper, standing in front of him. He had some kind of welt rising up on his hand, like something had bit him.

"What do you want?"

Mr. Floyd chuckled to himself. Then he limped over to the bench and sat down.

"You put your homo hands on me, old man, and I'll kill you."

The grounds keeper seemed to ignore him, just rubbed his thigh, grimacing. Brimstone winced with disgust.

"Trying to get excited?"

He didn't even see the hand reach out and grab him by the throat. The old man's face was suddenly centimeters from his. He could smell his sour breath: cigars and alcohol.

"You say something like that to me again, boy, and I'll rip your friggin' eyes out."

Brimstone's voice was charcoal in a chute.

"I'll. Kill. You."

Mr. Floyd slapped him across the face. The boy struggled and kicked, but the old man pressed his thumb into his Adam's apple.

"You stop, and I'll stop. You don't, and I won't."

Brimstone paused, thinking about fighting back. How long would he be able to do anything with Mr. Floyd's thumb in his throat? Could he at least land one blow? Then, as if reading his mind, Mr. Floyd pressed down even harder, and he went limp, and Mr. Floyd waited, waited, and finally relaxed his hand, but still kept it in place.

"My parents—"

"Your parents don't give a rat's ass about you, boy. If they did, they'd have bribed enough people to set you free in the first place, not send you here, with people like me." He put his face close again. "If it were up to me, I'd put you all out in the woods first night you get here. Let you play around with what's out there, have some fun. See who comes out walking on their own two feet and who comes out in my shovel."

He threw Brimstone's head away from him with a disgusted grunt, and the boy keeled over the bench arm, coughing and gagging and retching.

When he was able to speak, he wiped the tears from his cheeks and said, "Get away from me."

He could still feel the bastard's thumbs on his throat, and it made him want to gag even more. Mr. Floyd withdrew a flask from his jacket, unscrewed the cap, took a pull.

"Can't do that. I need you to do something for me."

"Why would I do anything for you?"

Mr. Floyd offered him the flask but Brimstone knocked it away. The old man shrugged and took another pull.

"I think you'll like this job," he said. Another pull, and he re-screwed the cap, slipped the flask in his pocket. "You know, when I was your age, there was a few guys in school who acted different from everybody else."

"Oh God."

"Shut up. When I was your age, there was a few guys in school who acted different from everybody else, I said. Problem was, they didn't know they was different, and they didn't seem to care. Talked queer. Had queer voices. Looked queer. Did queer things. Had queer names. They should have been shaking in their shoes at the sight of me, but instead they had the nerve to talk back, and they was always making me feel stupid."

Brimstone grew silent. The hate in his eyes had dimmed a little, replaced by a cold, emptiness that was somehow more frightening.

"I see you know what I'm talking about now, don't you?" When Brimstone didn't answer or nod, he punched him in the arm and said, "Don't you?"

"Ow! Yes! I know what you're talking about."

"Good. You know what I did?"

"No."

"I didn't let them get away with it, that's what I did. I let them have theirs, but it didn't work, see? If I insulted them, they just gave it back ten times worse. If I beat them up, they just fought back. And then one day I realized the reason they kept giving it back was because they weren't afraid of me. So I decided to make them afraid."

Brimstone stopped rubbing his shoulder.

"What did you do?"

Mr. Floyd suddenly laughed his wheezing laugh and shook his head.

"Oh no. Not until we make a deal. You see, I'll let you know what I did, but you gotta promise me something first."

Brimstone thought for a minute. What'd the old guy want him to do? Something sick and perverted? Well, he'd just agree and then not do it.

"Okay. What?"

"If I tell you how I made them afraid, you gotta promise to follow through. All the way. Until it's done."

That was much easier than Brimstone thought.

"Okay. Sure, whatever, you old freak."

Mr. Floyd nodded and adjusted himself on the bench. His bad leg stuck straight out, and he looked like he was digging around in the back of his pants for something.

Brimstone held up his hands.

"Wait a minute, whoa, whoa."

Then the old man brought out the most beautiful thing he'd seen in a long time. Held it out in front of him. Twirled it in the air. A knife. The blade was long, and sharp, with serrated edges. The handle looked like it was made out of curved bone, like the jawbone of some disgusting animal. The grounds keeper put the sheath over the blade, and when the ends came together it formed an ugly, wide mouth with huge white teeth.

"This give you any ideas?"

Zorn stored the chimera in the secret room so he could move about freely without drawing attention to himself. It worked out relatively well. The chimera, contrary to what he'd initially believed, didn't show very much interest in destroying the room, though it did use one of the chests as a litter box. Most of the time it found a comfortable spot curled up on one of the chairs and slept, though it did like to perch on the door frame and attack people when they came in. He fed it with scraps from The Grotto, usually beef and chicken, though he did trap the occasional wild mouse for the snake, and the goat head seemed to enjoy lettuce and handfuls of grass.

Winter snuck up on them. One week it was fifty five and sunny, the next it was twenty five and overcast. Then the sky darkened and a Nor' Easter pummeled the mountain for three days straight. When it was over, the entire campus, the surrounding woods, the athletic fields, Lake Perish, everything was covered in a thick mantel of pure white. Gertrude imagined the blood on the cobblestones being soaked up by the snow, cleansing the school of sin.

An uneasy peace settled over the dorms. There was no joyousness at the impending winter; no sudden burst of snowball fights to ease the tension of studying for exams. Instead, the grounds remained devoid of life. Even during the day, students choose to use the bridges and overpasses that connected each dorm and each academic building rather than traverse the open spaces. Another attack had not, as Topher anticipated, occurred.

"As well it should not," he bragged during lunch. "We dealt their numbers a severe blow. They're most likely mustering forces for a far deadlier attack at the end of *this* month."

I, Dennis forked a sausage into his mouth.

"What are you talking about?"

He'd taken his helmet off and put it on the table next to him, exposing his puckered and scarred scalp, and Topher couldn't look at him.

"I forgot. Poindexter has been in the basement since he rescued us."

"How goes the physics project, I, Dennis?" Zorn asked. He elbowed Gertrude. "I, Dennis is making rocket boots."

"Rocket boots? Is that safe?"

I, Dennis scratched his scalp.

"I've got some power and trajectory problems to work out in the heels, but I think they should be taken care of soon. I'm going to try and upgrade the leather to something less flammable."

"How are you getting the equipment for this?" Topher asked. "Who's your source?"

"I don't have a source. Nobody can get anything in here that isn't searched by the guards."

"So what do you use?"

I, Dennis ignored him, focusing instead on his breakfast.

"How about you guys? What are you building?"

"Oh," Zorn replied. "Well."

"Uh-huh. Haven't started yet, have you?"

"On the contrary. Our project is complete. We just have some bugs to work out."

Zorn collapsed on his bed.

"We haven't even begun to think about our crossbow!"

"Calm down, Zorn," Topher said. "You'd be done by now if you listened to me the first time."

"How can I calm down? The project is due in a week, and I, Dennis already finished a rocket fueled boots."

"Are you required to use just bow and arrow?"

Gertrude glanced at Zorn, nervous.

"Well, it doesn't say so in the assignment." He had no idea where this might lead, but the last time Topher became involved in his schoolwork, he ended up writing and producing a mimed version of the balcony scene from *Romeo and Juliet*. The humiliation of miming had been bad enough, but the D minus (the minus for 'effort') stung worse than a thousand jeers.

Topher pressed on.

"Are you limited in your budget? Restricted to certain materials?"

"Not necessarily."

"Uh huh, uh huh."

Topher went to his desk and sat down. He leaned back in his chair. He crossed his legs. He folded his hands gently in his lap. "Gertrude? Can I ask you a question?"

"I think so?"

"Are you a pussy?"

"What!"

"A pussy. A weak male human. A fag, a neeerd, a geek, a drip, a bore, a dork, a wad, a dorkwad, piss-ant, pip-squeak, sand in the face, throws like a girl, dipshit." He leaned forward. "Pussy."

Gertrude was too shocked to respond.

Topher sat back. His chair creaked.

"Because faced with unlimited options and funds and the assignment to create a projectile firing device, only a pussy would choose bow and arrow over, oh, let's say, a monster death-missile!"

As if to punctuate his point, he put both feet on the floor, pushed off and leaned all the way back in his chair, placing his hands behind his head. At that point the trap Gertrude set was sprung. The trigger holding Sally to the wall clicked, and the ketchup covered mannequin, held together by wire and duct tape, swung straight at him.

"Good Lord!" he screamed, and tumbled off his chair just as she swooped overhead.

The mannequin swung back, hit the wall with her feet, and remained still, her mouth open in silent, accusatory ridicule. Zorn laughed until he fell off his bunk bed. Gertrude stood up and clapped. Topher eyed him from the floor.

"Your work?"

Gertrude continued to clap.

"A good prank." Topher grunted and got to his feet. He pointed at her middle. "Is this barbed wire?"

"Zorn nearly killed me when I was dusting her. She had to be mended."

"Where did you get it?"

"The basement."

Topher shook his head.

"This is the most negligent detention center ever. It's almost like they're just leaving this stuff out so we can hurt ourselves."

"Okay," Zorn said, regaining his bed. "Levity achieved. I think I'm ready to hear what you have in mind for our project." He fingered his poster.

"I'd definitely exploit the professor's lack of guidelines."

"I don't know if that's such a good idea."

"Oh, come on! Where's your sense of competition? Better still, where's your sense of roommate spirit? If anything, you should beat I, Dennis simply for the sake of not embarrassing me."

"There are a few restrictions," Gertrude lied. "Nothing made of metal, for one. Nothing that uses gas. Nothing that can explode."

"Very well. Have you any designs yet?"

"I drew this at lunch."

He removed a wadded up napkin from somewhere within his fur and threw it at Topher, who let it land on his desk before picking it up by pinching a corner between his thumb and forefinger. He flicked the napkin over, removed an antenna from his drawer, and picked it apart like a surgeon opening an alien.

"This is it? Ha!"

"What's wrong with it?"

"From the minds of babes." Topher swiped the offensive wad from his desk. Nobody noticed when it disappeared seconds later, deposited neatly in his metal trash bin, which had been scrubbed clean. "I have plans in my possession that will both satisfy my need for hyperbole *and* earn you an A."

He then withdrew from his bottom drawer a rolled up blueprint, not even the least bit cognizant that the stack of blueprints he kept there, blueprints of various machines he'd designed (including the failed hornet shot), had been categorized according to predicted use (killing, maiming, productivity), method (for killing and maiming: evisceration, explosion, or entropy; for productivity: word processing, multi-media, and accounting), and then alphabetized. Even if he had noticed, he would have attributed the feat to himself. Perhaps he had done it in his sleep. He was a genius!

"Here's what I had in mind," he said, unrolling the print and smoothing it out over his clean desk.

Upon it was a diagram of a massive, wooden crossbow, approximately the size of two small houses. The bolt was leviathan, capable of skewering a Kraken like a hot marshmallow.

"We'll have to scale it back a bit."

Gertrude appeared nauseous at the thought of building a machine of such mass destruction, but Zorn started to bounce on his bed.

"We're in," he said.

Contrary to Topher's plans, which called for pressure-treated lumber, and, if not newly pressed, at least somewhat straight screws and nails, Zorn and Gertrude were forced to scavenge whatever they could from various basements on campus. They were surprised at the number of weapons they found. Knives. Shivs. Slingshots. A few homemade arrows. Without a working forge, they couldn't melt them down, so they hid whatever they found in the secret room. The most useful items they came across were broken wooden desks, and the discarded metal bed frames and bedsprings. At one point they found a fully functional pool table, and an argument ensued over whether or not they should repurpose it. Gertrude opposed its use from a moral standpoint; he simply couldn't abide the employ of a working engine of gambling for an academic pursuit.

"The ivory tower is assailed enough by the powers of ignorance and religion. Using an agent of avarice will only provide for them fodder for further attacks. You know I'm right, Zorn."

"Oh please, Gertrude. Not again."

"I'll not sully my hands, or my mind, by touching such a filthy thing."

"Ridiculous!" Zorn cried, and he thumped the surface with his fist to emphasize his point. It collapsed.

Gertrude clapped and beamed. "Now we can use it."

They also used whatever they could find in Chainwrought, so long as they looked during the day. Most of the trees were too petrified with cold to be cut down. Not even a limb would snap. However, Gertrude found a massive trunk of a recently fallen tree under the snow where they had buried the ingredients for the Homunculus a few weeks before. It did occur to him to check on their golem, but he remembered Zorn's warning and he didn't want to wake a half-baked midget fetus from its incubatory sleep.

Tools were a greater problem. There were no hammers, screwdrivers, crowbars, band saws, or jigsaws to be found. They considered breaking into Mr. Floyd's room but immediately thought better of it. So they used rocks from the creek to hammer the nails they scavenged from the broken furniture, and their various knives and blades to screw the semi-straightened screws.

They constructed the crossbow out on the playing field, close to where they found the mangled body months before. If students were being eaten there without anybody noticing, Zorn reasoned, they could build a siege engine without any problems. Gertrude was just happy that they didn't have to haul all of the materials back to the dorm. They spent a whole Saturday laboring under the winter sun. It was cold, and they slogged valiantly in the snow, hammering and screwing, breaking frames over their knees, and hammering some more.

If anything, Zorn learned this: the construction of siege weapons was not something to be attempted by amateurs. The integrity of the stock, for one, was a concern, not to mention the trigger device, neither of which Zorn or Gertrude felt was of any importance. Nothing was balanced, or particularly well affixed, or designed correctly, or properly measured, and Zorn had a habit of replacing the number three with the letter E, which understandably threw off the calculations. A confused Gertrude chose the number eight to replace Zorn's dyslexic three, for it was a logical collusion of the E and the 3, as well as his lucky number.

"My eighth year was one of pure joy," he informed Zorn as they worked. "I won an overstuffed lion at the traveling carnival, earned five hundred reading points, and ate lunch with the principal."

Zorn stopped what he was doing.

"Why are you telling me this?"

"Because you're using the letter *E* for an eight."

"No I'm not."

Gertrude showed him one of the measurements.

"That's Euler's number," Zorn said.

"Who on Earth uses Euler's number in carpentry?"

"I do."

By the end of the day they'd managed to create exactly what one would expect from an assortment of broken bed frames, one shattered amusement device, and a tree trunk, which is to say an assortment of broken bed frames, a shattered amusement device, and a tree trunk shaped vaguely like a crossbow.

"This is an amazing feat of engineering," Zorn said. He patted it and something shifted and it listed to the right.

Gertrude covered his mouth with his hands.

"Don't touch it anymore!"

It fell over anyway, and they left it there, on the verge of total collapse, disheartened and exhausted.

Gertrude returned alone at six the next morning. He'd been thinking about their project all night and woke early with an idea of how to fix the bow. He wanted to work on it before Zorn arrived. Clouds, dark and full, had settled in overnight. They looked about ready to burst. The air was crisp and cold, but not icy yet, just the right weather for another storm. The paths and fields were still unplowed, and he had to push through the snow, taking pleasure in the exercise and the plumes of fog that he breathed with each step. Ah, how Emerson would have loved this! He reached the practice field, trudged another twenty yards, and stopped in his tracks. The crossbow was still sitting there, but in place of the piece of junk they built the day before there stood a fully functional engine of destruction, perfectly measured, balanced, sanded, stained, and varnished.

He approached it carefully, wary, afraid. Who had? How had? A cold breeze blew, rattling the blueprints that had been left neatly folded on the stock. The creases from where Zorn had balled them up in frustration were smoothed and flattened. Gertrude pushed through the remaining distance and circled the crossbow slowly. The detail was undeniably, astoundingly intricate. Topher had included in his plans unnecessary decorations that were to be burned into the wood: Celtic knots and runes, ankhs, calligraphy, and a hodgepodge of other cultural symbols, some contradictory in meaning, many canceling one another out. He and Zorn had long ago decided not to include them, but there they were now, branded as if by an expert. The bow was sleek, and looked to have been made from the silken strands of millions of worms. The bolt was amazing, a solid, steel shaft with real feathers. The head gleamed, sharp and deadly. He examined the trigger mechanism; it was set on a hair.

The leaves in the bushes to his left rustled.

"Hey!" he cried. "Who's there?"

The rustling stopped for a moment, then whatever it was skittered along the row. Gertrude's curiosity overwhelmed him. He lurched along with it, catching up to the runner with eight, long strides. The creature in the brush stopped in its tracks, and though Gertrude did not see where it was, he knew generally where it might be. For a moment he faltered and stood erect. Would Mr. Floyd come barreling over the horizon like he had the morning they found the dead boy?

He swung his head around. Nobody. Not a soul. They were allowed to sleep in on Sundays. No brutal rousing from the Assistants. Most likely they were just rising, or shuffling in pairs and groups to The Grotto for hot oatmeal and toast. His belly growled. The thing in the bush made a minuscule noise, and Gertrude stooped, studied the leaves, and with a sudden decision thrust his hand inside. He grappled for a moment, yanked the thing out, and gasped.

He held in his hand a miniature replica of himself, had he chosen to dress in squirrel pelt, which he had not done since he was a boy. It kicked its legs furiously, trying to shake free. Before he could utter a word, however, a shout from the fields wrested his attention.

"Gertrude?"

Zorn.

The homunculus took advantage of his distraction and bit him. Gertrude cried out and dropped it, and it zipped away into the woods. Zorn emerged from the path and looked around.

"Over here!" Gertrude called.

Zorn turned and waved and hurried over, plowing through the snow. He stopped short when he saw the crossbow.

"Did you do this?"

"Um."

Zorn circled the weapon.

"It's phenomenal!"

"Thank you. I did it. I did it all by myself."

Zorn laughed.

"Shall we show Topher?"

When they returned, Brimstone and Burr were standing outside their room, holding the door open. Brimstone nudged his friend as they approached, and they both looked up and graced them with evil smiles. Zorn was about to ask what they thought they were doing when Stoneman's head peeked out from inside.

"Ah, Michael, Kenneth," he cooed. "So nice of you to join us. Do come in."

"We were just on our way to breakfast."

"Not anymore."

They entered their room, heads down. Topher stood next to his bed, stricken.

"Please, both of you take your place next to your bunk," Stoneman ordered. "Your presence here is a privilege. If you say anything else I shall have you removed."

Brimstone kicked over a trashcan and half-heartedly toed at the contents. He supposed the old man expected him to be happy that he'd asked him to come along on the raid, but he was wrong. He didn't give a rat's ass, and had it been any other room, he would have said no.

"Have you uncovered anything of worth in that wastebasket, Phyro?"

"Nah."

Stoneman gave him a look of disapproval, and the boy stammered, "I—I mean, no, sir. Nothing, sir. Nothing yet. Sir."

"Then look harder, boy."

Something caught the headmaster's attention: Sally, hanging in the corner behind him. He performed a double take and leaned away in disgust. His face threatened to turn red, but he mastered it, and soon he'd regained his pleasant countenance. "Sick," he hissed, pronouncing the final two consonants with a revolted click.

The two Assistants destroyed the place. They pulled out drawers and emptied them onto the floor. They threw all of their toiletries out of the bathroom, emptied the toothpaste and shampoo bottles into the sink. They pulled the sheets off the mattresses, folded them over, cleared out the wardrobes and chests, tore Sally down from the ceiling, ripped posters from the walls. They gathered all of the boys' books together and stacked them on Topher's desk.

"These are all the books we could find," Brimstone said.

Stoneman strode in front of them.

"Straighten the spines so they all face me."

Brimstone elbowed Burr, who did as he was told.

Stoneman kicked through the piles of clothes and other debris to get to Topher's desk, never deigning to remove his hands from behind his back. He leaned carefully over and inspected titles. He straightened.

"What are these, Phyro?"

"Books, sir."

"Textbooks, you idiot. I told you the book I'm looking for is a different kind of book!"

Zorn and Topher glanced at each other. Brimstone frowned, confused.

"Like, story books?"

"No! Not like story books." Stoneman's eyes fell on Zorn, boring holes into him. "You." He kicked through the clothes and ripped up posters, thrusting toward the rather large and hairy boy. "You were the one who had the painted stick, yes?"

Zorn shook his head. Stoneman breathed heavily out of his nose and tore open his jacket. "Don't lie to me, boy." He thrust his hands into the pockets, finding nothing but a few candy wrappers and stale crumbs from an old roll he'd smuggled out of the Grotto. He patted the boy's chest and legs, cursing and muttering under his breath, until he finally gave up, thoroughly aggravated.

"Take off your shirt!"

Zorn blanched.

"What?"

"Mr. Stoneman," Topher said. "I don't think that's absolutely nec—"

"Shut up! Take off your shirt, or I will rip it off your back."

Zorn stared at him for a moment in disbelief.

"Do it!"

He slowly peeled his shirt off, revealing nothing but his broad chest, which was hairier than expected, and his square torso, and his thick, muscular arms.

"Turn around."

Zorn did, staring straight ahead. When he made a full revolution, the old man swallowed a cry. He spun upon Brimstone and Burr, who had watched the proceedings with mingled horror and glee.

"You're sure you searched everywhere?"

The pair nodded slowly.

"There's nowhere else you can look?"

They shook their heads.

Stoneman stared at them a long time. Then he looked at Gertrude's wardrobe.

"Is this it? Is this the wardrobe you were talking about?"

Gertrude started to say something, but Topher shushed him.

Stoneman followed the exchange.

"It is, isn't it?" He ripped the doors open, stepped inside, and started pounding on the back. After a moment, he came back out and marched up to Zorn. "Open it!"

"Open what?"

Stoneman threw his finger at the wardrobe. "Open it!"

"It is open!"

"You know what I'm talking about! Now do it, damn you. Do it!"

"I don't know! I don't know!"

Stoneman stared at him again, chest heaving. His hair was mussed, and his eyes wide and red and angry. They broke from Zorn's face and wandered, and he seemed to see himself as they saw him. Very slowly, very calmly, he shut his mouth and stood up straight. He smoothed the graying hair on his head. Buttoned his suit.

"I know you have the book. I don't know how you got it, but you have it. I want that book. I need that book. And one way or another, I'll get it."

He pulled himself smartly away and marched toward the door.
"Brimstone, Burr."
The two Assistants startled and scrambled out.
Then they were gone.
The room was silent.
Zorn bent over and retrieved his shirt.
"Good God," he muttered. "Good God."

The boys hadn't enjoyed the secret room since they escaped Stoneman's first murder attempt. Certainly, Zorn used it to house the chimera, but his visits amounted to retrieving his pet, or feeding it, and he never spent more than a few minutes at a time. The maps were still spread out over the coffee table, and his book, his magic book, still sat beneath them. Safe.

Zorn whistled for the chimera when he entered and stuck out his thumb, and Gertrude started the fire. Soon they were sitting on the hearth, enjoying the warmth of the flames. He stroked the lion's mane, reflexively avoiding the snake's bites and batting the goat's head aside. He stared at the coffee table, thinking. Gertrude watched him, worried.

"Maybe we should just give it to him."

Topher strolled along the wall, studying the tapestries again.

"Nonsense," he said.

Zorn said nothing, just sat and stared, sat and stared.

"But look at what it's done to Zorn."

"I'm fine," Zorn said. "I'm just thinking."

"I can't make heads or tails of this," Topher grumbled, turning away from the wall. "Everybody but the unhealthy looking, pale-faced goon is dead. And he isn't even armed. Maybe the answer's in the book."

Zorn shook his head, but said nothing.

"No?" Topher asked. "You've read the whole thing?"

Zorn inhaled deeply and let it out in a fat burst, seeming to shake off the confrontation with Stoneman.

"No, I haven't. Just the introduction and a couple of spells. You know, the one for the mouse, and the big dragon thing, and the chimera, and the homunculus."

Topher threw himself down in the chair next to the fire.

"That's it? You have a magic book and all you do is read the instructions?"

"It's not like I've had a lot of time, exactly. If we're not running out into the woods to fight werepyres, or running into the courtyard to fight werepyres, we have class and homework. Besides, everything in there is instructions."

"Like how to make magical things?"

"Yes. Like a cookbook for magic. Only there's nothing in it about how the things are supposed to be used, or how to control them, or why anybody'd want to make anything like it in the first place."

"Still," Topher said. "It's a magic book. Stoneman's willing to ogle your chest for it, so it must be worth something."

Zorn pulled the book out from beneath the maps. He felt immediately better, if dizzy. After the rush passed, he thumbed through the pages.

"Hello Zorn," he read aloud. " . . . average rainfall in Portland, instructions for the painted stick . . . ." He read silently for a while, paged forward, read silently. "There's a lot of gibberish about animals in here. Drawings, et cetera. I think the author was into taxidermy."

Topher held out his hand.

"Give it to us."

"Hold on. What's a 'Cursine'?"

"It's a magic book. It would make sense if there were, you know, spells and curses in there."

"I don't think—"

"Just hand it over. Let me see."

Zorn shut the book and started to hand it to his friend. He had every intention of doing just that, putting it in Topher's outstretched palm and letting it go, but he couldn't.

"What is that? Are you having a stroke?"

Zorn willed his arm forward. It didn't move. He willed it again, and only his wrist rotated outward a bit, so that he sat there, arms resting on his lap, with the book barely extended out.

Topher sighed.

"You are what is commonly known as an imbecile."

He grabbed the book. Zorn still didn't let go. Topher thought he was kidding. He pulled. Zorn held on. He pulled again, twice. Zorn held on. Twice.

"Okaaay. Let it go."

"I'm trying."

"Let. It. Go."

A sorry, confused smile twitched at Zorn's lips. Topher startled and pointed in the air above his head. "My God, what is that!"

Zorn stood and spun, releasing the book, saying "What? What?"

Topher caught it and strutted away, chuckling. He tucked it under this arm.

Zorn sat down, neither upset nor amused. He felt a little better, honestly. While the book had given him a small thrill, a dizzying jolt, the longer he held onto it, the more ill he became, like a child who had eaten too much sugar. He breathed a deep sigh of relief and went back to petting the chimera. Topher ignored him. He found a seat away from his friend and paged through the book.

In the meantime, Gertrude pored over the maps, reorganizing them. At one point he left the room to retrieve a pencil and straight edge from his desk, then returned and started drawing lines on them with crisp, sharp movements. Zorn stoked the fire. The chimera fell asleep, and he put it down on the chair and rose to search through the chests. He found some of the books on blacksmithing, flipped through them, then settled on the old yearbook with all of the students who had been marked for death in it.

Topher strode over to the tapestry of Lord Burleigh. He pointed at something in the book, then gazed up at the tapestry, flipped through some pages, repeated the motion.

"I think I understand."

Zorn looked up from the yearbook.

"What do you understand?"

Topher paced back and forth.

"Sword, dead, arrow, dead, mace dead."

"What does that mean?"

Topher turned around.

"Each knight that's dead is armed in these tapestries."

"So?"

"Except this one." He ran over and pointed at Lord Burleigh. "He's not armed. He has a book, and a stick, and there are huge shadows in the trees."

"Topher, you're not being very clear."

"He has a book. And a stick."

Zorn suddenly understood. He pulled the stick out from under the maps.

Gertrude finally looked up. Topher scurried excitedly back to his seat, the magic book open in his palm.

"It's all in the way it's organized. Look, Zorn, what was the first thing that you created?"

"The chimera."

"Right. And how did you get the spell?"

"I don't know. I just kind of flipped through and found something interesting."

"Right, so it was about the middle?"

"No, more toward the end."

"The very end?"

"Kind of the middle of the end."

"Exactly!" Topher chortled. "Exactly! And what was the second thing you made?"

"That little, rainbow colored mouse. The one that exploded on the cobblestones."

"End, middle, or beginning?"

"Huh?"

"Of the book!"

"Oh. Um—"

"It was the beginning, right? In fact, it was the first spell in the book."

Zorn frowned.

"If you knew, why'd you ask?"

"Shut up! The third thing you made was the horrific, rainbow-colored dragonfly! It, too, exploded on the cobbles." He flipped through the pages, found what he was looking for, and plunked his finger down to mark the spot. "End of the beginning."

"And the homunculus spell was toward the end," Zorn said. "So what?"

"This book isn't just a book of recipes. It's a document. A series of magical experiments, from beginning to end. Whoever wrote this was no experienced wizard. Exploding mouse exhibit number one. But as he went on and tried again and again, the results were better and better. Gigantic, flying, yet exploding gay dragonfly exhibit number two. Fast forward to the end and you have a functioning mythical creature, then a homunculus."

He trailed off, staring with sudden realization into space.

"What is it?" Gertrude asked.

"My theory is wrong," Topher whispered. "The homunculus didn't work." He threw the book down. "Dammit!"

"Er, that's not . . . actually . . . true."

"Excuse me?"

Gertrude thought for a moment, and then turned around and grabbed a handful of dirt and crumbled bark from the corner of the hearth.

"See?" he said, holding it up.

Topher gave him a ridiculous look. Clearly his hand was full of dirt and bark.

Gertrude dumped the handful on the floor.

The brown blur streaked by, and the handful of dirt and bark was gone

Topher's mouth dropped open.

"The homunculus," he said. "In the courtyard. Out in the woods. My theory is right."

They were all silent for a moment, allowing the knowledge to set in.

"When we tried to use weapons on the monster, somebody gets hurt," Zorn said. "But when the chimera and homunculus are involved, we win."

"What's the last spell in the book?" Gertrude asked.

Topher shook himself out of his reverie. He bent over to pick it up, but before he even reached it, Zorn said, "Cursine."

Topher picked the book up and flipped to the last page.

"He's right."

"What's that?" Gertrude asked. "What's a Cursine?"

Topher didn't immediately answer. He shuffled over to the tapestry and looked up at it.

"Well. What is it?"

Topher closed the book.

"It's awful."

Christmas was celebrated with a ham dinner at The Grotto. Many of the boys received packages from family members, but since the Assistants were given the privilege of checking all incoming mail for possible weapons and contraband, not very many survived the screening process. I, Dennis was initially ecstatic when he opened his. Boxes for new computer equipment were stacked inside, and on the bottom, a year's worth of Linux magazines. He brought the package into the trio's room, beaming, and proceeded to withdraw the contents one by one.

"A new motherboard, a wireless keyboard and mouse, and a 3T thunderbolt! This is incredible!" But when he opened the boxes, there was nothing inside. He stared in disbelief, then threw them across the room with an anguished cry.

Topher, who didn't get anything, said, "Your mother must hate you."

"My mother loves me, you idiot. My father's the one who sent me here. And those bastards Brimstone and Burr stole it all."

That afternoon, at lunch, Marvin Grimm filled his plate with two steaks, a bowl of pasta salad, another steak, a chicken leg, and a bowl of peas. He dined after his fashion, calm and quiet, and when he was done he put his tray in the dish line, strode over to the table where Brimstone and Burr were sitting, grabbed each one by the back of the head, and smashed both their faces down into their plates. He would have held them there until they suffocated to death had not another brown shirt smashed a chair over his head.

The ensuing riot resulted in four broken legs, a host of smashed noses, and legions of lacerations. Doctor Bowls was overwhelmed. Marvin was banished to solitary for a month, and the rest of the school was put on lockdown for the entirety of the break. New Year's Eve passed and nobody noticed. Meals were deposited at doors precisely three times a day, at six, noon, and six. Cold sandwiches, bottled water, and some kind of fruit, usually a banana.

In the middle of the second week it was not unusual to hear the muffled sound of screaming. Long simmering resentments boiled to the surface, and thumping and crashing periodically carried through the walls. Suicide season started early. Zorn saw three bodies being carted away in black bags, bouncing in Mr. Floyd's payload on the way to the stackhouse.

The trio used the secret room to get away, even ventured down the tunnel for fresh air until Gertrude heard a rumor that there were guards roaming the forest.

"Where did you hear this rumor?" Topher asked. "We've been cooped up in here, together, for over two weeks."

Gertrude said, "When I'm bored, I roam the secret passages." He blushed. "The things these boys do and say."

"I don't think you should be spying on people."

"You're one of the worst!"

At the stroke of midnight on January fifteenth, Topher looked out his window just in time to see a body streak by. It landed with a splat, its head exploding like a ripe watermelon. The snow surrounding him stained pink, then red, then maroon. He simply closed the shades and went back to his book.

Lockdown ended the next day. The boys poured out of the dorms and into the courtyard, screaming with joy, laughing, running around like maniacs. Friends from separate dorms hugged and jabbered at one another. Nobody seemed to care about the cold. They were too happy to just be outside, alive, survivors. Games of tackle football broke out, as did snowball fights, races, anything to expend the thirty days of energy and terror that had built up inside them like steam in a kettle.

After lunch, and after an invigorating game of Slaughter in the courtyard, Gertrude took the opportunity to visit the library. Nobody wanted to be inside, not now, but as strange as it seemed, he desperately wanted to read up on the history of Raleigh's Prep. He'd read through Zorn's magic book, looked at the pictures, was repelled by the drawing of the Cursines. As far as he could tell, the idea for the beast was borne from the successful chimera experiment, only whoever had written the book wanted to combine two creatures that were large enough and powerful enough and vicious enough to truly keep the werepyres from escaping the immediate area, possibly eradicating them altogether. He finally settled on rottweilers and grizzly bears.

The spell managed to exaggerate every deadly aspect of both animals. The pointed snouts sprouted sharp and crooked predator's teeth. The keen ears stabbed the air. The beady eyes glinted in the moonlight. It was as huge as a bear but lacked the fat, its body tight with sinew and bulging muscles. It had cleavers for claws, and a long tail for ballast. An altogether gruesome, horrific animal.

And Gertrude wanted to find out more about them, and about the person who made them.

Scathewort Library was open until midnight, and though he thought it a dark and slightly menacing place, at least it was heated, and at least it was away from his roommates, or any other people for that matter. He didn't even know Raleigh's had a library until one afternoon after morning classes when he decided to explore the campus, walked all the way through Merton, exited out the other side, and found himself upon the Lawn, one of the most beautiful places on campus.

Certainly the courtyard was handsome, but in more of an organized, neoclassical way, with its access to all of the dorms and academic buildings, it's marvelous, alabaster clock tower, and the intricate system of tunnels and bridges, all of which combined to create the approximation of a miniature city. The Lawn, however, was romantic and feral. Twenty thousand square feet of grass, trees, and flower beds. The middle section was, yes, mowed tight and trim, and yes the Lawn was shaped like a perfect rectangle, but in the spring and summer the gardens in each corner grew untamed, branches and bushes tangled together, like healthy gothic sentries, and flowers grew in patches, overflowing with color. The undomesticated look had been carefully created, though. Gertrude could tell this by the way the chaos of the gardens was not allowed to grow beyond a certain point, and by the way the paths were carefully manicured, and by the way the benches were set at even intervals around the grass.

Now, however, everything was dead.

The branches and brambles were weighed down with snow, sagging, depressed and forlorn, into the usually well-maintained paths. The Lawn was a single white blanket; the benches were funeral mounds. Flakes of snow swirled in the air like the aftermath of a plane wreck.

On the opposite end stood Melville Residence, where the instructors lived. Melville was a stately building that looked just like the dorms in the courtyard, only in much better repair. Its Doric columns were pristine and white (no doubt they painted them once a year), but rather than a flat, rectangular roof, this one had a tall, white steeple. At its top, Gertrude thought he could make out a bell.

Scathewort was located to the left. On the outside it was squat and dark. The windows were tinted, and the doors hissed on air-pressured hinges when opened. When he'd asked a librarian why, she told him the hinges were a security measure against a riot or uprising. Should a riot occur, the doors automatically slammed shut and locked from within.

"And believe me," she said, smiling. "You don't want to be caught in there if that happens. A few years there was a riot, and a student tried to stop the door by sticking his arm inside while it was closing." She clapped, and Gertrude jumped. "Cut his arm clean off! He bled out before we could do anything. Died alone, sad, crying, a disfigured, pathetic, stupid little boy who didn't listen to me."

The inside of the library was dingy, and it only had one floor at campus level. Four more burrowed underneath. Most of the wards referred to the belly of the library as The Hive, and that's exactly what it felt like. The lights in the sub-levels were overly bright tubes that buzzed and flickered incessantly. The Hive was very quiet, but not in a way that suggested peace or safety. Rather, it felt like the silence one experienced moments before someone leapt out of the shadows and stabbed him in the stomach. The one time Gertrude tried to study there, he kept looking over his shoulder, expecting to be attacked by zombies.

So now, merely four hours after they'd been let out of their confinements, Gertrude used shortcut between Croix and Merton to get to the Lawn, and stole down the covered sidewalk. Hooligans pranced about, pelting passersby with snowballs. A few had taken sniper positions in the trees, and they bombarded him as he passed. He merely hunched against the onslaught and continued on, seeming to flow forward in his massive furs, a dark mass penetrating the washed-out whiteness of snow and setting sun. He merged with the shadows, appearing once more when he opened the door to the library and slipped within.

Scathewort was, of course, entirely empty. Not even a librarian was to be seen. Gertrude felt both comfortable and profoundly ill at ease. At least nobody would bother him while he studied, but once again he found himself on the lookout for zombies. The section he was looking for was on sub floor three, the belly of The Hive. When he got there, his ears tensed and twitched at every sound, every click and tang of the radiator, every swish of the air vent. He once thought he heard someone laughing in a distant part of that floor, so he strode around, poking his nose down every aisle, but nobody was to be found.

Eventually he relaxed enough to find what he was looking for, a book titled *An Unauthorized History of Raleigh's Prep*, written by somebody named Anonymous.

"Must be Greek."

He found a comfortable couch near an emergency exit, sat down, and began to read.

Much of the early history of the school bored him. Founded in blah blah blah, as an alternative school for Juvenile Delinquents guilty of blah blah blah. The part about the original school burning down held his interest for a chapter or so, if only because dozens of people were killed, but Anonymous never detailed who did it or why, and soon it was back to descriptions of former headmasters and when the additions were made and blah blah blah. In fact, nearly half of the book was blah blah blah until he reached the chapter about one of the more recent former headmasters (or in this case, headmistress) titled Mistress Chainwrought.

"Now we're cooking," he muttered, ogling her portrait. She was at once cold and sexy, with wide set, doe eyes, a cupid mouth and upturned nose. Her cheekbones looked like they were modeled after the cliffs of Kilimanjaro. She had the shoulders of a swimmer, and wore an expression on her face that was either a come on or a cuss word. She was beautiful, stern, and buxom; Gertrude wondered what she would look like in a hockey mask. No, naked. No, naked *and* wearing a hockey mask.

He read. And read. And read. When he was done, three hours had passed. He'd read the chapter three times, first with curiosity, then with disbelief, and finally with complete and utter terror. It was all her fault. This whole thing. The werepyres, the cursines. If the unauthorized history was correct, then, well, there were too many things he had to do. Too many for him to do alone. He had to tell Topher and Zorn.

Nobody was at the checkout counter, and after waiting for several minutes, Gertrude finally just left. The alarm pierced the silence of the library, echoing into its dim recesses, but he didn't care. The door shut behind him when he left the building, compressed air hissing, sealing all sound within.

It was well past ten. Night had come, and with it, more snow. So much snow, in fact, that he could barely make out the lamps that illuminated the sidewalk just in front of him. The knowledge of Mistress Chainwrought and her role in all of this thrilled him and creeped him out all the same. He pushed through the snow on his way back to the courtyard and Burleigh's; the tree limbs were heavy with it, and the plants hung low to the ground, as if bearing a sorrowful burden. He walked as fast as he could, frequently looking over his shoulder. The snow shushed. He may have found it soothing were he not so paranoid.

Wait. What was that?

He turned around. Nothing but the Lawn, blanketed in snow. It was so much deeper than when he first left the library.

"Just an echo," he murmured, and he turned and began to walk again, this time a mite faster than before. Then he heard it again, a distinct crunch, as if someone or something were stepping very gently behind him onto the packed snow. Sometimes the acoustics of the surrounding buildings amplified and refracted everything, especially in the colder months, so that someone whispering in the northeast corner could be heard in the northwest. The noise could have come from anywhere, but Gertrude was quite sure of a presence other than his. He stopped again, hugging the book close to this chest. Perhaps it was a creepy librarian, come to force him to check it out?

"Hullo?"

His voice echoed in the corners, a muted, dead echo dampened by the snow.

Nothing.

He turned again and began to jog. He wanted to be elsewhere, immediately. Where was the brown blur? His little homunculus? He hadn't seen it since it bit him and zipped away into Chainwrought. Had it been eaten? Didn't Topher tell him something about it turning on its master? In the distance he could hear laughter and hooting from the courtyard, no doubt students at play in the blizzard. They could help him! With their . . . with their snowballs? He was doomed. The only way he'd survive this would be to make it to Burleigh's, run up three floors, into his room, into his wardrobe, down the secret passage, into the secret room, grab an axe and cut the thing's head off, assuming there was just one. And if there more than one? But what about Topher and Zorn? Could they offer him protection, or would he be bringing death to them, a horrible death in the form of a hulking, bubbling mass of fur and fangs, and red eyes, and drool?

A new sound came from behind, a grunt, guttural and gargled. His jog turned into a sprint, and as he pushed ahead, the lights went out. He threw a terrified look over his shoulder. Behind him, four pairs of red eyes lit up.

Four of them. Galloping right at him, gaining fast. He poured on as much speed as he could, putting his head down to keep the snow out of his eyes, grunting with effort. He looked up just in time to see a dark blur in front of him, and then he ran into it, something burly and solid, and it grabbed him and wouldn't let him go, and he looked up into its face and . . .

"Mr. Floyd! Thank God it's you!"

"Easy, boy."

"No, they're right behind us! We've got to run! Where's your truck?"

"Don't need it for this."

Then he did something Gertrude had never seen him do. He smiled, and the smile turned into a roar of laughter.

Zorn sat up in total darkness, stirred awake by a horrible dream of teeth and fur and blood and bone that ended with the howl of wolves. Topher was standing by the window, staring out into the night. The falling snow cast shadows upon his face, which was illuminated by the full moon.

"What're you doing?"

Topher didn't move.

"The lights are out and the werepyres are back."

Zorn rubbed his eyes. His onesie made him hot and uncomfortable, so he unzipped it down to his chest.

"Is anyone in the courtyard?"

"They were. Brimstone and Burr and some other idiots. They fled as soon as the wolves howled."

"Thank God we're in here," Zorn said. He stood up to wake Gertrude, patting the lump on the bed. It collapsed, empty. He plunged his hands into the comforter. It was cold.

"Where's Gertrude?"

Topher snapped his head away from the window.

"He's not here?"

"Oh no."

"Now calm down. Maybe he's in the secret room. I'll check."

He returned five minutes later, panicked.

"Get dressed," he said, darting for his wardrobe. When Zorn didn't move, he said, "Hurry!"

"He's not there?"

Topher pulled out a white parka.

"Where are you going?" Zorn asked.

"To get Marvin Grimm and I, Dennis. If we're going to get Gertrude out of this alive, we'll need people." He shrugged the parka over his shoulders and moved to the door. "Besides, I, Dennis might have rocket fuel." He yanked it open, and there stood Warren Crews. Topher leapt for his throat, crying, "Bastard!"

Crews fell back, using Topher's momentum to flip him up and over and into the far wall, which dented. He slumped to the carpet. Crews stood slowly up and dusted himself off and looked at Zorn.

"We don't have time for this."

Zorn had just taken off his onesie when Topher opened the door. Now he just stood there, shocked, holding his onesie up over this chest.

"Okay.

Crews pointed at the courtyard.

"They're out there, right now."

Topher slowly dragged himself off the ground.

"They have him," he said.

"They have who?"

"Gertrude."

Topher pressed his hand against his hip as he pushed past Crews and back into the room.

"Then he finally made his move," Crews muttered to himself.

"Who, Gertrude? Just what are you implying?"

"Floyd."

Topher snorted.

"You're crazy. Mr. Floyd's our friend. He helped us escape that first time in his truck. You were there!"

"Mr. Floyd is not your friend. Who do you think knocked you out, tied you up, and left you in the woods to die?"

"You did! And your master, Stoneman!"

"I wanted to escort you away from Stoneman's office. I practically begged him."

"Of course you did. So you could bring us out into the woods yourself."

Crews shook his head in disbelief.

"Really? You really believe that?"

"It's what happened. And I'm sorry to report that your little plan didn't work. Mr. Floyd alerted Marvin Grimm and I, Dennis, and they rescued us."

Crews stared at him, a cruel little smile curling up in the corner of his mouth.

"I alerted Marvin and Dennis. I wrote them the note. I shoved it under their door while I was making rounds with Stoneman."

Topher was struck by something.

"How did you know it was a note?" Suddenly he was able to look Crews in the eye.

Crews relaxed a little.

"I'm telling you, Mr. Floyd was the one who put you out there, not me. Not Stoneman. We're trying to help you."

"Stoneman?" Zorn asked. "But he wants the book."

"Yes! So he can keep it from Floyd and those things." Crews ran a hand through his hair. "Look, I don't have all day to explain this to you. Stoneman's a bit of a tool, but he's finally getting it, and if Floyd really has

Gertrude, he's in danger."

Topher was nonplussed. Everything he'd believed had just been turned upside down. He shook his head. "What do we do?"

Crews smiled. "Come with me."

Zorn jogged toward the secret room, bristling.

Topher left with Crews. Just left. Told him to "go get the things" and he left. Sure. He'd get "the things," but what good was it? What could they possibly do? Five adolescent boys and two mythical creatures verses an entire army of supernatural monsters? Plus, he'd just made another painted stick and hadn't had a chance to try it out yet. What if it didn't work? What if Stoneman filched it from him again? Nothing worse than a filcher, but an adult filching from a child? That was just depraved.

It was colder than usual in the passage, and his breath steamed out of his mouth. Topher and his orders and smug self-righteousness. And those stupid poems he wrote and kept in that huge wad of balled up paper. And he picked his teeth and sucked on his teeth, and he left the sink in a constant state of funk, and he hated that little curly-haired, linen-suit wearing, speck of a—

The door was open, just a crack, but it was open. Maybe it was Gertrude! Maybe he'd just been hiding in there all along! He stepped up to it, leaning toward the crack.

"Gertrude?"

Something shifted inside. A brief, hushing noise.

It was completely dark inside. He squatted down, pushed his eye into crack, thinking he may be able to see something, anything at all, even a shadow. Nothing. He glanced back down the passage. He didn't have any time. Gertrude was in trouble, he needed them.

Another sound echoed from inside the room. Zorn's head whirled around, and he thought he saw something move.

"Who is that?" he asked.

Then the door exploded, and a werepyre burst out of the room.

I, Dennis checked the note for the third time, mouthing the words as he read them. So here he was, standing outside The Grotto, just like it said. Where was Topher? He hugged himself tightly against the cold. The snow was only a light shower when he left his dorm, but now it was coming down heavy and thick, and his plastic outfit didn't keep him very warm. He pushed the eye plate on his helmet down to check the time. Not even midnight. What good did it do, meeting at this time? And where had Marvin gone? He wasn't in his bed when that thunderous knocking woke him up, another note sliding under the door.

That bed, that poor bed. So bowed in the middle that the springs nearly touched the floor. It was only a matter of time before the legs gave out completely. He didn't know why Marvin didn't just sleep on the floor. That looked like it would be a lot more comfortable.

Anyway, the note had specifically been addressed to "I, Dennis" not to Marvin Grimm, so whatever it was Topher needed him for required skill and expertise, finesse and grace, not brute strength and violence. Unless his skill and expertise required something violent, that is. Perhaps the violence didn't matter so much, then, just as long as it was carried out with elegance.

He cast a loving gaze down at his rocket-powered boots. They were black with soot and fuel burns from all of the trials, but they worked! They worked! He'd surely take the prize in the physics competition, especially in comparison to Zorn and Gertrude's pathetic crossbow.

A horrible thought struck him. Clearly Zorn and Gertrude hadn't begun their physics project yet. They talked about it all the time, but he hadn't seen it yet. What if Topher had called him out here in the middle of the night to assault him and steal his boots? He suddenly found himself wishing for Marvin Grimm and his brute strength and violence. Nothing like a hulking giant with Asperger's to fill his enemies with fear.

Something was moving in the distance. What was it? A shadow, no, two shadows, walking toward him from the direction of the courtyard. But . . . but they weren't walking, were they? He couldn't tell. The snow thickened as he stood there, making it even more impossible to see. If only the dratted lights on the path didn't shut down after lights out.

"Conserves energy," he muttered.

There, again, the shadows. God, they were fast. Must be running. Didn't blame them. Cold as the dickens out there. Still, he wasn't sure if he was seeing things, so hugging himself and shivering, he leaned forward to peer, uselessly it seemed, into the dark and the snow.

Marvin sat on the ground near the hole in the forest. The snow hissed all around him, heavy and hard. His trench coat provided sufficient warmth against the cold, but he didn't have any gloves on, and his boots weren't really weatherproof, and his second supper only consisted of a loaf of lightly toasted wheat bread, a jug of apple cider, two chicken breasts, a half pound of potato salad, a can of peas, a couple of potato rolls, and another chicken breast. Had he known he'd be asked to meet out in the middle of the woods in the middle of a snow storm, he would have packed his third and fourth dinners.

He wondered dimly if he should duck into the tunnel to get out of the snow, even if the note specifically told him not to. Wait outside the tunnel, it said, and the word "outside" had been underlined. He didn't get it. What difference did it make to Topher where he waited, just as long as he was there? Oh well, better to do as he was told. Topher could be a bit of an idiot about things if you didn't do it his way and his way *exactly*.

To be honest, Marvin was proud at having been asked separately from I,

Dennis. Clearly this was a task that required brute strength and violence, not some namby-pamby with a computer chip lodged in his brain. What's that? We're facing down a drooling monster with blood dripping off its fangs? Let's Google it and see what some geek in Sweden says we should do. And when I'm bored, I'll tease you about your weight.

"I swear, Marvin, those bed springs are only about an inch away from the floor." Over and over. About a million times. If he didn't have lasers or rocket boots or whatever hooked up to his body, he would have wailed on him a long time ago.

He shook his head, sending a half inch of snow scattering all around him. Jesus. If that linen-suited pansy didn't show up soon, he was leaving. Right as he finished that thought, he heard something crunching in the snow toward him.

"Finally," he sighed.

He stood up, muscles creaking, and dusted the snow off his backside and shoulders. He peered around him to see which direction he was coming from.

Topher squatted behind Gertrude's dead boxwood. The snow was coming down so hard now that he doubted he needed to hide at all. His white parka over his white linen suit should have been camouflage enough.

Marvin and I, Dennis were not in their room, and Crews had gone off without him.

"'Meet me in the clearing,' he says. Well, please, Warren, which clearing would you be talking about? The first clearing, with the succubi and incubi? Or the second clearing, where we were tied up and left for dead? Or would it be an entirely different clearing altogether, I wonder?"

He swiped at the snow on his sleeve, surprised at how thick it had gotten.

And where was Zorn, that oaf? Was he not aware of Gertrude's predicament? Probably off stroking his chimera somewhere. This made him laugh a little, and then he shivered, and then off in the distance there was a concussion, as if from an explosion. A bright, red star shot up into the sky from the direction of The Grotto, climbing higher and higher, up over the buildings, and arcing toward him. For a brief moment, he thought that the werepyres had acquired missiles, but then realized how ridiculous that was. Werepyres didn't even have opposable thumbs.

The red star grew closer and closer, warbled over the courtyard, then began to descend, and that's when he saw a large black object attached to it, or rather, hovering above it. The flames sputtered about fifteen feet off the ground then gave out all at once, and the black form plummeted to the cobblestones where it cried out.

"Who is that?" Topher shouted. "I have a knife!"

The form rolled over.

"Topher?"

Topher recognized that voice. Nasally and whiny, a bit cracked, a result, no doubt, of endless nights playing Dungeons and Dragons, or narrating poorly written fantasy novels to geeklings in the library.

"I, Dennis! Your spaceman boots work!"

He ran to his friend's aid, but I, Dennis was already pushing himself up off the ground.

"They're not spaceman boots. They're rocket boots."

"Six to one, half dozen to another. It's so fortunate that you're here. Gertrude's been kidnapped, and the werepyres are on campus."

"Yeah, I know." I, Dennis pulled something out of his pocket and handed it to Topher. "I waited by the Grotto, but you never showed up. Did you want me to be attacked by those things?"

Topher inspected the note.

"I didn't write this. The handwriting is atrocious, and the 'I's aren't even dotted." He pushed it into I, Dennis' face. "I always dot my 'I's with little, perfectly formed circles."

I, Dennis ignored him. His face had screwed up in pain, and he pressed on his lower back.

"Dear Lord, you were attacked by the werepyres. Did they bite you?"

I, Dennis didn't respond at once. Just continued to press on his back.

"No," he finally answered. "That landing was a bit rough, though."

Something shifted in the snow. A shadow. Topher frowned, looking over I, Dennis' shoulder.

"What's that?" he asked.

I, Dennis turned around.

"What's what?" he said, and then he was punched in the face.

Finally, he thought. After all these weeks, finally.

He backed off, just like the old man said. Bided his time, waiting. The old man seemed to be everywhere, sometimes shoveling snow or making repairs, or sometimes just sitting there, watching without watching. But he never acknowledged the boy, or any of the boys for that matter. Then a few hours after lockdown ended, there he was, sitting on the same bench from before. Brimstone ignored him as usual, just passed by. Burr finished some gay joke, and Brimstone laughed, letting his eyes slip over to where the old man was sitting, and the old man looked right at him.

"Hey, I forgot something back in The Grotto," he told Burr. "I'll meet up with you later."

He waited in the entrance until he was sure Burr was out of sight, then joined the old man on the bench.

"Tonight's the night," Mr. Floyd growled.

Brimstone could hardly contain his excitement.

"When? Where?"

"In the courtyard."

The boy licked his lips.

"Give me the knife."

Mr. Floyd got up off the bench, squinted up at the clouds.

"Not until the signal," he said, and limped away.

"What signal?"

"You'll know. Check the tunnel."

Brimstone threw up his hands.

"Which one?"

"You know which one."

Later, he was in the courtyard when he heard the howls, and he knew, right then he knew. He and Burr ran back to the room, and once they were in, he kissed his roommate on the lips, and Burr responded.

"I knew you'd change your mind," he whispered.

Brimstone smiled and turned around, acting like he was unbuttoning his pants, but really he was removing his blackjack from his pocket. He waited until Burr was busy taking off his shoes and then spun and struck him on the head as hard as he could, knocking him to the floor.

"Faggot!"

Burr held up his hands to ward of the blows, but Brimstone struck at them, snapping his fingers.

"Think I'm gay? Think I'm queer like you, faggot?"

"Phy, please," Burr wept.

"Don't call me that!"

He brought the blackjack down hard against Burr's temple, and Burr collapsed. Brimstone slapped him in the face a few times just to make sure he was really out. Not even a moan. Then he dragged him out of the room, down the hall, and into the lobby. He propped the front door open with a chair from the front desk.

Another howl sounded nearby.

It was time to get rid of Topher Bill. He looked out at the snow covered courtyard, then back at Burr. But there wasn't any reason why he couldn't get rid of this mistake, too.

The knife was right where he thought it would be, in the corner of the tunnel where he and Burr hid from the wolves the first time. He waited there for a while, peeking around into the courtyard. Then he saw I, Dennis shoot into the sky, though he didn't know it was I, Dennis until after he landed and heard his voice. Hadn't seen his bitch until he stood up from behind that dead bush. No wonder. The asshole was dressed all in white. He waited until he was sure they wouldn't hear him, and then he trotted across the courtyard, the snow masking his steps.

"What's that?" his bitch asked.

"What's what?" the geek asked, and as he was turning around, Brimstone smashed him in the nose. He crumpled in a ball, blood spewing out into the snow.

"Brimstone!" Topher yelled. Brimstone slashed at him, but he was too excited and the knife went wide. "What are you doing?"

Brimstone launched himself forward and tackled him. Topher pushed his hand up into Brimstone's chin, scratched at his eyes. He tried to punch him, but Brimstone knocked his arms aside easily, purposefully not using the knife. No, no. He wanted to see the fear in his queer little eyes when he slit his throat, wanted to see them widen as his blood leaked out, watch his hands try to cover the hole. So he struck him first with the back of his hand, then he picked his head up by the hair and slammed it down three times. The snow was hard enough to make it hurt, but cobblestones would have been better.

Topher lost consciousness. He came around slowly, black spots in the corner of his eyes. He tried to move his arms but was too weak. His head throbbed. Could barely breathe. Something heavy on his chest. Brimstone. Kneeling on him again. He leaned down so that their noses almost touched.

"How's my dog? How's my bitch?"

"Fuck you."

Brimstone backhanded him again, and the stars rocketed in his eyes. When they cleared again, Brimstone was waggling something in his face. It looked familiar.

"My knife!"

"No, bitch. *My* knife."

Topher coughed, his chest wracked with pain.

"Got any smart ass comebacks now, faggot?" Topher coughed again. "Didn't think so. Looks like you fucked with the wrong guy." He dragged the knife along his cheek. "See, I was just going to slit your throat, watch you bleed out. Watch you know you're bleeding out. But now I think that there's no reason to have a little fun first."

He swiped the point under Topher's eye, slicing a two inch gash into the flesh. Topher screamed, but Brimstone hit him again, cutting it off.

"Shhh, shhh," he hissed into his ear. "Can't let our friends in the woods know you're here. Not yet."

"Brimstone," I, Dennis said.

Brimstone looked up. I, Dennis was holding his boot up to his face. A bolt of fire exploded out from the bottom, sending the boys flying in opposite directions. Brimstone landed in the tunnel, completely engulfed in fire. He stood up, his screams winding higher and higher as he ran for the snow. He threw himself into a bank, extinguishing the flames, then lay still, smoke rising off his body. The sickly sweet smell of burned flesh and hair filled the air.

Topher didn't dare move. It had all happened so fast. Was Brimstone dead? Where did I, Dennis go? His face throbbed, and he remembered the cut. He grabbed a handful of snow and pressed it to his cheek, numbing the wound. When he was able, he stood up and looked around the courtyard. I, Dennis lay on his back a dozen feet away, staring up at the sky. Topher stumbled over to him.

"Are you okay?"

I, Dennis blinked.

"The snow feels good on my back." He raised his head. "Is he dead?"

Topher looked back at the charred body.

"He hasn't moved yet."

I, Dennis let his head fall back on the snow again.

"Good."

"He was going to kill me."

"I know."

"You saved my life."

"My pleasure."

Topher reached out his hand.

"Well, come on. Zorn was supposed to meet me out here, and we need your help. Gertrude's been kidnapped. We're going to get him."

"Kidnapped?"

"I don't have time to explain. Crews said to meet him in the forest. We can use the tunnel to get there."

I, Dennis didn't move. He seemed like he was measuring his options.

"What are you going to do?" Topher asked. "Stay here?" He pointed at Brimstone's corpse. "You heard him. Those things are all over the place."

I, Dennis shifted in the snow.

"Still safer than the woods."

"Sure. For now. But you were just attacked on campus, right? How long until they infiltrate the dorms? Two weeks? Two days? An hour?"

I, Dennis pressed down on his side, grimacing.

Topher threw up his hands.

"Are you coming or not?"

I, Dennis said nothing.

"Bah!" Topher snapped, and stalked away toward the dead bush and the secret door.

Howls sounded all around, muffled and damp, but near. I, Dennis slowly sat up, wincing in pain. He cast a worried glance over his shoulder in the direction of The Grotto.

"Topher!" he cried. "Wait!"

The cut under his eye throbbed and ached, but it wasn't deep, and by the time they reached the secret room it had clotted. The door was broken again. Shards of wood stuck out of the walls as if it had exploded out into the passage. In fact, there was nothing left of it but scraps and debris. Topher scanned the passage for the doorknob, but couldn't find it. Then he stepped on something that crunched under his shoe, and when he bent down to investigate, he found a shaved-off portion of gold plating.

"What do you think?"

I, Dennis stood behind him, pale and sweating, his eyes rimmed red.

"They bit me," he said.

Topher slowly rose from his crouch.

"What?"

"I'm okay." He gasped and sucked in his breath. "I'm okay."

"Where," Topher croaked. He swallowed hard and took a deep breath. When he spoke again, his voice was stronger. "Where were you bitten?"

I, Dennis said nothing for a moment. He scratched the back of his neck, staring straight ahead with hollow eyes. Then he shuffled around. A huge, gaping hole had been torn out of the lower left hand side of his back. Raw meat and bone stood out, red and white against a black foreground. He did not turn back around.

Topher started to back into the room, then stopped, wondering if the thing that shredded the door was still inside, drooling, waiting for him. His foot slid backwards a little. He'd stepped on a part of the door, the thick middle section from the original wood. It was about two feet long and two inches thick, and ended in a neatly squared off plane. He leaned carefully down and picked it up.

I, Dennis grunted.

His back heaved and hiccuped, and he struggled for breath. Topher saw the muscles under his friend's plastic outfit twitch and swell. His body convulsed, and the violence of it sent him to his knees. He moaned, low and feral, bordering on growl.

"Dennis?"

He adjusted his grip on the board, forced himself to take a step forward toward his friend. If this was really happening, he didn't want to give him room to rush him.

I, Dennis convulsed again. He was down on all fours now, his knuckles resting on the earth, his back arched. A wave shot through his spine. His neck snapped up and he cried to the ceiling, only the cry came out as a howl.

Topher slammed the wood pane over I, Dennis' head and I, Dennis collapsed.

"Ow!"

"Oh my gosh, are you okay?"

Topher reached forward to help, wondering if he'd knocked the monster out of his friend, but then I, Dennis shuddered and whipped his head around. His eyes were red and angry, and his brow swelled, and his teeth cracked as they grew larger and sharper. Topher swung, knocking his helmet off, exposing the puckered flesh, the blue veins, the crepe-like skin. He swung again, striking the temple and cracking the wood. The beast yelped and collapsed, and Topher raised what was left of the board again, swung down again, and again and again. Blood spattered his arms and face, and he cried for his friend and he cried for his heart and he cried for his soul, his shoulder burning, his lungs burning, his back burning, stopping only when there was nothing left to smash and stab and crush, and I, Dennis was nothing more than a mess of pulverized bone and tissue, indistinguishable from the pulpy shards of wood Topher held between his shaking hands.

Zorn dove behind one of the couches when he heard the voices coming down the passage. There was not enough time to whistle for the chimera, or rummage around in the chest for a suitable weapon, or even hide the carcass. Then there were those strange gurgling noises, and more talking, and a howl, and grunting and crying and wet thuds, over and over again. He dared not speak or cry or do anything more than just close his eyes tight and wait for it to be over. When the wet thudding ended, he a soft clunk from the hallway, at which point he realized the chimera was feasting on the carcass of the werepyre that had attacked him, smacking loudly.

Something was standing in the door. He hadn't looked yet, but he knew. It was out there, looking for him. He could continue to hide, cower there behind the couch and pretend it wasn't there and hope it went away, or he could stand and fight. He could face it. He could face it and the chimera would help. He might die or he might not, but at least he wouldn't quiver and quake like a coward, waiting to die. All of the sudden he didn't care anymore, didn't care if the chimera helped or not, didn't care if he'd get hurt, he was just tired of being afraid. He stood up, stood up straight and strong and said, "Who are you?" and the something in the door shouted, "Hey!" and a beam of light pierced the darkness, and oh crap he wasn't as brave as he thought he was, and he ducked back down, his eyes skittering around for something to use as a weapon. Nothing. The sword chest, a foot too far. The chimera was his only chance.

Zorn threw himself up and held out his thumb. The chimera, startled by the motion, jerked up from eating the werepyre's face, its muzzle painted red, and leapt for it. He was just about to throw it when the thing in the hallway stepped into the room and said, "Zorn?"

"Topher? Is that you?"

Topher stepped into the room, wearing I, Dennis' helmet on his head. He tripped over the wolf the chimaera had been eating and fell and I, Dennis' helmet rolled away.

Zorn bustled over to help him, pulling on his elbow and Topher shook it hand off.

"Why were you wearing I, Dennis' helmet?" Zorn asked.

"I had to kill him."

"What?"

"He'd been bitten. What happened to the door?"

Zorn told him about the motion in the dark, how the door exploded at him, and how one of the beasts leapt at him.

"Its jaws were inches from my throat, and then the chimera leapt on its face and poked its eyes out. It whipped around, and they fell back into the room. A few minutes later, I heard footsteps. I thought it might be more creatures, so I hid behind the couch."

Shuffling sounds came from the tunnel leading out into the woods, something big and breathing heavy. Topher put his finger to his lips and snatched I, Dennis' helmet off the ground.

"Who's there?"

Zorn backed over to the weapons trunk, threw open the lid, picked out a short sword.

The shadow spoke.

"Topher?" Into the room stepped Marvin Grimm, beaten and bloody, holding his left arm in his right. "Where were you?"

Topher tried not to look disgusted. He said, "What do you mean 'where were you'? Where were *you*?"

"I got a note from you, telling me to meet out in the woods."

Another note. Just like I, Dennis said. It could only be one person.

"Crews."

"What?"

"Crews, that traitor. He did this to us. He set us up. Separated us so that we'd be easy prey."

Marvin shook his head.

"I don't think that's true."

"What happened to you?"

Marvin motioned in the direction of the tunnel, where it emptied out into the woods.

"Those things."

"You were attacked!"

"There were three of them."

"Were you bitten?"

"I'm fine. Only a few scratches."

Topher took a step forward.

"Take off your clothes. We need to see."

"No."

He grabbed Marvin's wounded arm and twisted. Marvin winced, but didn't move.

"Let me see your body!" Topher said.

Marvin tugged free and shoved him away.

"Get off me."

"Look, Marvin. If you don't at least show us your arm, I'll be forced to —Zorn will be forced to run you through with his short sword."

Marvin rolled his eyes.

"Fine."

Using his right hand, he struggled to remove his left arm from the sleeve. His coat slipped off his shoulder. Underneath he wore a heavy red flannel, the sleeves of which were rolled up past his elbows. He twisted his torso so they could see his arm without having to straighten it out. It was swollen, and an ugly purple and yellow bruise ringed his elbow, but there were no puncture wounds.

"I told you I wasn't bitten." His eyes fell on the helmet in Topher's hand. "Is that I, Dennis'?"

"Yes."

Marvin frowned. "I, Dennis wouldn't part with that thing for a million Majic cards. What're you doing with it?"

Speechless, Topher just shook his head.

Marvin saw something there, seemed to understand.

"Give it back."

He took a swipe at Topher's hand, trying to get the helmet.

Topher dodged it.

"Marvin, listen."

"Give it back."

"No."

He lurched toward Topher, who darted to the dead werewolf and jumped over it, and Marvin, who didn't know it was there and couldn't see it, stumbled over the carcass sprawled across the floor. He didn't move. He just lay there, face down.

"Give it to me," he finally said. "That's I, Dennis' and he'll want it back."

"No," Topher replied, sadly. "No he won't."

"You had no right to steal it from him."

"I didn't steal it from him. Not technically, anyway."

"You had no right."

"Marvin, I'm sorry."

Silence hung heavy in the room. Finally, Marvin said, in a very quiet, small voice, "How."

"He got a note, too. Told him to wait by the Grotto."

"Go on."

"He didn't tell me he was bit until we were down here, looking for Zorn. I had to do it."

Zorn dropped his head; even the chimera wilted.

Marvin remained on the ground for a long time. Then he asked Topher to help him up, which he did. Then he asked to see his roommate's body, so Topher and Zorn escorted him to the door and into the passage and over to the spot where I, Dennis' corpse lay twisted and mutilated amongst the debris. Marvin gave a shocked little choke. Topher had tried to cover his head with a few shards of wood, but it wasn't enough to hide the blood and pulverized bone. Marvin squatted down and put a hand on his dead roommate's foot.

"Do you really think Crews set us up?"

Topher nodded.

"Marvin? I hate to be rude, but Gertrude's been kidnapped. We think Crews took him. We think he wants Zorn's magic book."

Marvin seemed to think for a moment, and then he stood up.

"I saw him."

"Who? Gertrude?"

"No, Crews. I saw him in the woods."

"You're sure it was him?"

Marvin looked uncertain.

"I didn't see his face, but he shouted and waved to me right before I dropped down into the tunnel. Shouted something about 'over the hill'. I didn't know what was going on. I thought it was another trick. Plus I was already hurt."

"Then that's where Gertrude is," Topher said. "Over the hill, in the clearing where he tried to kill us before."

James Noll

OF GATES AND CROSSBOWS

The three of them lay flat on the top of the hill, staring down at the clearing below. Each bore a weapon from the chest in the secret room. Topher wore a short sharp blade, Zorn a line of daggers tucked into his belt, and Marvin a long, honed, impossibly heavy sword, which he wielded with great ease. The snow had stopped for the moment. Topher traced the cut under his eye his finger. It ached and throbbed, so he held another handful of snow against his face to numb it some more.

Gertrude was standing on a stool in the middle of the clearing. He was gagged and blindfolded, and his hands and feet were bound. A noose encircled his neck, the other end tied to a sturdy branch above. A large bonfire burned and crackled and hissed before him, melting all of the snow around it. Other than that, the clearing was empty.

"What are we waiting for?" Zorn asked.

He pushed himself off the snow, but both Marvin and Topher pulled him back down with a grunt.

"Don't move, you idiot. Can't you see it's a trap?" Zorn stared at him, uncomprehending. "You've got the book, remember? They want you to go down there half-cocked. Alone. Then—" He drew his fingers across his neck. "And the book's theirs."

Marvin slapped Topher on the back with a huge paw.

"Crews," he whispered, and pointed to a spot down below.

Topher followed his finger, and indeed there he was, skulking around the edge.

"The rat! He's down there, waiting for us."

Now it was his turn to push himself off the snow, but before either Zorn or Marvin could stop him, he darted down. Zorn quickly followed, hissing, "Wait! What about your half cock?" Marvin jumped after them both, and the hill was soon misted with three clouds of white snow as they bounded after one another, weapons clinking. I, Dennis' helmet fell off Topher's head. He ignored it and continued, reached the bottom, and started the arduous task of wading through the snow as quickly and quietly as he could. Two things happened at once: Crews turned to him, both shocked and grateful at his presence, and Mr. Floyd stepped into the clearing right behind Gertrude.

Good, Topher thought. *Now we can bring this traitorous little twerp to justice.*

Crews had just enough time to say, in a very low voice, "Topher, where have you—" before Topher cocked his right arm and struck him full in the face. He went down in a lump, his nose broken. Fresh, red blood stained the snow.

"What are you doing!"

Topher picked him up by his shirt and smacked him.

"Shut up." He grabbed him by the hair and marched him toward Mr. Floyd.

Crews fought back, but Topher was in a passion. Zorn and Marvin pulled in and marched alongside, grim and silent.

"Mr. Floyd!" Topher cried. The heat of the bonfire struck him full on. His body relaxed, even if it was too hot. He hadn't realized how cold it was outside. Mr. Floyd put his hands on his hips.

"Stop where you are, boy!"

Topher obeyed. He shoved Crews toward the fire.

"We found him skulking around the ring. He was trying to kill you before you rescued Gertrude."

The fire crackled and popped. Mr. Floyd stared at him, waiting.

"You bring the book?"

"Yes, of course."

"Let's see it."

"Okay." Topher turned to Zorn and nodded.

Zorn withdrew the book from inside his jacket and held it up in the air.

Mr. Floyd said, "Bring it here, now."

"What about Gertrude?"

Mr. Floyd put his hand on Gertrude's back.

"Quick, boy! Before they get here."

Zorn took a step forward, but Topher put his hand gently on his chest. "Wait."

"Bring it here, Goddammit! We don't have time."

Topher looked over at Crews, who was packing snow against his nose. Blood washed over chin and wetted his shirt. He looked back at Mr. Floyd, standing there, one hand in his jacket pocket, the other now on the back of his neck, not moving, but rigid, as if his body were full of untamable electricity, as if he were about to burst.

"Cut Gertrude down, then you'll get the book."

"Don't be a fool, boy. They're coming."

Topher turned his head slightly. Zorn, Crews, and Marvin all looked around them, panicked.

"Who's coming?"

Mr. Floyd smiled.

"Them."

All around them in the woods, bright, red eyes flared up.

"Oh my God," Zorn gasped.

"Give me the book!"

Topher grabbed Crews by the back of the neck, whipped out his blade, and shoved it up under his jaw.

"Topher, let me go."

"You two are in on it, aren't you?"

"No, Floyd's with them."

Topher ignored him.

"Cut Gertrude down, or I'll kill your little spy here!"

Mr. Floyd's face crumbled, red and disgusted. His mouth trembled up into a sneer, and then he burst out laughing. Topher was shocked, immobile. He glanced around at Zorn and Marvin. Zorn hardly noticed; his eyes remained fixed on the dozens upon dozens of hot, red coals glaring out at them from the edge of the clearing. Marvin raised his sword. Low growls darkened the air.

"Spy?" Mr. Floyd shouted. "Spy?" He whirled his hands in the air. "Go ahead! Please. Kill him. One less of you I'll have to deal with."

Crews gently pushed Topher's hand off his neck. He bent down and picked up some more snow to rub on his nose.

"What now, professor?"

Topher looked around him in a panic. There stood Gertrude, blind and bound. There stood Marvin and Zorn, looking to him for instruction. There stood Mr. Floyd, guffawing like a madman. And there were the eyes, glowering from the shadows. Gertrude uttered a muffled call against the gag.

Topher snatched one of Zorn's daggers from his belt, turned, and threw it at Mr. Floyd. It parted the air, end over end, zipping toward its target, and it might have sunk into his chest had Topher been any good at knife throwing. As it stood, it merely thudded off the old man's chest and plopped into the snow. Mr. Floyd staggered backwards a few steps, stunned, but when he saw the knife lying helplessly before him, he broke out in laughter again. His mirth disappeared as quickly as it came.

"Kill me? Don't you get it? I'm the only one holding them back. I'm the only one who can get you out of here alive, you idiot. You kill me and them red eyes'll pour in here and tear all of you to pieces. Rip your lungs out, eat them whole."

Topher didn't know what to do. His thoughts flew from him.

"I told you to give up, didn't I?" Mr. Floyd said. "Told you more than once. But you didn't listen. You had to get involved, and now you got to give me the book. Give me the book, and I'll let your friend go, and you can get back to your rooms and everything'll be alright."

Topher looked at Zorn.

Zorn shook his head.

"Topher, no."

Topher snatched the book out of his hand. He pushed through the snow, heading for the smiling Mr. Floyd, but when he reached the fire, ripped a page out of the book and threw it into the fire. The page, so old and long dried out, went up immediately. One of the pairs of red eyes in the woods winked out. The werepyres let up a howl.

"Did you see that?" Zorn said.

"What?"

"You burned a page and one of them disappeared."

"You've got to be kidding," Topher said. "That's all we had to do this whole time?"

"It's not the way it works, boy," Mr. Floyd said. "There's more of them then there are pages in that book."

Topher ripped out another page.

"Fine," he said. "Then you won't mind if I burn another one."

"No! Don't."

"Then let Gertrude go."

Mr. Floyd glared at him.

"No."

The second page was reduced to crispy ashes, and another pair of eyes winked out. Topher ripped out a third. Mr. Floyd cussed.

"Wait!"

He limped up behind Gertrude, whipped his hunting knife out of his pocket, and cut his bindings, cut the rope from around his neck, cut the blindfold, cut the gag.

"Topher?" Gertrude called out, squinting and blinking in the glare of the firelight.

Topher ran to him, held him up, and guided him off the stool and away from his kidnapper.

"Idiot, boy," Mr. Floyd spat. "You burn that book, you'll kill us all."

And before he knew what he was doing, Topher spun, withdrew his blade, and stabbed Mr. Floyd in the stomach.

The old man's eyes grew wide. He staggered back, and his hands found his middle, and he sat down hard in the snow. He stared at his belly in disbelief.

"You killed me," he muttered. Then, louder, "You run me through, you cocksucker! Now we're all dead!"

The eyes burned in the area behind them. Mr. Floyd held his hand over his stomach and stumbled to his feet, lurched into the wood line and disappeared. Topher pulled Gertrude forward.

"Marvin, come get him."

Marvin did. Topher spotted a pile of branches sat near the bonfire, and he snatched one up and stuck it into the fire. It was dry caught easily. The red eyes in the woods pressed forward, growling.

"What do we do about them?" Zorn asked.

"Leave that to me."

By the time they reached the bottom of the hill, half the book lay burning on the ground behind them, a glowing trail of red, orange, yellow, and black in the snow. The red eyes followed. Anytime they threatened to break the invisible barrier of the wood line, Topher quickly ripped out and burned another page, and the eyes receded, growling. Twice they had to stop to break off and light another branch as the prior one started to sputter. Twice the eyes on the verge took advantage of the opportunity and struck. Marvin decapitated the first, cut the second nearly in two, but not before it swiped a chunk out of his thigh.

It was hopeless. Mr. Floyd was right. There were more monsters than there were pages, and the monsters knew it, too. The attacks became more brazen as they mounted the hill, despite the fact that when they reached the top Topher tore a huge chunk out of the book out and set it ablaze. He tossed it as far as he could. It sputtered and went out in the snow, and a beast fell upon it, took it up in its mouth, and retreated into the woods.

"Run!" Zorn cried.

They launched themselves toward the hole, snow flying. A beast threw itself at Topher, and he shoved the burning branch into its mouth. It squealed and tumbled away. Two leapt for the limping Marvin. He ducked lamely on his wounded leg, fell, and thrust his sword into the air, slicing one in half as it flew over him. The second was met by the chimera, and they tumbled to the bottom. Crews fell behind, crying out. A wave of beasts swarmed over him. His shrieks turned to squeals, and his limbs jutted out of the mass of fur, and the squeals wound impossibly high and cut off entirely. The boys took advantage of the diversion and dropped one by one into the hole.

Gertrude could see nothing; none of them could. He heard their shuffling footsteps, heard their breathing and grunts, heard their gasps of pain, boxy and metallic in the tunnel. There was no use turning around when the monsters dropped in after them. Grunts and snarls mingled with their own noises. Somebody cried out. He didn't know if it was him or not.

"Right behind us!" Marvin screamed. He was right behind him.

"The door!" someone yelled.

Gertrude felt Marvin's weight disappear.

"Marvin!"

"Too many!"

More confusion and percussion, squeals and yells, then he was pushed forward through an opening. He hit a wall and slid to the floor. The door slammed behind him.

Thuds and wails from the other side. Zorn yelled, "Look out!" and Topher shouted something. Inhuman shrieks, garbled cries. Something heavy and hard thudded into the wood. It rattled. Gertrude scuttled a little farther down the hall toward the secret room. Another howl. He couldn't tell if it was human or animal.

He sat completely still, sure of only the sound of his own breathing. He couldn't believe he was alive. He ran an inventory of his body, every ache and pain, every cut and stitch. His head still throbbed where Mr. Floyd had knocked him unconscious before, his wrists and throat burned from the bindings, his mouth felt like it still had the gag in it, and just thinking about the gag made him gag. He coughed and sputtered and sat up on the cold floor. A warm, yellow glow filled the short hall. Someone had started a fire. He looked at the door to the tunnel. The knob twisted, but stopped halfway. Something slapped at it.

A voice moaned, "Gertrude."

He groaned as he got up off the floor.

"Topher?"

Nothing.

"Zorn? Marvin?"

The knob turned again, even less than before. A light slap against the bottom of the door. A whine.

Gertrude could barely stand. He heaved for breath, the floor spun, and he was suddenly sick. When he was done, he stood to his full height and took a deep breath. He could leave. He could hide out in the secret room until the morning, and then when the sun was firm and high in the sky he could gather his things and try his luck escaping on his own. He did fine before he met Topher, better in fact. There was no reason to stick around for him, stick around this place. This was the same boy who killed his own parents. Killed Zorn's parents. Tried to kill his mother, maimed his father. Who cares if it was an accident! Who cares if it was supposed to be a joke! And then they're sent here, and he drags him into this cursed rubbish at this cursed school.

He made a deal with himself. If he heard any noise, any human noise, he'd open the door.

Nothing. Nothing. Nothing.

He was just about to turn and walk away when it came.

"Gertrude?"

It was Topher.

"Gertrude. Help us."

Every square inch of the tunnel was packed with carcasses. The dirt walls were splattered and dripping, and limbs and claws and snouts and teeth jutted out of the pile in a way that might have been strangely poetic. So much death. So much carnage.

Topher had been lying with his head against the door. When Gertrude opened it, he flopped out. Zorn was a little farther in, lying twisted on the ground under a pile of beasts. Gertrude dragged them both into the hallway. He couldn't see Marvin. He toed a few stray parts away from the jamb, but it wasn't enough, so he pushed and he shoved, and though he was weak and saw stars, he was finally able to shut it tight. Turning the lock felt ridiculous, but he did it anyway.

The yellow glow invited him in, and though he was wary of who lit it and why, he was more afraid of staying where he was. One at a time he pulled his friends through the passage and into the room, placed them on the couches before the fire. When he was done he collapsed into an empty chair. He felt a draft. The door Marvin fixed was no longer there, but he was too tired to investigate. He drowsed in the heat for a bit, listening to his friends' breathing. Were they badly hurt? Had they been bitten? He could barely lift his eyes, and the heat amplified his exhaustion. He dozed off.

He gradually became aware of the presence of the other in the room, feeling it the way one feels a stare upon his back in a crowded place. He started then, and sat up straight, for there in the chair opposite sat a short old man in a rumpled, brown suit. His hair was white and wispy, and his face jowly, but not fat. His belly poked out like a little beach ball inside his jacket, and the legs of his pants rode up so high that Gertrude could see his hairless, bony shins.

And he was smiling at him.

There was such a look of tenderness and love in that smile that Gertrude felt immediately at ease. Then he thought that the smile might be a trick, as if those soft eyes and that cheerful mouth would suddenly go wide with rage, and the old man would pull out some kind of unpleasant, angry, sharp instrument, and scream "Die!" and leap across the room and skewer him with it. Considering what he'd just gone through it would have actually felt like a relief. Still, his body tensed, and his face fell completely blank, and tears welled up in his eyes.

"Oh my dear boy," the old man said, the smile disappearing from his face. "Please, please, all is well. I mean you no harm."

His voice was thin and high, grandfatherly, and Gertrude nodded, unconvinced. His mouth turned down in the corners. The old man nodded toward Zorn and Topher, unconscious and bleeding on the couch.

"Your friends are not well, I see?"

"I don't know if they were bitten."

"Well, I'm sure there's nothing to worry about with that." His voice was soothing, reminding Gertrude of weekend mornings with his family. He rose out of his chair, stooping, and used a cane that had been leaning against his chair to totter over to Zorn. He peered into his face, checked his pulse, examined his arms and legs. He motioned for Gertrude to join him.

"Could you roll him on his side, my boy? I need to see his back."

Gertrude did as he was told, and the old man pulled up his shirt.

"Ah! There we are," he said. "Hmmm. Some bruises and cuts here, deep, yes, but nothing too deep. Now let's see about your other friend."

When they were done, the old man nodded, worried but satisfied. Patting Gertrude on the shoulder, he said, "I see no bite marks on your friends, my boy. They're beaten and bloodied and bruised, but they're not in any immediate danger. No worse than the other boys when they tried the same approach." He gestured to the tapestries. "Excuse me," he added, and Gertrude moved out of his way as he shuffled back to his chair by the fire. "Old bones don't weather the cold well." He eased himself back, his arm shaking as he put his weight onto the cane. "Ahhh. That's better."

Gertrude sat back in his seat, too.

"You knew those boys?"

"Knew them? I trained them!" The old man chuckled and sighed. "They were so young and strong, so good with their weapons. And I was young, too. Thirty five doesn't sound young to you, I realize, but trust me, it is. Not a boy, but not quite wise enough to make the decisions I made. And idealistic! Even here, in this place." He gestured vaguely around him. "I thought I could do something good, something noble. Read too many romantic adventures, if you ask me. I truly thought that they'd be able. But no."

Gertrude felt his strength return just being in the old man's company. The bruise on the back of his head throbbed, but he no longer focused on it. And his legs and arms and body, so weary and worn out after his ordeal, no longer plagued him so. He leaned forward, eager to hear what he had to say. The old man, however, didn't make a sound. He just sat there, smiling whimsically and closing his eyes to enjoy the warmth of the fire.

"Are you Lord Burleigh?" Gertrude asked.

The old man's eyes flew open.

"*Lord* Burleigh?" Then, as if suddenly remembering something, he half turned toward the tapestries and grumbled, "Ah, yes. Well, let me be the first to tell you that they were not my idea. Fisher always was a bit melodramatic."

Gertrude clearly didn't understand, so the old man said, "Yes, my last name is Burleigh, but please, just call me Jonathan, or Mr. Burleigh, anything but 'Lord'."

"You were in charge before Mr. Stoneman. And after Chainwrought."

Burleigh winced. "The night is evil enough as it is without bringing up her name." He regarded Gertrude thoughtfully. "How do you know about her?"

"I read one of the histories in the library. Is it true? About the experiments?"

"Oh, yes, quite true, quite true. We tried to put an end to it, you know, the boys and I. We made our own weapons! Learned how to defend ourselves. And it worked! At least for a while."

"They're all dead," Gertrude said, meaning the knights on the tapestries. "Mr. Floyd told us so."

Burleigh's eyes narrowed, and his face screwed up into a disgusted sneer.

"Floyd. If it hadn't been for him—" he caught himself. The anger left his eyes, and his shoulders relaxed. "He was their friend, you know. Right up to the very end, when the fear took hold of him and he sold them out. I never trusted him, and I told them he wouldn't do. But boys can be exceedingly loyal, without even knowing what loyalty means, especially boys like these. Never had a family, never would. Their friends become their family. They get all wrapped up in the group, can't separate themselves from it.

"After he turned on them, they tried to fight back, but to no avail. There is not much we mortals can do against an evil as powerful and as willful this one. In the end, after they were all dead, she rewarded the traitor. With a curse. That he should never rest, and that he should be here until the end of his days, never a part of their world, never a part of his. A pariah among pariahs."

Gertrude stared at the fire. He thought about his friends. About Topher and Zorn. Marvin was dead. He wondered why I, Dennis had not come out to help him. Had he felt a bond between them? Was this just a phase? Something his adolescent mind invented?

"That yearbook you have?" Burleigh said. "That's his. Floyd's. One by one he marked out their faces, and one by one they succumbed to his treachery. I found out only too late, so I did the only thing I could think of. I stole her book, and I ran. Cowardly, I know. I didn't get far. The book. Does your friend still have it?"

"Who? Zorn? I think so. Would you like me to find it?" He half rose, waiting for an affirmative.

Burleigh's eyes struggled with something deep and painful, something that Gertrude, in his youth, could never understand. Desire burned there, sick and sweet, and guilt, and regret, and lust, and a host of other contradictory emotions. He looked away at the fire and let out a shuddering little breath.

"No. Keep it away from me. It's a vile, awful thing, and I'm glad to be rid of it. I never want to see it again."

"Okay." Gertrude sat back down.

Burleigh's eyes sought him after a moment, and they were rimmed red. His cheeks were wet.

"This place is bad. Your parents and everyone else who props it up, they're bad, too. It was only a matter of time before it attracted someone like that woman. I came here because I thought I could do some good. She came here because she saw an opportunity to control other people. She used her power to torture those poor boys. Turned them into, well, you know. She was a bully, and there's nothing a bully hates more than someone smarter than she is.

"I wrote that book. I researched it, put everything I had into it. I used it against her, you see. And it worked. And then I thought, maybe, if I used it to get rid of her, I could use it to get rid of *them*." He sighed, his chest shaking. "But of course that didn't work out, did it? And now we have the Cursines." He gestured to the chests next to the door. "Look in the bottom drawer there."

Gertrude padded over and turned around, eyebrows raised.

"Yes, yes," Burleigh said. "Bottom drawer."

Gertrude opened it, and at the bottom lay a colorful, folded up tapestry. He picked it up and let it unfurl. Another knight was featured on this one. He had no weapon in his hands, and he rode no horse. Across the bottom, someone had burned a hole in a portion of the knight's name, but enough was visible for Gertrude to know who it was.

"Floyyde," he read. Then, as if to clarify, "Mr. Floyd."

"Her most loyal traitor. Fisher made that for him as a gift. Almost like a promise. They were training him on the bow and arrow. Tried to burn his name out after he turned on us."

Gertrude put the tapestry down on the chest, covering the drawers.

"Why are you here? What do you want from us?"

"Want from you?" The old man shook his head. "I don't want anything from you, my boy. Not anymore. I admit, I thought you and your friends here might be able to do a better job with it than I. To make the book work, to rid this place of the evil she created. But after tonight."

He stood up, leaning on his cane. He paused a moment by the fire. Then he looked up, his face dancing in shadows. "I came here tonight, Kenneth, to tell you all to get out. Get rid of that book. Leave. This place will bring you nothing more than sorrow, nothing more than death."

He tottered away toward the passage, leaning on his cane.

"But wait!"

Burleigh paused again and raised his eyebrows in question.

"How do we get past the gate? How do we get past the Cursines?"

Burleigh thought for a second, then said, "You have a crossbow. Use that." His cane clonked on the floor as he walked away. "And don't worry about the Cursines. If you're smart, it won't be you they're interested in."

Then he turned and shuffled away toward the door and the carnage.

"Mr. Burleigh! Don't go down—"

He stopped when he came to the opening. There was nobody there. The old man had simply disappeared.

Behind him he heard his friends groan.

They were waking up. They'd need water.

Topher told him all about the battle at the door. How Marvin Grimm went down in a maelstrom of teeth, and how the chimera was swallowed whole.

"I thought we were done for. They kept jumping in, piling onto each other, more and more and more. It was like a snarling waterfall. They pushed us back to the door. It got to the point where we couldn't swing our weapons."

And then the homunculus came, cutting through the wolves before they knew what hit them. Those in front continued to fight, but those in the rear turned on their little attacker.

"I never saw it after that. Zorn went down, and I thought he was dead, then I was hit by something and my head hit the door and I blacked out. The next thing I knew, I woke up here."

"The homunculus finally returned then," Gertrude said. "I could have used it when Floyd kidnapped me."

"If it makes any difference, I think it was trying to get to you this time." Gertrude stoked the fire.

"There was an old man in here," he said.

Zorn perked up.

"An old man? Did he have a cane?"

Gertrude nodded.

"It was Lord—Mr. Burleigh. He came to tell us something."

Zorn jabbed a finger at Topher.

"Ha! I told you I didn't kill him."

"Shut up, Zorn. What did he say, Gertrude?"

Gertrude told them everything. About the book, Chainwrought, the boys who came before them, the last tapestry.

When he was done, Topher said, "So we were right. We must continue the fight."

Gertrude shook his head.

"He said we should escape. 'Get rid of that book,' he said. 'This place will bring you nothing more than sorrow, nothing more than death.' Those were his words."

Silence settled over the room, each boy in his separate world.

Zorn stirred first.

"But what about the gate."

"We have a crossbow," Gertrude said.

The realization dawned on the other two at the same time.

"How convenient," Zorn said. "It's almost as if this whole thing were planned out for us."

Topher clapped his hands on his knees and stood shakily to his feet.

"So we escape. We storm the gate with the crossbow. We'll blow it to smithereens, and cut down anything else that gets in our way."

"Before we go," Zorn said. He took the book and the painted stick, which had broken in half, out of his pocket. I think it's time."

He took a deep breath and closed his eyes. He wanted to throw them both into the fire, but his arm wouldn't move.

"Heh," he said, opening his eyes again. "Topher? If you would be so kind?"

"Don't be a pussy, Zorn. Do it yourself."

"I can't!"

"Oh goodness sake."

Topher got up to take the items out of Zorn's hand, but the latter punched him in the chest and knocked him to the ground.

"Zorn, you idiot!"

"I didn't mean to!"

While they were both distracted, Gertrude swooped in, snatched them from Zorn's hand, and tossed them into the flames. Zorn shrieked and leapt after, but Gertrude held him back. The stick caught immediately, sending sparks up the chimney. The book took a moment more. It smoked at first, the leather cover resisting the blaze, but then the heat built up and it burst into flames. Thick, black smoke filled the hearth and hovered there, and Gertrude thought he saw red eyes staring out at them. Then, with an eerie howl, it was sucked out of the chimney and into the night.

They grabbed a few things from their room: clothes, Zorn's poster, a toothbrush. Gertrude whined about leaving Sally, but in the end conceded that she would be an unwelcome burden.

The snow had resumed, stronger this time. It covered Brimstone's body in the courtyard. Topher toed the corpse with his foot.

"He was such an asshole," he said.

They cut between Merton and Croix, nervously eyeing Chainwrought.

"Where will we go after we escape?" Zorn asked.

"I know of some places," Topher said. "First we'll need something to eat. I found a restaurant right before the, er, right before we . . . a certain establishment."

"What kind of restaurant?"

Topher cast his glance from side to side, as if there were people eavesdropping.

"One of questionable repute."

Zorn frowned.

"Oh?"

"Yes, yes. Yes, yes. They employ scantily clad waitresses."

"Strippers!"

"No! They're clothed. Kind of. It's suggestive."

"Suggestive of what?"

"Well, certain parts are exposed. Not in full, but little is left to the imagination."

Zorn pondered this.

"Exposed. Like their forearms?"

"Are they wearing hockey masks?" Gertrude asked.

Topher frowned.

"There were hockey masks on the walls."

Zorn and Gertrude shared a lecherous glance.

"They really expose their forearms?" Zorn asked.

"Yes! But think of a sexier part."

"Sexier than a forearm?"

"Yeeess."

Zorn pursed his lips.

"They expose their knees!" Gertrude shouted.

"Knees are not sexy!"

"The back of the knee is."

"No, it's not."

Gertrude waggled his eyebrows.

"Have you ever seen the back of a woman's knee?"

"These waitresses expose something sexier than knees and forearms!"

Zorn and Gertrude stared blankly at him.

"They wear tight shirts! Designed to draw attention to their hee-haws and doo-waps! Get it?"

Gertrude's face flushed.

"And we can go to this place?"

"As soon as we get out."

Gertrude and Zorn picked up the pace, bulldozing through the snow.

Security Officer Mark Larkham felt unusually relaxed. At first he thought it was because he'd napped for well over an hour, but then he realized it was because his neck had been cocked at an odd angle the entire time, and it cut off some oxygen to his brain, thus numbing him. He stood up, rubbed the kink out of his muscles, adjusted his uniform, and looked out the window.

Three large boys were wheeling a siege weapon into the middle of the road.

One of them ran forward and touched a flaming branch to the huge bolt they'd knocked.

It burst into flame.

"Hey!" he cried.

The shack was well insulated, so the cry did not penetrate the glass.

He ran to the front door and yanked it open. The boys didn't scatter as he expected them to.

"Good God, man!" one of them said. "What are you still doing here?"

"Put the bolt down!" Larkham ordered. "I mean out!"

The boy hurried over, beckoning impatiently.

"Come along, now, father. You don't want to be caught here. The place is overrun."

Larkham allowed himself to be led gently away.

"Overrun? With what?"

Topher patted his hand again.

"We're leaving. You should, too."

"Where? Out there?"

"Well, of course. Unless you know of a better way out."

Larkham eyed the trees dubiously. Stoneman had warned him not to go out there. Ever. Every morning he was driven to work in an iron-plated Humvee. He had never been allowed to roll down the window (which was dark and mirrored), but one time he had spied something large and hulking out there, a bulky silhouette in the early morning light. Before he'd had a chance to say anything, the massive thing melted into the woods.

Somebody cried, "Fire in the hole!"

Larkham turned around. The bolt in the crossbow was now completely on fire. One of the boys yanked on the rope tied to the trigger. The bolt launched into the air and struck the gate, which exploded.

"Jesus!" Larkham cried.

A tremendous howl, as if from the mouths of hundreds of animals, rang out from the direction of the campus. The boys ran for the gate. The bolt had damaged it, twisted it open a little, but it was made out of rarefied iron and steel. It would take more than a flaming log to break it. Not that it mattered. They'd cut the electricity. Dying blue flashes of it leapt between the sharp spikes of each rung. All they needed was an opening.

"Hey," Larkham cried. "Stop!"

The boys didn't pause. The first one to the gate kicked it as hard as he could, bending it back just enough for him to step through.

"Hey!"

Another howl pierced the night, closer now.

Larkham jogged up to the gate.

"Do you like pizza, sir?" Topher asked.

Larkham fumbled with his taser, but Zorn stepped forward and snatched it out of his hands.

"Topher, stop toying with him. Sir? It's time to leave."

He held out his hand.

Larkham turned around, wondering about the source of the howling. When he turned back the boys had backed away.

"Wait!" He squeezed through the crack.

Zorn attempted to shut the gate but found that the lock was shattered beyond repair, the iron bars twisted, and it couldn't be shut at all. He slammed it with increasing futility until finally Topher snapped for him to stop.

"Excuse me," Topher said to Larkham. "Do you have a pair of handcuffs?"

Larkham automatically put his hand to his belt.

"They're in the shack."

"You'd better hurry," Gertrude said, pointing. "They're coming!"

Indeed, a small group of rotting monsters spun around the corner in the road. They lurched forward at the sight of their enemies.

"Go get the cuffs!" Topher cried.

Larkham was too busy staring at the pack.

"What are those things?"

Topher grabbed the guard by the arm and shoved him forward.

"Go!"

Larkham stared at him.

"We'll lock the gate with them," Topher said. "Get the cuffs!"

Larkham suddenly understood. He squeezed sideways through and sprinted to the shack. Gertrude saw his head bob around in the window.

The wolves were a mere fifty yards away.

"It's too late," Zorn whispered.

Larkham must have thought the same thing, because instead of leaving through the front door, he opened the back window, swung out, and crawled up onto the roof.

"He's going to jump the fence!" Topher cried.

"Gertrude!" Zorn snapped. "Help me hold the gate!"

"What for?"

"To hold it!"

"But they'll bite us."

"They can't fit their heads through the rungs, you idiot! Now help me hold it closed until the guard can get over here!"

Gertrude grumbled; he sullenly approached and leaned half-heartedly against the iron.

Larkham, while sixty years old, was still quite spry. He took a few steps back, threw a terrified glance over his shoulder, then ran forward and leapt into the air, sailing high, the handcuffs in his left hand twinkling once in the moonlight, up and up and up, arms working, legs pin wheeling, a look of joyous fear slapped across his mug, and just as he reached the apex of his arc, just as he soared out over the spikes of the iron gate, seconds from freedom, from safety, a werepyre leapt off the roof and caught him in his middle. They plummeted, and Larkham was impaled on one of the spikes. The beast squealed as it's belly ripped open. The guard's carcass slid down the rung, cuffs dangling from his fingers, his last breath hissing out of him.

Topher leapt forward and snatched them from his dead hands. He quickly fastened them around both sides of the gate, and he and his roommates dashed away without even looking to see if it would hold. They heard the percussion of the first beast as it slammed against the iron, and a squeal as the handcuffs scraped against the metal. Only Zorn dared to cast a look over his shoulder.

"It held!"

One of the monsters leapt on the roof, its form silhouetted by the moon. Then another appeared, and another.

"They're on the roof!"

Topher looked back.

The first wolf reared and leapt, but it, too, failed to judge the distance correctly and was impaled on the spikes. The second suffered the same fate. But the third was stronger, and it sailed into the air, high over the spikes, its red eyes focused, two hot beads in the pitch black. It landed and skidded a few feet with the force. The lights winked out once, then lighted again. It came for them.

The boys put on as much speed as they could, but it was no use. The eyes loomed larger.

Ten feet away.

Gertrude cried out and stumbled.

Five.

Topher slowed to pull his friend up.

One.

The boys screamed and launched themselves forward, waiting for the pain as their insides were torn outside. Then the ground beneath them quaked, and a monstrous roar, like a thousand crashing trains, filled their ears. Gertrude squeezed his eyes shut, but Topher rolled onto his back, ready to fight. And that's when he saw it.

The Cursine.

It was huge, and black, and terrible, and it stood between them and the wolf, which was actually backing up, its tale between its legs. Though it bared its teeth, and though a growl rumbled deep in its terrible chest, Topher knew it was scared. The Cursine's back heaved as it breathed. Its claws hung from its massive paws like butcher's knives, and its body was tense with thick muscle. Suddenly it threw its head to the sky, and Topher saw a black snout and beady glowing eyes. It roared again, and all three boys wailed and clapped their hands to their ears. The wolf leapt, and the hulk swung one of its paws forward, impaling it on its talons. It let the beast writhe there for a moment, squealing in pain, before shoving it into its mouth and crunching, once, twice. Bones crunched. When it was done eating, the Cursine fell to all fours and lumbered away toward the gate, where more wolves had gathered.

Zorn helped his friends to their feet. He and Gertrude started to run again, away from the terror of Raleigh's Prep. Topher, however, stopped to look.

"What are you doing?" Zorn asked.

Topher didn't reply, just nodded back toward campus. Zorn and Gertrude followed it.

The roof of the guard shack was swarming with monsters; several were already airborne. But the woods on their side was alive as well. More hulking shadows streamed toward the campus, like sharks to the frenzy. They were feasting on the werepyres, snatching them from the air like children swatting gnats. Some caught the beasts in their jaws and ripped them apart with their teeth. Those werepyres that did make it over in one piece soon realized their folly and tried to scramble into the woods. There they were beset by packs of younger ones. The trio watched with horror and glee.

"So that's what he meant," Gertrude said.

Topher and Zorn gave him a look.

"Mr. Burleigh. Before he disappeared, he said, 'Don't worry about the Cursines. If you're smart, it won't be you they're interested in'."

"Maybe we should go just in case." Zorn said.

Gertrude saw one of the Cursines rip a werepyre in half.

"Good idea."

On either side of the drive stood tall, crooked trees, the variety of which Topher had seen only during his stay at Raleigh's. He wanted to say that they were oaks, but during the spring and summer, long, stringy grass, like Spanish moss, hung from their limbs. They were sharp to the touch, and the sap that ran down the needles was foul and sticky. In the winter, the snow coating the needles often melted before anything else, even in freezing weather. He was sure that if they tried to dash into the woods they would cut them to ribbons before they even made it four feet.

The squeals and growls faded into the distance as they limped toward freedom: Zorn on the left, Gertrude in the middle, and Topher on the right. Topher rather liked the image. If he ever wrote a book about his life, he was sure include it in his narrative.

EPILOGUE

Stoneman awoke from nightmares feeling predictably ragged. His room was ice cold, the end of his nose and his cheeks and ears were freezing. He looked over at his alarm clock and was not surprised to see that the power had gone out. His watch lay beside the clock, so he picked it up and read the time. Six thirty in the morning. At least he hadn't overslept. Soon the radiator on the opposite wall ticked, and the cold air gradually turned tepid, then warm, then warm enough for him to get out of bed.

The ancient floorboards popped when he put his weight on them, and continued to crack as the heat infused the room. He padded to the window and pulled the heavy curtains aside. It always refreshed and rejuvenated him to look out upon the empty campus in the rays of the rising sun. Reminded him of purity, the purity of his purpose here, to pilot these misguided boys through the rest of their troubled adolescence so they could rejoin society, renewed, reformed, reborn. Oh yes, he and the Regent's Board had had some heated discussions about that, but the only way he'd take the job, he explained to them, was if he was able to change the very purpose of the school, to turn it from a factory of death into a rehabilitation center.

Fine, they said. Just get rid of Chainwrought's beasts, and the school's all yours.

They didn't think he'd be able to do it.

For a moment, the campus was shrouded in the pre-dawn dark. Then the sun peeked over the tops of the trees in the forest.

Stoneman gasped.

The entire school was blanketed in snow. At least four to five feet deep. The top of the clock tower, the cobbles of the courtyard, the roofs of the dorms, the arches of the tunnels, all of them were coated in a cozy, veil of white. The sun rose higher, and the snow reflected its beams, nearly blinding him.

The night's bad dreams fled from his thoughts. He opened his window with a creak and a crack, and the fresh, pure air flooded into his now warm room. He closed his eyes and breathed in through his nose, a deep, satisfying breath.

Today would be a good day! He wondered what it had in store.

Thank you for reading *Raleigh's Prep*! If you liked it, you'll be pleased to know that the adventures of Topher, Zorn, and Gertrude continue in *Tracker's Travail*. Turn the page to read an excerpt!

THE ZOMBIE APOCALYPSE

The dead man lay on his back on the gravel. He was naked, a fact that Deputy Jeter tried to overlook, because this was a particularly attractive dead man. All in all a wonderful specimen of manhood, if one could ignore his lack of it. And the fist-sized hole in his forehead. His roommate, much thinner, lay a few feet away, also on his back, also naked. The hole in his forehead was much larger, in the sense that nearly the entire top of his skull had been ripped open. Jeter squatted, squinting. He tried to think of the man as a thing, for that's all he was now, an empty vessel, a shattered gum ball machine. The only light in the basement was a single naked bulb swinging on a stringy cord from the ceiling, so he pulled a penlight from his coat and shined it into the ragged hole. It was empty, totally scooped out, like a pumpkin, like a—

"Like a bowl of ice cream," a voice behind him said.

Jeter nearly toppled over the corpse. His hand shot out for balance, landing square on its chest, then he leapt up as if stung by a bee.

"My God, man! No need to molest the dead. He's been through enough, don't you think, without some backwoods deputy groping him like a horny eighth-grader."

Jeter spun around. A man in a white linen suit was standing on the stairs, stooping down to peer into the basement. He was of medium build, a tad portly. On his head sat a wide-brimmed Panama hat; in the other he gripped a large leather briefcase. He took off his hat and held it against his chest.

Jeter would have thought him magnificent were that not so gay. Not that he, Jeter, was gay. No one was gay in Fredericksburg, not even the gays. Not even the gays at Merrimen's, dancing all night, sweating to the incessant throb of techno music, drinking wine coolers, and dancing, oh so much dancing. Dammit!

"Who are you?" Jeter said.

The man on the stairs opened his mouth, but before he could answer, he was interrupted by a stampede from behind. A deep voice called out, "Topher! Topher! Zorn broke the bulbs in the spotlight and he was going to blame it on me but it's not true because I was nowhere near it!"

Jeter peered up the well. The basement was at least seventy years old, and the ceiling was only six feet high, which made seeing up the steps difficult, unless, like the man in the linen suit (his name was Topher, was it?), he were standing at the bottom. All Jeter could see now, though, was a tremendous pair of legs in fur pants, and very large black boots, and very large hands, which were worrying the waistband wrapped around a very large waist.

"Not true! Not true!" another voice roared. More footsteps rattled the staircase, and another set of legs and boots and hands joined the *soiree*.

"Gertrude was angry because he wanted to do the lights but I wouldn't let him so he dropped the lights and stomped on them on purpose!"

"It's my turn to do the lights!" Gertrude cried.

"No it's not. The schedule says it's *my* turn."

Gertrude's boots spun to Topher in a panic. "I didn't drop them on purpose. It was an accident."

"And he kicked out a window and made several unfavorable comparisons about you."

"That's a bald faced lie!"

"Your face is a bald faced lie!"

"See! He hates your baldness."

"Gentlemen, gentlemen, please," Topher said. "Shut the hell up!"

There was a momentary silence during which Jeter could imagine the jaws of the other two men hanging agape, then one of them said, "Well there's no need to be rude."

Topher stomped into the basement, shoes crunching on the gravel.

"We have a job to do here, you morons."

The two pairs of boots tromped down after him, making the steps creak and groan, and into the basement stepped two of the largest, hairiest men Jeter had ever seen. They were so wide that the first one had to get out of the way before the second could squeeze through, and they were so tall that they had to stoop at least half-over in order to fit in the basement.

"Did they build the basements like this on purpose?"

Topher set his leather suitcase down on the gravel and said, "Of course, you oaf. Southerners are naturally stumpy. It's because of all of that tobacco they ate. And cotton. Unlike we, their robust and towering brethren to the north. And by 'we' I mean 'me.' They built these cellars in the hopes that they'd be too small for the behemoth Union soldiers. It's where they stored their gold and unmentionables."

"The southerners ate tobacco?"

Topher snorted and knelt next to the body.

"And cotton. Stupid, I know. Why eat tobacco to make you short when you can smoke it and die of lung cancer? Which they did in droves, by the way. It's why they lost the war." He unclipped the lock on the suitcase and lay it open. Shining instruments sat neatly organized on a soft suede field. "No one ever accused the south of cornering the market on intelligence. Or enlightened attitudes towards France, for that matter."

"Uh—" Jeter began.

Topher faced him.

"Ah, yes, the local Barney. Be a dear, will you, and go fetch us some iced frapaccino? I prefer mine mocha. Zorn? Gertrude?"

Gertrude opened his mouth to reply but was cut off by Zorn, who said, "No thank you" and stooped farther into the basement to have a look at the other body.

Jeter puffed out his chest.

"Just who do you think you are? No unauthorized personnel are allowed down here. Can't you see this is a crime scene?"

Topher waved him off, grimacing in concentration at the hole in the corpse's head.

"Gertrude? Please see to the lights."

Gertrude clapped and ran to the stairs, pointing at Zorn

"Ha ha."

Topher slid a long, shiny, metal instrument from the case. There was a tiny procuring mouth at one end and a complicated trigger at the other. He sat a pair of glasses on his nose, withdrew a little flashlight from his pocket, and leaned over the corpse, his tongue poking out between his teeth.

"Hey!" Jeter protested.

Topher ignored him.

"Hey!"

"This one's naked, too," Zorn observed.

Topher pushed the instrument around.

"Ah, yes."

Zorn put his hands under the corpse, preparing to flip it.

"Has anyone had a look under it?"

"Don't touch that!" Jeter barked, startling Zorn, who stood straight up and banged the back of his head on the beams above. Dust and dirt sifted and pattered all over the body.

"Zorn!" Topher snarled. "Please try not to contaminate the crime scene!"

Footsteps thundered overhead and on the stairs, and more dust and dirt sifted into the basement, and then Gertrude appeared holding a candle and a box of matches.

Topher frowned.

"Candles, Gertrude. Really?"

"I told you. Zorn broke all of the lights."

Jeter took out his gun.

"Godammit, all of you freeze!"

Zorn laughed and resumed his work, and Jeter, who'd never experienced that kind of response, turned the gun on Gertrude.

"Put that thing away," Gertrude said.

Topher sighed and turned his attention back to the empty skull, trying to ignore the Barney in the corner who was now shouting into his cell phone, pausing only to shout at Zorn, who shouted back. Then Gertrude joined the shouting, though he wasn't sure why and couldn't decide who to shout at or what to say, so he just started yelling, "I'll break your neck! I'll stab your guts!"

In a moment their voices faded into the background. All of his attention was pinpointed on the empty cavity before him. He was close enough now that he could smell the dead man's cologne. He might have kissed his forehead, had there been any forehead left to kiss. The inside of his skull did indeed appear to have been scooped out like a pumpkin, but it was no spoon that performed the scooping.

Topher panned across the back of the skull with the light, twisting it to catch the corners. He'd long since gotten over the nausea that used to threaten the back of his throat whenever he did this. Once, in the early days while investigating a case in an abandoned warehouse in Danville, he vomited directly into an empty head. The building had been turned into a punk rock squat by teen-aged miscreants, most of whom had gathered around their now dead friend. They all vomited, too, when they saw what happened, though thankfully not into the same opening.

Nothing really bothered him anymore. In fact, he found it hard to suppress the icy butterflies of excitement, for the sight of a human skull emptied of all brain matter no longer represented the gore and viscera of human biology, but the tantalizing yeti of mystery, the fantastic chimera of knowledge, the golden dolphin of adventure. He looked forward to it so much that he sometimes felt himself grow aroused by the promise of a new case, though at that particular moment he was more than aware of the inappropriateness and possible legal ramifications of such stimulation. And while intellectually he had no aversion to the idea of necrophilia, he was certainly aware of the imbalance in the relationship (what if *it* took advantage of *him*?) just as he was certainly aware of the fact that he'd just used the word 'ramification' in referring to sex with a corpse, "ram" reminding him of mountains and goats and curly horns and—wait a minute. The instrument had caught against something in the back of the skull.

"What's this?"

He peered closer, deeper, striving to see. There. A sliver caught in a web of gore. He pulled the trigger ever so slightly, ever so carefully, let it close around the thing, and pulled it out, triumphant.

"Aha!" he cried, holding it in the air. He twisted to show his friends, then gasped.

Four Fredericksburg police officers surrounded him, guns trained on his head. Zorn and Gertrude were on their knees, hands cuffed behind their backs.

"Can I help you gentlemen?" Topher asked.

~

The bloody fingernail sat in a clear evidence bag on Sheriff Pitts' desk. Next to it sat a copy of *The Free Lance Star*. "CHINA INVADES SOUTH KOREA" the headline screamed. "United States Mobilizes Troops." Pitts glared at fingernail, squirming uncomfortably. He was a heavy man, possessing the build of a former linebacker gone to pot, which was ironic for two reasons: 1. he never played football, and 2. he was currently the regional champion of the Highlander Games. His specialty was the caber toss, though he also excelled in the stone put and the hammer throw. All of that flesh, seemingly loose and jowly beneath his uniform, was really a solid sheet of muscle. This only increased the embarrassment he felt at his current injury: a broken coccyx, earned two weeks before while chasing Donny Motts, a local drunk who'd stolen a cue ball and $500.00 from Spirits. He'd chased Donny all over town, somehow ending up on the roof of Sammy T's, where they both slipped and skidded over the awning and landed in the middle of Caroline Street, Donny on his shoulder, Pitts on his ass.

"And he said they were what?" Pitts growled.

Deputy Jeter sat on the other side of the desk, fidgeting. It was he who deposited the evidence bag on Pitts' desk, he who had to explain how he allowed his own crime scene to be contaminated, he who stammered, with as straight a face as possible, the words, "Zombie hunters, sir" as a response to his boss's question.

"Zombie hunters?"

"Yes, sir. Among other things."

"Other things?"

"Yes, sir. Here. He gave me their card."

Jeter placed a business card on the desk between them. It was the nicest card he had ever seen. On one side was printed this:

On the other, this:

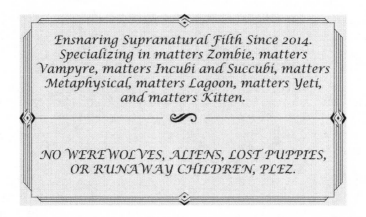

Ensnaring Supranatural Filth Since 2014.
Specializing in matters Zombie, matters
Vampyre, matters Incubi and Succubi, matters
Metaphysical, matters Lagoon, matters Yeti,
and matters Kitten.

NO WEREWOLVES, ALIENS, LOST PUPPIES,
OR RUNAWAY CHILDREN, PLEZ.

Pitts picked it up and read it with what could only be described as an incredulous frown. Then he tossed it on his desk, folded his hands over his solid belly. What kind of kook plants a bloody fingernail in the skull of a corpse?

"You say these idiots ransacked your crime scene?"

Jeter gulped.

"Well, yes. Sir. They kinda just showed up. At first I thought they were from the lab, and before I knew it they were moving the bodies, and the one in the white suit stuck a metal thing inside one of 'em and came up with that." He pointed at the bloody fingernail in the evidence bag.

Pitts breathed out of his nose. Finally he said, "Bring these morons to me."

He heard Topher a full minute before he saw him.

". . . about bloody time you retrieved us from that hell hole!" he shouted from the hallway.

"Topher, please."

"No, I will not 'please', Gertrude. And thank you very much! I'm unaccustomed to this kind of treatment. Bars on the windows, a single toilet in the corner. How do they expect me to contemplate the night in such primitive surroundings!"

The voices stopped right outside Pitts' door.

"I don't believe this is the kind of situation in which one can properly mull over the esoteric qualities of the evening."

"Oh but it is the kind of situation in which someone evacuates his bowels in front of his peers and enemies, no matter how egregious the effluvia."

"Shut up!" Jeter barked.

"You shut up!"

The door opened, and Pitts saw a medium-sized man in a ridiculous white, linen suit, with a tan Panama hat clapped on his head. Behind him stood two giants dressed in furs: fur jackets, fur pants, fur boots. The man in linen stepped hurriedly into the room, clearly judging the decor. The other two had to duck to enter, and when they were all inside there was very little room for them to do much of anything else other than stand.

One of them said, "That's not the point, Topher."

"No, it is the point, Zorn. I, unlike Gertrude's beloved Thoreau, view any visit to prison as an assault upon my person. I will not, like Gertrude's illustrious pencil-maker, upon release from said assault upon my person, join a huckleberry party and repair my shoe."

"I still don't see your point."

"My point is that if I choose to muse upon anything anywhere at any time, I should not be hindered from doing so by some iron symbol of tyranny, or the rancid stench of feces."

"Mr. Bill," Pitts said.

Topher held up a finger.

"I will not be hindered—"

"Mr. Bill!"

Topher shook his finger.

"I will not—"

Pitts grabbed the wiggling digit and bent it backwards. Topher cried out and sank to his knees.

"You listening now?" Pitts said.

Zorn's eyes bulged. Gertrude held his own finger in sympathy. Topher pressed his lips together and nodded.

"Good. I'm going to let go of your finger, okay?"

Topher nodded again.

"And when I let go of your finger, you're going to do two things. Would you like to know what those two things are?"

"Yes," Topher squeaked.

"You're gonna sit down. And shut. The fuck. Up."

He released Topher's finger and leaned back in his chair.

Topher slid up into one of the three chairs on the other side of the desk. Pitts eyed Zorn and Gertrude, who quickly scuttled into the other two, the latter shoving his hands deep into his pockets.

"Deputy," Pitts said. "I'll handle this from here."

"How dare you," Topher grumbled as the door shut "My hexing hand is permanently damaged."

"Hexing hand?"

Topher threw up his arms in disbelief.

"Yes. My hexing hand."

Pitts frowned.

"They'll be none of that here."

"Says the expert on the supernatural."

"Didn't I tell you to shut up?"

"Just don't come looking for me the next time you need a vampire heart staked or a squid monster red-eyed."

Pitts rolled his eyes.

"Lord Jesus." He picked up the evidence bag containing the bloody fingernail and shoved it at the trio opposite him. "What the hell's this?"

Topher said, "A bloody fingernail, of course."

"Did you plant this in that victim?"

"What?" Topher looked to Zorn and Gertrude for help.

"Er," Zorn coughed. "We're Trackers. Suggesting that we planted evidence is an insult."

"Unless one were Reinholdt Smythe-Webly," Gertrude said. "Remember the time he set that pumpkin on fire and shot it through that poor old woman's window?"

"Mmm. Tried to tell her she had a poltergeist. Dropped a hand-grenade in her parlor."

Gertrude pointed at Pitts. "Now Reinholdt. He's a fraud." "Wouldn't trust him with a dead kitten."

Topher reached for the evidence bag, but Pitts snatched it away.

"Sheriff Pitts, I'll try to explain this without sounding too crazy," Topher said. "That fingernail is broken off of a Class IV Zombie. Judging by the state of those poor young men, you've got a pretty nasty one on your hands."

"Or two pretty nasty ones," Zorn corrected.

Pitts shook his head.

"Smythe-Webly? Class IV Zombie?"

"Well," Topher said. "He's no Jerry Irons, granted, but I wouldn't go so far as to rank him among the filth of the supernatural."

"Mr. Bill. You just interfered with a criminal investigation."

Topher leaned forward. "You've got a lethal flesh grinder loose in your city. And a possible infestation under 312 Hawke Street. You better act soon before it turns into an all-out attack."

"You're aware that tampering with evidence is a felony?"

"Mr. Pitts. Sheriff. Please. If you don't allow me to eradicate the meatcicle that is probably at the moment wandering around your fair town, a trumped-up felony charge will be the least of both our worries."

"Jesus H. Christ on a crutch. You're as crazy as a shit-house rat."

"A shit-house rat?"

Zorn leaned toward Gertrude.

"Rats live in houses made of shit?"

"Oh yes. Positively filthy creatures, them."

Pitts adjusted himself on his donut. He breathed out of his nose.

"I know what you are. I've seen your kind before. Grifters. Travelers. Some other horseshit title you give yourselves to feel important. But I got one name and one name only for piss-ants like you."

"Oh!" Gertrude piped. "Is this a regional title?" He beamed at Zorn. "You know how I love colloquialism."

"In Massachusetts they call us Spookers," Zorn said.

"Oh yeah? Well here in Fredericksburg we got a special title for people like you." Zorn and Gertrude waited, eager and expectant. "Shit stains."

The smiles disappeared.

"That's right. Shit stains. You can't come into my town, jilt a few gullible old ladies out of their savings by getting rid of some imaginary spooks you cooked up for them. Bang on a few pots. Have your friends moan in the basement. Call it what you want, but you're all the same in my book. Frauds. And fraud is a felony."

Topher glared.

Pitts said, "I'm going to tell you what I'm going to do. I'm going to run your name through our database here. See, it's a national database. And if you're wanted on anything, and my gut tells me you're wanted on a load of charges, then I've got you. And you're screwed. And you're going to prison. Not jail. Prison."

Topher snickered.

"We've seen worse."

"I doubt it."

Pitts grunted as he pushed his chair away from his desk and rolled towards the computer behind him. Zorn shot Topher a panicked look. It had been over twenty years, but was the warrant for their escape from Raleigh's still out? Had Stoneman even issued one?

"You won't find anything," Topher said.

Pitts put a pair of glasses on and squinted at the monitor.

"Uh huh."

"Maybe a traffic violation or two." The keyboard clacked. "Just ask Bob Sewell."

Pitts stopped typing. He turned around and peered at them over the rims of his glasses.

"Are you trying to tell me that you know Bob Sewell?"

Topher sat back, satisfied, and crossed his arms over his chest.

"I'm telling you that I know Bob Sewell."

"*Sheriff* Bob Sewell?"

"Of Danville, VA."

"Bob Sewell. *Bob* Sewell?"

Topher spread his hands. Zorn's terror-stricken stare remained fixed. Gertrude smiled like an idiot. Pitts swiveled in his chair. Left right. Left right. His eyes never left Topher's.

"You're clearly acquainted," Topher said. "Why not give him a jingle."

"I will. But if you expect me for one second to believe that this is anything other than a stalling tactic, that Bob Sewell would vouch for a slime ball like you, you're sorely mistaken."

"Vouch for me? Vouch for me? My dear Mr. Pitts. Who do you think recommended this place to us in the first place?"

Pitts stared at him long and hard. Topher couldn't tell if he were angry or constipated. Finally the sheriff, keeping his eyes firmly fixed, reached into his upper right-hand drawer and withdrew an aged, brown, moleskin address book. He licked his thumb and flipped through it, found the number he was looking for, plucked the receiver from the cradle of the landline on his desk, and punched at the numeral pad.

"Hello?" he said after a moment. He spun all the way around so that his back was to the trio. "This is Tucker Pitts. I'm the sheriff up here in Fredericksburg. I'm doing fine, thanks. Listen, is Bob Sewell in?"

When it was clear Pitts was no longer paying attention to them, Zorn pinched Topher's arm.

"Ouch!" Topher hissed.

"You idiot. Sheriff Sewell hates us!"

"So?"

"You told him he recommended us!"

"Not really. I said he recommended this place to us."

"You mean after he kicked us out of Danville?"

"Now you're thinking. Look, Sewell hates us so much that he'll say anything to keep us out of his little city."

Topher cut himself off as Pitts swiveled back around to face them.

"Bob! This is Tucker Pitts. I'm the sheriff up in Fredericksburg. You might not remember me, but we met down at the sensitivity training in . . . Yeah, yeah, that's me. Everything's going fine, thanks. Still got my fill of drunks and druggies. You know the deal. Danville still a ghost town? Not no more, huh? Well, good for you! Uh huh. Uh huh. Listen, Bob, I'm not one for beating around the bush, so I'll get straight to the point. I've got this boy up here, name of Topher Bill, and—"

The shout on the other end of the line was so loud that even Gertrude winced. Jeter suddenly opened the door.

"Sheriff? We got a lot of phone calls coming in all the sudden."

"Get out!" Pitts snapped, and Jeter nodded and shut the door.

"You have the spare van keys, right?" Topher whispered to Zorn.

"So you know him?" Pitts continued. Sewell's voice yammered away on the other end of the line. "Uh huh. You don't say? A sewer creature? In a public toilet?"

"One of our dirtiest jobs," Topher said.

Zorn and Gertrude nodded solemnly.

"A swamp monster? Digging tunnels underground. Suckin' people down through the . . . uh huh."

"The mole-rat," Zorn whispered.

Gertrude shuddered.

Pitts glanced up at Topher, baffled and weary.

"Well, yeah, it does sound kinda crazy. Comes highly recommended, huh? No, no need to apologize for not calling. We're taking care of this right now. Okay. Okay, you too. Thanks for the intel."

He set the receiver gently down in the cradle, leaned back in his chair to think.

After a moment, Topher said, "So, *Monsieur* Sewell confirmed?"

"Not another word," Pitts growled. He stood up, wincing, and swept the evidence bag off his desk. Gertrude leaned forward, staring at the headline of *The Free Lance Star*.

"Oh dear," he said. "Look at that."

Pitts buckled his utility belt.

"We're taking a ride over to Hawke Street. You're going to explain this happy horseshit to me."

Topher stood up, too, ready and eager.

"I will explain the happy horseshit until the cows come home."

~

Pitts drove through the streets of Fredericksburg squirming like a cat with a hernia. He moseyed down Route 1, then took a right on Stafford and wandered around the streets of College Heights, eyes constantly scanning the tree-lined sidewalks. He turned onto College and headed to William, passing duPont and Seacobeck. Topher sat in the passenger seat, counting the money in his wallet, eager to pick a fight if even one dollar was missing. Zorn and Gertrude hulked in the back, staring gloomily out the windows. The rearview was so filled with their heads and hair that Pitts didn't even bother to look in it. Jeter followed in his own cruiser. The radio crackled with dispatch calls, and Pitts turned it up a little.

"Something's going on."

Topher widened his eyes and nodded. Duh.

Zorn stared out the window at the passing college campus.

"Mary Washington looks very pretty." He saw a large group of students running around an open commons. "Do the students often gather there?"

"That's Ball Circle. They're out there all hours. Playing hacky sack or some other shit. While we're on the way, why don't you boys explain this zombie crap to me. Not that I believe it for a second, but Bob Sewell's a friend of mine, and Bob Sewell swears by you, so spill it."

"Er, this is a textbook Class IV Zombie Attack," Topher replied.

"Uh huh."

"As opposed to a mere Class I Zombie Infestation. Class I's are placid, subservient, usually subject to some kind of curse from a priest or a priestess." The leather upholstery on the seat squeaked as he, like a professor at lecture, relaxed and settled into the comfort of his subject. "Some say the television, the 'electric teat,' is a modern version of the zombie priest; in recent years the Interwebs, and now Facebook, seem to have supplanted the teat in that role, and . . . forgive me, I digress."

Pitts sighed, already exhausted. Topher continued, oblivious.

"Class I's aren't dangerous at all, at least to others. Actually the concept is fairly laughable. Class II's are nomads, either set free by their priest or priestess, or subject to some kind of familial curse. Non-flesh consuming, of course. They expire within a few days."

Pitts rolled to a stop at the William Street intersection and put his blinker on. His radio squelched, and a female voice said, "Unit 9, unit 9. 101 in progress."

The light changed, and he turned left. The bleak, iron fence that surrounded UMW intrigued Zorn, as did small groups of people who were gathered on Sunken Road, just standing there, staring. A few others ran in the opposite direction, shooting frightened glances over their shoulders.

"Class III zombies are the one's you really need to worry about," Topher continued. "Fully reanimated, usually coffin-bound, extremely hungry. They'll usually claw their way out before they attack, but for some reason they won't bite."

Popping sounds echoed in the night. Topher looked out the window to see what they might be. They passed Hurkamp Park. Families and elderly couples were sitting on the grass watching a folk trio perform. There were more gathered in the trees in the distance, seeming to shuffle forward into the darkness.

"Music in the park series," Pitts said. "Kids bring firecrackers."

He turned left onto Prince Edward. The houses were stately and well-maintained.

"So," Topher went on. "Class IV zombies are the real worries. Active, mobile, hungry and violent. Many live underground for long periods of time. Metro or subway tunnels, ancient catacombs, crypts, tombs. Sometimes, like we saw last night, they hole up in a basement. They surface when their hunger is too much to bear. They'll attack anybody in the immediate area before going back to ground. We call it a 'base site'. They can exist that way for decades, sometimes centuries, before their bodies finally fall apart or someone like me kills them. Since their main diet consists of brains, most of the time an infestation won't occur. But every now and then one will get it in its head leave the base site, and then . . ."

Suddenly the street was filled with people running in all directions. Many were partially dressed, as if they'd been forced out of bed. A woman in a red nightgown limped by, crying, her hand covering a bloody gash in her neck.

"You have a full-on Class IV Catastrophic Zombie Event."

If you're interested in reading more short stories and continuing the Topher Trilogy, check out *You Will Be Safe Here*.

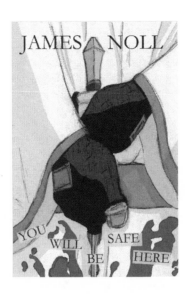

Come travel down the dark recesses of the human mind, accompany the doomed inhabitants of a distant planet on their dangerous final mission, and tour the paranormal corners of Fredericksburg, Virginia with four more short stories and a new novel from the author of *A Knife in the Back*. Who would have thought such a quaint little town could be so lethal?

"My favorites were "The Unan" and "Savages." (These two stories actually tie together.) There were elements to "The Unan" that reminded me of the world of Stephen King's The Dark Tower series, and I imagine the Gunslinger would have fit in pretty well in this setting. Recommended, especially for fans of sci-fi fantasy or readers who simply appreciate a diverse and interesting collection of stories."-- Dr. Gonzo, Amazon Reviewer

Get your copy here:
http://www.jamesnoll.net/safe

Hey you slugabeds! Topher here. That roustabout Noll was too busy napping to write this, so he begged me to do it for him. Seeing as I am considered quite the talented wordsmith, a man of letters, if you will, I cannot blame him. Also, he has the tact and charm of a drunken car salesman.

Unfortunately, he actually makes a living from the books he writes, if what he does can even be called writing (I liken it more to the random appearance of letters on a page.) Nonetheless, he needs help from readers such as you. Please review *A Knife in the Back* so he can write more books, particularly anything that feature me, like *Raleigh's Prep* and *Tracker's Travail*, and my personal favorite, *Topher's Ton*.

ABOUT THE AUTHOR

James Noll has worked as a sandwich maker, a yogurt dispenser, a day care provider, a video store clerk, a day care provider (again), a summer camp counselor, a waiter, a prep. cook, a sandwich maker (again), a line cook, a security guard, a line cook (again), a waiter (again), a bartender, a librarian, and a teacher. Somewhere in there he played drums in punk rock bands, recorded several albums, and wrote dozens of short stories and a handful of novels. He has published short fiction and poetry in *Whurk* (www.whurk.org) and the Fredericksburg Literary Reivew (www.fredericksburgwriters.com).

Contact him online at:

www.jamesnoll.net

Also by James Noll:
A Knife in the Back
YOU WILL BE SAFE HERE
Burn All the Bodies
Don't Turn Around

COMING SOON:
Bonesaw

THIS IS A BLANK PAGE!!!!!

AHHHHH! ANOTHER BLANK PAGE!

Made in the USA
Middletown, DE
20 February 2017